SWEET TORMENT

"Oh, Sabra. Sweet, sweet, Sabra," he whispered against her mouth before he pulled her into his warm embrace.

Winding her arms around his neck, Sabra tangled her fingers in his thick dark hair, eager for his nearness.

At first he merely brushed his lips across hers in a tormenting series of slow, shivery kisses that set every nerve in her body atingle. Then, boldly, he explored the sweet recesses of her mouth. When she tilted her head back, giving him greater access, white-hot passion exploded within him. He was consumed with a yearning to ease her to the ground, to let her sweet, sweet body lessen the pain in his heart, the hunger in his soul.

Desperation ran through Hawk when he finally pulled away. He had to stop before her gentle healing love bound him completely. He had to stop now—or he'd never let her go. . . .

WATCH FOR THESE ZEBRA REGENCIES

LADY STEPHANIE (0-8217-5341-X, $4.50)
by Jeanne Savery

Lady Stephanie Morris has only one true love: the family estate she has managed ever since her mother died. But then Lord Anthony Rider arrives on her estate, claiming he has plans for both the land and the woman. Stephanie soon realizes she's fallen in love with a man whose sensual caresses will plunge her into a world of peril and intrigue . . . a man as dangerous as he is irresistible.

BRIGHTON BEAUTY (0-8217-5340-1, $4.50)
by Marilyn Clay

Chelsea Grant, pretty and poor, naively takes school friend Alayna Marchmont's place and spends a month in the country. The devastating man had sailed from Honduras to claim his promised bride, Miss Marchmont. An affair of the heart may lead to disaster . . . unless a resourceful Brighton beauty finds a way to stop a masquerade and keep a lord's love.

LORD DIABLO'S DEMISE (0-8217-5338-X, $4.50)
by Meg-Lynn Roberts

The sinfully handsome Lord Harry Glendower was a gambler and the black sheep of his family. About to be forced into a marriage of convenience, the devilish fellow engineered his own demise, never having dreamed that faking his death would lead him to the heavenly refuge of spirited heiress Gwyn Morgan, the daughter of a physician.

A PERILOUS ATTRACTION (0-8217-5339-8, $4.50)
by Dawn Aldridge Poore

Alissa Morgan is stunned when a frantic passenger thrusts her baby into Alissa's arms and flees, having heard rumors that a notorious highwayman posed a threat to their coach. Handsome stranger Hugh Sebastian secretly possesses the treasured necklace the highwayman seeks and volunteers to pose as Alissa's husband to save her reputation. With a lost baby and missing necklace in their care, the couple embarks on a journey into peril—and passion.

Available wherever paperbacks are sold, or order direct from the Publisher. Send cover price plus 50¢ per copy for mailing and handling to Penguin USA, P.O. Box 999, c/o Dept. 17109, Bergenfield, NJ 07621. Residents of New York and Tennessee must include sales tax. DO NOT SEND CASH.

Arizona Vixen

LaRee Bryant

ZEBRA BOOKS
KENSINGTON PUBLISHING CORP.

ZEBRA BOOKS

are published by

Kensington Publishing Corp.
850 Third Avenue
New York, NY 10022

First printing: February, 1989

Printed in the United States of America

10 9 8 7 6 5 4 3 2

For my very special parents,
Marihelen and Lou Jetter.

ACKNOWLEDGMENTS

My sincere thanks to a very special couple, Ruth and Bob Hoppe of Bisbee, Arizona, for sharing so many memories; to Doris Lemke for the grand tour of Bisbee; and to the Fort Huachuca Museum personnel for their much appreciated help.

And a very special thanks to my sister, Michele, for making my Arizona research trips so much fun.

AUTHOR'S NOTE

Today Fort Huachuca (Wah-choo-ka) is the only active Army garrison left of the more than seventy military posts established in Arizona during the frontier era. Although the buffalo soldiers (a name Indians bestowed on black soldiers after comparison of their hair with that of the shaggy animals) served extensively in this area, they are not reported at Huachuca until 1892. Because I felt these gallant men played such an important role in the taming of the West, I took the liberty of adjusting this date so that Hezekiah could take part in my story.

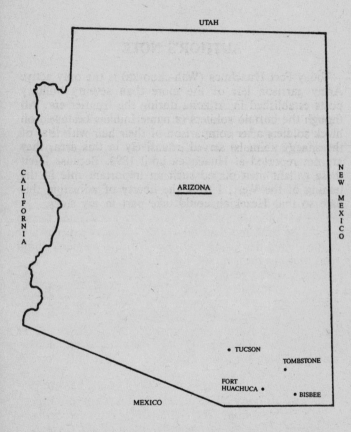

Prologue

Powers! The name leaped from the page. My God, could it truly be him? Was it possible that the man referred to in the faded newspaper article was the same Powers that had haunted Sterling Hawkins' dreams since adolescence?

Hawk drew a long ragged breath, his trembling hand clutching one page of the aged newspaper which had been used for packing material in the now-forgotten crate at his feet. Golden lamplight glinted off his nutmeg brown hair as he bent and held the ragged scrap of paper nearer to the light, devouring the words like a formerly blind man viewing the sun for the first time.

The headline read: "POWERS AND HIS MAGICAL MIRRORS TO JOIN ARMY'S SEARCH FOR GERONIMO," and the article went on to give a vivid description of the U.S. Army's long crusade to capture the elusive Indians led by the renegade Chiricahua Apache chief. Hawk's gaze skipped down the long column of spidery print, desperately searching for more information concerning Powers.

> *. . . have been pursuing the tenacious Apache since he and his band broke from the reservation on May 17, 1885. Among the additional personnel being transferred to the Arizona Territory to aid General Crook and General Miles in their seemingly endless crusade is Lieutenant Logan Powers, a recent West Point graduate. Powers will lend his expertise to the newly initiated heliograph system. . . .*

11

Hawk's heart sank. *Logan Powers*. It wasn't the same man. How could he have been so foolish as to believe fate would so casually present him with his enemy's whereabouts after all these years?

The yellowed paper slowly began to crumple within his fist and he drew back his arm, ready to consign the perfidious page to the blazing flames within the fireplace. But the pain became too strong, the mental pictures conjured up from the accounts he'd heard and read over the years too overpowering.

Wearily his arm dropped. With a soul-deep sigh, Hawk slumped against the back of his chair, his face etched with anguish as the familiar haunting drama once again played itself out against the screen of his shuttered eyelids.

He could almost smell the acrid odor of gunpowder, the scents of fire and sweat and fear defiling the sweet spring morning air of the small Indian village. A cacophony of sounds echoed in his head: the booming of gunfire, the shrill whinnies of horses plunging madly through the panicked people trying to flee the soldiers, the war cries of the braves as they desperately attempted to defend their homes and families, the heart-rending wails of women and children as they fell beneath the merciless onslaught of bullets and bayonets and flying hooves.

Oh, God. Dear God in heaven. Why was it still so vivid, so real? Had the spirits of his mother and father cried out to him that day in the last moments of their agony, reaching across the miles to find him within the safe haven of his aunt's house? Why had he been spared when the parents he adored had been massacred?

Great shuddering breaths were pulled into Hawk's belabored lungs, cleansing draughts to wash away the bitter memories.

Why? *Why?*

Questions had reverberated endlessly through his mind for years. Why had two of the kindest, most loving people in the world been so cruelly struck down? Why had Ten Bears sent word of his pending marriage at just that time? Why had Hawk's parents decided to journey to their old friend's village to join in the festivities? And what strange whim of fate had caused them to send their

12

son for his annual visit with his white relatives two weeks early that year?

He should have been with his mother and father. He would have, had they not been so determined that he learn the ways of both societies. They'd made sure he divided the time in his formative years between his Cherokee father's village and the small lumber-milling town where his mother's family lived. His parents had wanted their son to have the best of both worlds.

And then, suddenly they were gone and there was no peace for Hawk in either world.

The Indian way of life that he loved so dearly was dying—slowly, surely, inevitably. And in the white world, aside from his mother's hometown, he was an anomaly. At first glance, educated, wealthy Sterling Hawkins was readily accepted in the outside world because the silver blond coloring of Maria Hawkins had effectively muted the legacy of his Indian blood. Ah, but later, almost without exception, when the whites learned of his mixed heritage, things changed.

As the half-breed Silver Hawk, he often found himself subjected to the same prejudices suffered by all red men. He learned to pretend not to see the wary glances, to ignore the instinctive backward step many took when he approached, to show no emotion when a family suddenly found it inconvenient for him to continue calling on an eligible daughter. He had stoically endured it all, never revealing any of the pain he felt inside, waiting, hoping for things to improve. But they never did.

Eventually he'd turned away from the outside world. The business had become the center of his universe; he'd poured all his energy and passion into making the lumber mill the most successful in that part of the country, as if that would in some way prove his worth as a human being. And after a while it had simply become easier to send another when a business trip was necessary. Hawk preferred to stay within the confines of the town; at least there he was known and accepted.

Hawk's thoughts returned to Powers, and hatred speared through him, then he knew again that ache deep in his gut, so familiar it had become an accepted part of his being. Andrew Powers, the man who'd given the order for the raid, the man responsible for the deaths of Hawk's parents, and the destruction of Hawk's innocence, still walked free, and was revered and honored for his military endeavors on behalf of a society that called itself civilized.

"Someday," Hawk hissed vehemently. Someday Powers will pay, he thought.

Hawk squinched his eyes tight against the nightmarish pictures racing through his mind, fighting to control the whirlpool of fear and frustration and despair that always accompanied the return of these heart-wrenching memories.

Dragging his thoughts back to the present, he smoothed the rumpled page against the hard surface of his thigh and continued to read. Finishing the article would at least give him the satisfaction of once again reliving the story of how one small band of ragtag Indians held the mighty U.S. Army at bay. A fleeting hard-won moment of victory in the bitter struggle between red man and white.

Hawk knew that Geronimo and his men had eventually surrendered and had been banished from the wild free land of their forefathers, shipped like so many cattle to a reservation in Florida. Oh, but what a delicious fiasco that fifteen-month chase had been while it had lasted. A handful of Apaches, leading God only knew how many expensively outfitted soldiers on a merry chase through the southern Arizona Territory, through the parched deserts and up and down the craggy Sierra Madre Mountains.

American and European newspapers had had a field day with the story. Geronimo had been reported killed no less than three times during those wild months. And overly enthusiastic editors had penned versions of his surrender as many as five times before it actually took place in September of 1886.

A sharp hiss of air escaped Hawk's lips. He blinked hard and scanned the last lines of the article again, his mind refusing to believe what he'd just read.

14

. . . Lieutenant Powers will be joining his father at Fort Huachuca. Now serving as second in command at the fort, Major Andrew P. Powers is best known for his part in the Stone River Battle. . . .

Hawk's heart fluttered within his chest like a wild creature's. *Andrew Powers.* He read the name again, one long bronze finger brushing across the printed words as if to reassure himself of their truth. His gaze darted to the dateline of the gazette. More than a year had passed since Logan Powers had been ordered to Arizona Territory. Would he still be stationed there, now that the Apache Wars were over? And what about Major Powers? Was there any possibility he would still be in command at Fort Huachuca?

Hawk offered up a silent plea to the Great Spirit. If there was a chance, even the smallest chance, of finally facing his nemesis, of finally gaining the peace which had eluded him all these many years, then Hawk had to pursue it. Perhaps the fates would be kind to him and allow him to keep the vow he'd made so long ago.

He pulled a small leather pouch from his pocket, loosened the strings, and tipped it over. A delicate golden ring fell on to his palm—his mother's wedding ring, returned after that fateful day by an old Indian woman who'd somehow managed to escape the slaughter. Hawk's fingers curled inward, closing tight around the talisman.

He smiled. Vengeance would be sweet. So very, very sweet.

Chapter One

Arizona Territory — 1887

Rank upon rank of Indians filled the street. One hundred strong they rode behind their leader, lending a wild and barbaric flair to the festive parade. They were streaked and daubed with paint of many hues, bedecked with a colorful array of feathers, and armed with every species of weapon imaginable — primitive war clubs, bows and arrows, hatchets, knives, and the most up-to-date rifles. Their small, sinewy ponies pranced and snorted in response to the excitement filling the crisp autumn air.

"They're Papagos," Daniel Reed explained above the swoosh of carriage wheels and the rise and fall of cheers. "The hereditary enemy of the Apaches."

Sterling Hawkins bit back an instinctive response. He knew more about Indians than Daniel Reed ever would, but he dared not let anyone realize it. Shrugging against the confining cloth of his impeccably tailored jacket, Hawk momentarily envied the Indians the freedom and comfort of breechcloth and moccasins.

Quickly he pushed the errant thought away, aware of just how important it was that he maintain his cover story. Forcing himself to assume a look of rapt attention, he listened carefully as the *Arizona Sun* reporter continued with his rambling discourse on the local Indians.

Skies of breath-taking blue crowned the ragged mountain ranges surrounding Tucson. The fast-growing desert town sprawled haphazardly across a large flat plateau within a fairy ring of majestic peaks. Never quite tamed, the desert somehow seemed only to tolerate the sprinkling

17

of buildings and abodes atop its sandy chaparral-scattered surface.

From the corner of Pennington and Main, Hawk and Reed watched the parade honoring General Nelson A. Miles, heroic captor of the mighty Geronimo, snake its way through Tucson's evergreen- and bunting-bedecked streets. There were few spectators for the grand event, most of the town's citizens taking part in the spectacle themselves and the rest awaiting the arrival of the cavalcade and the guest of honor at the site of the bandstand in Levin's Park.

The parade was quite an extravaganza. It was made up of mounted policemen, a spit and polish military band, various army units, wave after wave of open carriages filled with dignitaries and officials, the fire chief with his hook and ladder company, school children and members of the Mexican Society enthusiastically marching along, Chief Asuncion Ruis and his mounted Papago Indians, and mounted citizens bringing up the rear.

"Guess we'd better get on our way or we'll never get close enough to the bandstand to hear the speakers," Daniel finally prompted.

Sterling Hawkins cast one last glance at the slowly moving spectacle before following his companion's lead. They hurried the short distance to the wooded park and then weaseled their way through the mass of humanity filling the festively decorated area, managing to reach the edge of the raised speakers' platform just as the last notes of the military band's patriotic opening number faded away and the official ceremonies began.

Once again Daniel began a discourse on the events leading up to the momentous occasion unfolding before them, eager to share his knowledge with his newfound friend and "fellow writer." He ended with a whispered who's-who litany on the few people seated upon the platform.

Hawk only half listened to the opening address and to the reading of letters and telegrams from dignitaries who were unable to attend. His deep-set eyes of midnight blue, as restless as his body was still, were searching face after face while he wondered if there was the slightest chance

18

any of the splendidly uniformed men in attendance might be his quarry.

The introduction of the principal speaker piqued Hawk's curiosity, and he turned his mind back to the drama being enacted on the stage. Judge William H. Barnes's voice rose in passion as he pontificated on the necessity of ridding the country of a deadly scourge. The muscles of Hawk's sculptured bronze jaw bunched in response to the man's vituperative tone.

"The Indian savage has lurked in every bush, hidden behind every tree, ambushed in every valley, and with his deadly war whoop at every moment of cowardly vantage, has rushed upon the sturdy emigrant, tomahawk and scalping knife in hand, following a volley of poisoned arrows, intent on every act of fiendish cruelty his savage cunning could invent."

Barnes paused for effect, his gaze sweeping the enthralled audience before he continued.

"His hand has never stayed, not even at the mother's breast, and with ecstatic joy he has dashed out the brains of infants torn from their mothers' corpses. His squaws in fiendish glee have held high carnival over scenes of carnage too brutal for description."

Heads bobbed. Excited murmurs of agreement rippled through the crowd.

Bile rose in Hawk's throat, and he longed to spew forth his anger at this blanket condemnation of a whole race. Clenching his fists at his sides, he refused to let more than mild interest show on his face. He hadn't traveled this far, waited this long, to ruin it all now in a fit of rage.

No one here knew him as Silver Hawk. He was simply Sterling Hawkins, a wealthy *bon vivant* and freelance writer, come to Arizona to gather material for a treatise on the "real story of Geronimo." He had carefully chosen his guise, wanting one under which he could move with ease throughout the territory. Such freedom hopefully would enable him to track down the information he was really after — the whereabouts of his hated enemy, Major Andrew P. Powers.

Barnes's rhetoric continued. "The Indians spread terror and devastation. Ranches were deserted, mines were abandoned, prospectors left the mountains and came rushing into the town for safety. The number of citizens killed within a few months was over two hundred—every one assassinated from an ambush without provocation or warning."

Hawk grimaced. Ah, yes, the standard oration—the villainous Indian, guilty en masse of unspeakable horrors. Why was there never a mention of the many equally abhorrent acts perpetrated by the whites over the years? Why was the story always so one-sided? Once, just once, couldn't someone publicly admit that the whites had committed their fair share of atrocities? Or even acknowledge that both races had been cursed with a number of brutal, selfish men? Why was it always the Indian who was at fault? Why were the actions of a few sufficient evidence to condemn a whole race of people?

Barnes's voice rose again, this time in an eloquent eulogy to their lauded guest.

"But then General Miles assumed command of the Department of Arizona. White-winged Peace has at last folded her frightened wings and has come to rest on a silver crag in yonder mountains. Prosperity has descended from the rocks where she is poised, and at last the most deadly of all the tribes of the Apaches has been sent from this country. Away from the mountains made famous by the raids of their ancestors, away from the land whose every rock and peak and mountain spring and water hole is an invitation to these savages to emulate the crimes of their fathers. Away from the people whose property they have destroyed, whose homes they have desolated, whose lands they have laid waste. And there let them remain, their red hands hanging powerlessly by their sides."

The crowd roared its approval, and Hawk recoiled from this indictment of his people. He forced himself to remain still, however; hiding the tremble of rage that seared through his tall frame. Only years of practice at cloaking his feelings allowed him to maintain an impassive, almost disinterested expression.

But, internally, he fought an almost overwhelming desire to express his umbrage at the continuing tirade that assaulted his ears, his mind, his soul. Frantically, Hawk turned his thoughts inward, striving to tap the pool of patience his father had spent years instilling in him.

As a young child, the legacy of his white mother—her natural exuberance—had frequently been at odds with the centuries-old tradition of his Indian heritage. But through practice and a fervent desire to please his father Hawk had persevered. He'd learned to hold his tongue, to listen, to see, and to decipher the smallest sign. He'd become proficient at the slow and deliberate art of tracking, and was better than most at lying perfectly still for long periods of time while waiting for the quarry to come close enough for the arrow to find its mark.

But this time the wellspring of patience seemed beyond his reach. This time he'd been pushed too far. He felt the insulating layers peel away one by one, leaving behind only a raw rage, a blinding desire to just once strike out in retaliation. Panic washed through him as he felt his control ebbing away.

Desperately Hawk pulled his attention away from the speaker. In an effort to shut out the man's offensive remarks, he tried an old trick. Starting at the far right side of the stage, he deliberately scrutinized first one, then another, of the figures seated on the platform, concentrating hard on every small detail.

But this time the diversionary tactic failed to work; he could still feel his tenuous hold on composure slipping away like sand sifting through one's fingers.

Suddenly a movement at the left of the stage caught his eye—a flash of robin's egg blue—as a beruffled parasol bobbed unsteadily. Overhead a soft breeze soughed through the stately cottonwoods sheltering the stage. The leaves rustled pleasantly as bright beams of light spread through the trembling boughs, spattering the platform and its occupants with a dancing pattern of sunshine and shadow. The frilly parasol dipped again, and the sun's daffodil glow caught and lingered lovingly on a shining mass of golden curls.

Hawk's heart gave a disconcerting hitch-and-hold beat before resuming its erratic thumping against his breastbone. The woman was beautiful, breathtakingly beautiful . . . a cool, refreshing oasis of serenity for his thirsting soul in the midst of bleak and barren wastes. Hawk fastened his gaze upon her, letting the soothing sight blot out the hateful words that had been tearing at his heart.

She must have felt the intensity of his regard, for she grew as still as a startled doe, then turned her head, her gaze moving curiously over the faces at the edge of the platform. He knew the minute she picked him out of the crowd. He could read her reaction in every tiny movement. Her eyes widened slightly, and then he clearly saw puzzlement in their deep brown depths when she realized he was a stranger. He waited for her frown, for an imperial toss of her head and the delivery of a chastising look.

But the rebuff never came.

Across the distance their gazes continued to hold. Then, surprisingly, gloriously, her full coral lips turned up, deepening a small dimple in one cheek. Hawk was shocked to feel the heat of his anger drain slowly away, leaving him with only the warm glow of the woman's smile.

The world receded, grew misty and distant in his battered mind. Even when the woman turned her attention back to the speaker, Hawk continued to watch her, and was inordinately pleased when she darted several more glances in his direction.

He hardly noticed when Barnes called for the token of the people's gratitude and appreciation to be brought forth. Murmurs of awe rippled through the crowd when the specially crafted Tiffany sword was presented, but they hardly registered on his mind. The gilded scabbard, engraved with scenes of Miles's successful battles against the Indians of Arizona, sparkled in the sun's rays, but Hawk gave it scarcely a glance. To him, its brilliance paled in comparison to the woman's golden beauty.

Hawk gave one quick look in the general's direction when Miles grasped the splendid sword and raised it. Then, almost immediately, his gaze returned to the woman. The multitude's cheering response to their hero's gesture barely penetrated his consciousness, although it was several minutes before the crowd quieted long enough to allow their honored guest an opportunity to speak. Hawk scarcely heard him.

"Thank you, thank you for this touching tribute. I

accept this token not for myself alone, but in behalf of the noble men who labored with me in putting down the Apaches."

The crowd roared its approval. Music rang out once again, and then a beautiful bouquet of brightly colored flowers was presented on behalf of the ladies of Yuma.

Miles smiled broadly as he accepted the floral token. "Mere words cannot express my thanks for having received such a token from earth's most beautiful creatures."

The festivities went on around Hawk, but for all he cared, the rest of the world could have disappeared. It had been a long time since he'd allowed himself to experience the simple pleasure of a beautiful woman's smile. He knew the moment would end soon. What's more, deep inside he knew it would never have happened if she had been aware of who he was; *what* he was. But suddenly, almost desperately, he wanted to wrap himself in the sweet warmth of her glances, to hold on to the small comfort they gave him, if only for this short while.

All too soon, it seemed, the speechmaking came to an end. The dignitaries on the stage rose, ready to take their leave. The woman cast one last shy smile in Hawk's direction before turning to accept the hand of the gentleman who had been seated next to her.

With a surge of sudden resentment Hawk watched the handsome soldier assist her to rise, then tuck her hand protectively through the crook of his arm before leading her from the stage. For an instant Hawk hated the unknown man. Hated him for the familiar way he touched the woman, and took her out of his sight.

Hated him for being all that Hawk himself was not . . . and never could be.

As the crowd surged forward, Hawk was jostled roughly. He caught his balance, and craned his neck to follow the progress of the golden-haired beauty, but she was lost in the milling crowd.

The sun dipped low over the mountains and a flag-stirring breeze feathered through the air. But the chill that whispered through Hawk owed its birth to a strange new feeling of loss rather than to the waning sunlight.

With an unbidden sigh, he gave in to the increasing press of people wanting to shake hands with their hero. Stepping to the side, he moved away from the eager flow of bodies until he at last stood alone at the edge of the crowd. He continued to watch quietly, almost sadly, as the band played the closing tunes and the throng slowly began to shuffle away.

But all the while his midnight blue eyes hungrily searched the shifting crowd for one last glimpse of the woman.

"Well, have you seen enough?"

Daniel's voice jerked Hawk back to reality. "What? Oh. Yes. Yes, of course. I'm ready to leave whenever you are," Hawk replied.

"The festivities are far from over," Daniel quickly said when he noticed Hawk's bleak look. "There are parties and soirees and socials planned for every evening this week."

"So I've heard."

"I thought you might be interested in tonight's events. There's to be a reception and ball at the San Xavier Hotel. Why don't you come with me? Everyone who's anyone will be there, and quite a few of the soldiers who participated in the Geronimo campaign will be present. I'll make sure you get to meet as many as possible."

Hawk's pulse quickened as his mind returned to his quest. "Sounds interesting. I certainly appreciate your inviting me to come along."

The reporter withdrew an engraved watch from the pocket of his embroidered vest, snapped it open. "Looks like we'll have just enough time to freshen up and change before the ball begins. It should provide some good material for your book."

"Then I suppose we'd best be on our way," Hawk responded, suddenly eager to return to the hotel, and once again anxious to take the next step toward fulfilling his vow of revenge.

The San Xavier's large dining room had been draped with bunting in the national colors, and the teasing

24

aroma of evergreen hung in the air, intensified by the hundreds of candles casting a warm glow over the festive scene.

"It might help if I had a little background on some of the people attending the ball tonight," said Hawk, determined to play to the utmost the role of inquisitive writer.

"Sure," Daniel agreed. "Just point someone out. I'll do the best I can."

Deliberately Hawk scanned the opulently decorated room. Paying scant attention to the cluster of officials surrounding General Miles and his party at the north end, he instead pointed out a random selection from the crowd. He then listened patiently to Daniel's comments, being careful to murmur appropriate phrases in all the right places.

The band in the far corner struck up a merry tune, and people shuffled toward the center of the floor, eager to begin the dancing. The brightly hued women's dresses looked like scattered jewels among the men's somber evening clothes and dark blue dress uniforms.

"Isn't that the same band that was at the park?" Hawk asked, raising his voice a little so he could be heard over the music.

"That's right. The Fourth Cavalry band. They do a good job, don't they?"

"Quite commendable for a frontier unit," Hawk agreed, his restless gaze still surveying the room.

A hiss of surprise escaped his lips as he spied new arrivals. He glanced sharply at Daniel, hoping the reporter hadn't noticed his unguarded reaction, but his next words were out of his mouth before he could hold them back.

"I . . . uh . . . I suppose I ought to think about adding a little color to the text. Some background on Mrs. Miles, or perhaps a little information on some of the other ladies present. For instance, that young lady over there . . ."

"Which one?" Daniel asked, turning to peer in the direction Hawk indicated.

He knew he should stop the crazy game right then. But he couldn't. The words continued to tumble out despite his misgivings. "That one. Over there by the windows—the one in the lavender gown. Do you know anything about her?" Hawk's breath hung in his throat as he waited for an answer.

Daniel craned to catch a glimpse of the young woman through the milling crowd. With a small shake of his head he turned back to Hawk. "No. No, I can't say that I recognize her."

"Oh."

The reporter's trained ears caught the faint tone of disappointment in Hawk's voice. He grinned up at his friend. "But I can see why she caught your attention. She's certainly lovely."

"Yes. Yes, she is," Hawk murmured softly.

The mental lecture Hawk had delivered to himself earlier while changing into formal attire had been wiped from his mind the moment the woman had entered the ballroom. All his vows to forget the disconcerting episode in the park, to concentrate on the task at hand, had disappeared like smoke on a warm desert wind.

Undeniable jealousy surged through Hawk when he recognized the man at the blond beauty's side, the same man who'd ushered her off the park platform. Who the hell was he anyway, and what right did he have to stand so close to her, to let his hand linger in such a familiar manner against the small of her back?

Hawk's hungry gaze caressed the woman, absorbing each tiny detail. He judged her to be three or four years younger than himself, surely no more than twenty-one. She was small, her head barely coming to the soldier's shoulder. The gossamer ruffle edging the low-cut neckline of her dress shimmered with each movement, paying homage to her soft curves, and her glorious mass of blond hair was swept upward from the sides, then caught at the crown with a cluster of purple ribbons. Streamers from these flowed and twined amongst her long gilded tresses, and when she tilted her head, ringlets of molten gold swayed against the rich cream of her bare shoulder, finally coming to rest against the gentle swell of her breast.

Hawk tried to look away, but it was hopeless. Deep

26

down he knew his full attention should remain on his prime goal, that all his energies had to be targeted toward fulfilling his vow. But despite this knowledge, a small insistent voice continued to whisper in his heart.

What was it about this woman that tugged at him so? She'd offered him no more than a friendly smile. Why this sudden, almost consuming, desire to touch her, hold her, even if just for a few moments?

Unconsciously, Hawk reached to knead the tightening muscles at the base of his neck, as he considered approaching her. He had far more important things to worry about. And, besides, what good would it do?

That discomforting pit-of-the-stomach jealousy flared again as Hawk watched the man solicitously bend his head toward the woman.

". . . How about it?"

"Uh? What?" Hawk's head snapped around. "I . . . uh . . . I'm sorry. I didn't quite hear what you said. The music . . ."

"I asked if you were about ready for a small drop of liquid refreshment," Daniel repeated with a wry grin. "How about it?"

"No. Uh, no, thank you." Hawk shifted his weight restlessly. "I think I'll just stay here for a while longer. But, please, don't let that stop you. Go right on."

"All right. I'll see you later." With a wave, the dapper little reporter disappeared into the shifting throng.

Once again Hawk's attention returned to the woman. Giving himself a hard mental shake, he continued his internal expostulations. What on earth was he thinking of? The soldier could easily take offense at a stranger approaching his . . . his . . .

No! Not wife. Not betrothed. Hawk refused to even acknowledge the possibility.

She didn't belong to the soldier. *She didn't!*

However, even if the soldier didn't object, Hawk had no way of knowing how this woman would react. In polite society, ladies expected proper gentlemen to wait for formal introductions.

Still, what had impeccable manners earned him in the past? Bitterness flashed in indigo eyes as Hawk thought of how often over the years the narrow-minded pillars of polite society had refused to accept him. Why in hell should he continue to worry about what was right and proper?

A dance, the tormenting voice whispered. Just one dance. What could it hurt?

Tiny furrows etched Hawk's prominent brow as he continued to observe the couple. The woman tilted her head to one side, laughing at something the man said, and Hawk longed for it to be his words that called forth that bright cascade of sound.

Suddenly his pulse quickened as the woman's rose-petal lips turned upward in a quick smile. The soldier leaned forward, murmured another word or two. She responded with a quick nod, and the man turned and left.

She was alone.

For a moment Hawk forgot to breathe. "Why not? Why the hell not?" The words slipped out on a ragged sigh. And then he gave in to temptation, eagerly embracing the justifications buzzing in his head.

My God, was he less than human? Didn't he deserve a few moments of sunlight in a world that had become increasingly gray and lonely? Tomorrow would come soon enough, and he'd leave Tucson and the woman far behind while he continued his crusade.

A small acerbic smile played on Hawk's lips. After all, who knew what might happen if he found Powers? There was no guarantee he'd even survive.

Resolutely Hawk started across the room.

Chapter Two

The lilting melody of the waltz wafted through the room. Sabra's feet moved to the music, the full skirt of her satin dress swaying softly with her unconscious motions. Head swiveling this way and that, she tried to see everything at once, with childlike eagerness perusing the crowded room, delight at the kaleidoscope of sounds and sights and aromas evident in her every move, every expression.

It had been a wonderful day, so exciting, so different from her sedate life back East with her grandparents. She almost wished it would never end. But somehow she knew this day had been only a taste of what was to come. The future unfurled before her, so bright and shining, so promising. She felt almost radiant in the expectation of wonderful things to come.

"I couldn't help but notice how you're enjoying the music."

The words laced through the melody-laden air. Sabra gave a tiny gasp of surprise, and turned toward the speaker. Her gaze first encountered nothing but the pristine starched surface of a beruffled shirt framed by ebony lapels. The man was tall, very tall. Golden curls brushed against the small of her back as Sabra tilted her head to view him, and her heart fluttered like a leaf on the wind when she recognized the man from the park.

"Could I be so bold as to request the pleasure of a dance with you?"

His voice was deep, assured; as caressing as black satin against her skin. With an elegant offer of his arm, he tilted his head questioningly toward the dancers in the middle of the room, a hopeful smile tipping the corners of his chiseled mouth.

Surprised to see him again, Sabra hesitated, and for the tiniest fraction of a second, something other than assurance flickered in the bottomless blue depths of the stranger's eyes. But the change in expression was gone so fast Sabra credited it to a trick of lighting.

In the very next instant her mind was made up. "I'd love to dance. Thank you for asking."

Hawk's heart soared as he watched her lips once again curl upward in that delightful, accepting way. And when that beguiling dimple deepened in one peach-blossom cheek, he was almost overwhelmed. He marveled at how her eyes, deep brown and inquisitive as a newborn fawn's sparkled even more brightly when she smiled.

His answering smile—hesitant at first, then widening, though never quite touching the secret depths of his eyes—sent a rush of warmth through Sabra. The smile crinkled the corners of his eyes, pulling golden skin taut over high cheekbones, and she thought again how handsome he was. Something about the smooth, angled planes of his face, the proud slope of forehead sheltering deep-set eyes of darkest blue, reminded her of exotic lands and of the noble princes in the fairytale books of her girlhood.

"I'd love to dance," Sabra repeated bravely, tucking a dainty hand through the proffered crook of an arm covered by finely woven black broadcloth.

Relief surged through Hawk when he felt the soft touch of her fingers on his arm. Her shining innocent smile washed over him, unknowingly finding a tiny chink in the protective armor he'd worn for years and gently warming him deep within.

Unknown to Hawk, something strange, something totally unanticipated, began to happen—a tiny seed of long dormant, almost forgotten emotions put down tender quavering roots in the bleak wasteland of his soul.

Placing one hand protectively, almost possessively, over the small hand tucked within the bend of his arm, Hawk expelled a contented sigh and proudly led Sabra to the edge of the dance floor. Her bright, trusting smile blossomed once again when he turned to take her in his arms.

As he touched her waist, Hawk fleetingly thought he could easily span its small circumference with his two hands. Then he reached out for her hand. Her fingers, delicate and fragile as a hummingbird's wings, fluttered against his left palm, and his heart mimicked that beat.

Thought fragments tumbled through Sabra's bedazzled brain. He was so tall, so imposing, so male. Her hand, cradled in his, seemed lost in the vast expanse of his palm. And when his long fingers closed gently around hers, she suddenly felt . . . safe.

As the music washed over them, Sabra followed Hawk's strong lead with total trust, her view of the world narrowed to broad shoulders and midnight blue eyes. Each move he made was satin smooth, each turn and sway and swirl of the dance as gentle and flowing as the morning mist on the soughing wind.

Blue eyes gazed down into brown ones. Lean tanned fingers unknowingly tightened against satin-shrouded flesh, urging her closer, just a tiny step closer.

Words seemed unnecessary.

The crowded, noisy room faded away as they turned and twirled to the dulcet strains of the music. It was enough to just touch and look and savor the strange magic of the moment.

And then, too soon, their dance was over.

The music ceased, and the band left the room to take a short break. For moments Hawk and Sabra stood, eyes locked, frozen at the edge of the dance floor.

His hand tightened convulsively at her waist, as though loath to give up its hold on her. Her fingers pressed closer to the heated strength of his palm as the strange frissons that seemed to radiate from their joined hands accelerated, tingling their way up her arm and pulsating in the most delicious manner throughout her whole body.

He drank in the way her thick silk lashes cast a velvet shadow on blush-tinged cheeks.

She feasted her gaze on the tiny pulsebeat at the corner of his jaw.

His heart beat faster as her delectable mouth parted

31

slightly and the tiny pink tip of her tongue darted out to moisten rose-petal lips. For one wild, wonderful, tormenting moment he ached to lower his head and claim those lips for his own.

Madness.

Sheer madness.

Hawk yanked himself back from the precipice of forbidden desire. It was impossible.

More than impossible.

They came from different worlds, worlds that could never meet, never blend. And he'd sworn a vow . . . a blood vow.

It was time, past the time, to end this impossible dream.

Chapter Three

Sabra was startled out of the delicious state that had embraced the two of them when Hawk suddenly stepped away from her as if he'd been brushed by flames. Emotion flickered in the blue depths of his hooded eyes, then disappeared as quickly as it had come.

Remorse? Regret? She wasn't sure.

The warmth and openness seeped from his features, leaving his face an inscrutable sculpted bronze mask.

Turning quickly on his heel, Hawk took Sabra's arm in an unfaltering grip and hastily guided her through the press of people and off the dance floor before his staunch resolutions were swept away like so many feathers on the wind. With great determination, he ignored the bewildered lash-sheltered glances she cast in his direction as he escorted her to her original place by the window.

"Thank you for the dance," he said when they reached their destination. "You were most kind to indulge a stranger's request." Even to his ears, the words sounded aloof, almost stilted.

"Y-you're welcome," Sabra stammered. She was more than a little perplexed by this man's abrupt behavior.

Despite his intentions, Hawk lingered before her, his gaze roaming over her perfect features as if to memorize them. The delicate pulse at the base of her throat held his attention for a long agonizing moment while he struggled against a growing desire to lead her back to the dance floor so he might take her in his arms once again.

He bit back a curse. What folly! He had to get hold of himself. There was, after all, no point in prolonging the situation.

She was an extraordinarily beautiful woman, and dancing with her had been a rare pleasure, but that had to be the end of it. This was but a moment of innocent indulgence before he knuckled down to the all-consuming goal at hand. Nothing more.

Hawk was well aware that there was no time for foolish pleasantries. He still had a dozen tasks to accomplish before the stage to Fort Huachuca left in the morning. He should be seeing to them instead of spending his time on nonsense such as this.

His mind once again on track, Hawk gave Sabra a perfunctory nod of his head and, like a puff of smoke, silently slipped away.

"Well, my goodness gracious," she murmured in surprise as she watched him disappear into the crowd, her eyebrows lifting in a puzzled arc.

His abrupt departure left her slightly off kilter. What could have caused his sudden change in attitude? Mercy's sake, she thought. It wasn't as if she'd stumbled over his feet while they'd danced. Not at all. The dance had been as enjoyable for him as it had for her. She was positive of that. No hint of dissatisfaction had flared in his eyes as he'd held her in his arms and moved to the lilt of the music.

Sabra's mouth turned downward in a perplexed frown. A minute shrug of her creamy shoulders set the lavender ruffle aflutter. The whole incident seemed decidedly peculiar, even a little annoying.

She was honest enough with herself to admit she wished the stranger had stayed around a while longer. There was something terribly intriguing about him. Something besides his dashing good looks and the expert way he'd guided her about the dance floor . . .

"Here's your punch."

The words shattered Sabra's bemused speculations. "Oh! Thank you," she said, accepting the proffered cup and taking a quick sip to cover her discomposure. "Ummm. Delicious."

"Come along," her companion urged. "There're some more people I want you to meet."

"Yes, of course."

Quickly pasting a bright smile on her face, Sabra turned to follow her escort's lead. But even as they crossed the room, her eyes restlessly searched for one last glimpse of the tall dark stranger.

Boot heels tapping in unison, Hawk and Daniel Reed walked toward the stage depot. Nestled in the ring of protective mountains, the town was quiet. The majority of its citizenry were evidently recuperating from their long night of revelry, resting up for the parties still to come before the Miles celebration came to an end.

"Well, Hawkins, be sure to look me up if you ever come through Tucson again." Shielding his eyes from the bright new sun, Daniel slowed long enough to grin up at his new acquaintance.

"I will," Hawk replied. He sounded sincere, but deep inside he knew there was only a slight chance he'd ever see the little reporter again. "I want to thank you for all your help the last few days."

Daniel's lopsided grin blossomed again. "You're quite welcome. Oh, and good luck with your research. I'll be looking forward to reading your work in published form someday soon. Now, remember I expect you to keep me informed. Let me know how it goes."

"Thanks. I'll be sure to do that." Hawk quickly buried the twinge of guilt he felt at once again having to lie to someone who'd been so accepting and helpful to a stranger.

His purpose justified the falsehood. He just had to keep remembering that.

"Your bags already loaded?"

"Yes. I brought them over before breakfast."

Daniel nodded approvingly. "Well, 'pears they're about ready to head out. You'd better get aboard before they leave without you." He delivered the statement with a jerk of his russet-haired head in the direction of the stage-coach waiting down the street. "Looks like the rest of the passengers are already inside."

A restless horse's snort and the jingle of the team's

35

harness underscored Daniel's remark.

"Easy there, fellas, easy," the grizzled stage driver called out in a whiskey-roughened voice that rode the chill morning air with ease. He tightened his hold on the long leather lines threaded through his callused fingers, and the shuffling horses immediately quietened under his skillful hands.

At that moment the shotgun rider exited the stage line's small office. He headed for the waiting coach, never breaking stride as he mashed a battered broad-brimmed hat down atop his shaggy head. Cradling a weapon almost as long as he was tall in the crook of one flannel-clad arm, the guard quickly clambered up the side of the dilapidated stage to take his place beside the driver. Once settled, he turned and cast a baleful look in the direction of their lagging passenger.

Hawk took the hint. "Well, thanks again." He thrust out his hand for a farewell shake.

Daniel's bony hand gripped Hawk's, pumping it up and down enthusiastically. "Have a good trip. And keep in touch; don't forget."

"Sure."

Hawk hurried forward. Three long steps and he was beside the scarred brown cab of the coach and reaching for the door.

His fingers closed over the handle. A quick turn and the door swung open, its hinges emitting a soft squeak of protest. With one fluid motion, Hawk grasped the edges of the doorframe and agilely pulled himself upward, his bulk filling the small rectangular space and blocking out the searching yellow fingers of the early morning sun.

At the very next instant he froze in place, totally nonplused by the sight of his fellow passengers.

It couldn't be. It simply couldn't be.

But it was.

Seated inside the coach were the blond temptress he'd danced with the past night . . . and her relentless escort.

"Here, let me get that out of your way," the man said, swiftly reaching to remove his hat and thereby making room for Hawk on the seat next to him. His smile wide and white and friendly, he slid a few more inches to the far side.

"Thank you," Hawk replied in a voice that revealed no hint of his discomposure. He was grateful that the next few seconds were taken up by the small necessary tasks of shutting the door and getting settled on the narrow leather seat opposite the woman. It afforded him time to begin an assessment of the situation.

Hawk had barely taken his place when the driver's voice rang out. "Yee-ha!"

The stage lurched forward.

Jostled by the sudden movement, Hawk's knee lightly bumped the woman's. Another bounce and the contact was broken, except for the soft folds of her skirt which continued to brush his trousers with each sway of the coach.

Hawk's gaze snapped upward, troubled eyes of darkest blue meeting the woman's curiosity-filled gaze.

She gave a small acknowledging nod, the hint of a hesitant smile tilting one corner of her mouth as she waited expectantly for some sort of recognition from him.

Now what? Hawk questioned silently. He darted a quick sideways glance at the man occupying the other half of his seat.

The soldier was big, a couple of inches taller than Hawk himself, and just as broad shouldered. The man shifted in his seat, adjusting his bulk against the hard backrest, and sunlight glinted off the silver bar on his collar. An unruly mop of curls, the deep bronze gold of old coins, feathered across the smooth plane of his forehead. An aura of raw strength surrounded him.

Hawk's attention returned to the woman. Had she told her companion about their dance? Probably not. The soldier had given no indication that he recognized Hawk as more than a total stranger.

Should he pretend he'd never seen her before? Or would it be more in tune with the role he was playing to admit that he'd seen both of them at the park, that he'd spoken to the woman last night, that he'd held her in his arms. . . .

He couldn't decide. He'd leave it up to her.

"Uh, mornin', ma'am."

37

The noncommittal words were accompanied by a quick tug of his hat brim, after which Hawk quickly looked out the window, pretending to study the landscape. As Tucson slowly receded into the misty distance, he struggled to recapture the initial interest he'd felt when viewing this area from the train that had carried him to the little desert town.

The land was a collage of browns and tans and dusty greens. Flat and barren in some places. Tangled with an intriguing array of extraordinary foliage in others. He'd recognized cypress and pine and juniper, but he'd had to ask Daniel Reed to identify the other growth. The little *Arizona Sun* reporter had been more than happy to provide a multitude of lyrical names—ocotillo and cholla and yucca and paloverde. The melodic words had fairly rolled from his tongue.

But, try as he might, the magic of the chaparral didn't beckon Hawk today.

For a long while the silence in the coach contrasted with the thunder of hooves, the incessant rumble of the wheels, and the soft whistle of the wind. Then the man next to Hawk cleared his throat and shifted in his seat, his ham-sized right hand extended toward Hawk.

"Since we have an all-day trip ahead of us, I suppose we ought to get acquainted."

"Yes. Yes, of course," Hawk replied quickly, gripping the soldier's hand for a quick shake. "Hawkins. Sterling Hawkins."

"Glad to make your acquaintance, Mr. Hawkins. I'm Logan Powers."

An invisible fist delivered a blow to Hawk's solar plexus. *Powers!* My God, he had to be kidding! What kind of crazy coincidence could have created this situation? But Hawk's silent ruminations were swept right out of his mind by the man's next words.

"And this charming lady is Sabra Powers."

Powers. Denial twisted deep in Hawk's gut.

"My sister."

For a split second Hawk was speechless. *Sister?* His heart gave an unexpected lurch of relief. The soldier wasn't her husband, or even her fiancée. Her brother. Just

38

her brother.

Hawk's gaze flickered to the woman's face, and he was inordinately pleased to see the tantalizing smile teasing at her lips once again.

Then the real import of the man's words sank in. *Sweet heaven!* That made her Major Powers's daughter.

Chapter Four

Sabra's eyes studied the stranger. The dim lighting in the coach caressed the planes of his face, making his high cheekbones even more prominent. And there was something almost regal about his high-bridged nose, though his hooded eyes were unreadable indigo pools, shaded by a prominent forehead and twin slashes of crow's-wing brows.

His hair reminded her of the rich, tempting color of the dark chocolate bonbons old Mrs. Sinclair used to display in the glass case at the front of her store. The ones that had always made Sabra's mouth water.

She like the way the not-quite-straight locks brushed against the black broadcloth of his collar and curved ever so slightly over his ears. Her fingers flexed unconsciously as she wondered if that dark mass of hair could possibly be as thick and as soft as it looked.

Continuing her surreptitious examination, Sabra cataloged the strong line of jaw, the square, almost chiseled, chin. Cautiously she allowed herself an upward glance. His upper lip was long, fuller than the bottom one, and gave his mouth a hint of sensuousness that contrasted intriguingly with his very masculine features. When he smiled, the even line of his teeth was startlingly white against his deep tan.

Sabra's gaze dropped to hands resting casually on knees that occasionally whisked against the skirt of her dark blue traveling suit. Something fluttered deep within her breast as she remembered the way those long fingers had closed around hers, how small her hand had felt enveloped in his.

The man, seemingly quite at ease, swayed gently with the roll of the coach. But somehow Sabra sensed that underneath his calm, easy demeanor lay a coiled-spring readiness. Steel cloaked in velvet.

Suddenly she realized that this man was studying her with almost the same intensity with which she was regarding him. A rosy flush stained her cheeks and she quickly averted her eyes.

He was an enigma. And he fascinated her more than she dared to admit.

Outside, the sun's bright rays had burned away the early morning mist and had stolen the chill from the air. The temperature of the stage interior had risen with the sun. The subtle aroma of Sabra's fragrance drifted through the confining space, mingling most pleasantly with the faint smell of dust and desert.

Hawk's outward deportment revealed nothing of the turmoil that was raging inside him. *Sabra*. His lips longed to shape the word aloud. Sabra. A fitting name for one so lovely, so refreshingly open and accepting. But he allowed himself little time to dwell upon such thoughts. More disturbing concerns were echoing through his mind.

He should be feeling overpowering joy at finally finding a link to his quarry. Instead, undeniable relief surged through him because Sabra wasn't married. Why that should be so important to him, he simply didn't want to analyze. Meanwhile, his mind was doing its best to avoid dealing with the connection between this woman and his sworn enemy.

What did it matter anyway? Nothing had changed.

Neither Sabra Powers nor his unquestionable attraction to her would make the smallest difference in his plans. He'd made a blood vow, and by everything honorable he had to fulfill it. His strange fascination with her could not be allowed to interfere.

Indeed, the fulfillment of that vow would effectively destroy any chance for even a casual friendship with Sabra, and if that were not the case, Hawk had to consider the stigma of his Indian blood.

No, things weren't going to change. He knew it was

useless to dwell on what might have been if circumstances had been different.

Atop the stage, the driver snapped his snakelike whip over the heads of his team. The horses strained harder against the harness, and the coach picked up speed, rumbling over the rutted road.

The shotgun rider clamped his rifle between his knees while he dug a worn tobacco pouch out of his coat pocket. Stained fingers secured a wad of chaw and expertly transported it to his mouth. Jaw bulging, the man retrieved his rifle from its resting place and once again nestled it into the familiar crook of his arm.

The right front wheel hit a deep rut, and the springs creaked in protest as the coach body dipped wildly toward the undercarriage. Inside, the passengers were jostled roughly before the vehicle settled back into a normal swaying motion.

"Is your trip to Fort Huachuca business or pleasure, Mr. Hawkins?"

Logan Powers's question jarred Hawk out of his revery. "Ah . . . both, I suppose. Yes, a little of both." Hawk turned slightly, appearing to give the man his full attention. "I've always wanted to see the West. And my current project gave me the perfect excuse. You see, I'm conducting some research on Geronimo, for a book."

"A book on Geronimo?" Logan repeated with a quizzical lift of one taffy-colored brow.

"Yes. My ultimate goal is to write the real story of what happened." The lie rolled off Hawk's tongue effortlessly. Why shouldn't it? He'd told it a dozen times before.

"Well, in that case, your visit to the fort may be quite a lengthy one," Logan replied with a flash of smile. "Many of the military maneuvers were directed from Huachuca."

"Yes, I know."

"And what, may I be so bold as to ask, prompted your interest in the subject, Mr. Hawkins?" Sabra's voice was softly inquisitive. Her dress rustled as she wriggled to settle herself more comfortably against the hard leather cushion.

Hawk shrugged. He'd long ago prepared what he hoped was a proper answer.

42

"Simple curiosity, I suppose. And perhaps a touch of frustration after reading at least twenty different accounts of what happened. Every newspaper seemed to have its own version."

"And just what approach will you take in your report, Mr. Hawkins?"

"I'm looking for the truth. It's as simple as that," Hawk answered quietly, his dark eyes unconsciously assessing the graceful way her fingers smoothed the lapel of her jacket. "Perhaps it's time people were told the whole story."

Logan's laugh was good-natured, but a touch derisive. "Well, the truth is that Geronimo and his renegades played merry hell with the settlers of this territory for over fifteen months. Ran the Army absolutely ragged. They were cruel, ruthless men who thought nothing of the innocent lives they took—"

"I'm sure some of them were," Hawk stated, his voice still firm and controlled. He turned his piercing gaze upon Logan. "But, can you honestly say that there haven't been white men equally as guilty? Remember, there are always two sides to every story."

Logan cocked his head to one side, perusing his fellow passenger with a bright-eyed interest that threatened to slip into mild irritation.

"Surely you aren't implying that the whole affair was covered only from the Army's point of view?"

There was a sudden coolness in Hawk's voice, a coolness that hadn't been there before. "You might say that," he finally replied.

"Ridiculous!" Logan declared with a snort. "And what's more, it's senseless to drag the damn thing out again if all you want to do is exonerate Geronimo."

"Really?"

"Yes, really," Logan said, with an exasperated shake of his head. "Lord! Sometimes I wish this damn country had never kept pushing west. I often think we'd have been a whole lot smarter if we'd just left the land and the Indians alone."

"I have no doubt the Indians would agree with you." The corner of Hawk's mouth tilted in a bitter smile. He speared the man beside him with an assessing gaze. "I would have pegged you as a sensible man, Lieutenant Powers. Surely you don't object to someone telling both sides of this story." Deep in Hawk's stomach, a familiar knot began to form. "Or is it Indians in general that you object to?"

Sabra squirmed with discomfort at the turn the conversation had taken. Then she saw Logan's jaw tighten and her apprehension flared higher. She had to stop him before he dredged up matters she'd fought long and hard to forget.

"Now, Logan," she interjected quickly, "please don't go and spoil our nice trip by getting into some silly ol' political debate."

A long look passed between brother and sister, an acknowledgment of something Hawk couldn't begin to fathom. But there was no denying the unspoken plea in Sabra's eyes. Obviously, the topic under discussion made her quite uncomfortable.

"All right, honey, I won't. Don't worry." Gentle reassurance laced Logan's voice.

Hawk watched the tension slowly seep out of Sabra, an uncomfortable flush of remorse spreading through him. He shouldn't have baited Logan Powers. He almost felt ashamed. Sabra was sweet and innocent and totally enchanting. And, after all, she hadn't chosen the man who would be her father. Fate had played them all a dirty trick.

One day soon, Hawk would be responsible for bringing great sorrow to Sabra's life; there was no need to cause her discomfort in the meantime.

By unspoken agreement, the trio dropped the subject, and rode in silence for a long while. When conversation began again, it was if they had each made a personal pact to steer clear of further unpleasantness.

Hawk had been studying the ragged line of mountains framed by the stage's window. Finally, clearing his throat somewhat nervously, he asked the name of the range.

Logan answered quickly. And then, rather than letting the conversation die down, he continued with an informative discourse about the land and its history, as if suddenly eager to make up for the harsh words exchanged earlier.

"Ten years ago, Captain Whitside was given the task of establishing a camp near the Mexican border. He led Company B of the Sixth Calvary south and finally chose a canyon at the foot of the Huachuca Mountains—"

"Huachuca, an Indian name." Hawk's words were more statement than question.

"Right," Logan said with an affirmative nod, as though pleased that their companion had caught on so quickly. "It means thunder mountain. And the area certainly lives up to its name any time a storm hits."

Hawk gave an appreciative deep chuckle in response to the small joke.

Logan continued. "I'd have to agree that Whitside picked the perfect site. The area's heavily wooded, on high ground, and there's plenty of water. Huachuca Creek flows into the Babocomari and then on into the San Pedro River. There was even an established Indian trail leading from the canyon to a ford across the river."

"And the fort has served its purpose well, from what I've read."

"Yes. They managed to put a drastic halt to the raiders working out of Mexico. Did such a good job, in fact, that settlers started moving into this part of the territory late in seventy-seven."

Hawk's gaze returned to the vast panorama outside the window. His keen eyes caught a quick glimpse of a rabbit, nose atwitch as it carefully hopped from the shelter of an isolated dusty green bush. The sandy tan coloring of the area surrounding Tucson had slowly given way to ground streaked with rusty red. Coarse grass did its best to blanket the roughly rolling land with thick bleached-green clumps.

"It sure doesn't look like this land's been settled. I haven't seen a sign of people since we left Tucson."

"It's a vast country, Mr. Hawkins. Miles and miles of it open, and lots of mountains—some hardly more than hills, some truly awesome peaks. Believe me, I know what I'm talking about," Logan said with a low chuckle. "Thanks to Army orders, I've ridden up and down a good many of them."

Hawk and Sabra exchanged amused looks at her brother's sally.

Logan drew his brows together in reflection. "This land is special, filled with a sort of magic. It's unlike anything I've ever known, unbelievably raw and wild. And just when you think you might be taming it a bit, the heavens open up and deluge us, or one of those damned earthquakes hits and the very ground moves like liquid beneath you."

"They had a big one in May, didn't they, Logan?" Sabra interjected. "I'm rather sorry I missed it."

Logan shook his head to negate Sabra's whimsical remark. "You'd better be glad you did. Earthquakes are nothing to wink at. Mankind's not equipped to deal with such forces. Let me tell you, I was more than a little scared myself."

"What happened?"

"It started in the afternoon. One big shock, and two smaller ones spread out over a couple of hours. Shook the whole area around the fort like a dog playing with a bone. By four-thirty there was thick black smoke hanging over the San Jose Mountains. Next, a huge gray column sprouted from the highest peak of the Whetstones. Then night came and we could see that the entire top of the Whetstone Mountains was in flames. It looked like something lifted right out of Hades. All red and orange and gold, kind of suspended between the black of the mountains and the black of the sky."

"Mercy," Sabra gasped, her eyes wide at the awesome picture her brother painted.

"During later reconnaisance we found the flow of several creek beds completely altered. And over in the Mustang Mountains, tons of rock had cascaded down the eastern side. We were lucky; it only did slight damage to the buildings at the fort.

"It didn't affect any populated areas?" Hawk asked.

"Not that I'm aware of. Not too many settlers around here except for those clustered around the fort, and a good-sized settlement over in the Mule Mountains. But the area's growing. Yes, sir, it's growing. Someday this will all be different. Civilized."

The thought filled Hawk with a sudden sadness. Sadness at the possibility of the raw beauty of the land being swallowed up by the white man's cluttering buildings. Sadness that the clean crisp desert air might someday be desecrated by belching smokestacks like those that fouled the air back East.

But Logan Powers prophesied correctly. Progress, for better or worse, was coming.

For the most part, the Indians had already been banished from their ancestral lands, isolated on dirty, crowded reservations, forced to rely on handouts from the white man to survive.

Hawk's heart contracted at the knowledge of how rapidly the Indian's way of life was dying out. God, how he longed for just one more opportunity to enjoy the freedom he'd known as a young boy, running wild and free on the vast open plains surrounding the small Indian village of his father's people.

But it was useless to wish for the impossible. Hawk suppressed a sigh and pushed the troublesome thought away. "I seem to remember reading about you in the newspapers," he said to Logan. "Something about heliographs, wasn't it?"

Logan grinned, not the least bit self-conscious. "That's me, all right. I was sent out here to help set up a system of heliograph outposts during the . . . uh . . . Geronimo campaign."

Logan glossed over the word, as if hoping to avoid the previous animosity about the subject. Hawk played his part well, listening with no apparent sign of his earlier irritation.

"The whole thing was really Miles's pet project," Logan went on to explain. "I helped set up several of the other stations, but mostly I took charge of the one on a peak up in the Huachucas overlooking the fort."

The time had come to obtain some much needed information. His face carefully composed, Hawk proceeded. "Did the fact that your father was stationed in Arizona influence your decision to take a post here?"

Logan's wide, friendly smile appeared again. "In a

roundabout way, you might say that's the case."

"Oh?" Hawk prodded.

"My instructor at West Point was an old friend of the family, and when I suddenly found myself in a bit of a scrape over an officer's wi—"

Logan hastily bit back the word. He darted a quick look in his sister's direction before winking broadly at Hawk.

"Well, let's just say, he deemed a post in the faraway West the best solution to what could have become a rather sticky situation. I'd had training in the craft of heliograph messages, and Miles was desperate for men to run his stations. And, so"—Logan spread his hands wide—"here I am."

"Is your father still stationed at Fort Huachuca?" Hawk's breath stilled in his chest as he waited for the answer.

"Yes, he is," Logan answered. "He's second in command under Lieutenant Colonel George Forsyth. And it looks like he's going to stay at this posting for a while. Actually, that's the reason for Sabra being out here. Right, sis?"

Hawk watched greedily as that wonderful smile wreathed Sabra's face once again.

"Absolutely right, Logan dear," she said with a gentle nod of her head. Then she turned her big, brown eyes full force on Hawk. "You see, Mr. Hawkins, I'd been living back East with our grandparents since I was a small child. I was delighted when I found out Father might be at Fort Huachuca for an extended period of time, especially since Logan was also stationed there. I hadn't seen much of either of them for several years. I suggested that the time had come for me to join my fam—"

"Suggested!" Logan said amidst hoots of laughter. "That's an understatement if I ever heard one."

Sabra's eyes narrowed threateningly. "Now, see here, Logan."

"The truth is, we received a letter stating she was coming, like it or not. Nothing Father said dissuaded her. We could either help her make plans for her arrival or wait for her to show up on our doorstep." Logan's words held

48

the teasing, loving tone older brothers so often use with little sisters.

"That's not exactly the way it was," Sabra protested insistently.

Logan's rich, full laughter rang out again. "Don't you believe it for a minute, Mr. Hawkins. The little lady can be as stubborn as a mule when she sets her mind to something."

"Logan!" Blotches of bright color appeared on Sabra's cheeks and she glanced nervously at Hawk, hoping Logan's wild allegations wouldn't influence his opinion of her. Somehow the thought that he might consider her anything less than a most proper lady bothered her.

A lot.

Chapter Five

"See? What'd I tell you? There it is. Civilization coming up."

Logan's words were light, almost teasing. Obligingly he leaned back from the window so Hawk could have a clear view of the fast-approaching way station sitting all alone on the vast desert land.

The horses strained against their bits, eager to reach the place where water and fresh oats awaited. Automatically the driver applied more pressure on the long lead lines twined through his fingers, effectively reducing the speed of his team despite their reluctance to slow their pace. The wallowing coach dipped, then adjusted its motion, slipping into a slow easy sway as the revolutions of the big wooden-spoked wheels decreased.

They ground to a stop in a cloud of pale dust beside a cluster of weathered buildings. Startled, a family of quail scurried from the safety of a clump of earth-hugging brush to the right of the corral gate. Little black head plumes bobbing comically, they hastily took flight on whirring wings.

The jingle of harness and hitches had barely died away when the door to the relay station was thrown open and a muscular little man stomped out, calling his welcome in a voice that belonged to someone twice his size.

"Well, howdy there, Horace!" His spade-shaped beard, a gray-streaked red, bobbed against his chest as in a ground-gulping rush he approached the vehicle. "And Max, good to see ya again."

"Howdy, Wallace," the driver called down. The guard merely nodded.

As the station master reached the side of the stage, he pulled a dented watch from his pocket and popped the lid open. "Yep. Thought so." A touch of pressure from his thumb and the timepiece snapped shut. Satisfied with his findings, he shoved it back into his pocket. "You're a mite ahead of schedule. Figured I had at least another half-hour before you got here."

"Yeah," the driver said, bobbing his head in agreement. "Been making good time today. Ain't hard to do now that we got shed of them damn pesky redskins."

Horace's wrinkled face folded into a lopsided grin as he leaned forward to secure the long leather lines before standing up. Placing his hands against the small of his back, the driver stretched sideways, then backward and forward to work the kinks of the bone-jarring ride out of his spine. Finally, he straightened, dropped his hands from his back, and climbed down from the stage.

The guard said nothing, merely leaned and spit a stream of tobacco-brown juice over the side of the front boot before scrambling down from his perch. Still silent, he joined the driver and the station keeper and they began unharnessing the horses, the fluid synchronization of their movements evidence of the countless times the trio had performed the chore.

The red-headed gnome stopped his work long enough to shout instructions as first Logan and then Hawk exited the coach.

"Jus' go on in. The missus has plenty of good grub ready. Make yourselves right to home."

"Much obliged," Logan said, his attention momentarily on the laboring threesome when Sabra appeared in the stage's small doorway.

But Hawk had eyes only for her. He responded instantly, reaching up to fit his large hands against her narrow waist. A quick rush of pleasure surged through him, and he realized how eagerly he'd been waiting for just such an opportunity. Too late he wondered if he should have waited for Logan to assist his sister. But he quickly pushed that thought away and simply let the enjoyment of Sabra's nearness wash over him.

She felt as light as thistledown as Hawk lifted her and

51

eased her to the ground. Her full skirt billowed slightly, and the hemline brushed, whisper soft, against his trousers. Although he felt her feet touch the sandy surface, he made no move to release his hold on her. Lord, but it felt good to touch her again.

For a long moment they stood, eyes locked, his hands snugged against her waist, hers resting lightly on his shoulders.

Sabra's heart skipped a beat when Sterling Hawkins' powerful hands continued to bracket her waist. His warmth seemed to sear right through the layers of material separating his fingers from her tender flesh. Her mouth suddenly felt as dry as cotton.

Mesmerized, she stared up into eyes of darkest blue, eyes that reminded her of the winter sky just before a raging storm. Her fingertips registered the sudden, almost imperceptible tightening of the shoulder muscles beneath her hands, and an unfamiliar tingle coursed through her. A confusing medley of emotions were assaulting her mind, feelings quite pleasurable and, at the same time, strangely disturbing.

Hawk felt himself sinking into the lambent brown depths of Sabra's eyes. A heat far greater than that generated by the sun's amber rays slowly seeped through him, and pooled deep in the pit of his stomach.

Sabra tilted her chin just a fraction, and a spear of sunlight caught in the soft tumbled locks framing her face, making them shimmer like molten gold. Hawk marveled at the effect.

How could it be that each strand of her hair was a different shade? All the golden tones of mother earth seemed to be present in those gently disarrayed curls. The gleaming yellow of spring jonquils, the tawny hues of ripe wheat, silver blond and bright brass, platinum and buttercup, copper, cadmium and daffodil.

If he were bold enough to thread his hands through it, would all that bright sun-kissed beauty warm his questing fingers as her smile had warmed his heart yesterday at the park?

"Well, shall we go inside and see what they have to offer? Personally, I'm so hungry I think I could eat anything that isn't still moving."

The sound of Logan's voice startled Sabra and Hawk out of their trance. Quickly, they stepped apart.

Belatedly remembering her manners, Sabra murmured a tardy "Thank you," and ducked her head to hide the blush creeping into her cheeks. To disguise a sudden case of nerves she turned her attention to brushing the wrinkles from her skirt with hurried little strokes.

Dropping his suddenly empty hands to his sides, Hawk responded with a muffled "My pleasure," his reply barely discernible over the nonstop chatter of Horace and the station keeper. Max remained quiet, and for a moment Hawk's only coherent thought was a fleeting question: what would it take to get the guard to speak?

Damn! Hawk silently swore. She'd done it again. Filled his senses so that he'd forgotten everything but her nearness. Sweet heaven! What was wrong with him? He was a warrior, trained to control his emotions, schooled to remain at all times alert to the goal at hand. He'd always prided himself on the stoic strength he'd learned from his father; but now it suddenly seemed that his mother's passionate nature was making itself known.

What in hell was it about Sabra Powers that made him forget everything but her? No other woman had ever affected him quite so completely. He didn't have time for such nonsense. The fulfillment of his plan depended upon maintaining total control. He couldn't allow his mind to wander like that of an adolescent in the throes of a first crush.

Well, Hawk vowed with determination, he'd just have to concentrate harder, and be careful when he was around her. Very careful.

He swallowed twice and hoped that his voice didn't sound as shaky as he felt. "After you, Miss Powers." Then, using the time to regain his badly slipping composure, he waited for brother and sister to mount the small step and cross the weathered porch.

Suddenly aware of the mouth-watering aroma wafting through a nearby window, Logan never noticed the byplay between his sister and their fellow passenger. In eager pursuit of food, he took three long strides across the silver-gray boards. Grasping a tarnished metal handle, he gave it a hearty yank, and the door swung open with a shrill squeal.

Sabra cut one quick glance in Hawk's direction, the corners of her coral mouth hesitantly turning upward—a tantalizing, teasing reminder of the glorious smile she'd bestowed on him at the park. Then she hurried after her brother.

Hawk's heartbeat threatened to double in pace. He drew in a deep breath and, with a stubborn thrust of his chin, crossed the porch and followed them into the dim room.

Although sparsely furnished, the interior of the way station was clean and neat. The red-headed bantam's wife, no bigger than a minute herself, darted toward them, hastily drying work-roughen hands on the tail of her faded red calico apron.

"Welcome, welcome. Come right on in. I'm Mrs. Borg. Food's almost ready. Jus' take me a minute or two to finish up."

Clucking and muttering to herself about the endlessness of dust and chores and time schedules, the little woman hastily provided speckled blue basins of water for washing before returning to her stove, one for Sabra and another for Logan and Hawk to share.

Sabra hurriedly removed the jacket of her traveling suit. With quick, efficient motions she rolled up the crisp sleeves of her pale blue shirtwaist and unfastened several buttons at her throat. The temperature of the coach had risen with the sun, and the water felt delightfully cool against her heated skin. Time and again she plunged her hands into the clear liquid, splashing refreshing handfuls over her cheeks and throat, enjoying the feel of errant water droplets as they traced a damp trail downward to the shadowed valley of her bosom.

Finally, she straightened and reached for the threadbare towel which hung from a nail nearby. With efficient little pats she dried her hands and face, then pushed her collar aside to dip inside her bodice in search of the last elusive beads of moisture.

Across the table, Hawk drew a ragged breath and

jerked his eyes away from the intriguing sight. Thrusting his hands into his pockets, he silently cursed Sabra's brother for doing such a thorough job of washing. Then he forced his eyes to begin a survey of the room . . . they flickered back to Sabra. He tried to concentrate on Mrs. Borg as she bustled about the stove like a honeybee at a flower. That didn't work either.

Just when it seemed as if Logan would never complete his ablutions, the big man finally finished and moved aside. Hawk quickly stepped up to the table, gratefully bending over the basin to sluice palmfuls of cooling water over his face.

Sabra and Logan were already seated at the scrubbed plank table when Hawk finished. Across the room, the station master's wife was busy ladling up generous bowls of stew. Hawk hurriedly scoured the moisture from his face, returned the towel to its bent nail, and joined the others. Within seconds Mrs. Borg set the fragrant provender before them, and then added a heaping plate of cornbread and mugs of steaming coffee.

Hawk hastily turned his attention to the savory meal. At least the food gave him something to think about besides Sabra and the disquieting feelings she stirred within him. For long minutes, all three of them dispensed with idle talk and concentrated on filling their hollow stomachs.

Once the edge was off his appetite, Logan was ready to resume his discourse about the region. As before, anecdotes and jokes were sprinkled liberally amid the chunks of history. Although Hawk was determined to concentrate on the monologue just in case Logan happened to impart anything of importance to his quest, he again found his attention wandering.

Once he shifted his foot and the toe of his boot came into contact with the edge of Sabra's slipper. Two pairs of eyes snapped upward, met, then quickly looked away. Hawk hastily withdrew his foot.

Another time they both reached for the same square of cornbread. Hawk jerked his hand away and they had a polite verbal skirmish over who would take it. Sabra finally relented and placed it on the edge of her plate.

Then Hawk passed Sabra the bowl of butter, and lost another long moment watching the graceful movement of her small hands as she buttered that same square of cornbread.

As time wore on, it became a sweet agony to listen to the frequent trill of her laughter in response to one or another of Logan's witticisms. Every minute in her company, every smile, every teasing look chipped away at Hawk's resolve.

"Want that warmed up, miss?" Mrs. Borg asked, hovering near the table with a steaming pot of coffee. She'd already topped off Logan's and Hawk's cups.

"What?" Sabra's gaze darted first to the station master's wife and then to the nearly empty mug in her hands. "Oh. Yes. Thank you." Her mind had been on things far removed from the beverage.

Quickly, she set her cup down and leaned back so Mrs. Borg could pour. Then, once again cradling the refilled cup between her palms, Sabra sipped slowly at the hot liquid. Over the rim of her mug, she scrutinized the two men who shared the table with her.

Sterling Hawkins's unexpected arrival at the stage that morning had sent a flash of sheer, unexplainable joy through Sabra. She couldn't begin to understand why someone she'd only seen twice could have such a hold on her . . . but there was no denying it was so.

Thoughts of the handsome stranger had tiptoed through her mind ever since that first look at him in the park. She'd been inexplicably pleased to see him at the dance, plagued with a strange sadness ever since his abrupt departure, and considerably more troubled at the thought of never seeing him again than she should have been under the circumstances.

And right now she could hardly believe that the fates had given them another opportunity.

A small breath of relief whooshed against the rim of her cup as she eyed Logan. Thank heaven, he seemed to like Sterling Hawkins. It certainly wouldn't hurt to have him on her side in case their father became difficult.

Her gaze softened as she watched her brother. She knew she could count on Logan; it had always been that way. Through the years he'd been there for her—playmate, champion, friend.

She'd missed him terribly when he'd gone off to the military academy, feeling more abandoned at the loss of Logan than she had when her father had left the two of them in the permanent care of their grandparents. They'd been used to the major's prolonged absences; so, except for sorely missing their mother, life hadn't been too different than before. Their grandparents had been loving and kind, and as always Sabra had had Logan to depend upon.

The fact that Logan had been stationed at the same fort as their father had played a big part in Sabra's recent decision to come West. It had been touch and go for a while whether she could convince either of them to see things her way. But Logan had finally capitulated, giving in to Sabra's desires just as he'd always done when they were children. And despite the major's loud and prolonged grumblings about a fort being no place for civilians, her father had seemed pleased to have her with him the last three months. In fact, he'd taken to the role of full-time parenting with a bit more dedication than Sabra had expected.

Indeed, several incidents that had occurred since her arrival at the fort had disclosed how very opinionated and obstinate the major could be when it came to his only daughter. More than once, Sabra had been subjected to a stern lecture regarding why this or that young officer wasn't worthy of her attention. So far the major had been able to justify his proprietary admonishments by pointing out that he'd known the man in question for many months before Sabra had arrived on the scene, and therefore he was more qualified to pass judgment. Nothing had come easily, especially getting permission to accompany Logan on the trip to Tucson.

Sabra had taken her father's occasionally gruff demeanor as a sign of affection, assuming his attitude was partly due to his military background and partly because he wasn't yet accustomed to having her around. Given the family's past history, she felt certain it was only natural for him to be a bit overprotective. And to be perfectly honest, none of the young officers had piqued her interest enough to argue the point. It had been far more important to get acquainted with the father she had seen only rarely in many years. And there had been the added pleasure of once again being with her beloved brother. Yes, Sabra had been content to let things be.

But all that had changed yesterday in the flicker of a heartbeat. While none of the young officers had seemed worth arguing over, she was sure that Sterling Hawkins might well be.

She contemplated how pleasant it would be if her father approved of Sterling Hawkins calling upon her. Given an opportunity to get acquainted with him, her father was bound to recognize what a charming and intelligent man Hawkins was. Surely, oh surely, the major could have no preconceived notions in this case. Sterling Hawkins was, after all, a total stranger.

A wonderfully handsome, deliciously intriguing stranger.

If she could just steer the major away from his usual notions of what and who was proper for her, who could know what might happen?

Sabra suppressed a sigh. While the theory was sound, underneath she was afraid it wouldn't hold true when put to the test of reality. A small spark of rebellion flickered within. This time the major might be surprised to find his daughter not quite so meek and pliant as in the past. Come what may, Sabra had every intention of getting to know their traveling companion better during his visit.

What might happen after that, her innocent young mind hadn't even considered.

Peculiar though it was, she had felt drawn to Hawkins from that very first moment at the park. Why was that so? She wasn't sure.

It wasn't based merely on the fact that he was dashingly handsome. Nor had she simply been influenced by the aura of strength and mystery which seemed to surround him.

No, it had begun with that first glance into Sterling Hawkins's eyes. Those wonderfully beguiling eyes. Such a startling deep blue. They'd held such an undercurrent of raw emotion . . . a strange mixture of . . . of . . . what?

Sabra couldn't quite put her finger on it. A touch of sadness? A flicker of hope? She didn't know. Whatever it was, before being quickly suppressed, that fleeting flash of reaction had tugged at her heart.

Suddenly Logan's bright laughter blossomed forth, drawing Sabra out of her musings. A small smile of satisfaction curved her mouth. Yes, Logan definitely seemed to like Sterling Hawkins. If bad came to worse, she could count on her brother to intervene on her behalf.

Full at last, Logan abandoned his spoon in his empty bowl and leaned contentedly back in his chair. "Delicious, Mrs. Borg. Absolutely delicious. That's the best stew I've had in a long time. I do believe you've quite stolen my heart. Mr. Borg had better watch out. I know a dozen fellows who'd be mighty tempted to steal such a talented lady right out from under his nose." The compliment flowed from Logan Powers's silver tongue with ease, his easy flirtatious manner as natural as breathing.

Mrs. Borg blushed bright scarlet, and giggled like a young girl. "Get on with you, you young scalawag," she scolded in soft simpering tones.

Logan's attention was drawn back to his dinner companions when Hawk and Sabra joined in to offer their praises of the meal.

Not a bad sort of fellow, Logan mused as he contemplated the man sitting to his right. Not a bad sort at all. Hawkins had proved to be a pleasant traveling companion—intelligent, well educated, good humored in a quiet way. His stay at the fort would provide a pleasant change from the usual humdrum activities of military life.

Logan smothered a grin as he scrutinized his sister's glowing face. Apparently he wasn't the only one who was looking forward to Mr. Hawkins's visit. There was a definite sparkle in Sabra's eyes every time she looked at the man. Well, as long as Hawkins treated her properly, Logan could see no reason to protest. He'd found no fault with their companion.

Stranger or not, at gut level Sabra's brother felt Sterling Hawkins was a man worthy of his respect. And, for Logan Powers, that was the first step toward friendship.

Meanwhile, Hawk's thoughts were moving in a very different direction from those of his table mates. While they were pleased at possibly having made a new friend, he was considering the sheer folly of what was happening.

There was no doubt in his mind that it would be foolish, perhaps even dangerous, to become too familiar with the offspring of his sworn enemy. To do so could play hell with his conscience . . . not to mention the fulfillment of his goal. Things were complicated enough as it was. He shouldn't even like them.

He didn't want to.

But he did.

There was a zest to Logan Powers that was undeniably appealing. His happy devil-may-care attitude was almost contagious. Even the touch of wildness hinted at by Logans, earlier West Point story added to Powers's charm.

Perhaps it was this contrast in their personalities that drew Hawk to Logan. Hawk had held himself in for so many years, been rigid, controlled, and leery of close relationships after so many disappointments. Now it felt so good to relax, to be accepted — if only for a little while — for who he was, not what he was. To just be Sterling Hawkins, man, human being.

And Sabra. Ah, Sabra. She was special. No doubt about it. If things were only different . . .

Hawk forced his mind away from the risky thought. Things *weren't* different, and he'd be a fool to forget it.

Still, what would it hurt? a little voice within said relentlessly. After all, he wasn't going to be at the fort for very long . . . certainly not long enough for anything more than a casual friendship to develop. What harm could there be in that?

Besides, wouldn't it be smarter for him to cultivate a relationship with Logan and Sabra? After all, he needed enough time to develop a plan that would allow him to fulfill his vow. There was no denying that such a relationship might divulge information impossible to obtain otherwise. Information essential to his goal.

Why, such a relationship might even make it easier for him to achieve his objective and escape undetected. Who would suspect a friend of the family? He'd be a fool not to pursue such an advantage. Wasn't he honor bound to follow any possible source that might prove beneficial to his quest?

Of course he should take advantage of the situation. How could he possibly pass up such an opportunity? He couldn't. There was no getting around it. Spending time with Logan and Sabra was necessary.

More than that.

It was his duty.

By the time the station master stuck his head in the door and told them that it was time to board the stage again, Hawk had managed to convince himself that he was following the only path open to him.

His head hadn't needed to put forth much of a struggle, not when his heart agreed so completely.

The sun was descending rapidly, a glowing red-orange ball in the darkening sky, when the fort finally began to take shape on the horizon. Eager for his first view of what would be his stalking grounds, Hawk leaned forward to peer through the window. He braced one hand against the bottom of the frame as the stage bounced and swayed over the last stretch of almost indecipherable road.

Through the gathering twilight he could barely discern the scattering of desert-hued adobe and plank-sided buildings huddled at the foot of purple-misted mountains. Then, as they drew nearer, he couldn't believe his luck. The buildings appeared to be wide-spread and easily accessible from almost any angle. There was no stockade surrounding the sprawling military encampment. No gates to swing shut at the first cry of alarm.

"Well, Mr. Hawkins, what do you think?" Logan asked.

"It's perfect," Hawk replied with a slow smile. "Absolutely perfect."

Chapter Six

"Things have changed considerably since the fort was established. Living conditions were quite primitive until eighty-one," Logan explained. "Mostly because of the excessive rainy season between July and September. But the fort was designated as a permanent post that year and things began to look up. General Sherman visited and picked out the location for the formal parade ground. And a railroad spur was finally completed, terminating about seven miles from the post. It made supplies easier to obtain and life considerably more pleasant."

"I'm sure," Hawk replied, suddenly eager to spend the last few minutes of their ride listening to whatever details Logan chose to impart. There would be many pieces to the jigsaw puzzle of his plan; he dared not ignore a single scrap of information. "This is all very interesting, and it's wonderful background for my book. Please tell me more."

"Well, we're not quite so cut off from the rest of the world anymore. The California newspapers arrive a mere three days after publication. And there's a telegraph system."

Hawk cataloged that bit of news away for further consideration.

"Fort Huachuca's quite a thriving little community now. Most of the married men have brought their families with them. Really nice people, for the most part. Oh, the wives are just like army wives all over the country—they talk about the heat and complain about the dust and the sandstorms, but they've made this fort their home. And no one's more sharing or helpful than a bunch of military wives. They do a great job of helping newcomers settle in."

"Yes, they do." Sabra's voice was full of enthusiasm as she joined her brother in praise of the settlement. "I haven't been here long, but I can assure you everyone is very friendly. People go out of their way to make you feel welcome. I must say new arrivals are greeted with an enthusiasm I never experienced back East."

Deep in Hawk's mind lurked the knowledge that he'd never be the recipient of such a welcome if the truth about his heritage were known. He swung one long muscular leg over the other, and took up the thread of conversation again.

"Naturally, most of the activities still center around the military routine, but the ladies have prevailed upon the post commander to provide something more in the way of entertainment than daily retreat ceremonies. There are sewing bees and afternoon teas. And we have a brand new amusement hall that the womenfolk make sure is put to use for dances on most Saturday nights."

Sabra's eyes twinkled merrily as a thrilling scene came to her mind. What fun it would be to arrive at the Saturday night gala on the arm of the fort's handsome new visitor. Wouldn't the ladies all be pea green with envy? Why, when they saw how well Sterling Hawkins waltzed, they'd be falling all over themselves to be the next partner in his arms.

Sabra's delight faded as a troublesome thought penetrated the rosy mists of her daydream. There were half a dozen young ladies near her age at the fort, most of them the oldest daughters of officers. For the most part they were genteel, pleasant and polite. Except for one—the spoiled and pampered daughter of the post's trader.

Melissa Henderson was black-haired, buxom, bold as brass, and totally without scruples when it came to chasing the eligible men on the post.

Sabra stole a quick glance at Sterling Hawkins, praying that Melissa was still smitten with Sergeant Woodley, too smitten to set her sights on the fort's new visitor.

A strange new feeling had bloomed within Sabra, a

feeling utterly foreign to her and quite disturbing. Never before in her young life had she experienced such a surge of jealousy. She'd always had an abundance of friends, both male and female, and never had she felt the compulsion to tag any of them as her exclusive property. She'd shared the beaus of early womanhood with the same good-natured abandon as she had displayed with toys in her childhood years.

It was quite shocking to realize that she had absolutely no desire to share Sterling Hawkins's attentions with anyone, especially Melissa Henderson . . . not even for one dance.

To make things even more confusing, Sabra couldn't understand why she felt so strongly about someone who was a veritable stranger. She'd only just met the man. Why did he affect her so?

What *was* it about him? . . .

Sabra's appraising gaze lifted to the man in question, and she instantly noticed the row of tiny furrows marring his brow. Her own disturbing musings drifted away as she began to wonder at the cause of his concern.

Could he possibly be apprehensive about their eminent arrival, or perhaps the thought of meeting new people? She quickly dismissed the idea as ridiculous. A man as handsome and poised as Sterling Hawkins was surely used to dealing with all manner of folk, both in business and society. What possible challenge could Fort Huachuca or its inhabitants present to a gentleman of his caliber?

Hawk's mind was grappling with thoughts of the impending arrival at the fort, but not in the way Sabra suspected. He wasn't afraid to meet and mingle with the citizenry of the post. Far from it. He'd been successfully pulling off his masquerade for several weeks now, and he felt certain he could continue to do so. Fooling people was easy. All he had to do was live a lie.

Living the lie.

That was what bothered Hawk.

He'd always refused to hide the truth about his heritage. To do so would have made him feel he was denying his mother and father and the very special love they had shared.

Oh, there'd been times when he was younger that he'd been tempted, so very tempted. What a relief it would have been to avoid the wary sidewise glances, to no longer hear snide, loudly whispered remarks about "dirty savages" and "tainted blood."

Yes, it had been tempting. But he'd never given in to that temptation.

Hawk would never forget the first time he'd realized he was different from other boys, the first time he'd been hated simply because Indian blood ran in his veins. He'd been barely eight years old.

A group of travelers had stopped over in town, deciding to take advantage of Hawkinsville's clean, well-stocked inn for a few days before continuing on their travels. Hawk and his friends had been engaged in a rowdy game of chase. Attired in the buckskins and moccasins he normally wore only when staying at his Indian father's village, Hawk had rounded the corner of the inn, head down, scrawny long legs churning as he charged after Tommy Hunsacker. Intent on the game, he hadn't seen the woman stepping through the inn's doorway until it was too late.

He'd tried to swerve around her, but the small bow and quiver looped over his shoulder had somehow caught on the flounce of her elegant cape and before he'd known what had happened, they'd both been sprawled on the boardwalk. Scrambling to his feet, he'd been quick to offer an apology, but the woman had only stared at him, eyes wide and frightened, mouth agape. When he'd reached out to assist her to rise, she'd shrieked and flung herself away from him.

At that moment, the woman's husband had appeared in the doorway, his face red and twisted with outrage. "Get away from my wife, you filthy little savage!" the man had yelled. Shocked at the outburst, Hawk had sputtered another apology and had grabbed for the woman's flailing arm, anxious to get her upright before his mother found out how badly he'd neglected his manners.

Hawk had barely laid a hand on the blue cotton fabric of the woman's sleeve when the man had grabbed a handful of his hair. With a vicious backward yank and a hard shove, Hawk had been forced away from the still-shrieking woman.

The rest of the incident was a blur of motion and sound. Hawk vaguely remembered the innkeeper coming out and taking up his defense, assuring the strangers that the "dangerous savage" was merely the son of Maria Hawkins, intent on nothing more than a childhood game. Humiliated at having caused such a commotion, young Hawk had paid scant attention to the shocked questions that had followed that revelation. All he could think about was escaping to rejoin his playmates . . . and to nurse his smarting scalp. His head had eventually quit hurting, but the wound to his heart had never healed.

The woman's departing words had seared through him like flame. As the couple had stalked off down the boardwalk, she had proclaimed in her shrill voice, "Can you imagine? A white woman actually *marrying* one of those revolting heathens. Well, I for one say she's no better than a common whore! It's blasphemy, that's what it is. Blasphemy. Any decent white woman would kill herself before submitting to the touch of one of those repulsive barbarians! Makes my skin crawl. And that disgusting little half-breed savage . . ."

The couple had departed the next day. Hawk had never known if they had left voluntarily or if someone in the town had advised them they were no longer welcome.

It didn't matter. The damage had been done. Hawk had never again taken it for granted that his world would always be loving and secure. The episode had been a cruel introduction to reality. The lifelong acceptance he'd experienced in his small hometown had done nothing to prepare him for that first vicious attack, nor for the ones that had followed over the years.

Before that day, it had scarcely crossed Hawk's mind that he was different. Oh, he knew that the other little boys didn't spend most of the year living in an Indian village. He'd simply considered himself luckier than they were.

And, truth be told, the boys of the town heartily agreed with him. They'd have traded places with young Sterling Hawkins without a second thought. What young boy

66

wouldn't consider learning to make a canoe or stalking a deer with bow and arrow infinitely more exciting than chopping wood or drawing water? What youngster wouldn't have happily exchanged stiff Sunday suits and even stiffer high-top boots for soft buckskin clothing and moccasins? And certainly it was much more appealing to take school lessons on a sun-drenched river bank than in the stifling confines of a building.

But in the course of a few cruel minutes, Hawk had learned that the white world he'd experienced in Hawkinsville had been very rare indeed.

Later he'd realized there'd been good reason for that special environment. The small town owed its birth to Hawk's grandfather, Lazarus Hawkins. It was the efforts of Lazarus, his wife Suzanna, and their children that had pumped lifeblood into the fledgling community, and made it what it was. The townsfolk never forgot that.

Although Lazarus had been lucky enough to come to the territory with what was considered a sizeable inheritance, it was his old-fashioned sweat and determination that had brought prosperity to Hawkinsville and had eventually made the Hawkins family the wealthiest in town. Yet old Lazarus had never asked of others what he wouldn't do himself.

Over the years his small lumber business had grown, providing a steady supply of good-paying jobs. People trickled into the territory. Many continued west, but some stayed, eager to put down roots in a community that offered the promise of stable employment and a safe, law-biding environment for their families.

In some towns, old Lazarus' domination might have caused ill feelings. But not in Hawkinsville.

From the very beginning Lazarus was a benevolent leader. He believed that what benefited the community, benefited the family, and he practiced what he believed. Hawkins's money funded the white clapboard church on Main Street and the school around the corner. And Hawkins's money lured a fine young doctor to the town and made it worth his while to stay.

Whenever there was illness or need, Lazarus or one of the Hawkinses was there. If a man was hurt on the job,

Hawkins saw to it that the family had enough funds to survive until the head of the household could return to work. And more often than not, for the first few evenings anyway, Suzanna could be found in the worker's cabin, a pot of her special stew brewing on the stove while she tended to the children so the mother of the family could care for her injured husband.

Under Lazarus's tutelage, his sons began to take responsibility for the business and the town. And his only daughter followed in her mother's footsteps. When barely more than a slip of a girl herself, Maria nursed the sick and helped teach the younger children their lessons in the small one-room schoolhouse.

Maria Hawkins was well loved in the town. She had proved to be as good as she was beautiful, and her white blond beauty was synonymous with sunlight to the town's people. Perpetually optimistic, Maria was sweet-tempered, dependable, unselfish, and hard working. She approached life with a joyous, sometimes impetuous, enthusiasm, embracing each new challenge with determination and passion.

When she decided to spend one summer living and teaching in an Indian village, the townsfolk simply nodded their heads and remarked that it was typical of Maria. And when she fell in love and married a young Indian brave, although a trifle taken aback at first, they eventually accepted that, too. After all, she was still their Maria.

As Maria's son, Hawk had enjoyed the same loving acceptance.

And then, suddenly, Hawk's parents were dead and he was left in the custody of his uncles. It had been a confusing time for an adolescent boy. He'd longed for the life he'd always known, the freedom of the long months he'd spent each year at his father's village. His uncles had been kind and attentive, his aunts affectionate and doting. But he'd missed his parents terribly.

Eventually his uncles had begun to take him on occasional business trips to the East, and for a while he'd even been enrolled in an academy. Those little excursions into the "real world" were supposed to bolster young Hawk's confidence and prepare him for the day he'd take over the family business.

Though enthusiastic at first, Hawk soon grew wary of the world outside of Hawkinsville. He'd quickly learned that each journey provided opportunity for yet another humiliating incident, and the outside world all too often lived up to his worst expectations.

After one or two disturbing episodes, Hawk realized that he could circumvent the unpleasantness concerning his mixed blood by avoiding any mention of his heritage. Yet, to Hawk, such a deception would have shamed his parents' memory. And he couldn't—wouldn't—stoop to such disloyalty. No matter how much those incidents hurt, he refused to hide behind a convenient falsehood. To do so would have been a betrayal of everything he was.

Only one thing had compelled Hawk to live the lie . . . the sweet promise of revenge. But when this crusade was over—if he was still alive—he would return to the safe haven of his hometown and take up his quiet existence again, far from the stinging barbs of the white man's prejudice.

No, it wasn't fear of what was to come that was bothering Hawk. It was simply memories. Old painful memories.

He'd been unable to completely suppress a quick twinge of bitterness when Sabra had spoken of how friendly the people on post were and of how they made newcomers feel welcome. He knew better than to believe that the good people of Fort Huachuca would welcome him with open arms if they knew the truth about his background.

Suddenly weary to the bone of the mental turmoil such thoughts always brought, Hawk forced the bitter reflections to the back of his mind. Distasteful or not, he was forced to live the lie . . . just this once. For now, he must put the past behind him. The success of his plan hinged on the continued acceptance of his story. He dared not let memories destroy this opportunity.

Logan had continued talking while Hawk's mind had wandered. But before Hawk was put in the embarrassing position of having to respond to something he hadn't even heard, the driver gave a shout, and Logan's monologue ended abruptly.

The coach slowed and then jerked to a stop. They had arrived.

For several minutes the three passengers were caught up in the bustle of gathering their personal items and readying themselves to climb down from the stage. Muffled thumps and bumps resounded from the roof of the stage, followed by a succession of grunts and soft curses as the driver and the guard unloaded the luggage.

Logan exited first, then Hawk leaned forward to steady Sabra's elbow as she left the coach. Finally, pulling a steadying breath deep into his lungs, Hawk abandoned the false safety of the stage and stepped down onto the home territory of his long-sought enemy. He had turned back toward the stage to push the door closed when he heard Sabra's joyous exclamation.

"Father! I wasn't expecting you. How nice of you to meet us."

Hawk pivoted in time to see Sabra rush forward and rise on tiptoe to place a kiss on the cheek of a tall, imposing figure. The man slipped one arm around his daughter's shoulders and gave her a hug; a fancy plumed helmet was cradled in his other arm.

Hawk's heart thudded heavily. So this was Major Andrew P. Powers.

Standing quietly in the shadow of the stage, Hawk held his whirling emotions under tight rein as he assessed his enemy from head to toe.

There could be no denying the legacy of Powers's long years in the military. Although not required at this late hour of the day, the major wore an immaculate dress uniform. Bright brass buttons marched smartly up the front of his blue wool coat. Breast cords, tassels, and pipings added further splendor to his costume, and his high leather boots and wide belt were burnished to a soft glowing patina. Pinned with military precision to the stiff stand-up collar snugly encircling his throat, a gleaming gold maple leaf bespoke the importance of the man's rank.

The major's manner was brisk, almost formal, his carriage as ramrod stiff as if he were standing review on the parade ground. It was obvious where Logan got his build

70

and coloring. The major's hair was the same deep gold, except where time had liberally laced it with silver. Yet the eyes of father and son, though very similar in shade, were different. Andrew Powers's gaze held not the slightest hint of warmth or humor as he perused the stranger before him.

Here was a man who lived by the book, his whole life dictated by military tradition and his own inbred suspicions. For a moment, Hawk wondered if anyone or anything ever got beneath that rigid exterior.

Major Powers nodded in Logan's direction. Then his calculating eyes gave his son a thorough once-over, long years of habit evident as he automatically ascertained the correctness of a subordinate officer's attire and attitude.

"You had a pleasant trip, I presume?" Powers asked Logan, his words precise, clipped.

"Yes, sir. Very pleasant."

Hawk's keen hearing caught the almost imperceptible stress in Logan's voice. The younger Powers's usual wide grin had disappeared, and Hawk wondered at the reason for the peculiar tension between father and son.

Strange, thought Hawk. It was almost as if Logan were expecting some sort of rebuke. As if he were afraid he might not quite meet the expectations of his illustrious father.

Maybe Logan, with his carefree, light-hearted ways, wasn't sufficiently "spit and polish" for the major, Hawk mused. Maybe the major demanded too much of his children.

One look at Sabra and Hawk amended his last conjecture. Whatever the major's feelings or expectations concerning his son, they didn't seem to include his daughter. The senior officer's taciturn bearing melted like butter in the sun when he looked at her.

"And what about you, Sabra dear, did you have a good time in Tucson?"

"Oh, yes, Father. Everything was absolutely wonderful. Especially the ball at the San Xavier." With these words, Sabra slanted a quick glance and a dazzling smile in Hawk's direction. "You should have seen the sword they presented to General Miles. A sword made by Tiffany's!

71

Can you imagine! It was so beautiful. The scabbard was gold, and all engraved with scenes from Miles's Indian campaigns in Arizona. And Mrs. McDonald told me the grip was made from white sharkskin wound with braided gold. Oh, I wish you could have one just like it!"

Sabra's bubbling enthusiasm brought a hint of smile to the major's mouth. "You're very sweet, my dear," he said, his voice thick with indulgent fondness. "But I imagine General Miles would feel otherwise."

Sabra's silver laughter danced through the dusk. "I suppose you're right." She tucked her hand through her father's elbow, her full skirt swaying gracefully as she urged him in Hawk's direction. "Father, I want you to meet our fellow passenger, Mr. Sterling Hawkins."

Hawk momentarily froze in place as he once again came under the major's careful scrutiny. He called on his inner strength, forced a smile on his face.

Heels clicking audibly, Powers drew himself up even straighter, if possible, and extended his hand in proper greeting.

"Mr. Hawkins. How nice to meet you." The major's tone belied the pleasantness of his words.

Hawk had no choice but to match the gesture. "Thank you, sir."

Andrew Powers's handshake was indicative of the man himself—firm and strong and authoritative. Hawk felt the barely perceptible rasp of calluses against his palm. This was no limp-fingered dandy who'd spent his life behind a desk. At least the man would be a worthy adversary.

"And I must admit that I've been waiting for this opportunity for a long, long time."

"Oh?" Powers questioned coolly. "Is that so? Any particular reason, Mr. Hawkins?"

"I'm a great history buff. Naturally I've read about some of your military exploits."

"I see," said Powers, obviously unimpressed by Hawk's comment.

"And of course, I heard a great deal more about the fort and your military career during our ride."

"Ah." A hint of uncharacteristic amusement played at the corners of the major's mouth. His gaze turned fondly

72

to Sabra. "Well, you'd better take anything this young miss said with a grain of salt. I'm afraid she's a bit prone to prejudice when it comes to family."

"And why shouldn't I be?" Sabra demanded, her dark doe eyes sparkling. There was a teasing lilt to her voice, but Hawk recognized heartfelt conviction when he heard it. "Haven't I been blessed with the best father and brother a girl could ask for?"

"That's probably debatable, my dear, but far be it from me to try to dissuade you," the major replied with a small throaty chuckle; then he became all business again. "Now, shall we proceed to the house, Sabra. It's getting rather late."

"Are you coming, Logan?" Sabra asked, hoping that he would and that he'd bring Sterling Hawkins with him.

"No," Logan answered quickly. Almost too quickly, Hawk thought. "I'd better see that Mr. Hawkins gets comfortably settled."

"Oh, that's not necessary, Logan," Hawk intervened. "I don't want to hold you up. I understand there's a boardinghouse. If you'll just point me in the right direction—"

Logan interrupted with a dismissive wave of his hand. "Yes, there is, but I have a much better idea. I'm not sharing quarters with anyone at present, so why don't you join me? One of the rewards for being an officer on this post is a decent house. There's no sense in your putting up at the boardinghouse when I have all that room. Besides, it'll be more convenient when it comes to your investigation since I'll be able to show you around—"

"What a wonderful idea!" Sabra was quick to agree with her brother. Having their visitor under his care would surely help discourage the fort's single young ladies. That is, all but Melissa. But Sabra refused to dwell on such an unpleasant thought. "It'll work out perfectly."

"What investigation?" The major's sharp question interrupted Sabra's enthusiastic comments.

"Oh, I'm sorry, Father. I forgot, you don't know what we're talking about, do you? You see, Mr. Hawkins is a writer."

"Oh?"

"Yes, and he's come to Fort Huachuca to do some

73

research on the real story of Geronimo. Isn't that exciting?" Sabra's arm stayed lovingly looped through her father's, but her bright eyes were steadfastly focused on the tall dark stranger.

The major would have to have been blind and deaf not to notice his daughter's sudden intense interest in a subject she'd hardly acknowledged before.

"I see," the major said, and indeed he did. The ice was back in his voice, and his gaze once again probed the stranger in their midst, even more sharply than before.

No doubt about it, Powers decided in the flick of an eye, the stranger was the type of man who would catch a young girl's eye. Tall, too attractive by far. Expensive suit, expertly tailored. Obviously the product of one of those rich aristocratic families with nothing better to do than squander time and energy on senseless projects such as the one Sabra seemed so enthralled with. More than likely a real bounder just waiting to take advantage of some sweet naive young girl.

As instant distrust flickered in the major's eyes, his mouth thinned in irritation. Sabra was at such a delicate age, so impressionable. He certainly couldn't allow her to fall under the spell of such a man. The situation would definitely bear close watching, he decided.

Andrew Powers hadn't approved of Sabra's coming out West, but now that she was at the fort, he had no intention of losing her to some worthless scalawag. There'd be time enough for romantic nonsense in the years to come. Although he and Logan seemed to be eternally at cross-purposes, Sabra was a joy to be around. She sparked memories of the happier times in his life. He'd long ago given up trying to establish a good rapport with his son, but he still had a chance with Sabra.

No one, absolutely no one, was going to be allowed to disrupt the major's home life again. The relationship he and his daughter had just begun to share was more satisfying than he'd expected. Didn't he have a right to some happiness in his later years? A little joy to make up for all the lonely times. The years sacrificed to his military obligations, the years lost after Elaine's death.

No, he silently vowed. Nothing was going to interfere

with this chance for reacquaintance with his daughter. He'd missed so many special events in her young life. Her first words, her first faltering steps, her second *and* third birthdays. The next few years belonged to him . . . only him.

When he was young and ambitious, he'd scarcely given those special events a second thought. His career had been the most important thing. He'd foolishly assumed there'd be time later for family.

And there almost had been.

The two oldest children had barely been school age when he'd finally gotten an assignment at a fairly secure post. Elaine had pleaded with him to let her and the children come join him. He'd always thought it better that his family stay back East where they were safe, where the children could receive a proper education. He'd tried to convince her the area was still too dangerous, but she'd insisted . . . and he'd finally given in.

For the first time in their married lives—for just a few short months—they'd lived like a real family. Little by little, the Army had ceased to be the main reason for Andrew Powers' existence. He and Elaine had settled into a comfortable routine, Logan finally stopped treating him like an intrusive stranger, and Sabra became a real "daddy's girl." Little Mary was just beginning to walk. They'd been happy, really happy.

And then . . . Then it had all been snatched away—their newfound happiness, their hopes, their dreams, their plans—by a band of thieving, murdering renegades. Elaine and the baby dead. Andrew left with two small motherless children he hadn't the heart or the experience to care for.

The painful memory of the day he'd given his two surviving children into the care of their grandparents still rankled Andrew Powers. But what else could he have done? A career military man was hardly capable of raising two young children alone. So they had stayed in the East, and he had dedicated himself to his military career even more vigorously than before. The major camouflaged a sigh with a discreet cough. "Come, come, Logan. There's been enough dilly-dallying about the matter," he said, sounding even sterner than before. "What's it to be?"

"You're more than welcome to stay with me, Mr. Hawkins," Logan quickly declared despite his father's warning frown. "I hate being alone anyway. You'd be doing *me* a favor."

Hawk found the offer tempting. Too tempting.

He certainly couldn't discount the wonderful opportunities such an arrangement might provide. Finding out the major's routine should be child's play under such circumstances.

Besides, there was no sense denying that he liked Logan Powers; he'd enjoyed the time they had spent together. Too bad Powers was the major's son. Logan was the kind of man who, under different circumstances, could kindle a real sense of friendship in Hawk.

And then there was Sabra. Rooming with Logan would surely allow him to spend more time with her. That thought affected Hawk like fine wine.

"Are you sure it won't be an imposition?" he asked politely.

"I'm sure."

"In that case, I'd be glad to accept your invitation. And, please, let's drop the formalities. Just call me Hawk."

"Hawk it is," Logan said with a grin.

"Wonderful!" Sabra declared.

"Very well," Major Powers intervened testily. "Now that you have that settled, do you suppose we might proceed to our quarters before the stroke of midnight?"

Logan bit back a retort, but the major didn't even notice. His attention was on two passing figures.

"You there," Andrew Powers called out sharply, his brow furrowing as he squinted to identify the men through the gathering dusk.

"Yassir?" came a reply.

"Over here."

Two black soldiers materialized out of the deepening shadows. One was small and wiry, the other the exact opposite. As the big one approached, Hawk judged that he easily stood half a head taller than Logan.

76

"Ah . . . Private Kane and Private Morgan," the major acknowledged. "See that this baggage gets to the proper place. Morgan, you can take Miss Sabra's bags to our quarters."

"Yassir." The small man nervously shifted from one foot to the other while Sabra pointed out which pieces of luggage were hers. Eager to escape his commanding officer's presence, he then hastily hoisted the bags and staggered off under their weight.

"And you, Kane," the major ordered, "see that the rest of this baggage is taken care of immediately."

"Right away, sir," the big man answered smartly, his pearly white teeth gleaming against the chocolate color of his skin. Wrapping hands the size of hams around the handles of the two remaining cases, he lifted. The heavy bags might as well have been filled with feathers for all the effort it required to hoist them.

"Where to, sir?"

"My quarters, Hezekiah," Logan instructed.

"Yes, sir." Hezekiah Kane flashed another dazzling smile and disappeared into the darkness.

The remaining four fell into step, leaving the corrals behind as they headed toward the heart of the fort. The sounds of jingling harnesses and restless horses were soon replaced by the hodgepodge of muffled noises common to any small community. As they passed close to one of the long wooden barracks bordering the parade ground, a burst of hearty laughter interrupted the drone of male voices, then the sounds returned to normal. For the most part the fort was quiet, its inhabitants settled in for the night, enjoying the leisure time between the evening meal and slumber.

Hawk caught only an occasional glimpse of shadowy figures moving in the distance. If guards were posted, they were few and far between.

The cleared and raked parade grounds sloped upward ever so gently, easy going even in the dark. Across the way, the softly illuminated windows of the officers' houses beckoned them onward.

When they reached the bordering path on the far side of the parade ground, they halted once again.

Major Powers, Sabra still on his arm, turned to face Logan and Hawk. "We'll say goodbye here. I'm sure everyone is tired from the long trip. Especially Sabra. Good night, gentlemen."

"Good night, Father."

"Good night, Major Powers." Hawk's words came directly after Logan's.

"Make your goodbyes, Sabra," Powers commanded.

Sabra was far from ready for the evening to end, but her instinctive reaction was to obey the major's instructions. Slipping her arm from her father's, she stepped toward Hawk and into a pale yellow square of lamplight coming from a nearby window.

"Well . . uh . . . good night, Mr. Hawkins. I do hope you enjoy your stay with us." She offered her small hand in a reluctant gesture of farewell.

Hawk's hand closed around it, and his heart gave a crazy little *ker-thunk* as Sabra tilted her head and gifted him once again with that wonderful, warm smile. Light shimmered in her hair, rimming it with a golden halo. She was so beautiful she took his breath away.

Bittersweet sadness filled him, and he suddenly wished that the lie he was living was true. That he was who he was pretending to be, that he had nothing more on his mind but the pleasure of researching a book . . . that he was free to court Sabra Powers the way he longed to do.

Chapter Seven

Andrew Powers stepped forward and took his daughter's arm in a firm grip. "Come along, my dear. It's getting far too chilly for you to be out."

"Wait, Father," Sabra said impetuously. "I have a marvelous idea. Why don't we invite Logan and Mr. Hawkins to join us? It's still early, and I'm not a bit tired. Really. It's been a long time since our last meal. I'm hungry. Surely Logan and Mr. Hawkins are, too. It won't take me but a moment to make a pot of coffee and throw together a few things for a cold supper."

The major's tone was as frosty as the night air. "I think not, Sabra. I'm afraid you just don't realize how fatigued you are. I'll feel much better if we make an early night of it and you get some much-needed rest."

Sabra sighed. "Yes, Father," she said softly. The last thing she wanted to do was set him against Sterling Hawkins. It would be better not to push the issue. Besides, she silently soothed herself, it wasn't as if she wouldn't have ample opportunity to see the man over the next few weeks.

Hadn't Logan mentioned showing his guest around the fort the next day? She'd slip away and join them for the tour. Surely her father couldn't object to her showing hospitality toward a visitor. And there was always the Saturday night dance.

The thought of once again being in Sterling Hawkins' embrace sent little quivers dancing in the pit of Sabra's stomach.

Resigned to the futility of arguing the present situation,

Sabra gave Logan a quick hug and, casting a last smile in Hawk's direction, let her father guide her toward the nearest house.

Hawk watched the major lead Sabra up the steps and across the porch. The lattice-work screening surrounding the porch reduced their movements to no more than rippling shadows. Hinges creaked as the front door opened, and for just a moment Sabra was silhouetted against the bright rectangle of interior light. She turned her head toward them, and Hawk heard her call out a soft good night. Then the major mumbled something unintelligible and Sabra hurriedly disappeared into the house.

Without a moment's hesitation, Major Powers stepped within, and the door swung shut with a final firm thud.

A sudden gust of wind whipped across the deserted parade ground. Leaves whispered and danced in the darkness. Invisible fingers snatched a handful of sand and sent it whirling like a dervish before it peppered against the side of the house.

Hawk wished the door would open again, wished he could have just one more glimpse of Sabra.

"Don't pay any attention to him." Logan's voice shattered Hawk's reverie.

"Uh? Ah . . . what? I'm sorry. I didn't quite catch what you said," Hawk said, turning toward Logan.

"Father. Don't pay any attention to him. He's that way with everyone. Everyone but Sabra, that is. It doesn't mean anything. You just have to get used to it."

"Oh. I . . . uh . . . I really hadn't noticed," Hawk was quick to assure him. "Besides, he's quite right. Sabra does need her rest. It's been a long day."

"So it has." Logan shrugged, quite willing to drop the subject of his father's less than amiable actions. "We don't have much farther to go. My quarters are just a few houses down from the one Sabra and Father share."

"That sounds fine." Hawk forced an enthusiastic smile. "Lead on."

Resolutely turning his back on the major's house, he fell into step with Logan, and very shortly they were climbing the steps to the young Powers's quarters.

The two-storied building of sun-baked adobe was very

similar to the others on the street. All had latticed porches front and back, which offered shade from the summer heat or shelter from the biting winter wind. Some were two-family structures; others were clearly built for individual families. Logan lived in one of the smaller units.

One look at the inside of the dwelling confirmed that a bachelor resided there. Although spotlessly clean, it definitely lacked a woman's touch. There were no curtains, knickknacks, or photographs. The plastered interior walls were bare, the furniture serviceable but sparse.

"Hezekiah," Logan called out as he pushed the door shut. "You still here?"

"Yes, sir," the buffalo soldier replied, stepping into the living area through a back doorway, his bulk dominating the room. "I put the gentleman's luggage in the spare room."

"That's fine. Thank you."

"You're welcome."

"Hezekiah, come meet my guest. This is Mr. Sterling Hawkins. He's going to be staying here for a while."

"Pleased to meet you, Mr. Hawkins." Hezekiah's voice was a deep rumbling bass.

"Mr. Hawkins, Hezekiah Kane."

"Hawk, please," Sterling reminded Logan. "And I'm pleased to meet you, too, Private Kane."

Onyx eyes scrutinized Logan's visitor, politely but carefully. Struck by the vitality emanating from the huge soldier, Hawk decided then and there that Hezekiah Kane was a man to be reckoned with. It grew more evident by the minute that he wasn't the average soldier of color. For one thing, his speech indicated that he'd received considerably more education than most Negroes. Fleetingly Hawk thought that this big man with the ebony skin was someone he'd prefer to avoid if it came to a showdown fight.

"Oh, I made sure there's hot coffee, just in case you'd like some," Hezekiah reported.

"Sounds good. I believe I would. How about you?" Logan turned to Hawk, who nodded in agreement. "Why don't you pour us all a cup, Hezekiah, while I dump these bags in my room?"

"Yes, sir."

"You can knock off that 'sir' crap, Hezekiah. Father's not here and Mr. Hawkins isn't going to tell."

The corners of Hezekiah's mouth climbed upward as he returned Logan's broad grin before disappearing once again through the doorway. Bags in hand, Logan headed in the other direction. In a matter of minutes they were both back in the living room, Logan empty-handed, while Hezekiah carried a tray which held three heavy mugs of dark liquid that looked strong enough to stand alone. He distributed a cup to Logan and one to Hawk, discarding the tray on a side table and keeping the third cup for himself.

Crossing the room, Hezekiah sank down onto Logan's sofa, seemingly completely at home. The none-too-delicate piece of furniture groaned in protest as he settled himself against the cushions.

"Make yourself comfortable, Mr. Hawkins — I mean, Hawk. It's been a long day and we can certainly dispense with formalities now."

Logan discarded his hat on a table at the side of the room. His belt quickly followed, the metal buckle jingling lightly as he dropped it on the polished surface. Long fingers made short work of the brass buttons of his navy blue coat, which he carelessly threw across the back of a spindle-legged chair.

Hawk gratefully followed his host's lead, removing his jacket and placing it and his hat on a nearby highboy. Lastly, he unfastened the collar button of his shirt and pulled the constricting fabric away from his throat.

Logan folded himself into one of the two big oversized chairs opposite the sofa, and, with a sigh of pleasure, propped his booted feet on a nearby stool.

"Sit down, Hawk," he prompted. "Just consider yourself at home here."

Hawk nodded.

While his guest settled in the other chair, Logan hefted his coffee cup for a long swallow. Then he pinned Hezekiah with an inquisitive look. "Just where were you sneaking off to when Father caught you."

"Me?" Hezekiah replied in mock surprise, a flash of wariness in his eyes. "Nowhere in particular. Just out walkin', that's all."

Logan threw back his head and laughed. "You sly dog. I'd bet my next pay packet you were headed for Suds Row in hopes of getting a glimpse of the lovely Miss Jasmine."

Hezekiah squirmed nervously, acting for all the world like a kid caught with his hand in the cookie jar. "Now, Logan, it wasn't like that at—"

"Why don't you break down and let the lady know how you feel? I've been telling you for weeks that she's got her eye on you."

"Well . . . maybe I will . . . someday." Hezekiah downed the last of his coffee in one huge gulp, the cup all but invisible in his ham-sized hands. Nervously he turned the empty cup round and round. "But I think I'd best wait for a proper time."

"Proper time." Logan snorted in amusement. "The lady could be old and gray before you decide it's the proper time."

Hezekiah tried to change the subject. "I saw Miss Della last time I was in Bisbee. She said to give you her regards."

Logan grinned knowingly, well aware of Hezekiah's intention. "That's nice. I always enjoy hearing from a pretty lady. And speaking of pretty ladies—"

"Now, Logan." Hezekiah's soft self-conscious chuckle cut short his protest.

Meanwhile Hawk sat in perplexed silence, hearing with a sense of total confusion the casual bantering between the two men. The camaraderie between this unlikely pair had caught him completely off guard, and he had no idea what to make of the unusual situation.

It wasn't only that Logan was an officer and Hezekiah an enlisted man, Hawk would have thought that fact alone would have made friendship between them rather difficult. But here sat a black man and a white man, apparently completely at ease, joking and baiting each other in good-natured fun. That was something totally unexpected in the realm of Hawk's experience with the outside world.

83

As he continued to listen, some of the tenseness slowly began to seep out of Hawk. With amazement, he realized he was beginning to feel at ease, even comfortable, in the company of these two mismatched compatriots. A surprising thought fluttered at the edge of Hawk's mind. Somehow, he didn't think Logan and Hezekiah would react in the manner he'd learned to expect if they should learn the truth about him. The idea that he, too, might be judged by what he was, who he was, rather than by the blood that ran in his veins or the barely discernible color of his skin was exhilarating.

Not that they'd ever know of his mixed heritage. Oh, no. He could never allow that to happen. But the extraordinary realization that acceptance might actually be possible pleased Hawk immensely. It was gratifying to think these men wouldn't be shocked by his background, that he would still be welcome in their company.

Logan's hearty laughter interrupted Hawk's reverie. Raising his hands in melodramatic emphasis, he tried to stop Hezekiah's protestations at his latest jibe. "All right, all right. I give up. If you insist on leaving the little lady with a pining heart, I guess I can't stop you."

"Praise be," Hezekiah muttered, rolling his eyes heavenward. He relaxed again, slouching against the cushions, one arm carelessly thrown over the back of the sofa.

Logan grinned at his friend. "I guess it's time we turned our attention to other matters."

"I thought you'd never catch on," Hezekiah muttered.

Logan only grinned. "Why don't you tell me what's been going on around here while I've been away? Anything exciting?"

"Not much. Unless you want to count your daddy and ol' Mortimer Henderson having words."

"What? Again? What happened this time?"

"I don't rightly know what started it. I walked into the trading post right in the middle of their conversation. From what I heard of the argument, Henderson's been selling whiskey to the men on credit again. He must have been bitchin' about some of them not paying their bill promptly enough to suit him."

"Sounds like him."

"Well, your daddy told him in no uncertain terms that the easiest way to stop the problem was to quit selling to men who didn't have the money in their hands. Henderson didn't like that one bit."

Logan gave a loud snort. "I'll bet he didn't."

"You know Henderson," Hezekiah continued. "All he's interested in is how much profit he can turn. He knows if he lets the men have the whiskey on credit, he'll wind up with the biggest portion of their pay. If they have to wait till payday to buy, they'll just take their money to Tombstone."

"They'd be better off. He charges way too much, and I think he waters it down. Oh, that reminds me, Hawk. It might be smart to limit your purchases from our illustrious sutler. On some items I'm afraid Henderson's little better than a crook. If you need anything in particular, we'll take a run over to Tombstone or Bisbee the first of the week."

"Thanks for the warning, and the offer," Hawk said. "I'd like to see some of the surrounding country."

Of course he would. The more familiar he was with the area, the better his chance for escape if something went wrong later on. A sudden rush of guilt spread over Hawk. He hadn't considered how very uncomfortable it would be to sit in a man's house and plan the demise of that man's father.

"The only thing I'll need right away is a horse." Hawk's words tumbled out as he quickly pushed the troublesome thought away. "The rest can wait until a more convenient time."

Logan nodded. "There're plenty of extras on the post. Don't worry. We'll fix you up with a good one."

"I appreciate it."

"And Hezekiah and I'll show you around the fort tomorrow. Get you familiar with the lay of the land."

"Thanks. That would be most helpful," said Hawk. "I'm looking forward to seeing everything."

Logan waved Hawk's thanks aside and slumped further down in his chair. "Oh, by the way, there's a dance planned for tomorrow night. I'm sure Sabra will be looking forward to your attendance. Not to mention the other single ladies of the post."

Logan's good-natured grin broadened as he remembered the proprietary way his sister had studied their guest. If it came to a contest of wills among the ladies tomorrow night, he'd put his money on Sabra.

"Well . . . uh . . . thank you for telling me. I'm sure it'll be a pleasant evening." Hawk cared nothing about the "other single ladies." His only thought at the moment was that he'd see Sabra again. The prospect did strange things to the pit of his stomach.

He carefully scrutinized Logan, whose amusement at the whole situation was quite evident. What would happen if Logan learned about his Indian heritage? Was there the remotest possibility he'd still consider Hawk worthy company for his beloved sister? Hawk longed to believe it could be so. He was saved from further contemplation of the subject by Logan's next statement.

"Sorry, Hezekiah, I got off track there for a minute. Please go on with your story. Then what happened with Henderson?"

"The major said he might have to take some action against him if this kept up. Well, Henderson just glared at him with those little beady eyes of his and dared him to try something. He reminded your daddy that he'd been appointed to the post by Washington and that his patron had plenty of pull. Said the Army'd never be able to do anything to him."

"Oh, lord. I bet that ticked the ol' man off good and proper."

"Sure did." Hezekiah slapped his knee, his deep rumbling laughter filling the room. "You should have seen him. He turned about three shades of red and said 'We'll see about that' and then he marched out of there like he was on the way to a war." Hezekiah's laughter faded away, the amusement on his face replaced by a pensive look. "Do you suppose Henderson's telling the truth? Do you think he's got enough influence back in Washington to keep your daddy from putting a stop to his scalawag ways?"

Logan shrugged. "Could be. I've heard about post traders who're in so thick with some of those Washington politicians that they can get away with anything."

Shaking his head forlornly, Hezekiah muttered, "There's gonna be trouble for sure. I can feel it in my bones. Your daddy's gonna get his nose all out of joint over ol' Henderson's antics, and there'll be hell to pay around here."

Logan smothered a yawn. "Well, there'll be time enough to worry about that later. I'm beat. I think I'll turn in." He grinned hugely at Hezekiah, his dark eyes snapping mischievously. "Maybe you'll still have time to finish your evening walk."

Hezekiah's scathing look did little to subdue Logan's hearty laughter. Midst a last minute flurry of good-natured joshing, the three men said good night, and after Hezekiah left, Logan showed Hawk to the room that would be his during his stay, then disappeared down the hallway to his own.

Hawk noted with relief that the entrance to the kitchen was almost directly across from his room, the back door but a few steps away. A hasty exit might never be required, but he was glad to know that a way was available should it become necessary.

Logan had left a lantern burning low on the table beside the bed, and Hawk's gaze swept the Spartan accommodations, methodically placing each piece of furniture in his mind. From this moment on, light or no light, he'd be able to move about without bumping into anything.

Hezekiah had put his luggage on the bed for easy unpacking. With hurried efficient movements, Hawk emptied the case and placed his clothing in the wardrobe, wondering when and if he'd be repacking these items. Not knowing what the next few days might bring was strange to one accustomed to a very structured life.

He missed Hawkinsville, the friendly people he'd known all his life, the day-to-day mind-numbing bustle of running the family business. It would be good to get back to his normal routine, his safe, anesthetizing habits.

Hawk stood his now-empty bag in the corner of the room, then returned to the side of the bed. Shadows flickered across his troubled face as he bent to blow out the small dancing flame of the lamp. Still dressed, he eased his long frame onto the mattress, hands crossed behind his head.

A nagging little thought kept nibbling at the edge of his mind. Yes, it would be good to go home again. But going home meant not seeing Sabra again. And that rumination brought a sharp frown to Hawk's face, a dull ache to his heart.

This wasn't the way it was supposed to be. All his careful plans seemed to be dissolving, changing shape and texture, flowing and fading like puffy white clouds under the onslaught of a high, fast wind.

How had he managed to fool himself so completely? He'd been so sure he'd taken everything into consideration. It had seemed so easy.

It hadn't taken much thought to devise a new persona, one that would be readily accepted when he reached Arizona. Coming up with a believable story had been little more than an amusing mental exercise.

His biggest worry had been his family. He'd wondered how in the world he'd ever explain his uncharacteristic absence to them. But that, too, had proved ridiculously easy.

All he'd had to do was mention that he was considering an extended business trip and they'd all been thrilled. His aunts had been especially pleased with the prospect. He shouldn't have been surprised. They'd been none too subtle in the past about letting him know how much they worried about his self-imposed solitude.

There'd been a good deal of chatter and coy hinting that this trip might offer the perfect opportunity for their favorite nephew to meet a nice young lady. Such comments had been accompanied by the waggling of eyebrows and the exchange of knowing glances by the ladyfolk. Hawk was well aware of what all their theatrics meant. Find a young lady, fall in love, and bring her home as his bride.

Having long ago despaired of fixing him up with any of the local girls—Hawk simply had had no interest in them—his aunts were overjoyed at his sudden plan. Here was a chance for their darling nephew to remedy a malady they considered worse than death—bachelorhood.

How ironic, Hawk thought. He had let his aunts have their little daydream, had even played along with them. Anything to keep them happy, to keep them from suspecting the real purpose of his trip.

And now, here he was, caught smack in the web of his own deceit.

For the first time in his life Hawk had met someone so special that a mere smile from her could take his breath away. A young lady whose inner beauty promised to be even brighter than the soft golden comeliness with which she was outwardly blessed. The kind of young lady his aunts and uncles would adore on sight.

Hawk's deepest instincts told him Sabra might very well be the one and only woman who might give purpose to his aimless and lonely life. Somehow she'd managed to put a chip in his carefully nurtured protective shell, and in a scant two days' time. How was he going to keep her from burrowing even deeper into his thoughts during the next few weeks?

The whole situation was impossible. There was no way in hell anything could come of it. No matter how long his mind grappled with the facts, there was simply no workable solution. He couldn't stay in Arizona, and he couldn't take her back home even if she'd consent to go. He couldn't tell her the truth, and he couldn't live the lie forever. His careful scheming had become a trap.

It had all seemed so simple back in Hawkinsville. Just get to Arizona, fulfill his pledge, and leave. No doubts, no remorse, not a single thought for those he might meet along the way. But it wasn't working out like he'd expected.

Hawk's hatred for Major Powers was as strong as ever, his desire for revenge still the most powerful force in his life. But he was beginning to realize that the whole situation touched upon more than retaliation.

There were other people involved . . . real, living, breathing people. People who had been kind to him. People who had feelings just like he did. People who didn't deserve the hurt he was going to cause them.

How could he continue to justify his actions under

those circumstances? Then again, how could he turn his back on a blood vow sworn on the memory of his parents?

He couldn't. Honor simply would not allow it.

The walls of the room seemed to shrink, the atmosphere becoming as heavy and oppressive as the thoughts that swirled through his head. Suddenly all he wanted was to go outside, to pull a long draught of night air into his lungs, to feel the gentle wind on his face.

Cat-quiet, Hawk left his bed and made his way to the back door. He eased it open, hesitating in the entranceway long enough to hear the continued, slow even breathing that marked Logan's sleep, and then he slipped outside.

The night breeze had plucked the last bit of warmth from the land. Hands thrust deep into his pockets, Hawk silently walked away from the house, instinctively seeking the solace and solitude of the nearby wilderness. The chilly air nipped at his ears. Each breath tingled all the way to the bottom of his lungs.

Ahead of him, onyx mountains thrust against the black velvet sky, all but blending with it as a lone patch of sooty cloud scudded across the pale silver moon. A million stars studded the firmament.

Beset by a nameless unhappiness, filled with uncertainties, Hawk continued to gaze heavenward. Memories of the familiar constellations above Hawkinsville stabbed through him. Would he ever see them again? Resolutely he turned the doubt away, forcing himself to concentrate on the skies over Arizona Territory, to deliberately and methodically note the slightly different placement of stars he'd known intimately since childhood.

It was important. The time might come when he'd need their guidance for his escape.

Chapter Eight

Pale streaks of pink and plum and coral barely edged the jagged crests of the mountains ringing Fort Huachuca, heralding the coming of a new day. Tucked snugly in her bed, Sabra drifted in deep dream-filled slumber. . . .

She was all alone, embraced by a comforting cocoon of indigo velvet. Then the darkness began to melt away, leaving great puffs of mist that swirled and danced through the shadows, all silver edged and star sparkled. A gentle breeze, filled with the fragrance of a thousand flowers, feathered a golden curl against her cheek and rippled the gossamer lace edging of the low bodice of her gown. Reaching slender fingers to smooth the wind-blown ruffle, she closed her eyes for a moment and savored the angel-wing fragility of the moonglow white fabric.

In the distance she could hear the gentle haunting strains of a waltz. The music searched for her, found her, surrounded her, cherished her. Enchanted, she swayed to the beautiful notes, the ground beneath her feet as soft as any cloud. And then the music grew in urgency, calling to her, beckoning. Whispering soft urgings to hurry, hurry . . . hurry.

Expectation blossomed in her breast, unfurling like the petals of an exquisite rose, filling her with the beguiling promise of what lay just beyond the iridescent mists. Joy suffusing her face, she hurriedly lifted the skirt of her diaphanous gown and surrendered herself to the guiding melody.

A star-streaked silver glow began to fill the sky as she skimmed, weightless as smoke, across the petal-strewn field. Then the opalescent mists shimmered and parted, revealing a tall dark figure. Her breath caught in her throat and she froze in midstep.

He raised his head, and their gazes met and held. When he began to walk toward her, heat flickered in the depths of her soul, danced through her veins like summer lightning through the heavens.

His midnight black evening clothes fit him to perfection, the tight-fitting trousers caressing his long muscular thighs with each step he took, the jacket hugging his powerful shoulders like a lover. His skin was molten gold against the crisp pristine white of his beruffled shirt.

He was glorious.

And she knew from the look on his face that he thought her beautiful, more beautiful than the moon that floated overhead. His gaze caressed her from head to toe, a smile gently lifting the corners of his sensuously sculpted mouth. His worshiping eyes would have put the finest star sapphires to shame.

And suddenly he was standing mere inches from her, so close she could feel the heat of his body. She ached for him to touch her. And he was attuned to her every wish. No sooner had the thought been born than one strong arm slipped around her waist, drawing her into the safe haven of his embrace. He took her hand, his fingers closing ever so gently over hers. And then they were dancing, dipping and whirling, twirling and turning, floating with the shining stars.

She wished it would never end.

The music caressed them, bathing them in its beauty. His arms tightened around her and pulled her closer, and closer still until her breasts were pressed so firm against the broad rock-hard expanse of his chest, she could feel the racing beat of his heart.

Sweet anticipation filled her.

Hungry gazes locked, they slowed their steps until they were standing still. He bent toward her, a warm breath caressing her temple with the movement. Frissons of plea-sure shimmered through her as his mouth grazed the

tender flesh of her earlobe.
    And then . . . then his lips claimed hers—

Boom! The roar of the cannon rattled dishes in the cupboards of every house on the post and rudely interrupted Sabra's dream. Reveille.

"Sterling," she sighed, still half-asleep. Burrowing deeper beneath the bright patchwork quilt, she pulled a fluffy pillow over her head in an effort to shut out the discordant blare of bugles and the answering howls of the post dogs.

For several minutes she drifted in that misty sweet nothingness between sleep and waking, fighting to recapture the pleasure of her fast-fading fantasy. But it was no use. The familiar early morning sounds of a post stirring to life refused to relinquish their hold on her mind. No matter how much she wished it, sleep was not going to return and wrap her in its blissful cloak.

Finally, Sabra groaned and shoved the pillow away. Opening her eyes, she blinked sleepily and pushed a wild disarray of golden curls from her forehead. Smothering a yawn, she snuggled back into the plump feather pillows to savor the last remnants of the dream. The memory of it sent tingles all the way to her toes, and brought a blush to her cheeks.

"Mercy," Sabra whispered, thinking of the way Sterling Hawkins' lips had felt against hers in that ethereal world. Would a *real* kiss be as good?

Or better?

She had so little to base her musings on, having grown up well chaperoned and with little chance to experience such things. Oh, not that she and her friends hadn't managed to sneak a fair number of stolen pecks and hugs over the years, as young people are apt to do. But Sabra's only experiment with real adult kisses had come about under the tutelage of Phillip Marshall.

The first time Phillip had kissed her had been at her seventeenth birthday party. There'd been a few other similar episodes during the following year as young Marshall diligently wooed her, vaguely pleasant and quite innocent interludes that never advanced beyond hand-holding and a stolen buss or two. But by the time Phillip pledged his undying love and begged her permission to speak with her grandfather, she'd realized she wasn't in love with him. Phillip had been disappointed; Sabra had been relieved.

Funny, now that she thought about it, she realized that just dancing with Sterling Hawkins roused more butterflies in her stomach than the sum total of all of Phillip's fumbling displays of passion.

What was it about this stranger that sent chills racing through her at nothing more than a look from his intriguing blue eyes? He was so unlike the familiar, happy-go-lucky young men she'd grown up with . . . and that unclassifiable difference ignited tiny puffs of excitement deep in her belly. Somehow her reaction was all tied up with the strange haunted look she'd noticed in his eyes on several occasions, a look she was positive could only allude to some great hidden sadness. She wondered what might have caused such hurt . . . or who. Each time she glimpsed that peculiar expression, she longed to wrap her arms around him and soothe away the pain.

Sabra's fingers absently pleated the edge of the sheet as she contemplated whether the familiar post sounds had awakened Sterling Hawkins, too. Was he dressing so that he could view the morning formation? Perhaps he and Logan planned to begin their tour of the fort as soon as Logan finished with roll call.

Or was Sterling Hawkins still asleep in Logan's spare bedroom? That question generated a very alluring mental picture. Did he sleep in one of those silly nightshirts her grandfather had favored? Or perhaps his long johns? No, that picture didn't suit him at all. Her eyes grew wide. What if he slept in . . . nothing? Spots of rosy color blossomed on her cheeks at the decidedly wicked thought.

Sighing deeply, Sabra wiggled into a more comfortable position and deliberately turned her thoughts to safer things. Such as the clattering morning sounds outside her windows, which brought to mind the stories Logan had told her about the timeless morning rituals of soldiers stirring to wakefulness.

In the barracks the noncommissioned officers would be

clomping up and down the length of the room, bellowing insults and threats of drastic punishment for any man late to the morning formation. The men, in turn, would question the legitimacy of their officers' birth and make the standard early morning vow to desert at first opportunity. Logan had told her that similar scenes took place at posts all over the country, the soldiers stubbornly clinging to a routine that had become a comfortable and familiar part of their frequently mundane lives.

Despite the vast amount of belly-aching, the men would be in ranks by 5:40 A.M., just as the squad leaders began to make their reports. Daily duty assignments would then be made. At Fort Huachuca, Sabra knew those duties consisted of such things as escorting paymasters and survey parties, guarding railroad construction crews and equipment, and checking telegraph lines, which frequently needed repairs. Then, too, as always, troops would patrol the border.

The major held firm to the idea that hard work and rigorous training produced prime troops. Sabra had heard her father say at least a dozen times that too much slack time resulted in boredom, drunkenness, and desertion. He wholeheartedly believed that it was good for the men's pride to meet and overcome hardship and danger.

The sounds outside Sabra's window increased in volume, and she knew the men were beginning to line up across the parade ground. She stretched languorously and considered what the day might bring. Like the flag being raised outside, the coming hours unfurled before her, full of bright promise.

The muffled names of roll call reminded her she'd better hurry and get dressed if she wanted to accompany Logan and Sterling Hawkins on their tour of the fort. She ignored the fact that she'd been living on the post for three months now, that she'd seen most of what there was to see. Everything would look brand new when viewed while standing beside Sterling Hawkins.

And tonight, ah, tonight was the Saturday night dance. She could hardly wait. Much as she'd hate to relinquish even one minute of Logan's and Sterling's company, she'd probably have to excuse herself early in order to have enough time to bathe and wash her hair. She intended to look her very best. She didn't want Sterling Hawkins looking at anyone but her when she walked through the door of the amusement hall that evening.

Suddenly eager to sample the possible delights of the coming day, Sabra threw back the covers and thrust her long legs over the edge of the bed. She barely noticed the chill wooden floor beneath her bare feet as she sped toward the wardrobe in search of the perfect dress.

The new day was little more than a pale promise when Hawk stepped outside to watch the ritual of morning formation from the front stairs of Logan's quarters. Buttoning his jacket against the night-chilled air, he set about trying to estimate the number of active soldiers assigned to Fort Huachuca. He knew that a company might be composed of as many as a hundred men, but in most cases that number was drastically cut due to sickness, detached duty assignments, and guardhouse confinements. Hawk also knew that the total men on active duty could be further whittled down by desertions or the absence of soldiers on leave. In times of relative peace, any number of men might be granted extended leaves simply because they asked their commanding officer for time off.

Hawk's intense gaze traveled over the neat rows of blue-clad figures, cautiously assessing the degree of aptitude displayed by the soldiers. It wasn't exactly what he'd hoped for.

The soldiers had taken their places quickly, falling into rank with little confusion. They stood at attention, shoulders back, heads up, arms stiff at their sides; the spit-and-polish professionalism of the majority of them no doubt was attributable to the military-minded Major Powers.

Hawk gave a resigned shrug. He had hoped this isolated fort housed nothing more than a ragtag batch of society's dregs, but he'd never lost sight of the possibility that he might be up against crack troops. And that certainly looked to be the case.

Well, so be it. It wasn't his intention to confront any of

the soldiers anyway; his plan would be much more subtle than that. But if, in the end, it came to a showdown, he'd face them one and all. A warrior could do no less.

At that moment, Major Powers marched out of the gloomy residue of night and onto the field, straight and tall, and once again faultlessly attired in a braid-bedecked uniform. Although Hawk's stomach churned at the sight of his sworn enemy, his expression never changed. Once again Hawk noted Powers's ramrod-stiff posture and brusque demeanor, and he wondered how such a cold, inflexible man could have fathered someone as delightful and warm as Sabra.

Determined to subdue the familiar anger building within him, Hawk deliberately pulled his gaze away from Powers and turned his attention to a scrutiny of the numerous buildings bordering the parade grounds. He could guess the purposes of some of them; the others he would ask Logan about later.

The first pale yellow rays of the sun slanted their way heavenward as the assignment of the day's duties was finally completed. Then ranks broke, the men melting into a swirling mass of dark blue uniforms peppered with an occasional item of civilian clothing. Within seconds the soldiers had dispersed, eager to have breakfast and get on with the day.

Hawk spotted Logan and Hezekiah almost immediately. Their greater heights making them easy to distinguish in the milling assemblage, the pair threaded their way through the thinning crowd, sauntering in his direction. Hawk pushed himself away from the support post he'd been leaning against and went down the steps to greet them.

"Ready for the grand tour?" Logan asked when he drew near enough to be heard, his usual devil-may-care grin back on his face.

"Yes, I'm ready," Hawk answered, smiling in return. *More than ready.*

"Good. We'll have a bite of breakfast first and then be on our way."

Hawk bit back a suggestion that they skip the morning meal. Although extremely eager to explore the post, to discover a few more pieces of the puzzle, he knew better than to reveal that fervor to anyone else.

"Wonderful. I'm starving," he lied.

He could spare a few more minutes. After all, he'd waited years for this opportunity. No need to mess things up now by rushing. There were too many details to be learned from the promised promenade.

Hawk wanted to know what areas were heavily traveled, what sections of the fort were relatively deserted—where Major Powers's office was, and what hours he kept. Did the man have assistants that would prevent Hawk's undetected entrance to his inner chamber? Would Hawk be better advised to look for a place of ambush away from the fort? Perhaps the major took an occasional ride off post, alone.

Hawk needed to know all these things and more.

The November sun had begun its climb in the clear blue eastern sky by the time the three men had finished their breakfast at Logan's. Descending the stairs at the front of the younger Powers' home, they headed south, beginning their journey on the long eastern side of the formal parade ground.

"That's really the heart of the post," Logan commented, nodding toward the now almost deserted rectangle of open field. "The layout is typical of most Western posts, a parade ground in the middle, flanked by officers' quarters on one side, the enlisted men's barracks on the other."

Hawk recalled passing between two of the four barracks buildings on the way to Logan's house on the previous night. Now, in the daylight, he could see that these structures were sturdy two-story wooden buildings perched high upon stone piers. Outside stairways provided access to open porches that gave some relief from the oppressive summer heat and some shelter from the winter winds. Hawk was quick to note that under cover of night he could easily use the open space beneath the barracks to move unseen down that side of the post.

"Logan! Wait for me!"

At Sabra's breathless call the three men halted at the southeastern corner of the parade ground.

At the sound of her voice, Hawk turned eagerly to watch her approach, all thoughts of secret paths and hiding places gone like a puff of smoke at the sight of Sabra. Sweet heaven, he thought. She's more beautiful every time I see her.

This morning she wore an apple green calico dress, high-necked and long-sleeved. The fabric molded the sweet curves of her breasts, and hugged her tiny waist in a most delightful manner. Each hurried step she took caused the full bell-shaped skirt to sway seductively. He was pleased to see she'd left her hair loose. A waterfall of sun-kissed curls cascaded down her back, held back from her face by a band of emerald ribbon. Once again, Hawk longed to thread his fingers through her tresses.

"I hope I didn't miss anything exciting," she said, her warm velvet brown eyes cutting in Hawk's direction. Then she quickly rose on tiptoe to place a good-morning kiss on her brother's cheek.

"Not a thing," Logan assured her. "We were just getting started. Weren't we, Hawk?"

It took a moment for the question to register. Hawk had been too busy wondering how it would feel to have those sweet coral lips pressed against his own flesh. "What? Uh . . . yes, that's right. We'd just started."

"Wonderful." Sabra smiled her delight, that tantalizing little dimple once again winking in her cheek. She tucked one small hand through her brother's arm, the other through Hawk's. "Shall we proceed, gentlemen?"

And off they went, Logan, Sabra, and Hawk arm in arm, Hezekiah falling into step beside Logan. As they traversed the south side of the square, Logan pointed out the storehouse and the impressive new amusement hall where the dance would be held that night.

"And this is Henderson's trading post," Logan said as they neared the end of the square. He hesitated, torn between preference and duty. Duty won. "Guess we should stop in, since Henderson was here during the Geronimo campaign. At least give you a chance to meet him. I'm not overly fond of the man, but it certainly isn't

99

my place to censor your contacts. There's always the chance you might want to ask him some questions later on."

Sabra's heart dropped right down to her toes. It was all she could do to bite back the words of protest ringing in her mind. She could have strangled her brother for trying to be so helpful. Henderson's trading post, for pity's sake. The last place on earth she wanted Sterling Hawkins to enter.

Drat and double drat! Where had her mind been? If she hadn't been so caught up in the pleasure of Sterling Hawkins' company and the feel of his muscular forearm under her fingertips, she might have realized where they were heading, perhaps have steered them in another direction or given Logan some kind of signal.

Well, it was too late now. Logan was already headed straight for the store . . . and Melissa.

Sabra squeezed her eyes shut for a second and sent a small prayer heavenward. *Please, please, let Sergeant Woodley still be courting Melissa.*

The men's boots thudded against the plank flooring of the store's porch, completely drowning out the whisper-soft patter of Sabra's small, very reluctant steps. However, as Logan reached out to open the door, Sabra squared her shoulders and lifted her head, prepared to do battle if necessary. Through the opening she marched, the three men trailing behind.

The interior of the trading post was dim, but a dozen aromas lingered in the dusty air.

Sabra's apprehensive gaze swept the store the minute she was inside, sliding over the figures scattered about the room. Mortimer Henderson was in his usual place, poking through the contents displayed in two large cases lying open on his front counter.

A rotund little man, a stranger to Sabra but obviously the owner of the treasure trove in the cases, hovered nearby. He kept up a steady sales pitch as Mortimer picked up one gadget after another.

"Now, that's a real little jewel," the drummer declared with an emphatic nod of his head. The movement caused his thick glasses to slide to the end of his bulbous nose. A chubby finger pushed the wayward spectacles back into place, but the very next bob of his head sent them gliding again. ". . . Quite a little item, sold real well up in Tucson . . . oughta give that one a try . . ."

The salesman's incessant chatter barely penetrated as Sabra's restless eyes continued to search the store. Two officers' wives were fingering the yard goods on a side table, and near the back a private was checking the balance on a pistol.

It took a moment for reality to register, so ready had Sabra been to confront her nemesis. Then a surge of sweet relief washed through her as she realized Melissa was nowhere in sight.

Finally noting the arrival of prospective customers, the store's proprietor pushed himself away from the littered counter. The gnawed matchstick in his mouth bobbed from one corner to the other and then back again as he watched the foursome approach.

"Good day to you, Logan, Miss Sabra." The matchstick quivered with each word. Mortimer Henderson's tone was pleasant enough, considering the bad blood between him and their father. "What can I do for you this fine morning? You be needing some supplies?"

"Not today, Henderson," Logan replied, anxious to get the introduction over with and be back on his way. Something about the sutler always seemed to rub him the wrong way. "Just showing our visitor around a bit."

"Fine, fine. Say, Miss Sabra, you might want to take a look at this fellow's wares. Got some mighty pretty geegaws in those bags of his."

"Sure do, little lady," the drummer said, turning toward them for the first time.

Hawk's heart almost stopped beating.

A jovial smile wreathing his face, the salesman inserted his thumbs in the pockets of his plum-colored vest, causing the material to pull taut over his round little belly as he rocked back on the balls of his feet.

"Julian Hobart, at your service, ma'am. I got ribbons and lace and fancy buttons, plus lots of other necessities. Just feel free to have a look-see for yourself." The salesman's double chin wobbled a bit as he nodded invitingly in the direction of the open cases.

Sabra gave the contents a polite perfunctory glance, but was careful not to let her gaze linger on any particular item. She had no intention of doing anything that might prolong their time in the store. If they hurried, they might still be able to get outside before Melissa put in an appearance.

When Sabra failed to take the bait, the drummer's pale blue eyes, considerably magnified by the thick-lensed glasses again perched precariously on the end of his nose, flickered toward Logan and Hezekiah. He barely noticed Hawk, who had quickly stepped behind the other two men.

"You, too, gentlemen. Step right up and have a look. Don't be shy."

"It's kind of you to offer." Logan decided he'd leave Hawk's introduction for a later time. Traveling salesmen didn't often come through Fort Huachuca, and Henderson was apt to be busy for quite a while yet, especially when dealing with this garrulous little fellow. "But I'm afraid we don't have the time right now. We're on a rather tight schedule."

The glasses wobbled alarmingly as the little drummer nodded his head in empathy. "I understand. That's all right. You'll have another chance." A merry chuckle punctuated his statement. "I'll be back in a week or so, after I've made my other stops."

"Thank you, we'll be sure to keep that in mind."

When Logan moved toward Sabra, reaching out to take her arm in preparation for their departure, Hawk was caught unaware. A split second too late, he turned on his heel and took a step toward the door.

"Say there, young fella, don't I know you?" Julian Hobart's myopic eyes squinted up at the man who'd previously been hidden behind the other two.

"Me?" Hawk responded, despite the large lump in his throat. His worst fears were realized. He'd recognized the salesman at first glance, and had been concealing himself behind Hezekiah and Logan ever since. "No. No, I don't think so."

Hobart shook his head. "H'm. Can't quite put my

102

finger on it, but you sure remind me of someone. I'm not much on names, and the ol' eyes aren't what they used to be, but I've always had a good memory for faces." He dragged his glasses from his nose, polished them with a linen handkerchief he took from his vest pocket, and popped them back on his nose to peer upward once again. "Yep, you sure do look familiar."

"Sorry," Hawk said, shrugging his broad shoulders as he backed toward the entrance. "I'm sure we've never met." He cast an appealing glance toward his companions. "Shouldn't we be on our way?" He had to get out of there . . . and fast.

"Right behind you," Logan responded, as eager as Hawk to escape the talkative salesman's snare.

"I'll keep thinking on it, young fella. Maybe I'll have the answer by the time I get back."

Julian Hobart's parting words followed Hawk out the door.

"Whew! What a character," Logan declared once they were back outside, shaking his head in amusement. "We'll talk to Henderson later."

"Good idea," Hawk said. He was willing to agree to anything as long as it got him away from the store and the tenacious little salesman. He gladly followed the others down the path.

While Logan and Hezekiah discussed where they should go next, Hawk's muddled mind was trying to come to terms with the new hitch in his scheme. Never once in all the hours of planning had he considered the possibility of what had just happened. Who would have thought there'd be anyone within hundreds of miles that might recognize him?

But maybe, the fates willing, Hobart wouldn't remember that one time he'd come through Hawkinsville peddling his wares. Hawk breathed a silent prayer of thanks that Logan had never gotten around to introductions. At least that little man hadn't been given the additional clue Hawk's name might have provided.

Still, Hawk was going to be forced to make adjustments because of this odd quirk of fate. He dared not take a chance on the man remembering where he'd seen him or exactly who he was, for that might destroy any chance of being able to walk away undetected after Powers' death. If nothing else, Julian Hobart's imminent return meant that Hawk had less time to complete his plan than he'd hoped for. Less than a week to reconnoiter the fort and find out Powers's schedule. The deed had to be done and Hawk had to be back on the stage for Tucson before the drummer returned.

Hawk was almost grateful when Sabra interrupted his worried ruminations.

"Oh, look, Hezekiah, there's Jasmine," Sabra exclaimed happily as she spied a familiar figure headed in the direction of Suds Row, the cluster of buildings housing the fort's laundresses. "Come on," she urged. "Let's go say hello."

Hezekiah hesitated, dropping a step or two behind the others. "Maybe . . . maybe I'd better go on back—"

"Oh no, you don't," Sabra scolded sternly. "Don't be so silly. You're coming with us. Jasmine! Jasmine, wait!" Sabra called out.

The woman turned at the sound of her name, balancing a large woven basket against one softly rounded hip as she waited. As they drew near, Hawk immediately saw why Hezekiah grew tongue-tied at the mention of her. Tall and willow-slim, Jasmine carried herself with grace and dignity. Her high cheekbones and dark sloe eyes reminded Hawk of the pictures he'd seen of Egyptian princesses. Her skin was flawless, the color of coffee mixed with rich pure cream, and her deep brown hair had been pulled back, plaited, and pinned atop her head like a crown.

"Morning, Miss Sabra, Mr. Logan." A timid smile curved Jasmine's lips as her gaze slid to the stranger in their midst, but it blossomed when her obsidian eyes fastened on Hezekiah. "And a good morning to you, Private Kane," she said, her voice soft and sultry as the whispering wind.

Hezekiah whipped the cap from his head, nervously clutching it in front of him. Oblivious to the damage he was doing to it, he continued to turn the poor crushed topper round and round. Finally his broad pink tongue slipped out to moisten lips as dry as the surrounding desert.

"Uh, morning, Miss Jasmine," he croaked. Then he simply stood there, shifting from one foot to the other, his eyes worshipful.

Sabra finally took pity on Hezekiah and picked up the thread of the conversation. "Jasmine, I'd like to introduce our guest to you. This is Mr. Sterling Hawkins. Mr. Hawkins, Jasmine Sinclair."

"I'm very pleased to meet you, Miss Sinclair."

Jasmine nodded her regal head. "My pleasure, Mr. Hawkins." She turned back to Sabra. "I heard you were back from Tucson. Did you have a pleasant trip?"

"Absolutely marvelous," Sabra assured her.

For the next few minutes they discussed the festivities Logan and Sabra had attended in Tucson. Then Logan reminded them that they'd only covered one side of the fort and that they still needed to find a suitable horse for Hawk's use during his stay.

"Of course, I mustn't keep you any longer," Jasmine said quickly.

Logan noted the flash of disappointment in her eyes, and had a sudden inspiration. He gave Jasmine a quick conspiratorial wink, then turned to Hezekiah. "That basket looks awfully heavy. Why don't you lend Jasmine a hand, Hezekiah?"

Hezekiah gulped audibly, but Jasmine gave him no chance to refuse. "How kind of you to offer, Hezekiah," she said, deftly ignoring the fact that it had been Logan's idea. "You're such a gentleman."

Before the big black soldier knew what was happening, Jasmine handed him the basket, looped a hand through the crook of his arm, and led him off, like a calf to the slaughter, in the direction of Suds Row.

Logan's low chuckle accompanied Hawk's bemused perusal of the retreating figures. "I guess we ought to be ashamed of ourselves, sis."

Sabra gave an impatient toss of her head. "Don't be silly, Logan. I'm on Jasmine's side. If Hezekiah's too bashful to make the first move, then it's up to us as his friends to see that they get together. Now," she said brightly, summarily dismissing the subject, "let's get on with the tour."

Little by little Hawk's apprehensions regarding the drummer began to abate. Deciding he was being foolish to worry about something he couldn't change, he vowed to put the matter from his mind, at least for the time being. If he were lucky, Hobart would be gone before they returned to that side of the fort. If not, Hawk would just have to be extremely careful to avoid any further contact with the man.

While he'd been worrying over the drummer, minutes had been slipping away—minutes he could have spent enjoying Sabra. Determined not to waste any more of the precious little time he'd have with her, Hawk resolutely put the incident at the trading post from his mind and concentrated on the pleasures at hand.

Like the cozy feel of her arm tucked through his, and the gratification he felt at seeing her small hand curved so trustingly against his forearm. The flash of her familiar smile, and the way it did strange things to his breathing. Or the tilt of her head, the melody of her laughter, the feel of her crisp calico skirt brushing against his pants leg. Each memory he carefully collected and stored away for the long, lonely future.

The next few hours Hawk was shown the rest of the fort, including the various storage buildings, the guard-house, the post hospital, the chapel, and the surgeon's quarters. Long after the midday meal, the three of them finally made it to the corral. At Sabra's urging, Hawk picked out a magnificent white stallion. Inordinately pleased that he'd agreed with her personal choice, Sabra gifted Hawk with yet another dazzling smile, and he knew he'd gladly purchase a dozen horses if it would make her happy.

"What's out there?" Hawk asked inquisitively as they started to leave the corral area, for he'd noticed a cluster of dwellings set a good distance from the northwest corner of the fort.

"Out where?" Logan asked, turning to glance in the direction Hawk was indicating. "Oh, that . . . that's the Indian camp. The scouts and their families live out there."

"I see," Hawk said, wondering if the Indians had chosen to locate their camp that far from the post or if the army had purposefully segregated them by distance.

"Would you like to see it? Father will be expecting Sabra back for supper, but I think there's still plenty of time."

But before Hawk could answer Logan's question, Sabra spoke up, her eyes wide and anxious, her voice suddenly tense. "No, Logan. I can't go out there . . . uh . . . I mean, I shouldn't go. It's . . . it's getting late. Father will be worried." She backed away with small nervous steps. "Please, you two go on. I'll be fine. Really. I'll just run on home."

A confused frown furrowed Hawk's brow as he listened to Sabra's babbled excuses. What had precipitated her rapid change in attitude? His troubled gaze swept the distant camp once again. The Indians? Were they what bothered her? His mind rebelled at the possibility.

What then? Logan's mention of their father? Hawk could think of nothing else that might have caused her reaction.

His stomach knotted with distaste. Was Powers that difficult to get along with? Would Sabra be chastised for spending so much time with them? Surely not. The man appeared to dote on his daughter. Then Hawk remembered the major's despotic attitude. Had Sabra joined them without his permission? Powers was definitely the type of man who wouldn't like being crossed. The thought of Sabra being reprimanded by Major Powers made Hawk's blood simmer.

Well, to hell with the rest of the tour, he decided. It was far more important that they get Sabra home, and before she incurred the major's wrath.

"No," he said quickly. "I don't want to see the Indian camp. I've seen everything I want to see for today. I agree with Sabra; let's head for home."

Sabra's chin trembled. "Oh, dear. Now I feel bad about interrupting everything—"

"Don't," Hawk admonished softly, his gaze holding hers. "I don't care about the rest of it. You're absolutely right. It is getting late. Why, look how low the sun is; it

107

won't be long until it's time for the dance."

"The dance," Sabra repeated, a smile beginning to curve her mouth.

"Yes, the dance. I certainly don't want anything to interfere with the pleasure of the coming evening. I've been looking forward to it all day."

"So have I," Sabra whispered. "So have I."

Chapter Nine

Not long after dark the amusement hall began to fill with milling people, all eager to begin the evening's merrymaking. Decorations consisted of fragrant evergreen boughs bedecked with bits of bright ribbon, prettily arranged by the ladies of the fort, and the soft golden glow of candlelight sent velvet shadows flickering over the sturdy tables and chairs grouped along the walls. The post band, attired in splendid dress uniforms, occupied one corner, while the center of the large room had been left clear for dancing.

A half-dozen young ladies, all of marriageable age, had strategically positioned themselves near the main entrance. Word about the fort's handsome new visitor had spread like wildfire during the day, and they could hardly wait to see him for themselves. Twittering like so many magpies, they eagerly awaited his arrival.

"My brother saw him out by the corral this afternoon. He said he's almost as tall as Lieutenant Powers, and very good looking. And he has lovely dark brown hair, and dark eyes . . . Bubba couldn't tell exactly what color they were from where he was—"

"Oh, good grief, Louise, your little brother's only ten years old. How can you possibly believe anything he has to say?" Melissa Henderson snapped.

Louise was a handy target for the vexation that had plagued Melissa ever since the late-afternoon arrival of a note from her current beau. It was bad enough that he'd been unexpectedly assigned to field patrol and wouldn't be available to escort her to the dance, but he hadn't even given her enough time to try to find a replacement. In Melissa's mind that was almost unforgivable.

Louise Penrod's eyes grew round with surprise at Melissa's hateful tone. "Because I caught a glimpse of the man myself this afternoon. Besides, I was very careful when I questioned Bubba." She hoped her tone adequately conveyed her displeasure with Melissa's shrewish attitude.

Up went Melissa's nose. A dismissive "Humph!" left no doubt as to her opinion of Louise's interrogation skills or the accuracy of Bubba's description of the mysterious newcomer.

"Well," Mary Ruth Randall interjected, a self-satisfied look on her freckled face, "this evening, when my pa came home for supper, I heard him telling my mama about the stranger." She paused dramatically.

"Oh! What did he say?" Ramona Wilcox squealed, her eyes round with curiosity.

"Do tell, Mary Ruth," Louise pleaded. "Don't keep us waiting!"

"Yes, tell us all about it," chorused the Johnson twins, Susan and Emma.

Mary Ruth refrained from answering until she was sure she had everyone's attention, including Melissa's. "Well, his name is Sterling Hawkins." She cast rapturous eyes heavenward. "Isn't that the most romantic name you ever heard? And Pa said that he's some rich fellow from up East and—"

Melissa sighed in exasperation. "Of course he's rich, Mary Ruth! We could have guessed that all by ourselves. Who else but a rich man would travel around the country and do nothing but write stories? Everyone knows you can't make a living doing that. Therefore, his family *has* to be wealthy. Honestly!" The last word was delivered with a haughty toss of curls.

"You don't have to be so snippy, Melissa," Louise protested, still smarting from her friend's earlier snide comment. "I know what's wrong with you. You're just peeved because Sabra Powers got to him first. My little brother says she was with Mr. Hawkins and Lieutenant Powers most of the day. That's all that's wrong with you. You're jealous of Sabra."

A concerted gasp went up at Louise's indiscreet statement. Though it was obvious to each and every one of the girls that the post trader's pampered daughter had had her nose out of joint ever since Sabra Powers had arrived, previously no one had been brave enough to mention it.

Prior to Sabra's arrival, Mortimer Henderson's daughter had been considered the most beautiful of the eligible females on the post. Lacking even a smidgen of timidity, she had never hesitated to flaunt her obvious physical beauty or her unique position in the hierarchy of the fort.

Unlike the members of military families, who dared not forget that a future promotion or a coveted duty assignment might depend on the good will of a superior officer, Melissa and her father were under no compulsion to kowtow to anyone. Henderson's government appointment practically guaranteed the continuance of their privileged status.

Furthermore, while money was frequently tight for the families of soldiers, the Hendersons appeared to have no such problem. And Mortimer Henderson was generous to a fault when it came to his only child. Melissa's one source of irritation—until Sabra's arrival—had been her father's insistence that she occasionally work in the store. She hated the few hours she spent behind the counter at the trading post, fretting that such menial servitude was beneath her. She was positive that she was destined for far better things.

Day by day, she became more determined to find a wealthy beau and escape her mundane existence. But despite the relentless parade of suitors calling on Melissa, not one had possessed the qualifications she was looking for in a husband, the main one being money. Lots of it. Edward Woodley had come closest to being acceptable, so she had been content to sharpen her female wiles on him until a better candidate came along.

Although frequently disgruntled by Melissa's superior attitude, the other young ladies at Fort Huachuca had generally chosen to ignore it. After all, they couldn't deny she was beautiful. Her midnight black hair and magnolia-blossom complexion were envied, her voluptuous curves coveted. Besides, maintaining friendly relations with Melissa was in their best interest since they often benefited from the overflow of eager young soldiers hanging around the dark-haired beauty.

Such had been the situation at Fort Huachuca until Sabra Powers had appeared. Then, fickle as a mountain wind, the men had forgotten Melissa and flocked to the new girl's golden loveliness like bees seeking a nectar-laden blossom. Melissa had been furious. She'd conveniently ignored the fact that Sabra had done little to encourage all that attention. It was much more soothing to her wounded ego to think that Sabra Powers was simply feigning disinterest to further fuel the men's attraction to her.

Knowing the games she herself had to resort to on occasion, Melissa even went so far as to consider that Sabra might be pretending indifference to her eager admirers in an effort to appease her father. It was a well-known fact that the major had been less than pleasant to the young officers who had been brash enough to try to pay court to their superior's daughter.

What stung Melissa even more, however, was that Sabra was fundamentally everything she herself only pretended to be — sincere, caring, unfailingly pleasant, and eternally good humored. And, to make matters worse, Sabra Powers appeared to possess not one conceited bone in her body.

The young ladies of the fort welcomed Sabra into their midst almost immediately . . . all the more reason for the seeds of dislike to find fertile ground in Melissa. Playing second fiddle to anyone was not in Melissa Henderson's nature.

A good number of the fickle young men had eventually become discouraged because of Major Powers and, afraid to incur any further disfavor from a commanding officer, had straggled back to Melissa's ring of admirers. But by then the resentment Melissa felt toward Sabra was too deep rooted to be put aside. Over the weeks, the young woman's animosity had continued to grow, fed by one imaginary offense after another.

Louise's rash statement of the very thing they'd all been thinking caused eyes to widen and mouths to drop open in astonishment. Expectantly the group waited for the explosion they knew would come.

But for once Melissa fooled them. Her clear gray eyes greedily fastened on the front of the room, while her devious mind explored the germ of a wickedly tempting plan that had begun to unfold at the sight of the two men coming through the ornate doorway.

She patted her hair in an exaggeratedly feminine gesture, her small pink tongue slipping out to wet her full lips. Then she cast one last disdainful look at her erstwhile friends.

"We'll just see about that," she said. "If I set my mind to it, I can make any man—including Sterling Hawkins—forget that Sabra Powers even exists."

With that, Melissa haughtily gathered her voluminous skirts and began to sashay toward the main entrance, leaving her open-mouthed friends to speculate on what was about to happen.

Logan and Hawk had barely cleared the doorway when Melissa pounced.

"Why, Logan," the black-haired beauty exclaimed, provocatively fluttering her eyelashes as she swept down upon the two men, "how simply marvelous to see you tonight." Her Southern accent thick as honey, she rushed on before Logan could even open his mouth in reply. "I do declare, Logan Powers, this ol' fort just wasn't the same, what with you gone off to Tucson."

Logan smothered a droll smile and waited for a clue as to just what Melissa had on her mind. It didn't take long to find out.

Looking the very picture of flustered innocence, Melissa let her gaze drift away from Logan to sweep over the man standing at his side.

"Why, Logan, you sweet ol' dear," she gushed in mock surprise, "I see you've brought a guest to our little dance. How very nice! But what a naughty, naughty boy you've been."

"Oh?" Logan queried, amusement sparkling in his eyes. "Why is that?"

Melissa bestowed her most dazzling smile on Hawk. "You should have warned us how handsome your friend is. Why, I vow every female heart in the place must be beating at double time." Melissa placed slender fingers strategically against the ample bosom which swelled over the edge of her emerald green bodice. "I certainly know mine is."

Satisfaction flared bright in her eyes as Hawk's gaze obediently followed the gesture.

"Well, aren't you going to introduce your friend, Logan dear?" Melissa simpered, letting her lashes drop in another coy flutter.

"Gracious me," Logan drawled, feigning grave mortification. "I don't know what got into me. Why, it seems I've let my manners slip clean away. Sterling, allow me the honor of introducing you to the daughter of our illustrious post trader, Miss Melissa Henderson. Melissa, Sterling Hawkins."

A small frown momentarily marred the creamy smoothness of Melissa's brow. Was that a touch of sarcasm she heard in Logan's voice? Surely not. She dismissed the thought instantly, deciding it was more likely that Logan was simply jealous because she wasn't paying attention to him. Well, it certainly served him right if he was! And about time, too. Much to Melissa's annoyance, the handsome Lieutenant Powers was one of the few men on the post who had appeared to be immune to her charms.

Why, if things went right tonight, she gloatingly told herself, she might take more than one Powers down a peg or two. The thought cheered her considerably. There was also the added pleasure of punishing Edward for abandoning her tonight. A little jealousy was good for a beau, kept him in his place. But all that paled beside the final incentive. Sterling Hawkins' probable wealth.

Just then Melissa spied Sabra coming up the stairs on her father's arm. Quick as lightning she stepped closer to Hawk, tapping his arm with her fan in a playfully possessive gesture while she gazed up at him with soulful eyes.

Hawk scarcely noticed her actions. He was too caught up in watching Sabra. She looked even more beautiful tonight than she had at the ball in Tucson. The long waterfall of her hair shone like spun gold against the rich royal blue of her gown. A tempting tangle of curls had been caught atop her head with blue ribbons, leaving the rest to cascade down her back and dance against her shoulders, except the few feathery little wisps that had managed to escape their velvet bonds to curl enticingly against her temples and in front of her ears.

The bodice of her satin dress dipped beguilingly low, revealing creamy white shoulders and the most delectable hint of bosom. The gold locket suspended just above the shadowed décolletage almost revealing her full breasts winked and twinkled with every move she made. The delicate gold chain on which it hung highlighted the slender column of her throat. As Sabra approached, her tiny waist was emphasized by the gentle flare of the full, flounced skirt that swayed provocatively with each graceful step she took.

Hawk's breath caught in his throat as he remembered the feel of her soft flesh beneath his hands when he'd lifted her from the stagecoach. He could hardly wait for the music to begin so he could again hold her in his arms.

Hungrily Hawk watched Sabra pause just outside the entrance while she handed her cape to an attendant. His heart beat like a tom-tom when she once again moved toward the door, coming closer and closer with each step.

Sabra and the major stepped through the entranceway . . . and right into Melissa's staged scene. However, the silent reflections of father and daughter were drastically different.

Andrew Powers felt a rush of pleased relief when he spied Melissa with Sterling Hawkins. He fervently hoped she'd monopolize the man's whole evening because that would mean less worry about the insolent dandy spending too much time with Sabra.

As for Sabra, she was immediately engulfed by a slew of whirling emotions. Her very first thought had been of how handsome Sterling Hawkins looked in his ebony formal attire, and how the pristine white of his beruffled shirt made his blue eyes look even darker. She loved the way his hair hugged the nape of his neck and curled over the edge of his ears. He was so tall, so powerful looking, so very masculine.

When Sabra's eyes left Hawk long enough to take in the other people standing with him, the sight of Melissa Henderson firmly ensconced between Sterling Hawkins and Logan sent her stomach plummeting. For a moment she was too stunned to make any sense of the situation. Then Melissa slithered closer to Hawkins, gazing up at him like a desert predator who'd just spied a juicy rabbit.

A flash of pure, unadulterated jealousy surged through Sabra, and it was all she could do to keep from slapping Melissa's phony wide-eyed innocence right off her face. Only the necessity of keeping her father from realizing how upset she was at the sight of Sterling Hawkins with another woman allowed Sabra to keep her composure. She was still trying to sort through her tumultuous thoughts when Melissa began babbling at them.

"Major Powers. How nice to see you. And Sabra! Don't you look simply divine! I do envy you. That color would look quite garish on me, but you carry it off remarkably well, my dear."

Sabra wasn't sure if she was more offended by Melissa's backhanded compliment or by the exaggerated friendliness in the girl's voice. How dare this woman pretend they were friends! Melissa had barely a civil word for her since she'd arrived at the fort.

"Good evening, Miss Henderson," Major Powers replied with considerably more warmth than usual. He disapproved of the Henderson girl because he considered her behavior far too bold for a proper young lady. He'd been quite grateful that Sabra and Henderson's daughter hadn't taken to one another. She certainly wasn't the type of person he wanted Sabra around. But much as he disliked Melissa, at the moment he considered her a godsend.

Melissa continued her prattling, trying hard to look sincere. "I'm so glad you returned from Tucson in time to join us. I was afraid you might be so taken with the grand happenings up there that you'd forget all about our poor little social gathering."

Sabra finally found her voice. "And where's Sergeant Woodley tonight, Melissa?"

"I'm afraid he's out on patrol," Melissa answered, every

116

word oozing sugar and spice as she boldly slipped her hand through Hawk's arm. "Isn't it lucky that Logan brought this handsome gentleman along to keep me company?"

Sabra appeared calm but Logan could see hot sparks of anger and frustration in his sister's eyes as their gazes briefly met. He shrugged his shoulders minutely as if to deny any understanding of Melissa's actions. Sabra's dark brown orbs flashed in response, and then moved on to the man by Logan's side.

"Mr Hawkins . . . how nice to see you again. I do hope you're enjoying yourself."

"Miss Powers, I—"

But Melissa had no intention of relinquishing control of the conversation. Whatever Hawk had been about to say was abruptly interrupted. "Oh, don't you worry your little ol' head about that, Sabra. I intend to make sure he does."

"How thoughtful of you." Sabra forced the words through clenched teeth.

The sarcasm went right over Melissa's head. "I was just about to prevail upon Logan and Mr. Hawkins to tell me about the celebration in Tucson. I just know they'll have some wonderful stories. I simply can't wait to hear all about it."

Major Powers saw Melissa's statement as a golden opportunity to remove Sabra from temptation's path. "In that case, we won't hold you up any longer. I see Captain James and his family across the room. We really should go say hello. Come along, Sabra."

Melissa Henderson's smug look galled Sabra, but she bit back the words of protest forming on her tongue. She knew they would only make her father more determined to keep her away from their fascinating visitor. She also knew that the smartest thing she could do right now was accede to his wishes and hope that his attitude softened before the night was over.

Too late Hawk realized what was happening, but he was powerless to do anything but stand there. He could not free himself from Melissa's clutches without making a spectacle. Even more galling was the self-congratulatory look on the major's face as he took Sabra's arm and led her away. The man's satisfaction with Melissa's devious little ploy couldn't have been more obvious. But, for the moment, there was nothing Hawk could think of to change the situation.

He dared not chance a public confrontation. Such a clash would surely be remembered later if . . .

If?

Hawk's thoughts came to a jolting stop. No! No matter how Sabra affected him, he couldn't lose sight of the reason he'd come to the Arizona Territory. He slipped his hand in his pocket and fingered the small leather pouch. Not *if*, dammit, but *when* the major met his untimely demise!

Melissa frowned, wondering what thoughts lay behind the rigid, almost expressionless look on Sterling Hawkins' face as Major Powers and Sabra walked away. The fleeting reflection that Hawkins might have been looking forward to spending time with Sabra Powers tweaked at Melissa's self-centered brain, but she quickly dismissed the odious thought. Given enough time, she was positive she could dazzle Sterling Hawkins so thoroughly that he'd forget all about the major's daughter.

Just then the band struck up a tune, and Melissa hastily seized the opportunity to draw the handsome stranger's attention back to herself.

"Oh, my, Mr. Hawkins, do you hear that? I do believe that's a waltz they're playing." The look she cast from beneath sooty lashes was blatantly flirtatious. "And I have to admit there're few things I love better than a waltz."

The last thing in the world Hawk wanted was to dance with someone other than Sabra, especially a conniving, simpering little flirt like Melissa Henderson. But keeping up appearances was vitally important. Since it was obvious that Major Powers had no intention of letting him near his daughter, Hawk decided he might as well spend the time gathering what information he could.

Guilt consumed him as he realized just how lax he'd been since his arrival at the fort. He knew he'd let his goal slip from his mind far too often. Now would be the perfect time to make a little progress toward his mission, to reaffirm his determination to avenge the death of his parents.

The previous night's conversation between Logan and Hezekiah Kane had alerted him to the long-standing animosity between the major and Mortimer Henderson. The opportunity to find out more about a situation that might prove useful to him was practically being dumped in his lap. He couldn't afford to ignore it.

Hawk uttered a capitulating sigh. "In that case, Miss Henderson, may I have the honor of this dance?"

Melissa cooed her delight. With one last look of resignation in Logan's direction, Hawk pasted a false smile on his face and reluctantly led Melissa out to the center of the floor.

Logan felt bad about abandoning his new friend to Melissa, but his main concern at the moment was Sabra. He knew how much she'd been looking forward to the dance. Why couldn't their father realize that she was a grown woman now? How long was he going to keep her wrapped in cotton batting? Surely he wasn't foolish enough to think he could protect Sabra from life's dangers forever.

Fingers restlessly curling and uncurling at his sides, Logan contemplated the sad state of their situation. He was well aware that Sabra had been exceedingly tolerant of their father's overprotective nature since her arrival. She'd been positive he'd mellow with time, and there had been occasions when Logan had been tempted to agree with her. He'd been convinced that permission for the trip to Tucson was evidence of a marked change in the major's possessive attitude.

But just when Logan thought things were going to change for the better, the major had reverted to type, taking an immediate and unwarranted dislike to Sterling Hawkins. Logan considered Hawkins pleasant and extremely likeable. He could think of no sound basis for the major's attitude, only his father's awareness of Sabra's interest in their visitor.

Was Andrew Powers still so desperately haunted by the loss of his wife and his youngest child that his feelings for

Sabra were distorted? Was he now afraid of losing the daughter he'd so recently reclaimed?

An ancient weariness filled Logan. He and his father had never been able to recapture the closeness they were just beginning to enjoy at the time of his mother's death. He didn't blame the major for the distance that had developed between them. In fact, he knew that his own guilt had probably compounded the situation. How could he expect his father to forget the grievous way his son had failed him when Logan himself couldn't forget?

The words his father had spoken to him before riding away on that fateful day still rang in his ears: *I'm leaving you in charge, Logan. Get your chores done, and remember, no playing until you're through with all of them. You're old enough to take a little responsibility around here. I'm depending on you to take care of your mother and your sisters.* If he'd only obeyed his father. If he'd done what he'd been told to do . . . If . . . if . . . if. The word had tormented him for years. Still tormented him.

When the shame of that childhood failure overtook him, Logan often wondered if he and his father were doomed to be forever haunted by that terrible moment in their past. And since Sabra's arrival at the fort, Logan had developed a new fear. Was his sister's happiness destined to be sacrificed in order to soothe their father's bitter memories?

The guilt Logan had fought so long to subdue flared deep in the pit of his stomach. He couldn't change the fact that he'd long ago failed his family, nor was there any way to make up for that failure. Oh, for many years he'd tried to do so, even pursuing a military career he really didn't want in the hope that would please his father.

Foolishly, he'd even looked forward to his assignment at Fort Huachuca, wanting time to establish some sort of familial relationship. But he'd realized that was not to be. Although they'd never actually spoken of the tragedy, Logan soon realized that the major had never forgiven him for his failure, that he never would, that there was absolutely no chance that his father would ever feel anything more for him than polite tolerance.

But now he had Sabra to think about. Logan might be

120

to blame for her growing up without a mother, but he'd be damned if he would let an unforgiving old man's bitterness ruin the rest of her life.

Filled with a sudden fierce determination to make sure that Sabra didn't pay for his past mistakes, Logan squared his shoulders and crossed the room in pursuit of his sister.

"Feel like dancing?" he asked, when he found her standing forlornly at the edge of a circle of the major's cronies. She'd been so intent on watching Melissa whirl around the room in Sterling Hawkins' arms that she jumped in surprise at her brother's words.

Major Powers paused in the recounting of an old battle story long enough to give the hall a sharp inspection. A small satisfied smile tipped one corner of his mouth when he spotted Melissa and Sterling Hawkins on the far side of the dance floor.

"You two run along and enjoy the music," he told Logan and Sabra, giving a benevolent nod of his head. Smugly sure that the situation was still well in hand, he turned back to his friends and once again took up the thread of his tale.

Logan chuckled wryly. "I guess he thinks you're safe, now that Melissa's set her sights on Hawk."

Sabra's brown eyes blazed. "That . . . that Jezebel! Oh, how I'd like to get my hands on her—"

"Don't get so riled, sis," Logan said soothingly as he whirled her out on the floor. "And don't underestimate Hawk either. I'd be willing to bet he'll find a way to evade Melissa before the night's over."

Sabra cast a hopeful glance upward. "Do you think he really wants to?"

"Yes, I do. Most definitely. Poor fellow." Logan sympathetically shook his head. "He looked like a lamb being led to slaughter."

"Really?" There was a hint of blossoming mirth behind Sabra's question.

"Really," Logan assured her, glad to see her spirits picking up. "Just listen to your big brother. I want you to quit worrying and let me enjoy this one dance. Now that I've rescued you from father's protective custody, I have a feeling you'll have more men flocking around than you'll know what to do with."

Logan's prediction gladdened Sabra's heart. She cared not one whit about the prospect of being fawned over by the men to whom her brother was referring, but she was female enough to hope that such a sight might spur Sterling Hawkins to action.

Chapter Ten

Logan's prediction proved gratifyingly true. The music had barely ceased before there was an eager line of gentlemen waiting to take his place as Sabra's partner. And for once, blessedly, the major appeared content to stay with his associates and let his daughter enjoy the dance. Logan was quite sure his father's decision not to interfere with the flurry of eager young soldiers descending upon Sabra was simply a case of momentarily settling for what he considered the lesser of two evils.

While Melissa stubbornly continued to cling to Sterling Hawkins like a sand burr, Sabra pretended sheer delight at the arrival of each new partner and rapturous enjoyment of every dance. Any time a whirl around the dance floor brought her within reasonable proximity to Sterling and Melissa, she would gaze up into the face of her partner, and smile and laugh as if she were having the time of her life. Sweet gratification filled Sabra when Hawk's eyes grew increasingly more brooding with each carefully staged episode.

Meanwhile, Hawk's patience with Melissa was nearing an end. The time he'd spent with her had been a total waste. If her incessant chatter had revealed anything of consequence, he'd been too busy watching Sabra for it to register, and the gnawing frustration that had taken root as he'd watched Major Powers lead Sabra away had grown with each tick of the clock, making him more miserable by the moment.

During the course of the evening he'd tried several polite ploys to get rid of Melissa, but all had failed. She'd blithely sidestepped each and every subtle excuse, possessively clutching his arm, ohing and ahing over each new melody that the band played. Hawk was beginning to wonder if he'd ever manage to escape the silly little twit.

But what was worse, after watching the men swarm around Sabra for the last hour, he was consumed with the fear that she would have forgotten all about him by the time he could free himself from Melissa's clutches. Sabra Powers appeared to be having so much fun, he wondered if he'd even crossed her mind.

Maybe . . . maybe he'd misinterpreted her earlier actions. Maybe she had only been being friendly. Maybe she didn't experience the same strange stomach-rolling lurch he did every time he came near her.

The sight of Sabra bestowing one of her glorious smiles on still another soldier sent Hawk's already melancholy mood plummeting.

He fumed inwardly. No, dammit! He wasn't wrong! She did feel it! He knew she did. Whatever the strange attraction between them, she felt it, too. He'd seen it in her eyes.

And what if she does? his conscience goaded. What possible difference could it make? Sabra belonged to another world. A world that would never accept him if it knew the truth.

Yet he tormented himself with crazy thoughts of things that could never be. Even if she felt the same fascination he was feeling, it didn't change a damn thing. He'd come to Arizona to fulfill a blood vow, and not even his undeniable feeling for Sabra were going to change that.

But right now the last thing Hawk wanted to think about was his lifelong quest. He just wanted to make the most of the few weeks he might have with Sabra, to bask in the glow of her sweet smile, to feel the warm softness of her beneath his hands.

Oh, he'd keep his vow all right.

Eventually.

But until that time came, he was damn well going to enjoy what meager pleasures fate permitted. He'd take these few weeks with Sabra and savor every single second of the time they had together, then store the memories away in his heart for the lonely nights to come.

But first he had to solve one problem—get rid of Melissa.

Maybe the only way he was going to accomplish that miracle was by walking off the floor and leaving her standing on it, alone. Dare he risk such a rash move? While he doubted that Melissa would cause a scene, he was sure that someone would notice such a severe breach of manners. Women loved to gossip, and by tomorrow the story would be all over the post. Henderson would find out about it and take offense. Then the major would hear . . .

No, he was a fool even to momentarily consider such an insane idea. The last thing he needed to do was draw undue attention to himself. He'd have to think of something else, something practical.

Besides, there was still the major to contend with. Powers' earlier move to keep Sabra away from Hawk had been very obvious. What would the cantankerous old bastard do if he dared approach Sabra? Hawk could just imagine Powers descending upon them like an irate eagle protecting its only chick.

Oh, hell! he thought forlornly. There's got to be a way around all this mess. But what?

The music ceased, and Hawk gratefully escorted Melissa off the floor.

"Thank heaven," he murmured under his breath when it was announced that the band would take a short break. His searching gaze quickly found Sabra, near the punch bowl with her cluster of admirers.

"What was that, Sterling?" Melissa asked, maintaining her tenacious grip on his arm. "I didn't quite catch what you said."

Melissa's honey-coated words jerked Hawk's attention back to his predicament.

"What? Oh, ah . . ." Sudden inspiration bloomed. "I said, it's warm . . . yes, that's it. It's a bit warm in here. Wouldn't you like a nice cup of punch? And you must be tired by now. Why don't you find a chair, and I'll go get you something cool to drink."

But Melissa was too smart to fall for such an obvious

ploy. Her skeptical gaze swept the vicinity of the punch bowl and confirmed her suspicions.

"Why, I'd love a cup of punch, Sterling. But I believe I'll walk with you. I'm having far too much fun to be tired."

Sterling rolled his eyes in disgust and headed for the refreshment table.

Why doesn't he *do* something? Sabra fretted, as she surreptitiously watched Hawk cross the room, Melissa still in tow. Despite his seemingly calm exterior, she could sense the coiled-spring tension in him. She was positive that Sterling Hawkins was disturbed by all the attention she was receiving. Absolutely positive. He didn't like what was happening, not one bit. Those dark, sulky glances couldn't possibly mean anything else. So *why* didn't he do something about it?

The minutes kept racing by. If he didn't make a move soon, the dance would be over. Sabra nibbled her bottom lip in frustration as Hawk drew nearer.

Across the crowded table, their gazes met and held. In the twinkle of an eye all the emotions they'd been feeling were laid bare and acknowledged. Disappointment. Hope. Desire. And utter frustration.

Then fate stepped in.

A soldier hurried up the steps of the amusement hall. Winding his way through the milling crowd, he went in search of his commanding officer.

"There's trouble in the barracks, sir," Corporal Ferguson reported when he finally located Major Powers.

"Yes, Ferguson, what is it?" Powers queried.

"A couple of enlisted men, Major, drunk and fightin'."

"Well, get some men from the guardhouse and take care of it," Powers instructed irritably.

"Well, . . . uh . . . yes, sir. I could do that," the soldier said, nervously shifting his weight from one foot to another, afraid to continue his disruption of the major's evening and afraid not to. "But I thought you'd want to know about it since—"

Powers shot him a look of pure exasperation. "Will you get on with it, Corporal! What's so special about this situation?"

"Well, it seems that someone had a whole trunk load of whiskey, sir."

"In the barracks?" Powers demanded sharply.

"Yes, sir. In the barracks. And that's what the two that was fightin' got ahold of."

"Whose trunk was it?"

"Don't rightly know, sir. Nobody'll own up to it."

"Damnation!"

"Word is the whiskey came from Henderson's—"

"Henderson! Good heavens, man, if we can find out who stashed the whiskey in the barracks, we can prove the link with Henderson."

"Yes, sir."

"Well, this time I'm going to get the goods on that bastard if I have to talk to every last man. I'm sick to death of Henderson's larcenous ways disrupting the harmony of my post!"

"Yes, sir," Ferguson said again, bobbing his head in agreement.

Powers commended him, "You did right by coming to get me, Corporal Ferguson. Now, wait for me outside. I'll be right with you."

Relief flooded the man's face. "Thank you, sir. I was sure you'd want to know."

"Indeed I do," the major muttered under his breath.

Ferguson saluted smartly and retraced his steps while the colonel went in search of Logan.

Powers's instructions were terse when he found his son. "I've been called away . . . important business. See to it that Sabra gets home safely."

"Is there anything I can do to help?" Logan asked.

Powers gave a dismissive snort. "I'm quite capable of handling this matter by myself, Logan. Now, just do as you've been instructed and see to your sister's well-being."

Only the ragged twitch of a nerve at the corner of Logan's jaw betrayed his reaction to his father's acerbic tone. "Yes, sir. I'll see to her well-being. And that's a promise."

Hands clenched, Logan watched his father march across the room and disappear through the doorway. Then he turned sharply on his heel and hurried toward the refreshment table. As he shouldered his way through the congestion, the band members once again took their places and the first notes of music floated through the room.

Perfect timing, Logan thought. He was going to follow his father's instructions all right . . . more explicitly than the old man could ever have dreamed.

Sabra's "well-being" was uppermost in his mind as he marched up to Melissa Henderson and clamped a firm grip on her arm. Directing a casual "You'll have to excuse us" at Hawk, he propelled the surprised girl out on to the dance floor.

"Why . . . why . . . just what do you think you're doing, Logan Powers?" Melissa sputtered in protest as he deftly spun her around and took her in his arms.

She tried to snatch her hand from his steely grasp, but he only held on tighter and began to move to the music.

"Have you gone mad?" Melissa hissed, her eyes snapping with outrage.

Logan continued to dip and turn to the music. "Smile prettily, Melissa, so everyone will think you're having a wonderful time."

"Oh, my God! Is everybody watching us?" Her horrified gaze swept the room. Then a relieved sigh slipped past her lips when she was sure no one had noticed Logan's peculiar behavior. Her fears eliminated, her anger surged again. "Logan Powers, how dare you treat me in such a manner!"

Logan merely tightened his grip on her waist and kept on dancing.

"I demand to know what's gotten into you!" Melissa's words were punctuated by a stamp of her foot, a foolish move on her part for it caused her to stumble in a most ungraceful manner.

A wicked grin etched Logan's mouth. "Just shut up and dance, Melissa, before I let you fall right on your pretty little . . . face."

With open-mouthed astonishment, Sabra watched Logan and Melissa disappear among the whirling couples. Everything had happened so fast! She'd barely had time to catch a glimpse of her brother storming toward her

128

before he'd grabbed Melissa and hauled her across the floor.

Suddenly aware of Hawk standing next to her, Sabra raised her bewildered gaze to his, then asked, "My heavens, what do you suppose made him do that?"

A slightly dazed smile played on Hawk's lips. "Unless I'm much mistaken, I believe your brother just did me a very great favor."

"Oh," Sabra said softly. Her smile set his pulse to racing.

The lively music faded away and was replaced by the strains of a beautiful Spanish waltz.

Hawk hesitated, a thousand emotions filling him. Outwardly, he appeared calm, self-assured . . . but his eyes gave him away.

Sabra's heart contracted as she searched those midnight blue orbs. Never before had she seen such tenderness, such trepidation, such hunger mirrored in a man's eyes.

The joy inside her blossomed and spilled over, triggering another warm smile that melted Hawk's heart right down to the core. He opened his arms and she gladly stepped into the safe haven of his gentle embrace.

They managed to enjoy only a single dance before one of Sabra's earlier admirers came looking for her. Hawk caught a glimpse of the gentleman's determined face over her shoulder and his heart sank.

"Oh, no," he groaned.

"Is something wrong?" Sabra asked, her eyes following the direction of his gaze. There certainly is, she thought despairingly when she spied Harry Crutchfield strutting toward them. Her groan echoed his.

"Now what?" Hawk asked.

Sabra seized the first solution that came to mind. Grabbing Hawk's hand, she spun and ducked behind a group of people. "Quick! We've got to get out of here before he catches us!" and she headed for the back door, tugging him along behind.

In a matter of moments they were outside and down the stairs, running hand in hand across the moon-splashed ground like truant children.

Hawk's keen eyes spotted the dark silhouette of a pile

of large boulders. "Over here," he urged, pulling Sabra toward it.

They dodged a clump of brush and rounded the outcrop of rocks in a swirl of ruffled skirts. Sabra's silver laughter cascaded forth.

"We made it! We're free!" she cried joyously, flinging her arms wide.

Moving instinctively, they came together like playful puppies, Hawk catching Sabra in a bear hug, her hands pinned against his chest. He swung her around and around while their laughter filled the desert night. Finally, out of breath, he slowed his wild pirouetting. Setting Sabra's feet upon the ground, he kept his arms around her and fell back against a slab of rock to catch his breath. Sabra sagged against his chest, small giggles escaping now and then as she tried to still the thundering beat of her heart.

"My God," Hawk murmured in astonishment, a chuckle rumbling deep in his chest. "I can't believe we actually did that." It had been years since he'd felt so happy, so free. He hugged her in delight. "You're . . . you're marvelous!"

Their laughter rose again, blending, wafting heavenward as if to tell the stars of their joy.

"Listen," Sabra said, cocking her head to one side. "We can still hear the music."

"Ah," replied Hawk, "so we can. So we can." His smile was heart-stoppingly tender. "Perhaps I can have the pleasure of another dance without the fear of interruption this time."

"I can think of nothing I'd like better." Sabra's voice was as soft as a zephyr.

They stood for a long moment, simply looking at each other. Then her fingertips drifted down the front of his shirt, sending shivers of pleasure racing through his veins. Slipping her hands beneath of fabric of his coat, she wrapped her arms around his waist and laid her head against his chest. Hawk's arms tightened possessively, embracing Sabra with exquisite tenderness.

And they danced beneath the endless star-sprinkled sky. When the music ended, Hawk pressed a gentle kiss against the golden curl at Sabra's temple and then stepped away from her.

"Here, put this on before you get chilled," he instructed, shrugging out of his jacket.

He held it while she slipped her arms in the sleeves, reaching over her shoulders to tuck it against her throat. They laughed when she raised her arms and six inches of material flopped at their ends, her hands lost inside.

"I'll fix it," Hawk said softly. And he did, rolling the sleeves up until her fingers peeped from beneath the folds.

Then they joined hands again, fingers intertwined, and began to stroll. The pale moon bathed the landscape in an ethereal glow, making it easy for them to pick their way through several small stands of trees, around yucca and sagebrush and an occasional tumble of rocks. For a long time they simply walked, luxuriating in the warmth of their clasped hands, utterly content simply to be together. Night sounds gently surrounded them, the rustle of dancing leaves, the mournful call of a night bird, the whisper of the clean-scented desert wind.

Sabra was the one who finally broke the silence. "Tell me about yourself."

Hawk didn't answer at first, then he said, "What do you want to know?"

She tilted her head to look up at him, the too-large jacket slipping a bit as she gave a little shrug. "I don't know. Anything. Everything. About your home. Your parents. Do you have brothers or sisters?"

"No. I'm an only child."

"Oh? Weren't you lonely when you were little?" Her voice was full of concern. "I can't imagine growing up without Logan."

Hawk smiled and gently squeezed her fingers. "No, I wasn't lonely. Not when I was little. There were lots of children to play with, and I had the most marvelous parents imaginable."

"Tell me about them," she urged.

Tell her? If only he could.

He wished he could share the wonderful memories of growing up in the Indian village, wished he could tell her of the special love his parents had shared. Would she understand, or would she be appalled at the thought of a white woman marrying an Indian?

How could he ever explain how kind and patient his father had been? The long hours the man had willingly spent teaching a small boy how to track forest animals, how to make sure his arrow would find its mark, or telling him stories of their people, teaching him reverence for the world around him.

And how could he tell her that he'd always felt safe and loved and blessed until that all came to an end because of her father?

Hawk's sigh was the saddest thing Sabra had ever heard. She longed to put her arms around him and say, It's all right; whatever's troubling you, it's going to be all right. But she kept her silence, waiting patiently for his reply.

"They were very special people—"

"Were?" she asked gently.

"Yes. They've been gone a long time."

"I'm sorry." The words were delivered with utter sincerity, for Sabra understood full well the pain of losing a loved one.

Hawk forced a smile, determined that nothing was going to spoil the magic of this night. "Let's not talk of the past, or even the future. Not now." He stopped and turned to face Sabra, taking her other hand. "My mother told me something when I was small. She said you can't change what is in the past, and there's no guarantee you'll have a tomorrow. She believed we should take each day, one by one, and hold it close, wring every moment of joy out of it, because it's all we have for sure."

"That's lovely."

Hawk raised her hands to his lips, pressing tender kisses upon the tip of each finger. "I hadn't thought about that in years . . . maybe I should have. Somehow, being with you brought it all back again."

He tipped his head toward her, the luminescent glow of the moon highlighting the sharp planes of his face. His eyes were shadowed, almost haunted.

"Sabra, I . . . I want you to remember one thing."

"Yes?"

"No matter what happens, I want you to know that I'll always remember the days I shared with you. Always."

Sabra reached up and laid her hands against his cheeks with such unbelievable tenderness that his heart gave a lurch. Then she raised on tiptoe and pressed her lips against Hawk's.

"Oh, Sabra. Sweet, sweet Sabra," he whispered against her mouth just before he pulled her into his warm embrace.

Winding her arms around his neck, Sabra tangled her fingers in the thick dark hair at his nape, eager for his nearness. At first he merely brushed his lips across hers in a tormenting series of slow, shivery kisses that set every nerve in her body atingle. And all the while his hands traced the sweet contours of her body, caressing the soft curves of her shoulders, drifting over her back, skating down the delicate indentation of her spine, down, down to the dulcet swell of hips. As his fingers feathered across her flesh, she moaned low and leaned into him, relishing the heat and strength of his body.

She gave a tiny cry of protest when he freed her mouth, but it became a purr of pure ecstasy when he peppered tiny kisses along the line of her jaw. Her knees went weak when he paused to ravish the sensitive spot below her ear, and she convulsively tightened her fingers in his hair.

Then his mouth captured hers again, his right hand tracing her ribs one by one, in angel-soft caresses that moved upward until his fingers brushed against the swell of her breast. Fire blossomed deep within the pit of her stomach, and she strained against his trembling fingers, glorying in the way his touch made her feel.

He pressed her to him, seeking to fit the hard length of his body to her every fragile curve, exalting in the soft crush of her breasts against his chest. Her tiny whimpers of pleasure made blood pool hot and heavy in his loins.

Boldly his tongue explored the sweet recesses of her mouth, and when she tilted her head, giving him greater access, white-hot passion exploded within him. He was consumed with a yearning to ease her to the ground and bury himself deep within her, to let her sweet, sweet body ease the pain in his heart, the hunger in his soul.

Desperation ran silver-edged through Hawk when he finally pulled away. He had to stop before her gentle healing love bound him completely. He had to stop . . . now . . . or he'd never let her go.

Chapter Eleven

"I want answers. And I intend to get them." Major Powers's sharp gaze raked the row of men standing ramrod-stiff down the center of the room.

Although they'd been standing at attention for twenty minutes not one of them moved or said a word.

Powers nonchalantly smoothed the jacket of his spotless uniform, then crossed his hands behind his back. Chin high, eyes unreadable, he paced slowly down the length of the barracks, each measured step echoing against the bare wooden floor. At the far end of the room he turned smartly on the heel of his high polished boots and began a leisurely stroll back, his eyes once again scrutinizing the gaping wooden footlockers standing at the end of each cot.

The ransacked contents of the trunks were in sharp contrast with the otherwise orderly room. Each locker had been thoroughly searched by Corporal Ferguson but nothing had been found. Not a clue, no possible link to Henderson, nothing. Beneath his cool exterior, Powers was livid at the lack of results.

So far, no one had claimed ownership of the small trunk which had been found in a storage room. Sergeant Jennings, the noncommissioned officer in charge of these particular troops, fervently denied any knowledge of it, as did all of his men.

Finishing his promenade of the barracks, Powers stopped in front of the only two soldiers not in line. The arrival of their commanding officer had done wonders in sobering them up, but evidence of their dereliction of duty was still obvious.

Their uniforms were rumpled and dirty, their hair mussed. Private Monroe had hastily tucked his shirt back in his pants, but the tail end still straggled over the sagging waistband of his trousers. His left eye was starting to puff and discolor; he'd have a real shiner by morning. Blood from Williams' smashed nose had left a trail of rusty splotches down the front of his shirt. An effort to wipe away the final trickle with the back of his hand had resulted in a large smear across one stubbled cheek.

Powers paused in front of the two sorry-looking figures, the only sign of his agitation being the endless clasping and releasing of the hands he held behind his back.

"This is your last chance to reconsider." The major surveyed them up and down, his eyes like chips of ice. "Have you nothing to say for yourselves?"

"No, sir," they mumbled in unison.

Powers' gaze swept the room. "And no one else has anything to offer?"

Total silence pervaded the barracks.

"You won't be doing yourselves any favor by covering up for the guilty party," Powers continued. "I can promise you that." He paused again, waiting. "Very well, if that's the way you want it," he said tersely. He drew a long breath. "You've made your choice. Williams and Monroe will spend thirty days in the guardhouse."

Williams stifled a low groan.

The major's answering smile was frosty. "But first I believe I'll let you have the pleasure of disposing of this contraband."

Monroe and Williams cut a quick wary glance at each other and then at their sergeant. But Jennings' face was inscrutable.

"Uh . . . yes, sir, Major Powers. We'll put it in the trash bin right away."

"No, you won't."

"Sir?" Confusion echoed in their voices.

"I have something a little more memorable in mind. And since the other men have chosen not to cooperate, I believe I'll let them share in the experience. Maybe it'll jog someone's memory next time." The major's eyes glittered at the prospect of what awaited the culprits.

Sabra snuggled deeper under the covers, not in the least bit sleepy. Over and over in her mind she replayed the events of the evening, especially her tantalizing time with Sterling Hawkins. They'd had perhaps an hour alone before slipping back through the rear entrance of the amusement hall.

It had been the most wonderful, deliciously tormenting hour she'd ever experienced in her life.

They'd been loath to go back to the crowded dance, putting it off again and again until Sabra had reluctantly pointed out that the affair would soon end. And she'd been right. They'd barely gotten inside when the band had ceased playing and the hall had begun to empty.

Logan and Hawk had escorted her home, making sure she was safe inside before they left.

Now she smiled into the darkness, remembering those last minutes by the door. She and Hawk had stood there, just looking at each other, so very reluctant to part. She'd desperately wanted him to kiss her good night, and even in the pale lamplight from the open door she'd read the same desire in his eyes.

And Logan . . . he'd been such a dear, making a big show of being oblivious to their earlier absence. He'd deliberately waited on the top step while Hawk had walked her across the porch. Warm affection had curled within her at the sight of her brother's oh-so-casual stance, one shoulder propped against a support post while he made an absorbed perusal of the parade ground.

She'd almost gotten her wish for a good-night kiss. Hawk had stepped toward her, and she'd tilted her head, waiting expectantly, her breath frozen in her throat. But there'd been voices from several houses down on officers' row and Hawk had quickly backed away, murmuring his goodbyes in a husky voice.

Sabra had been surprised to find that her father had not returned to the house. Logan had told her that he'd left the dance on some unexpected Army business, but she'd assumed he'd have been home by such a late hour. She felt a bit guilty when she realized how pleased she was that he was still gone. His absence gave her time to quietly savor the strange magic she felt every time she was with Sterling Hawkins, and for that she was grateful.

She pressed her fingertips against lips that still tingled from Hawkins' kisses. She could hardly believe how his touch had set her head spinning. Philip Marshall's bumbling overtures had flown straight out of her mind at the first taste of Hawk's mouth.

And somehow she knew that no other man would ever affect her like this man did.

There were so many things she wanted to know about Sterling Hawkins, things she'd meant to ask him but had promptly forgotten in the glory of his embrace, the sweet rapture of his mouth.

During the stagecoach ride, he'd spoken of staying only a few weeks. A paltry few weeks. It wouldn't be long enough, not nearly long enough to bring to fruition any of the intriguing dreams spinning in her mind. She wondered if there was anything . . . anything at all . . . she could do to influence him to stay longer.

And she still didn't have even a hint of whether there was someone special waiting for him back home. The very thought of that made Sabra's stomach give a sickening little lurch.

Maybe he was in love with someone else. But how could that be? He was attracted to her; Sabra was absolutely certain. Something wonderful happened every time they were together. She didn't see how it could be so special for her and not be special for him, too. Did that mean he might come to love her, given enough time?

Or was he a confirmed bachelor? She judged him to be in his late twenties. Most men were married by that age. Why wasn't he? Surely he wanted a home and family. Didn't everyone?

Sabra groaned in frustration. How could she possibly find out any of those things if they didn't have some time together?

And, even if Hawk decided to stay longer, how, with her father acting like he was, could they manage to be alone? What on earth was she going to do about the major? Would she be able to change her father's attitude before Hawk had to leave?

Leave. There was that damn word again. Sabra was beginning to hate the very sound of it. She didn't want Hawk to leave. Not now. Not . . . not ever.

The thought stunned Sabra. Where had these strange wonderful feelings come from? How had they blossomed so fast, so totally? Was this the "love at first sight" she and her friends had whispered about? She'd done her share of adolescent giggling over that childish romantic fantasy, but that's all she'd ever really believed it was, a fantasy.

But what if it were true? What if some people were meant to be together? What if there were a few very lucky people who somehow managed to find that "intimate stranger" . . . a person that felt so right from the first moment that it was like finding a missing piece of yourself—one you hadn't even known was gone?

But what was she going to do? So many elements seemed stacked against them. Hawk would be gone in a few weeks and meanwhile her father was acting like such an old bear. It would be useless to try to explain "magic" and "belonging" to him. He'd never understand in a million years.

Weary with frustration, Sabra finally gave in to sleep. Her eyes fluttered shut, and once again Sterling Hawkins filled her dreams.

Hands behind his head, Hawk morosely stared up into the darkness, his mind filled with a dozen whirling thoughts. Was he in love with Sabra? Was this how it happened? Somebody filling your mind and your heart so fast, so totally that nothing else seemed to matter?

And even if it were love, what then? There was no way for it to end in anything permanent. Hadn't he been mulling alternatives over in his mind for hours?

The possibility that he could have her and keep his vow was inconceivable.

Holding her, touching her, feeling her sweet lips under

his . . . nothing he'd experienced before had made him feel the way he did being with Sabra. But fulfilling his vow would mean leaving her forever. He knew that with utter certainty. And something deep inside warned him that if he walked away from Sabra Powers he'd never feel this way again.

Never.

He finally relented, looked at the situation from the opposite angle just for argument's sake. Suppose he abandoned his vow. What then?

It wouldn't change a damn thing. He *still* couldn't have Sabra.

He couldn't stay at the fort, especially not if he let Powers live. The hatred he felt for the man was too deep. He'd never know a moment's peace if he had to face the major day after day.

Nor could he ask Sabra to marry him—sweet heaven, would she even have him if he did?—and come to Hawkinsville with him. My God, what insanity! The truth about his heritage would come to light in Hawkinsville in a matter of days, if not hours. And how would she feel when she found out she was married to a half-breed?

Her possible responses ran the gamut from mild shock to absolute revulsion.

Damn it all to hell! Wasn't there something he could do to ease her initial reaction? There must be some way to bind her to him so securely that, when the truth came out, she'd at least be willing to consider staying with him. Maybe he could delay their return to Hawkinsville until he was sure she loved him so completely that the truth of his past wouldn't matter. A few months together, a prolonged honeymoon, and then he could tell her about his mixed blood before they returned. She might be angry, and rightfully so, but by then surely she could forgive him.

Perhaps, just perhaps, she could handle that part of his life, but that wasn't the last obstacle standing between them.

He might be able to find an explanation for having deceived her about how he made his living. Sure. He

140

could say that writing had always been his dream, so he'd told his family he was taking a business trip and he'd given himself a few months to make that dream come true. She might even believe that story.

And why should she care how he earned his money, or whether he was a writer or a businessman? Especially if he was able to support her in a more than comfortable manner. After all, the lumber business was very profitable. He could easily give her the many little luxuries women seemed so set on.

But . . . what about the rest?

The town knew his history. And his aunts and uncles were well aware of who Andrew Powers was. When they heard that Sabra's maiden name was Powers, there'd be comments for sure. And she'd talk about her family . . . of course she would! Why not? She loved them; they'd been a special part of her life. How would she feel when she found out that her father was responsible for the death of his parents? Whose side would she take?

And it wouldn't be long before Sabra started asking questions about his real reason for being at Fort Huachuca? How much time would pass before doubts and suspicions killed that special light in her eyes? Maybe she'd never figure out that Hawk had planned to kill her father. But wouldn't she begin to wonder if his proffered love was as false as the tales he'd told? She might even decide that he had only used her in some bizarre attempt to get even with her father.

She'd never again believe a word he had to say, wouldn't believe that his feelings for her had been totally unexpected, had occurred in spite of and not because of the situation with her father.

Why should she? Not when almost everything else he'd said and done had been a lie.

One last option tugged at his mind. He could marry Sabra and go away somewhere totally new. Never return to Hawkinsville. Never tell her about his Indian blood or his parents or the part her father had played in his young life. Just keep living the lie.

Forever.

But deep within, Hawk knew he couldn't do that either. The business, his family, the town itself depended on him. What would happen to all of them if he disappeared? How could he possibly abandon his responsibilities so casually?

He couldn't. It was that simple.

And even if he could, he knew that he was incapable of living a lie for the rest of his days.

Oh, God! It was hopeless. Utterly and completely hopeless.

Powers eyed Williams and Monroe with distaste. "Get some shovels. Bring them and the trunk. Now!"

"Yes, sir! Right away, sir." Still unsteady on their feet from the effects of too much whiskey, the two soldiers scurried to do the major's bidding.

Sergeant Jennings watched from his position in the corner of the room, skittish as a barn cat. He wondered what the major had in mind. Was he going to assign extra duty to all the men for not cooperating? Or would the whole damn troop wind up spending a day or two in the guardhouse?

Hellfire, what a night! Jennings thought, suppressing his growing anger. All he could do now was pray that Powers would finish dealing out punishment, take the two men and the damned whiskey, and get the hell out of the barracks before something else went wrong.

But Jennings's prayers rose only as high as the ceiling.

"Sergeant," Powers called to him when Williams and Monroe staggered back with their shovels.

"Yes, sir?" Jennings answered warily.

"Get a lantern. Then have your men fall in and follow me." With that, Powers marched from the room.

Goddammit! It was getting late. What in hell was the man up to now?

Jennings's ill humor was obvious as he barked harsh instructions to his men. A few wary glances passed between the soldiers as they fell into line and followed Sergeant Jennings in pursuit of the major.

The moon's bright glow sent a double row of shadows

ghosting behind the soldiers as they marched away from the barracks. Monroe and Williams stumbled along at the end of the line, carrying the trunk between them and a shovel in their free hands. Jennings' lantern sent eerie zigzags of light over the ragged ground.

Finally, several hundred yards northwest of the camp, Powers halted.

"This should do it. The men can stand at ease, sergeant."

"Yes, sir," Jennings agreed although he hadn't the slightest idea of what was going on. "At ease, men."

His sharp words echoed through the clear night air. Behind him, the men shuffled to a stop. Still clutching their shovels, Williams and Monroe gratefully lowered their mutual burden to the ground. And there they all stood for a long, drawn-out moment, waiting in utter confusion for further instructions.

The forlorn howl of a coyote echoed in the distance. High above, a lone cloud scudded across the silver face of the moon, plunging all save the circle of light they stood within into deeper shadow.

With the toe of his boot, Major Powers drew a cross in the sandy dun-colored soil. "Monroe. Williams. Over here!"

"Yes, sir," they chorused, ricocheting off each other as they hurried forward.

"You can dig the hole right here."

"The hole, sir?" Williams questioned, his voice shaky. "Uh, how deep, sir?"

"I'll let you know," Powers answered quietly. "Start digging. Now."

Faces grim, Monroe and Williams squared off, side by side. They fell to their task with a fervor, quickly pushing the dull blades of their shovels deep into the loose soil and tossing aside one scoop of dirt after another.

Within twenty minutes a fine sheen of moisture had beaded their brows, while the other soldiers huddled together to escape the chilled night air.

Several hours later, the two hapless privates were more than waist deep in the hole. Filthy, reeking of alcohol-tainted sweat, and bone weary, they struggled to lift each agonizingly heavy shovelful of dirt up and over the edge of the gravelike pit. The other soldiers stood in a double line far enough back to avoid the haphazard spatters of dirt being tossed out of the growing chasm. Their hunched shoulders and gritty-eyed stares attested to how cold and tired they were. Now and then one of them was rash enough to wonder if he should have spoken up, but a quick look at Sergeant Jennings's scowling face usually sent that foolish thought packing.

"That looks deep enough. I suppose that will do the trick," Powers finally said.

The two men gratefully stopped their digging. Monroe wrapped both hands around the end of the shovel handle, resting his grimy forehead on them while little wheezing rattles punctuated his every whistling breath. Williams's shovel dropped from his blistered hands, and he draped one arm over the mound of dirt bordering the hole, clinging to it for support while he sucked in huge mouthfuls of air.

"Hand them down the trunk," Powers ordered, and two men scurried to obey.

Reeling from fatigue, Monroe and Williams managed to pull themselves upright in time to grab the trunk as it was hoisted over the side. With a loud grunt, they let their burden fall to the bottom of the hole.

"Now open it," said Powers. They did. "Pick up those shovels." Once again they obeyed. "Now use them to break the bottles. Every single one of them."

Shit! thought Jennings, who had already pinpointed the location of the buried trunk for future retrieval.

Only heads and shoulders showed as the two soldiers lifted their shovels and stabbed downward. The night air was suddenly filled with the loud clink and tinkle of breaking glass and the pungent reek of cheap whiskey.

Jennings rubbed a hand across his stubbled jaw, bitterly calculating the amount of money slowly seeping into the dry desert sands. *Interfering old bastard,* he thought, snatching a quick glance at Powers's ramrod stiff posture.

Their task completed, Monroe and Williams simply stood and waited, weary heads lowered against their chests.

"You may get out now," Powers said, his voice crisp and precise.

The spectators to this little drama had been shuffling from foot to foot to help ease the discomfort of the rapidly dropping temperature, but now they stilled their movements and gaped at their commanding officer. How could the man sound so fresh and rested at this time of night? Was he made of stone?

With great effort a weary Private Monroe lifted his shovel up and over the side of the chasm. Then he kicked the lid of the sodden trunk shut and used it to boost himself out of the hole, slumping to the ground as soon as he was clear. Still holding his shovel, Williams scrambled out behind him and collapsed beside his luckless partner.

Major Powers eyed the two exhausted men with disgust. "Now, bury it. And pack it down tight. I don't want to see one sign of this hole in the morning."

Monroe muttered something under his breath.

"Do you have something to say, Private?" Powers asked, his tone derisive.

"N-no, sir," was the weak reply.

Monroe struggled to his feet and offered Williams a trembling hand to help him rise. Once again they bent to the task, filling their blades with the desert soil.

Chapter Twelve

"Wake up, Sabra."

Sabra mumbled something incoherent and turned over, pulling the covers tight under her chin.

Major Powers gave his daughter's shoulder a gentle shake. "Sabra, listen to me, dear."

Eyes slightly unfocused, a sleepy Sabra peered up at her father. The room was still dark and she could barely distinguish his shadowy features in the pale flickering glow of the small lantern he held.

"What? . . ." She stopped for a yawn, then rubbed the backs of her hands against her eyes. "What is it, Father?" Pushing herself up on one elbow, she blinked away sleep and tried to understand what he'd been saying. "What time is it?"

"Almost dawn."

Sudden fear raced through Sabra. Her eyes widened and she swallowed twice before she got the next words out. "Is . . . is something wrong? Is it Logan? Is something wrong with Logan or . . . or Sterling?"

Powers frowned at the mention of the stranger's name, but he had no time to pursue the matter.

"No, my dear," the major quickly assured her, reaching to smooth an errant curl from his daughter's forehead. "Logan's just fine."

The lantern's small flame cast twin reflections of dancing light in Sabra's dark wide-eyed gaze. "Then what is it?" she asked.

"I just wanted you to know that I'm leaving for Tucson this morning—"

"Tucson?" Tiny furrows formed between Sabra's brows, betraying the extent of her confusion.

"Yes, my dear, I'm going to Tucson. I've already cleared it with Lieutenant Colonel Forsyth. He's given permission for the trip."

Sabra's frown deepened. By all rights it was still night. When had her father had time to speak with the fort's commanding officer? Good heavens, he would have had to wake the poor man up! What could have prompted such a breach of normal routine?

Sabra struggled upright, punched her pillows into a mound against the headboard of her bed, and wriggled into a comfortable leaning position.

"But why are you going to Tucson, Father? And so suddenly. Is Lieutenant Colonel Forsyth sending you on some sort of assignment?"

"Something like that, my dear. There's a bit of a problem I need to look into."

"Oh." Sabra knew better than to ask any further questions about the reason for her father's trip. "Well." She nibbled at her bottom lip, considering the portent of the major's pronouncement. "Well, then . . . how long will you be gone?"

"A week. Maybe two."

She nodded mutely.

"You'll be fine, dear. Logan will look in on you. Or if it bothers you to be alone at night, I could have him stay here at the house with you."

Night-tumbled curls bounced on her shoulders as she shook her head emphatically. "That's not necessary. I'm not afraid. And if I get lonely, I'll ask Jasmine to stay with me."

This time Powers frowned. "I . . . I suppose that would be all right under the circumstances, although I think you're becoming altogether too familiar with the woman. A colored laundress is hardly what I'd call proper company for an officer's daughter. I really wish you would—"

"Honestly, Father," Sabra protested with another insistent shake of her head. "Jasmine is quite nice, and I don't see what her job *or* color have to do with it."

Powers' mouth dropped open and then snapped closed with an audible click. Where on earth had the child gotten such outlandish ideas? He expelled an exasperated sigh, knowing he didn't have time to get into a discussion of such things at the moment. Not when the stage was due to leave within half an hour.

Andrew Powers scrutinized the stubborn line of Sabra's mouth, wondering if he was doing the right thing in leaving her alone. But what possible harm could come to her here at the fort? She was surrounded by experienced troops. Several dozen military wives were in residence and a diversified assortment of young ladies could keep her company. What could go wrong?

The only real hitch in the plan was the presence of Sterling Hawkins, but surely under the circumstances Logan could be trusted to watch his sister closely.

Besides, this trip could not be avoided. Andrew Powers needed to go to Tucson to speak with certain people concerning the problem with Henderson. Last night's episode involving the contraband liquor had been the final straw.

It had been barely four hours since Powers had left Jennings and his men beside the gaping hole in the desert and had returned to his office. He'd spent the next couple of hours pacing in agitation, discarding one alternative after another. The options for dealing with the post trader were quite limited.

There was no real proof that Henderson was involved in illegal trade, but Powers was positive that more was going on than met the eye. He knew he might never have enough evidence to force Henderson's withdrawal, but he refused to turn his back on the situation. Sure as the sun would rise in the east, the trader meant trouble for the post. There had to be a way to get rid of him despite Henderson's Washington patron.

Powers only briefly considered using the post's telegraph system to contact Tucson. He was almost positive someone had warned Henderson the last time he'd sent a telegram concerning the man's nefarious dealings. He had no intention of taking a chance on that happening this time. Going to Tucson seemed to be the only answer.

Dawn would be breaking soon. If Monroe and Williams weren't already incarcerated in the guardhouse, they soon would be. And now Jennings had probably herded the remainder of his weary men back to the barracks, where they would snatch an hour's sleep before having to rise and prepare for the Sunday morning inspection.

Powers knew the bizarre night would be talked about for months—and such had been his intention.

Although the two main culprits, Monroe and Williams, had borne the brunt of the unusual punishment—a fact their sore muscles and aching backs would testify to for days to come—the rest of the troops had paid a toll, too. It would be a long time before they'd forget the biting chill of the night air and the long wearisome hours of standing at ease while their friends excavated and then refilled a gaping hole in the desert terrain.

Maybe they'd think twice before covering for a guilty compatriot in the future. At least that's what the major hoped.

Powers yanked his thoughts back to the present. Precious minutes were slipping away while he stood around woolgathering. He must go.

Bending stiffly, he dropped a kiss on Sabra's forehead.

"Very well, Sabra, invite Jasmine if you so desire. I suppose there's no real harm in it. Just take care and don't leave the fort without a proper escort. Now go back to sleep, dear. I'll return in a week or so."

"Yes, Father." Sabra slid back down in the bed and watched her father's obsidian-shadowed figure glide toward the doorway. "Have a nice trip," she called after him.

Powers merely grunted in response to Sabra's final words, his mind already on the journey ahead. Placing the lantern on an entryway table, he shrugged into his coat and picked up his luggage.

Streamers of early morning sunlight were sifting through Sabra's curtains when she awoke again. She stretched hard before pushing wayward curls out of her

149

eyes and slipping out of bed to peek through her bedroom window. A bright smile curved her lips at what she saw.

The cloudless sky was a sparkling periwinkle blue, and an occasional soft breeze stirred the gold-dappled leaves of nearby trees. The square of sun-drenched planking under her feet grew warmer by the minute, and she knew that this November day was going to be one of the special ones, too rare to waste on anything as mundane as tennis or croquet, the fort's standard Sunday-afternoon activities.

It took but a minute for her quicksilver mind to come up with the perfect afternoon diversion.

Barefoot, the hem of her white dimity nightgown skimming the floor, Sabra bustled about the kitchen. Humming a little melody, she stirred the banked embers in the stove and then put water for her bath on the back burner. While waiting for it to heat, she checked the pie safe.

"Good," she murmured happily when she found two fruit pies still intact. A hurried tally of the pantry assured her of enough supplies to prepare a proper feast for the afternoon's adventure.

A sudden *rat-tat-tat* on the front door sent Sabra scurrying down the hall and across the living room. Carefully pulling the front window's ruby brocade curtain aside, she applied one eye to the narrow slit and confirmed her brother's presence on the porch.

Dropping the curtain back into place, she hurried to the door, pulling it open only a few inches.

Logan was greeted by the sight of a bodiless head poking around the door and well below it ten little bare toes peeping from beneath a white ruffle.

"Good heavens, Sabra, aren't you dressed yet?" he exclaimed, surprise flashing in his eyes. "Chapel starts soon."

"I know that," she said with a toss of golden curls. "I have something better planned." Her voice had dropped to a conspiratorial whisper.

Propping one shoulder against the doorframe, Logan shoved his left hand into his pocket and reached out with the right to poke at a smudge of white on Sabra's cheek. "What on earth have you been doing? And what is this stuff?"

A dainty hand materialized from behind the door. Each cheek received one distracted swipe before the hand dropped out of sight again. "Flour. Now, listen . . ."

Eyes sparkling with excitement, Sabra told Logan about her plan.

"A picnic?" Logan repeated. "Are you serious?"

"Oh, please say you'll help, Logan. It'll be so much fun!"

"I don't know, Sabra. You know Father'd be fit to be tied if he found out, don't you? Especially if he learned you'd skipped church services besides."

"How's he going to find out?" Sabra's bottom lip stuck out stubbornly. "Anyway, I'm simply not going to worry about that now. It's a glorious day, and I'm going on a picnic . . . with or without you."

Logan knew when he'd been bested. He threw his hands up in surrender, telling himself he'd done the best he could to talk her out of it.

The truth of the matter was that he found the idea as tempting as Sabra did.

"All right. All right," he conceded with a rumble of laughter. "You win. We'll go."

Sabra's eyes glowed with delight. "Wonderful! Now go get Jasmine and Hezekiah and—"

"And Hawk? You did want to invite Hawk, didn't you?" Logan teased.

"Yes, of course we're going to invite him," Sabra assured her brother in an exasperated voice, deliberately ignoring the knowing twinkle in his eyes. "Now, would you please pay attention?"

That disembodied hand reached out once again to swat at his arm. Logan dodged the playful blow.

"Yes, ma'am. I'm listening."

Five minutes later Sabra watched her brother skip down the stairs to begin rounding up the rest of the entourage for the afternoon's outing. By the time he cleared the bottom step his sister had closed the door and was heading toward the kitchen.

Just before church services were dismissed, five furtive figures carried a bevy of baskets and bundles to the back corral where three saddled horses and a small hitched wagon awaited.

As soon as the picnic supplies were stored in the rear of the wagon, Hezekiah shyly assisted Jasmine to climb on to the wooden plank seat. Once the dark beauty was settled, he drew a deep breath and clambered up, skittish as a colt, to sit beside her. The other three members of the party were already mounted and waiting by the time he slapped the reins over the backs of the mule team and urged them forward with a subdued "Yee-haw!"

The wagon, with riders strung out on either side, bounced and swayed its way across the grassy, yucca-stubbled valley, heading straight for the nearby foothills. Soon, only a thin haze of reddish-brown dust sifting slowly back to the ground divulged their passage. By the time the residents of Fort Huachuca trickled home from the morning worship services, the jubilant runaways had disappeared into one of the cool shaded canyons of the Huachuca Mountains.

They came upon a small gurgling stream, the runoff from a pure sparkling spring farther up the slope. Hastily a number of blankets were spread on the ground under a stand of majestic pines. Then Sabra and Jasmine took charge of arranging a half-dozen napkin-covered baskets on them, and of placing several jugs of cider in the creek for chilling. The men unhitched the mules and unsaddled the horses, hobbling one and all so they could graze freely.

When those chores were finished, the little party decided to explore their patch of paradise, poking and prodding their way along the striated terrain, marveling at each and every new revelation.

The discovery of two baby desert cottontails, twitchy little noses and long ears barely discernible beneath the scrub brush that sheltered their burrow, brought ohs and ahs of delight from the ladies.

Sabra had just knelt down to get a better look at the nervous little fuzz balls when the shadow of a high-flying hawk ghosted over the ground.

"Where's your mama, little bunnies? Has she gone off and left you all alone?" she crooned softly. She cast a quick glance heavenward, and then gave a quick flip of her hands. "Shoo! Get back in your nice safe house before that hungry ol' hawk spots you and has you for supper." The bunnies disappeared in a flash.

Sabra's tender-hearted concern for the small creatures brought a gentle smile to Hawk's lips. Indeed, her enthusiasm was fast coloring the whole group's attitude. As they clambered up and down scrub-covered gullies and over red-and-tan-and-brown-mottled rocks and precipices, they began to sound more like a gaggle of truant school children than five adults.

At first Hezekiah was shy, hanging back behind Logan and Hawk, mumbling only an occasional word in answer to Sabra's gentle attempts to draw him out. But finally even he loosened up, and before long he was talking a mile a minute to an enthralled Jasmine.

As Hawk ambled along beside the others, soaking up the blessed warmth of the sun and Sabra, he was suddenly overcome with a plaintive longing for the pleasure never to end, for the afternoon to go on and on and on. The days were slipping away so rapidly. Too rapidly.

"Shh!" Hezekiah warned as they rambled up a rocky slope. "Be still."

Obediently, they all froze as Hezekiah crept onward with exaggerated care. Suddenly he swooped forward, hands extended. "Ah-ha! Got it!" He turned and extended his cupped hands toward the other four.

"What is it? What did you catch?" the ladies clamored, eager and curious. Bending down, they tried to peer through Hezekiah's long dark fingers.

"This," he said, a huge grin splitting his face. With a quick movement, he gently pinned the hidden creature between thumb and forefinger. Balancing it on his huge palm, he showed them his prize.

"A horned frog!" Jasmine declared, eyeing the spiny flat-looking little lizard with distrust. "Be careful with him, Hezekiah. I don't want him getting mad and spitting blood out of his eyes. Um-um! He's an ugly little fellow, isn't he?"

"Not really," Sabra said softly, reaching out to stroke the tiny creature's dull gray head between the two backward protruding horns. "They're really quite harmless. Why, I even had one for a pet once . . . Logan caught him for me. Remember, Logan?" she asked, turning to grace her brother with a bittersweet smile.

"Sure do. That was a long time ago."

"Yes. Yes, it was," Sabra agreed in dulcet tones. "Mama gave me a bit of string, and sometimes we'd tie it around his neck and take him for a walk. It always made Mama laugh. . . ."

Ever alert to Sabra's moods, Hawk quickly raised his head as her words weakened and then faded away. A foreboding sense of bewilderment feathered through him as he watched a faraway, slightly haunted look appear in her eyes. A quick glance at Logan only heightened his sense of confusion. What had caused that sudden, almost hidden flash of pain on Logan's face?

Hawk's keen gaze fell on the remaining two members of their little group. Jasmine's attention was still on the tiny creature nestled in the big black soldier's palm, but Hezekiah . . . that was another matter.

Ah, thought Hawk, *Hezekiah knows,* or at least he's aware of something peculiar going on. With more than a touch of puzzlement, he noted the concern in the soldier's obsidian eyes.

Logan suddenly broke the strange mood. "Would you like to keep this one?"

Sabra's eyes lost that misty look, and she tilted her head back to smile up at her brother. "No," she said with a gentle shake of her head. "You can't bring the old days back. Let's give him his freedom."

Hawk's intense gaze never left Sabra as she watched Hezekiah slowly lower the little horned lizard to the ground and set it free. Her forlorn expression made his heart constrict.

"Oh, look!" Jasmine called out, pointing up the hill.

Sabra's face brightened a bit as a pair of quail scurried past with a cluster of fluffy little chicks. Then an Inca dove took wing from the lower branch of a scraggly sycamore, the rust-colored patches on its wings shining bright

154

in the golden sun. Shielding her eyes against the bright light, Sabra watched the bird flutter away, the tension around her mouth easing somewhat with the pleasure of the moment.

Logan's gruff voice once again interrupted the group's reverie. "I don't know about the rest of you, but I'm getting mighty warm. That creek looks perfect for wading. How about it?"

Relief rippled through Hawk as Sabra's face registered instant delight. "Oh, what a wonderful idea, Logan. Let's do it! Last one in's a rotten egg!"

She flung the taunt at them and took off, her laughter ringing like bells in the clear mountain air. The others exchanged surprised glances and then dashed in pursuit. The broken terrain wasn't very conducive to a real race, but amid shrieks of mirth the participants did their best, hopping and sliding and scrambling their way back to the creek.

Hezekiah's long legs outdistanced them all, and Logan came in second, throwing himself down on the grassy bank to join Hezekiah in hauling off boots and socks, and rolling pantlegs up. Although Hawk's Indian training would have enabled him to win the race he'd purposely hung back, keeping an eye on Sabra, wincing inwardly each time she took a slightly perilous step.

Logan and Hezekiah had already splashed knee-deep into the tingling water by the time he and the ladies reached the stream. Hawk promptly propped his lean hips against a boulder and began to remove his boots.

But the simple act proved to be an almost insurmountable task, for when Sabra kicked off her slippers and tucked her skirt into her waistband, Hawk was far too taken with the alluring sight of trim ankles and curving calves to pay any further attention to his own feet. As a result, he was the last one in the water, and the other four took great delight in telling him so.

"My heavens to Betsy!" Jasmine squealed as she held calico skirts high and cautiously inched her way deeper into the water's chilly depths. "This is cold!"

"You . . . ah . . . you'll get used to it pretty quick," Hezekiah assured her, his tongue stumbling over the words as he watched the water swirl temptingly around a pair of firm brown legs.

Logan noticed the slightly glazed look in Hezekiah's eyes, and ended his friend's sweet torment with a splash of frigid water. Then the fight was on. By the time it was over, the three men were rather on the soggy side; but at least they'd been chivalrous enough not to do much more than sprinkle the ladies.

Five tired, disheveled figures finally trooped out of the water, gathered up their hastily abandoned footgear, and headed for the blankets and food.

"Ouch!" Sabra cried, hopping on her left foot as she vainly tried to peer at the sole of the other one.

"What is it? A sticker?" Hawk asked, hurrying to her side.

"Yes. Ouch! Several, I think."

"Here, let me help."

With that he scooped Sabra up in his arms, his long legs pacing the distance to the blanket. Warmth radiated through Sabra as his arms closed around her. She looped her hands about his neck and enjoyed the short ride.

"Now, be still and let me take a look," Hawk commanded as he carefully lowered Sabra onto one corner of a blanket. Concern etching his face, he knelt in front of her, taking her foot in his hands and squinting at the sole.

"Uh-huh," he said with a little nod of his head. "You were right. Sand burrs. Three of them. Now, don't jerk your foot away. I won't hurt you."

The admonishment was totally unnecessary. Nothing short of an earthquake could have made Sabra pull her foot out of Hawk's gentle grasp. Little frissons of pleasure had started squiggling up her leg at his first touch. And now they were pooling in the pit of her stomach in the most intriguing manner before fanning out to pulse through her veins. She swore she could feel, in every pore, the stroke of Hawk's fingers.

How very peculiar, she thought. Somehow, the nerve endings in her toes connected with a sensory network that threaded through every single inch of her body. Most peculiar indeed.

But *most* enjoyable.

Hawk, his tanned brow furrowed in concentration, plucked out the offending stickers one by one, crushing them between his fingers before he tossed them away.

"Is that better?" he asked, sitting back on his heels and propping her foot against one rock-hard thigh.

"Yes."

The word sounded like a sigh.

"Good."

So did his reply.

Midnight blue eyes met deep brown ones and locked.

Long after it ceased to be necessary, Hawk's strong thumbs continued to knead the tender flesh at the base of her toes, his fingers possessively cupping the curve of Sabra's slender instep.

It felt so good to touch her. Hawk let his fingers reverently trace the delicate bone structure of her foot. She felt as fragile as the smallest bird, yet he knew better. He sensed an inner strength far greater than her satin-soft skin and petite stature evidenced.

Oblivious to the others, they continued to gaze at each other, their souls reaching out to meld.

The tiny pulse at the base of Sabra's throat fluttered faster. Her eyes became heavy-lidded, slumberous, and her lips parted, a sight almost too inviting to the man kneeling before her.

Hawk's lungs grew heavy, each breath becoming more difficult. As the banked embers of his longing flamed anew, heat licked through his veins to burn away his tightly held control.

Discipline died in the growing wildfire. His body responded.

"Isn't anybody else ready to eat? I'm starving."

Logan's lament evoked a hearty chuckle from Hezekiah. "You're *always* ready to eat," the big man declared emphatically.

Hawk jumped at the intruding sound of their voices. Jerking his gaze from Sabra's bewitching eyes, he quickly released his hold on her foot. An unfathomable sense of disappointment filled her as she watched him rise to his feet in one powerful movement.

"Uh . . . I'd better check on the horses first," he said,

his voice husky. With that, he grabbed his boots and bolted.

Intent on appeasing another kind of hunger, the other three were too busy unpacking picnic baskets to take much notice of Hawk's hasty departure.

Chapter Thirteen

"Hey, Hawk!" Logan called, brandishing a half-eaten drumstick in his upheld hand. "You'd better hurry. You're missing a great meal."

Hawk waved an acknowledgment from his position in the circle of grazing horses. "I'll be right there. I just want to check this last hobble."

Hezekiah grinned hugely. "Yeah, it's so great that if you don't get over here pronto, Logan's gonna eat everything in sight!"

"All right, you asked for it," Logan growled, pretending to aim his well-gnawed bone at Hezekiah, who in turn grabbed an empty basket and held it up in front of his face like a shield.

Sabra was in the middle of giving her brother a good-natured scolding about his table manners when Hawk finally returned. Surreptitiously she watched him fold those long lean legs, instantly recalling the feel of that firm muscular thigh beneath her foot.

As Hawk sank onto a corner of the blanket he cut a quick glance in Sabra's direction, then guiltily jerked his gaze away when he realized she was watching him. But no matter how hard he tried to keep his attention on the silly antics of Logan and Hezekiah, his eyes kept straying across the blanket.

Acutely aware of the effect Sabra had had on him earlier, Hawk looked for something, anything, to keep his hands and mind busy. First he fiddled with the cuffs of his shirt, making minute alterations in the folds on his muscular forearm. Then he raked his fingers through the shock of dark hair falling over his forehead . . . not once, but three times. Finally, he plucked a verdant twig of pine from a low overhanging limb and began to methodically strip it of needles, one by one.

Sabra tucked her skirts more modestly about her knees, clandestinely following every move Hawk made. She almost felt sorry for him. For a man who was generally the epitome of calmness, he certainly had a bad case of the fidgets. But she also had to admit that his obvious agitation was most gratifying to her womanly pride. She was positive his nervousness hadn't started until the incident with the sand burrs.

Was it possible . . . had he felt those crazy heart-stopping feelings, too?

The mere possibility of that sent a warm flush to Sabra's face. To hide her rosy cheeks, she busied herself fixing a plate for Hawk. She spent an inordinate amount of time picking the juiciest golden-brown chicken breast she could find. Then she finished filling the dish to overflowing with generous helpings from the other bowls and platters.

"Here, try some of this," Sabra said, offering the heaping plate to Hawk in the fervent hope that he'd be impressed with her cooking skills.

"Thank you very much."

His fingers brushed hers as he accepted the offering. His eyes snapped upward.

So did hers.

She smiled, almost shyly.

A tentative grin began to tip the corners of his mouth.

Her timid smile broadened, temptingly curving lush lips until that beguiling little dimple once again winked in her cheek.

Hawk's heart seemed to melt and ooze right down to the bottom of his boots. He thanked providence when Hezekiah's booming baritone broke the silence.

"You know what we forgot?" the big black soldier asked, grinning broadly at Jasmine and giving a quick nod of his head in Logan's direction.

"What?" Jasmine answered, her mouth already curving into a smile. She knew Logan was about to receive a liberal dose of ribbing from Hezekiah.

"A companion for Logan. Seems hardly fair that he's all by himself, what with him being such a lady's man and everything."

Logan refused to take the bait. He scooped up another piece of pie and simply ignored Hezekiah's teasing words, determined not to let his friend have the satisfaction of getting under his skin.

Hezekiah's dark eyes widened, the white showing all around. "I know!" he said, looking as if he'd suddenly had the most miraculous idea imaginable. "We could ride back and ask Miss Melissa if she'd like to join Logan. I'm *sure* she'd just love to."

"Like hell you will!" Logan declared hotly.

The whole group dissolved into peals of laughter at the horrified look on his face.

"All right, all right," he growled at Hezekiah. "I hope you're happy now that you've had your fun."

"I am. I certainly am," the buffalo soldier said, nodding his head emphatically. It wasn't often he got such a rise out of Logan.

"I can find my own company, thank you very much. And when I do, it won't be some pampered little brat like Henderson's daughter."

"Oh?" Hezekiah queried, one eyebrow quirked high in amusement. "That wasn't the story that was going around the barracks this morning. Why, they were talking about the dance last night, and from what I heard—"

"Enough, Hezekiah, enough." Logan groaned, raising his hands in surrender.

"Only trying to help," Hezekiah assured him innocently. "I wouldn't want you to be lonely."

Logan grinned. "Don't worry, that's one thing I won't ever be. There's always Bisbee and Della."

"What's Bisbee?" Hawk asked, trying hard to keep his attention on something other than the delectable picture Sabra made.

Logan popped one last bite of pie into his mouth, chewed, and swallowed before answering. "A mining town over in the Mule Mountains, about thirty miles away. Interesting sort of place."

"Oh? Why's that?"

"A portion of it's wedged into the bottom of the canyon, the rest of it rambles up and down the mountainsides. Kinda crazy. Some of the houses huddle on little ledges; others hang out over the canyon, propped up on long stilts. In some cases, there's more wood in the stairs that lead to the houses than in the buildings themselves."

"Yeah, you really ought to see it," Hezekiah put in. "It'd probably provide some good background material for your book."

Hawk nodded. "Maybe I should."

At the moment, keeping up a front about doing research for a book was the last thing Hawk was thinking about. Uppermost in his mind was the growing conviction that it might be a very good idea for him to get away from Sabra for a day or two. To get things back in perspective. It was becoming more difficult by the minute for him to concentrate on his goal. His mind was far too full of golden hair, deep brown eyes, and a smile that was more warming than the summer sun at high noon.

"Not a bad idea," Logan agreed, oblivious of the way his sister's interest perked up. "I can make arrangements, if you'd like to go."

Hezekiah's suggestion was sounding better by the moment to Logan. It had been several months since he'd seen Della. Sexy, fun-loving, comfortable Della. No strings. No problems. She was no more interested in a permanent relationship than he. All sweet little Della cared about was a good time. And that was damn sure the only kind of woman Logan Powers wanted.

Logan's mind was made up. This was a perfect opportunity to combine a little pleasure with the business of escorting Hawk.

"Are you going to go this week, Logan?" Sabra asked, the tone of her voice exceedingly nonchalant.

"Yeah, I think I'll run over. What do you say, Hawk? Do you want to go with me?"

"Yes. I think that would be a very good idea." Hawk declared, snatching at this opportunity for salvation.

"Anyone want this last piece of pie before I put all this away?" Sabra asked brightly, attacking the pile of empty plates and bowls as if nothing else were on her mind.

She was content to let the subject of Bisbee die for the time being; she had the information she needed. The major would be gone for at least a week, and Logan had promised several times to take her to Bisbee. Later that night or the next day she'd find the perfect opportunity to remind her brother of that. If Hawk was going, Sabra had every intention of being included in the forthcoming trip.

Everyone pitched in and shortly all the baskets were repacked and once again stored in the back of the wagon. Full of good food and drowsy from the warm afternoon sun, the five friends wandered back to the blankets. Logan flopped down and stretched out on his back, propping his broad-brimmed hat over his face. Within minutes soft snores were issuing from beneath the dusty Stetson.

Jasmine used one of the nearby pine trees for a backrest. With far less coaxing than any of them would have expected, Hezekiah was persuaded to pillow his head against her thigh. The ladies exchanged small satisfied smiles as he settled into place and closed his eyes with a contented sigh.

Sabra could hardly believe the progress Hezekiah had made during the day. He'd started out so shy, hanging back, barely talking. And here he was, curly black head bravely cradled in Jasmine's lap. The change in his attitude verified her belief. All it took was a little time and an opportunity.

Sabra's glance flickered toward Hawk. He'd propped himself against a large boulder, tilting his hat far down on his forehead. Deep shadows obscured his eyes, but the teasing little tingles that raced up and down Sabra's spine convinced her those dark hooded orbs were trained squarely on her.

Time and opportunity.

She was determined they'd have both.

Logan was the first to stir back to life, shielding his eyes with his hand and peering up at the sun. "Must be near to three o'clock," he muttered. He sat up and gave Hezekiah's foot a good shake. "Wake up, Private Kane. Much as I hate to think about it, we've got work to do."

Hezekiah mumbled sleepily and rolled to a sitting position.

Disappointment furrowed Sabra's brow. "Oh, Logan, no! Not yet. There's still several hours of sunshine left," she protested.

"It's been a delightful day, sis, but I'm afraid duty calls. Got a few things to take care of at the post. We'd best get back."

"Are you sure we have to go right now?" Sabra persisted. "Can't we stay just another hour?"

Logan shrugged. "Hezekiah and I have to get back, but I don't guess the rest of you need to leave right now. That is, if Hawk doesn't mind playing escort for a little while longer."

"Uh . . . no. No, I don't mind."

Hawk was as reluctant as the others for the wonderful afternoon to end. He couldn't remember the last time he'd been so relaxed and at ease around people other than his family. With surprise, he realized he hadn't worried once about his heritage or their possible reactions to it or to anything else to do with the past. It had been absolutely perfect. What harm could there be in staying with Jasmine and Sabra, in prolonging the pleasure a little longer? He could see no reason not to go along with Logan's suggestion.

"I'd be happy to stay," Hawk said, his smile broad and genuine.

Hezekiah hadn't said a word during this exchange, but the look of disappointment on his face as he glanced at Jasmine spoke volumes. This had been his first opportunity to spend any amount of time with the dark beauty who'd filled his thoughts for weeks, and he was suddenly saddened at the thought of the day coming to an end. Even worse, he was very much afraid that without the gentle pressure of his friends, he'd never gather enough nerve to seek her out again, once they were back in the familiar confines of the fort.

But, good soldier that he was, he rose to his feet. "What do you want to take back, Logan, the wagon or a couple of horses?"

"Well, I guess that depends on what the ladies want to

do," Logan responded.

Jasmine was well aware that Sabra had deliberately provided her with an opportunity to spend some time with Hezekiah. Her dark liquid eyes fondly traveled the long length of the big soldier, from the tip of his huge feet to the top of his curly black head. A tender smile curved her mouth as she considered how terribly shy her gentle giant was. But they'd made progress today, real progress. He'd actually talked and laughed, even done a little hesitant flirting himself. And getting him close enough to pillow his head on her lap had been a real coup. She had no intention of letting him slip away now, not after the afternoon had gone so well.

And, truth be told, Jasmine wasn't above a little matchmaking herself. From the first moment she'd seen the pair together, she had recognized Sabra's interest in the tall dark stranger. And it hadn't taken her long to sense that Sterling Hawkins was every bit as drawn to the golden-haired Sabra.

"Never mind all that," Jasmine said, quickly rising to her feet and shaking out her skirts. "I have a few chores to take care of, too. Why don't we go back just like we came? I'll ride with Hezekiah, and Sabra and Mr. Hawkins will still have their horses. Then they can return whenever they choose."

Hawk's attention was so riveted on Sabra that he caught only the last few words of what Jasmine said. "I'd be very pleased if you'd drop the 'mister,' Jasmine. Just call me Hawk."

Jasmine's pleasure showed on her face. Except for Logan and Sabra, she had rarely been treated as an equal by a white person. The whites' treatment of her more often fell somewhere between condescension and bias.

"Thank you, I'll do that," Jasmine agreed with gentle dignity. But being a woman—and Sabra's friend—her mind automatically went back to the situation at hand. "You don't mind staying with Sabra, do you?"

Jasmine's earlier words finally sank into Hawk's head. Sabra. Him. Alone.

Trouble.

Hawk knew he should find some excuse to leave with

the others. He had no business staying here alone with Sabra. His determination to kill Powers was already badly weakened. Why on earth did he keep subjecting himself to more temptation, more stress? The more time he spent with Sabra, the less sure he became that he could actually follow through with his plan.

The growing guilt Hawk felt at letting his lifelong vow so often slip from his thoughts hung heavy on his mind, but his need to be with Sabra proved too strong.

Sabra raised her eyes to find him watching her, a myriad of emotions in his midnight blue eyes.

"No," he finally answered softly, never taking his eyes from her sunlight-haloed beauty. "I don't mind in the least."

Within minutes Hawk and Sabra were shouting goodbyes as the wagon bearing Hezekiah and Jasmine rolled away.

"Don't let her talk you into staying too late," Logan cautioned Hawk, casting an affectionate look in his sister's direction. "It gets dark early, and fast. And the temperatures will start to drop the minute the sun goes down."

"I understand," Hawk answered with a solemn nod of his head.

Logan had put his trust in him and Hawk had no intention of letting him down. An hour. No more. Just a little time to talk and savor the pure pleasure of being with Sabra. That was all. Then he'd bundle her on to her horse and they'd head back for the fort.

Easy.

Logan gave one last wave of his hand and then spurred his mount, racing after the fast-disappearing wagon with an exuberant whoop.

Sabra and Hawk watched until he vanished from sight around a rise. Then a sudden awkwardness descended upon them. They exchanged fleeting smiles and ambled back in the direction of the one blanket that had been left on the ground under the trees.

"Well, what would you like to do?" Hawk finally asked, walking so slowly that his boots scuffed raspily against the short coarse grass. "A little more exploring?"

Sabra clasped her hands in front of her, the picture of demure uncertainty. "No, I don't think so."

"Oh." Hawk desperately searched his mind for another suggestion. "I . . . uh . . . guess we could go wading again. That is, if you want to."

Sabra drew her brows together in serious contemplation. "That was wonderful fun, but it's probably not a good idea right now; if we got too wet it would be a very chilly ride back to the fort."

"Sure," Hawk said, nodding his head in agreement. "I hadn't thought of that."

They walked along silently for a few more steps.

"We could just sit and talk for a while," Sabra finally suggested.

"Well, yeah. I guess we could do that."

Hawk sighed. What in hell were they going to talk about? He couldn't discuss his past, and he didn't want to know any more about Sabra and her family. What little he already knew was making his job far too tough. Better to let things remain as they were. Far better.

Sabra watched the hem of her blue calico gown swish over the rust-colored ground, her mind searching for a way to recapture the feeling of intimacy they'd shared the night before. Surely, now that they were alone, Hawk would stop acting like he was afraid to get within a six-foot radius of her.

Memories of the previous night swirled in Sabra's head. The way Hawk's lips had felt against hers. The utter tenderness of his embrace while they'd danced under the moon. The pleasure she'd felt at hearing such unrestrained laughter from him.

All those memories sent little tingles racing through her. Was she so wicked to want to experience those delectable sensations again?

Her father would probably think so. . . . No! Sabra's chin tilted stubbornly. Forget him, she told herself. He was far, far away, and what he might think had no bearing on the magical feelings evoked in her by Sterling Hawkins.

What harm could there be in a few stolen kisses? Absolutely none that Sabra could see. And they just might influence Hawk to stay around awhile longer.

Time and opportunity. That was what it was all about.

They'd finally reached the blanket, and with an exchange of shy glances, each took an opposite corner. When Sabra once again removed her slippers, placing them on a nearby rock, Hawk caught a glimpse of trim ankle and swallowed hard.

Research, he thought suddenly. The make-believe book. They could talk about the fort and Geronimo. At least those were safe subjects. He bumbled his way through half a dozen questions and Sabra did her best to answer them.

Then he picked up a couple of pebbles lying near the edge of the blanket, absentmindedly tossing them into the air and catching them. He missed one, and it rolled to the center of the blanket. After leaning over to scoop it up, he settled down again, a foot closer to Sabra.

Sabra finally flopped down on her tummy, wriggling into a comfortable position near the middle of the blanket. Chin resting on her folded arms, she chuckled softly as she watched a chaparral cock bob and weave in hot pursuit of an insect.

Hawk tired to concentrate on the chase, but he could manage only a couple of hurried glances before he turned his full attention back to Sabra. The way her calico dress molded her firm little backside was much more entertaining than the antics of some silly bird. The idle kicking of her feet had hiked one rumpled fold of her skirt almost to the backs of her knees, and the tempting display of firm curved calves made his mouth go dry.

Tossing another pebble heavenward, Hawk missed his catch. He watched it bounce across the blanket and roll to a stop against a pool of golden curls.

He reached for the pebble, hesitated, drew back.

Sabra sensed his movement and turned to look at him, her gaze soft, unafraid, totally accepting. A whole handful of sun-drenched curls shimmered off her shoulder and puddled on the blanket.

Hands clenched tightly at his sides, Hawk fought the wild desire to reach out and twine a gilded ringlet around his finger . . . and lost.

Eyes large and liquid, Sabra watched Hawk's hand

come nearer. Her breath caught in her throat as he reverently threaded his fingers through her hair.

Caught in the magic of the moment, lost in the deep blue depths of Hawk's eyes, Sabra slowly rolled on to her back. Her long silken tresses fanned out across the blanket in a river of gold, and the sun's radiant light danced along each individual strand, gathering, magnifying, highlighting shades of gold and silver and copper.

Completely attuned, they moved in unison, Hawk easing down to sit close beside Sabra as she turned, his left arm bracketing her shoulder, his right hand still possessively tangled in her hair.

Gently, ever so gently, he combed his fingers through her tresses, lifting them and letting them ripple from his fingers like spun gold.

As the last gleaming strands sifted away, Hawk turned his attention to tenderly tracing the line of her jaw, the slight trembling of his fingertips as they skimmed across her skin doing wild things to Sabra's senses. The gentle sough of the wind seemed to vanish, leaving only the matched rhythm of their rapid breathing. Hawk's nearness, blocking out the sky and the sun, became her whole world.

At the delicate curve of Sabra's chin, Hawk let his hand dip downward, trailing one finger after another along the slender column of her throat. His fingers hovered over the fragile pulsepoint nestled at the base of her throat, glorying in the runaway beat. Then his hand skimmed across the pale satin flesh left bare by the dip of her bodice, and finally curved possessively around the velvet flesh of her upper arm.

Their gazes locked, and her soft coral lips parted slightly, her breath coming in small shallow gasps as she watched him with eyes grown luminous, almost wondrous with expectation.

Sabra pondered the raw emotions in Hawk's eyes. Uncertainty. Perhaps a touch of fear. But mostly hunger, a consuming hunger that turned his eyes as dark as midnight.

Hawk could stand it no more. The ache in his heart was unbearable. He had to touch her.

A kiss.

Just one healing kiss.

That was all.

He slowly bent toward Sabra. Her eyes fluttered shut, and he caught with his own the gentle sigh that escaped her lips.

Sweet joy swept through Sabra as Hawk's mouth took hers. Had anything ever felt so good before?

The kiss began as something tender, almost reverent. A mere brushing of his lips against hers, soft as a butterfly's gossamer wings, so fleeting that it was almost torture. Then the tip of his tongue slipped out to trace the contours of her mouth, and she thought her heart would burst with rapture. How could anything possibly feel any better? But when his tongue slowly parted her lips, dancing against hers, exploring each hidden recess, she knew the ecstasy had only just begun.

Sabra tasted like honey, like life's own nectar to Hawk's starving soul. He couldn't get enough of her.

His tongue plundered her mouth, stroking the silken lining, gliding over perfect pearl-like teeth. Fever raged in his blood when she met and parried each sweet thrust.

But he made no move to touch her in any other way than the cherishing caress of his mouth and the trembling touch of fingers cupped around her arm.

Sabra arched her back, aching for more. The movement caused the heel of Hawk's hand to barely graze the swell of her bosom. There was instant response to his errant touch; her breasts grew heavy, swollen, the nipples pebbling, straining against pale blue fabric.

A moan broke low in her throat.

Hawk's hand froze. Almost instantly he relinquished Sabra's mouth and jerked his hand from the soft, utterly tempting mound of flesh. He had to stop. Now. Back off before it was too late, before his fevered brain became completely incapable of logical thought.

With supreme effort Hawk pulled away from her, gathering himself to rise. He didn't notice the confusion, the disappointment that flashed in Sabra's eyes. He only knew that, for her sake, he had to put some distance between them . . . and fast.

170

Sabra didn't think about what she was doing; she had no idea how near the edge Hawk was. She only knew she didn't want to lose his sweet nearness, the delicious heat that was racing through her veins. Reaching out, she laid a restraining hand on his forearm.

At the unexpected touch Hawk's breath caught in his throat, and his eyes jerked back to confront hers. The slight pressure of her fingers upon his flesh held him in place as securely as chains. A nerve ticked in the corner of his jaw as he struggled against temptation.

Did she know what she was doing to him?

His hungry, hopeful eyes devoured the rosy flush staining her cheeks, the telltale beat of the pulse at the base of her throat. Her wide-eyed gaze of deepest brown was somehow utterly guileless even as it spoke to him of passion and pleading.

How could he take advantage of her innocence?

"Don't go," she whispered.

How could he not?

Chapter Fourteen

Hawk was lost. Unable to fight the consuming desire any longer. To hell with the past, and the damned future, he thought. All that mattered was now. Holding this woman in his arms, letting her gentle heat thaw the frozen recesses of his soul, feeling the sweet healing beat of her heart against his.

Slowly he sank down, swinging his long legs around until he lay halfway across Sabra, her breasts crushed beneath his chest, his elbows propped on either side of her head.

Once again he threaded his fingers through the golden mass of curls spread across the blanket. Slowly, lovingly, his thumbs caressed her temples, then skimmed over cheeks as soft as ivory satin.

Sabra lay beneath him, calm, trusting. She could think of nothing but the pleasure of being so close to Hawk. How tenderly he held her, how very safe she felt within the confines of his embrace.

In response to his nearness, strange and marvelous things were happening to her body. Her nipples pearled against the broad muscled expanse of his chest; her breasts felt heavy and swollen. And deep within her belly, tiny tingles became frissons of longing that rippled through her from top to toe. Silently, wondrously, Sabra contemplated the strange little ache that continued to grow and grow, pondering the fact that the curious response only blossomed when Hawk was near, restlessly questioning if it were possible to assuage the tender torment.

Hawk's heart beat so hard he was sure Sabra could hear it. He wanted her more than anything he'd ever dreamed of. But still he waited, his eyes almost desperate as he searched hers. Did she even understand? Was she too young and inexperienced to realize the forces they were trifling with?

Contradictions whirled in his mind. He wanted to hold her, to possess her, yet he wanted never—ever—to hurt her. Desires in total opposition. How could he ever make the choice?

But then Sabra made it for him.

She could see the distress in his eyes, feel the tension in his body as he held himself motionless above her while his hands gently caressed her hair and his breathing rapidly rose and fell. Suddenly the most important thing in the world was to chase that haunted look from Hawk's eyes, to exorcise whatever devil tormented him.

Sabra's arms wound around his neck, her fingers tangling in the dark hair at his nape. With gentle pressure she pulled his head down to hers.

Hawk groaned in surrender, and with tender urgency his mouth claimed hers. Unconsciously he tightened his hold on her slender form, almost afraid she might somehow slip from his embrace and vanish before his very eyes, like mist when it meets the sun's golden rays.

Long minutes later he relinquished her lips to draw a ragged breath before peppering her throat with tiny love bites. A thousand butterfly-soft kisses were sprinkled down that long slender column, across the gentle slope of her shoulder. When Hawk paused and his tongue flicked across the tom-tom pulse at the base of Sabra's throat, she writhed under him, reveling in the growing fever that burned in her blood. Turning, adjusting, arching, she sought to press against the hard length of his body, needing to feel him closer and closer still.

Hawk's fingers tiptoed down Sabra's back to cup the delicate curve of her buttocks, rolling her toward him, cradling his manhood against her welcoming softness. A groan echoed deep in his throat as the heat from her body consumed him, flame by tiny flame.

Sweet agony swept through Hawk when Sabra tightened her embrace, his desire blazing as hot as the desert sun in summer.

She stayed snuggled against him as his hand continued its cherishing exploration, smoothing over the gentle swell of hip, dipping at the tiny waist, gliding upward over midriff to pause just below the rich swell of a breast.

Sooty lashes swept downward, and a small pleading whimper escaped as she tilted her face toward Hawk, a flower searching for the sun. He claimed her lips again, the taste of her sending his senses reeling.

Now Sabra's hands caressed Hawk's back, first savoring the great muscles that bunched and flowed under his skin and then examining the intriguing line of his spine, following it as far as she could reach. But it wasn't enough. She wanted to feel *him* under her hands.

Instinctively Sabra's hand slid to Hawk's side, and her fingers plucked in frustration at the offending fabric of his shirt.

Hawk raised his head, gazed at Sabra with eyes as dark as a midnight sky. He understood. His need to hold her close, without barriers, without restrictions, was even greater than hers. He angled away from her long enough to unbutton his shirt and lay bare the golden bronze expanse of his muscled chest.

Slowly, Sabra let her fingers trace the line of his shoulder, then follow the ridge of collarbone, all the while curving down, down. When her fingertip brushed one flat copper nipple, there was a sharp intake of breath from Hawk. Startled by the instant ripple of muscle and sinew her touch evoked, Sabra jerked her hand away.

Hawk's response was quicksilver fast. His hand snared her faltering fingers, dragging them back, pressing her palm hard against his chest, letting her know how much he welcomed her caress. Her eyes widened in awe as his heartbeat thrummed beneath her hand, and in the next instant, his hand swept upward to take possession of her calico-clad breast, his touch as gentle as the wind on a fragile flower.

And still it wasn't enough.

For either of them.

Hesitantly, Hawk's fingers slipped between them, find-

174

ing the row of tiny buttons at the front of Sabra's dress.
And all the while his hungry gaze never left her eyes. His
heart in his throat, he waited in agony for the expected
protest.

She said not a word, but the things he read in her velvet
eyes sent his fever soaring.

With agonizing slowness, he slipped the first button
from its mooring.

Then another.

And another.

Finally, they were all unfastened. His fingers trembled
as he swept the shirtwaist open, revealing a white chemise,
so finely woven that it did little to obscure the blush of
her nipples. Three tiny blue bows nestled in the valley
between her breasts. As he reached for the first one, his
knuckles brushed the gentle swell of her bosom, and a
low groan of desire rumbled in his chest. Anchoring the
fragile blue ribbons between thumb and forefinger, Hawk
gave each a tug. As the looped ties slithered from their
knots, the fabric fell aside, laying bare the most glorious
sight he'd ever seen.

Sabra's skin, almost translucent, was tinted the palest
shade of golden apricot. And her breasts, full and
rounded to perfection, were capped by pert coral tips that
grew even harder under his admiring scrutiny.

With a satisfied sigh, Hawk settled against her, his bare
chest brushing the smooth crest of one delectable mound.
For a long moment his eyes feasted on the miraculous
sight of her pale skin nestled against his own bronze
body. Then his gaze slowly slid upward and his heart
soared even higher when he saw the tender passion in her
eyes.

"Ah, Sabra," Hawk whispered reverently. "You're so
beautiful. I never dreamed . . ." A ragged sigh broke
from him, and cupping the lush fullness of her breast in
his hand, he lowered his head and gently captured the
proffered morsel.

His lips were petal soft as they closed around it, his
tongue hot and moist as it laved her aching flesh. Tremors
of ecstasy surged through Sabra at the exquisite feelings
his caress evoked, and lost in the rapture, she clung to his

175

shoulders, her nails biting into the hard muscles.

"Hawk." The word was a sigh, a catch of her breath, a plea.

The lazy November sun bathed the lovers in its golden glow as Hawk intuitively responded to Sabra's needs, claiming her lips again, thrusting his tongue deep into honeyed recesses, sipping her sweetness, letting her fevered breathing fill his soul with its healing balm. His knee slipped between her legs and she arched hard against his rock-hard thigh, burrowing against him, curving herself into the warm security of his embrace.

Her searching fingers feathered across the thick shock of hair hugging the back of his neck, then skimmed upward and she cradled his head between her palms, chaining his lips to hers, wanting the ecstasy never to end.

Suddenly Hawk stiffened, snatched his mouth away as his steely gaze searched the horizon. Sabra moaned a low protest at his abrupt retreat, and blinked to clear heated mists from her eyes.

"Shhh," he cautioned softly, slanting one long finger across his lips. "Listen."

Sabra's forehead puckered with concentration as she tried to hear something. Her hearing, not nearly as finely tuned as Hawk's, discerned no strange sound.

"Damn!"

Looking like a thundercloud, Hawk hastily pushed himself up and away, then reached to grip Sabra's hands and pull her to a sitting position.

"What is it?" Sabra asked, wariness in her voice. Her head swiveled this way and that, but she saw nothing, heard nothing.

"Someone's coming."

"Are you sure? I don't see anyone."

"Yes, I'm sure." Hawk surged upward, rising swiftly to his feet. "Damn! They mustn't see us like this. I couldn't bear it if your reputation were damaged because of my foolishness. We've got to hurry."

He held out his hands. The tone of his voice brooked no argument. Sabra let him pull her up.

He caught her as she came to her feet, steadying her shoulders with a quick grip. Then, almost instantly, he released his hold and began to fumble with the ribbons of her chemise, uttering another low curse when the tiny ties refused to respond to his hasty ministrations. Almost frantic, he abandoned the fruitless task and simply smoothed the gapping sides of the garment across her rosy, hard-peaked breasts before trying to force buttons through holes which seemed to have diminished in size in the last few minutes.

"Let me," Sabra finally said, the worried look on Hawk's face almost quelling the small smile that tipped her mouth at his tender show of concern. She didn't quite believe that anyone was coming, but she thought it very endearing that Hawk's first consideration had been to protect her.

Suddenly her initial pleasure at his chivalrous attitude gave way to a rush of embarrassment as she remembered the intimacies they'd been sharing.

Good heavens! Sabra thought with mild shock. From a kiss to . . . to . . .

Heat stained her cheeks as she stole a quick look at Hawk. What could he possibly be thinking of her? Would what almost happened have changed his feelings?

For better?

For worse?

She couldn't, wouldn't believe the latter. After all, his first thought had been of her well-being.

She analyzed her own feelings as she finished anchoring the last buttons on her dress. Except for that first flush of chagrin, she really didn't regret what had happened. It had seemed so right. It still did. She cared about Sterling Hawkins, and she wasn't ashamed to have revealed it.

Hawk finished putting his own shirt to rights, then raked a ragged furrow through his disheveled hair. Sabra, meanwhile, finger-combed her tumbled locks and smoothed the dampened wisps at her temples.

With quick, efficient movements he gathered the rumpled blanket and folded it; she shook the wrinkles from her calico skirt.

Just as Hawk bent to lay the bundled blanket behind a boulder, two mounted figures rounded a craggy fold of land and thundered in their direction, a red haze of dust swirling about the horses' hooves.

"Goodness' sake," Sabra said in a startled voice. "You were right."

"Who are they?" Hawk asked. "Can you tell?"

"I . . . no, I can't. They're too far away." A touch of anxiety crept into Sabra's voice. Shading her eyes with her hands, she peered questioningly at the dark silhouettes of the fast-approaching pair.

Hawk glanced toward the grazing horses, thinking longingly of the holster slung over the horn of his saddle. *Fool!* he railed inwardly. Why hadn't he thought to retrieve it when the others had left? His alert, uneasy mind measured the distance to the horses. With a fast dash he could reach the gun before the strangers arrived.

"Do you think there's cause for concern?" he asked. "Has there been any hint of trouble hereabouts?"

"No. Nothing I've heard of."

Hawk gave the gun one more glance, and then quickly discarded the idea of racing for it. Even if Sabra ran with him, the speed required to reach the horses in time made it almost certain that he would outdistance her. He simply didn't want to get that far from her . . . just in case. And there was always the chance that the strangers might interpret such a move as threatening. Who knew what might happen then? Hawk felt sure it would be smarter to stand his ground. He had his hidden knife. It would have to do, should there be trouble.

The echo of hoofbeats slowed and stopped as the men reined in their mounts at the top of a small ridge. Hawk knew the shadowed faces were scrutinizing the two of them. The riders watched for some moments, then one of them bent toward the other as if to confer about something.

Finally, the apparent leader nudged his horse ahead, his companion following behind. Within minutes the two were within identifiable distance. The wide brims of their hats still concealed their faces, but at least they were near enough for the bastardized army uniforms to be recognized. Both wore regulation navy blue pants topped by civilian shirts of faded calico.

Hawk heaved a sigh of relief. "I think it's all right.

178

They're wearing semblances of uniforms. I guess that's a good sign. Say, you don't suppose Logan sent them after us, do you?"

Sabra shook her head emphatically. "No. It's not that late."

Hawk quickly squinted at the low-riding sun. "Yeah. Maybe they're just on routine patrol."

As the riders drew nearer, details became easier to discern. One of the men was armed with a Winchester Hotchkiss repeating rifle. Both wore pistols strapped to their hips; that was to be expected on the frontier. What really caught Hawk's attention was their hair. Straight and black, it framed each blurred face—faces which seemed much darker than mere shadows could account for. And he noted the grace with which the riders sat their shaggy ponies.

"Indians," Hawk muttered. "Apaches, if I'm not mistaken." His head bobbed in a nod of conviction. "Got to be scouts from the fort, unless they're renegades roaming the mountains dressed in Army uniforms." He capped that statement with a half-chuckle, hoping the small joke would ease Sabra's mind.

"I-Indian scouts?" Sabra repeated, edging sideways until she stood almost completely behind Hawk.

Hawk's response was a quick frown and an even quicker glance over his shoulder. Then his eyes snapped back to carefully watch the two riders, but a good portion of his mind was now taken up by a picture of Sabra's pinched white face. He wondered what was causing her suddenly peculiar behavior.

Trembling, she pressed even more tightly against his back, her breasts rising and falling against him with her short rapid breaths. And her left hand gripped his upper arm with such alarming strength that he was grateful she didn't have that strangle hold on his knife hand.

The men were almost upon them, their broad copper-colored faces and high cheekbones quite recognizable now despite the overhanging hats. As the leader slowly lifted a hand in greeting, the pressure of Sabra's fingers increased.

"Is something wrong, Sabra?" Hawk questioned softly, not wanting the men to hear his query. "Do you know them?"

"N-no, not really. You're right, they are scouts. I mean, at least one is. The small one. I-I recognize him from the fort. I think he's the one they call The Apache Kid."

Hawk had no time to ask any of the other questions that were whirling in his mind because the men had reined to a stop about ten feet from them. Quickly, he assessed them. The one in charge was small. Though his build was wiry, Hawk suspected that coiled-steel muscles lurked under the thin faded calico. His face was the color of old pennies, all angles and sharp chiseled bones that stretched his skin high and tight across his cheeks. Flat black eyes, slanted so steeply they were almost Oriental-looking, never blinked as they slowly traveled over Hawk and Sabra. Hawk's scalp prickled in response to the small man's scrutiny.

The Indian's companion had a round, rather flat face and small piggy eyes sunk in extra folds of flesh that would soon turn to fat. He was a good half a foot taller than his companion, but Hawk considered him the lesser threat.

"Beggin' pardon, folks," said the smaller man, the one Sabra had identified. He reached one hand—not his gun hand, Hawk was quick to note—to tug with quasi-politeness at the brim of his Army-issue hat. Then he leaned forward and crossed his arms over the saddle horn, his onyx eyes seeming to bore right through Hawk and then settle on Sabra. "Ain't you the major's daughter?"

"Y-yes," Sabra answered, her breath hissing out against Hawk's shoulder.

"Everything all right, Miss Powers?"

"Yes, of course."

Once again the scout's inscrutable gaze flicked over Hawk. "We could escort you in, if you'd like." Harness jingled as his roan horse shook its head. The man expertly tightened his hold on the reins and the horse quieted down again. "Your father might be getting worried."

"My father's gone to Tucson. And I'm fine. Really. Logan—Lieutenant Powers—knows where I am. You can go on about your business now." Sabra managed to direct the barest semblance of a smile in the direction of the two riders.

Her tone of voice sounded almost normal, but her grip on Hawk's arm was still tight. He wondered if the scouts heard the tension in her voice as he did.

The two men exchanged a quick glance, but neither made a move to leave.

"Is there something else we can do for you, gentlemen?" Hawk inquired, his voice just a shade frosty.

Something was wrong with Sabra, and whatever it was had begun with the Indian scouts' arrival. Hawk wanted these men gone.

Now.

"Nope," the leader finally said. "Just wanted to make sure the lady was all right. The major'd have our hides if we was amiss in our duty. We'll be biddin' you good day, then."

Once again the smaller of the two tugged at his hat brim. At last, with a firm pull on the reins, he turned his sweat-stained horse toward the mouth of the canyon. His still-silent partner followed.

Hawk didn't move until the ponies' slow, even pace had carried them almost to the canyon's entrance. Sabra remained pressed against his back, her hand still clutching his arm. Inwardly Hawk struggled against the need to pull her into his arms and soothe her, to tell her everything was all right, that he'd take care of whatever was bothering her; but he dared not touch her until the scouts were out of sight.

Finally, after what seemed like eons, the riders covered the last few yards of scrub-covered ground and disappeared from view. Sabra slumped against Hawk with relief.

Turning quickly, he gripped the soft flesh of her upper arms. "What's wrong? You were frightened—"

"Me? Frightened?" she said, with a nervous little laugh. "No. No, I wasn't."

She despised the weakness she had just displayed, and was keenly embarrassed that, after so many years, she was still unable to conquer her fears. What had happened long ago had nothing to do with her present life. Why couldn't she just accept that?

Sabra's frustration edged toward anger at herself. What was wrong with her anyway? She was a grown woman, not a five-year-old girl. Why couldn't she put a little steel in her spine and stop reacting so childishly?

"I'm not stupid, Sabra," Hawk persisted. "Why don't you tell me what upset you?"

"Nothing," she insisted, pulling from his grip and flouncing away. She didn't want to talk about her reaction with anyone, much less Hawk. My God, what would he think of her?

She sent a stone skittering with an irritated kick of her toe. She knew exactly what he'd think. He'd think she was one of those silly, simpering, quivering females who got the vapors at the least provocation, that's what. And what would a man like Hawk want with a useless, infantile, clinging vine?

Nothing.

Absolutely nothing. And she wouldn't blame him, either.

Sabra's chin tilted stubbornly. She *wasn't* one of those empty-headed, weak-willed excuses for womanhood. She wasn't! The subject was closed as far as she was concerned.

Hawk scrutinized the proud stiffness of Sabra's back. He wasn't going to get any answer out of her, that was obvious.

He played the last few moments over in his mind. Everything had been fine until the scouts had showed up. Was she embarrassed? Maybe she was afraid the intruders had seen their wild abandoned embrace. Perhaps he should assure her that they'd been on their feet and presentable long before the men could see anything. Would that ease her mind?

No. Somehow he didn't think that was the case. She hadn't seemed unduly concerned when he was trying to convince her that someone was coming. If she'd been worried about being seen, it should have been evident sooner.

Then what was it?

She'd slipped behind him when he'd suggested that the riders were scouts from the fort. And when they'd come nearer. And then, when the leader had mentioned the major. . . .

The major! That had to be what it was. Damn Powers anyway. What had the old bastard said or done that made Sabra afraid of him? But something wasn't right about that assessment. She wasn't afraid of him all the time. The fear was triggered by something else. It seemed to come and go at random.

A sudden bitter smile etched Hawk's face. Yeah, it came and went all right. It came when she was with him. Her dear ol' daddy didn't want his precious little daughter to have anything to do with the likes of Sterling Hawkins. And Sabra was evidently very much aware of that fact.

Hawk gave a brief derisive snort. Even with the highfalutin false pedigree Hawk had concocted, Andrew Powers didn't consider him worthy of his daughter.

God damn the man.

God damn him to hell and back.

Chapter Fifteen

Why that lowdown, no-good, dirty skunk! Melissa fumed, quickly fading into the shadows so she wouldn't be seen.

She'd been roaming the fort all afternoon in search of Sterling Hawkins, determined to make one last try at snaring his attention. Her pale gold sateen dress, crisp and becoming when she'd donned it that morning, was wilted and dust-stained about the hem. The wind had plucked at her carefully arranged onyx curls until they were as droopy and frizzy as an old string mop. And, to make matters worse, her feet hurt abominably from long hours of prowling in new shoes.

How ironic that just when she had given up and was heading for home, she'd spotted the subject of her hunt riding toward the rear corral. There was only one problem. He wasn't alone. The major's snooty little daughter was riding at his side.

The last dying rays of the sun, streaked with pale coral and hot pink, backlighted the pair as they slowly picked their way through the scrub brush, angling in the direction of the gate. Hawk's mount paced so close to Sabra's horse that their figures more often than not blended into one hazy blur. Melissa's pretty mouth twisted into an unattractive pout as jealousy flamed anew in her.

"Brazen little hussy!" she muttered sourly. "Why didn't she just climb up in the saddle with him? That's the only way she could've got any closer."

Eyes full of resentment, the sutler's daughter watched the riders reach the enclosure. Sterling Hawkins dismounted, hastily flipped his reins over the top rail of the corral fence, and then hurried toward Sabra. A flush of anger climbed Melissa's cheeks when Hawk bracketed Sabra's waist with his hands then eased her to the ground as if she were a piece of precious porcelain.

"Good grief," Melissa grumbled as she watched Sabra's hands linger on Hawk's shoulders. "Would you look at that? She's hanging all over him! Humph! I'll bet her daddy'd have a fit if he knew they were out without an escort."

Melissa conveniently forgot that she'd spent a good number of hours the last year in the company of one or another of the young officers . . . without escort, frequently in much more compromising circumstances than those she was viewing, and most assuredly without her own father's approval.

Her eyes narrowed as she watched Hawk tuck Sabra's hand through the crook of his arm. "And him! Just look at him. He looks like a sick calf!"

Melissa's anger deepened. How could the man possibly prefer Sabra's pale washed-out looks to her own sultry dark beauty? Heaven only knew Sabra's figure came in a poor second when compared with her own. What on earth did he see in the Powers creature? Or, more to the point, what underhanded tricks had Sabra used last night to steal the stranger's attention?

For a while it had seemed that Melissa's spur-of-the-moment plan had been going to work. She'd had Sterling Hawkins practically eating out of her hand when Logan had yanked her away from his side. The next thing Melissa knew, the fort's handsome visitor was dancing with Sabra. And then they'd disappeared into thin air, leaving her feeling like an utter fool. It had been bad enough that Edward had deserted her, but to have Sterling Hawkins snatched from her grasp by that goody-goody-butter-wouldn't-melt-in-her-mouth Sabra Powers was more than her pride could stand.

Melissa hugged the shadows until Hawk and Sabra disappeared from view, then she stomped off toward home.

They'll pay, she vowed.

Yes, they'd all pay. Logan. Sabra. Louise and Mary Ruth . . . *all* of the girls. It would be a long time before

Melissa would forgive any of them for the veiled snickers and the taunting remarks she'd suffered at the dance after Sabra had stolen the handsome stranger right from under her nose. They'd all pay.

Melissa's mood was foul when she slipped through the back door of her house. In her absence the fire in the stove had gone out, and the kitchen was cold and shadowed by the coming night. She eyed the almost-empty fuel box with distaste, and contemplated how long it would take her to rekindle the fire.

Perhaps, she mused, she could talk her father into being satisfied with a slice of cold ham and the leftover apple pie. But the thought died aborning. Mortimer Henderson set great store in a hot evening meal, and he seldom relented in his desire for one.

"Damn!" The word erupted as a groan of frustration. Melissa kicked the toe-pinching slippers from her feet, sending them skittering across the floor, and then marched stocking-footed down the hall and into the living room in search of her father.

Her petulant mood increased when she didn't find him in his usual place. His easy chair was empty; the ashtray on the table at its side still clean. A quick glance at the clock on the mantel assured her that it was indeed past the hour for him to close the store. Surely he wasn't still rummaging around out there. The thought added to her irritation. At that moment, all she wanted was to get the evening meal over with as fast as possible and then crawl into bed to soothe her wounded pride.

Standing at the end of the front hallway, Melissa gazed at the closed side entrance to the store. Her father had probably forgotten all about supper, as usual. But Melissa had no intention of keeping the food hot for him. He could be at the table by the time she finished cooking or eat his meal cold, and she was just angry enough to tell him so.

Intent on doing that, Melissa stalked down the hall. Just as she raised her hand to grasp the doorknob, she heard the rumble of male voices. Her hand halted in midair. Who was on the other side of the door with her father? A dawdling customer?

Wonderful. Just wonderful. Now he'd come home even later, for he'd never close up if there was a chance to make a dollar.

Melissa sighed, knowing the extent of her father's tardiness would depend solely upon who was in the store with him. Well, there was only one way to find out.

Ever so gently she turned the knob and eased the door open a tiny crack. The rumble became words.

". . . tired of losing money because of his interference. Powers has messed with my business for the last damn time," Mortimer Henderson declared. "I intend to find a way to get rid of the ol' son of a bitch—and the sooner, the better."

Melissa's heart gave a little thump of surprise. Did her father really have the necessary connections to get Major Powers transferred to another post? She knew Mortimer Henderson had powerful friends in Washington, but were they that powerful? Lord, she hoped so. Because, if the major went, Sabra would go, too. Melissa almost laughed aloud at the pleasing thought, but the other man's words stifled her rash impulse.

"What do you have in mind?"

Melissa frowned, trying to place the voice, but it wasn't familiar enough to bring a face to her mind. Carefully bracing the door so that her full skirts wouldn't cause it to move, she eased forward and put one eye to the opening.

Her father was in his usual place behind the counter, his back to the door Melissa was peeking through. On the other side of the counter, a man slouched against a flour barrel, half-hidden by her father's bulk. She could barely make out the four stripes on the shoulder of his navy blue shirt.

A sergeant. But who?

Just then Mortimer Henderson shifted, moving several steps to the left and reaching out to close the journal which lay on the counter. The movement revealed a tall, sandy-haired man.

Jennings. Sergeant Leroy Jennings. His handsome face and decidedly male magnetism had caught Melissa's attention the first day he'd arrived at the fort. With great

187

reluctance, she had dismissed him as unworthy of further attention when she'd found out all he had was his monthly sergeant's pay. But now, as she watched him, she wondered if she had been too hasty. He might be just what she needed to bolster her decidedly slumping morale.

Strange, she thought. I didn't know Jennings and my father were acquainted, except as customer and proprietor.

Melissa considered the possibility of interrupting the conversation and hinting that her father invite Jennings to stay for supper. The thought was quickly dismissed. Her father disliked mixing business with his home life, and she wasn't that fond of cooking. She'd have to find another way to catch Jennings' eye. Her subconscious mind working on a solution to that problem, she turned her attention back to the conversation.

"Well?" Jennings prompted again. "Do you have a plan?"

"Maybe," Henderson said with a slow nod of his head. "Maybe I do."

A grin tipped Jennings's mouth. "Good. The sooner Powers is out of the way, the better I'll like it."

Afraid her father might catch her, Melissa eased the door shut. Her past irritation was forgotten in view of the pleasant thought of bringing Sergeant Jennings to heel and her steadfast conviction that her daddy was going to make sure the Powers family got their comeuppance.

Before long, Major Powers and his snooty daughter would be climbing aboard the stage and heading out of town. Why, much as Melissa hated to leave her cozy bed before midmorning, she might even rise early enough to wave goodbye. With a small chuckle, she headed toward the kitchen, her mood vastly improved.

Melissa's euphoria increased as the next two days passed, fueled even further by the successful beginnings of a liaison with the handsome Sergeant Jennings. She'd been a bit surprised, although more than happy to agree, when he'd suggested they keep their budding relationship a secret because her father would certainly disapprove, and Jennings hadn't cared that such an arrangement would allow her to keep Edward Woodley thinking he was the only man in her life.

Meanwhile Melissa kept a careful eye on Sterling Hawkins. She knew he was spending the bulk of his time with Logan and Hezekiah, and her mood was so good she didn't even fret over the few evening hours he shared with Sabra—always with Logan acting as chaperon, of course. One of two things was bound to happen soon. Her father's contact in Washington would negotiate the major's transfer, or Powers would return from Tucson. Either event would put an immediate stop to whatever foolish dreams Sabra was spinning.

And with Sabra out of the picture, by transfer or her own father's decree, who knew what might happen? Since Melissa found it inconceivable that any other female on the post was worthy of Sterling Hawkins' attention, she was confident he'd eventually see the error of his ways and seek her out. Indeed, her fantasy grew to such proportions that she began to practice what she would say in response to Hawkins' apology—*after* she made him squirm, of course.

Meanwhile, her increasingly frequent rendezvous with Leroy Jennings made waiting much easier than usual. And, with the eventual return of Edward Woodley in the offing, the renewal of his devoted courting, Melissa was more than content to bide her time and wait for her father's plan to come to fruition.

Her fondest dream was that a telegraph message would be waiting for Major Powers when he returned from Tucson. The mere thought of that possibility kept her mercurial spirits high. That is, until the afternoon she happened to pass Louise Penrod as she was returning from a tryst with Leroy.

"Have you heard the exciting news?" Louise asked, smiling as if nothing were amiss between them, although they hadn't spoken since the night of the dance.

Melissa was tempted to tilt her nose even higher and keep on walking, but her curiosity got the best of her. "What news?" she finally queried.

"About Sabra's trip."

Trip? Melissa's heart gave a sudden lurch. Surely, oh surely, Louise was referring to the transfer. Melissa's eyes shone with eager anticipation, a wide smile curving her mouth.

"A trip?" she asked in mock bewilderment. "Is Sabra's family leaving the fort?" Her breath caught in her throat as she waited to hear the longed-for news.

A tiny frown crinkled Louise's brow. "Family? Well, not the whole family. Just Logan and Sabra."

"Wh-what?" A knot of apprehension formed in Melissa's chest, making it hard for her to breath. Her previous good mood was fast evaporating. "What are you talking about? What about the major?"

Louise shrugged. "He's in Tucson . . . but you knew that, didn't you? I'm talking about the trip to Bisbee."

"Bisbee!" Melissa's hand snaked out to wrap around Louise's wrist. "Stop babbling this instant and tell me what you're talking about."

Louise's eyes widened in surprise, but she stood her ground, gratified to see that Melissa had taken the bait so completely. "Let go of me, Melissa, and I'll tell you all about it."

Melissa relinquished her hold immediately. Although she managed to paste the semblance of a smile on her face, inwardly she was seething. How could she have acted so rashly? The last thing she'd intended to do was let Louise see that she might be bothered by anything that had to do with Sabra Powers. Tightly clasping the cords of her reticule in both hands, she waited.

"I suppose what prompted the trip was Mr. Hawkins's research. But Sabra reminded Logan that she's never been to Bisbee and that he's promised to take her. Her brother thought it a fine idea that she go along."

Melissa's mouth dropped. "What? You mean just Sabra and Logan and Mr. Hawkins? That's all? No chaperone?"

Mousy brown curls swayed as Louise gave a dismissive toss of her head. "Don't be silly. It's perfectly proper for Logan to act as chaperon for his own sister."

"But—"

Louise interrupted, eager to finish her tale and rub a little salt in the wound. "They're going to stay at that fancy hotel and take their meals in the restaurant. And Logan told Sabra they'd even go to the theater and see a troop of traveling entertainers." Louise became rapturous at the thought of such luxury. Hands clasped to her small bosom, she tilted her freckled face heavenward. "Doesn't that sound simply marvelous?"

"Grand. Just grand." There was more than a hint of bitterness in Melissa's voice.

Louise peeped from beneath the shelter of pale lashes. A spot of high color on each of Melissa's cheeks betrayed her irritation.

Good! Louise thought. It's working. It gave her great pleasure to be the one to deliver such unwelcome news to Melissa Henderson. It almost made up for all the ill treatment she'd received at the dark-haired beauty's hands.

Melissa drew a deep breath and tried to put her thoughts in order. Maybe it wasn't too late. Maybe she could do something . . . stop them somehow. She couldn't bear the thought of Sabra having such fun while she was stuck at the fort. Perhaps she could complain to some of the older officers' wives, hint at how improper the whole situation was. Surely they'd step in and take charge since Sabra's father was absent and that stupid brother of hers had no sense of propriety whatsoever.

Melissa licked her dry lips. "Uh . . . I'm so pleased for Sabra. Perhaps I should drop by and wish her a pleasant trip. When did you say they were leaving?"

"Leaving?" Louise echoed, all wide-eyed innocence. "Oh, no. I guess I didn't make myself clear. They're already gone, Melissa. Long gone. They left at the crack of dawn this morning. And they won't be back for four whole days."

Melissa's mouth hung open. Too late. It was too late to do a damn thing! She threw Louise a scathing look, turned on her heel, and stomped away.

"Goodbye, Melissa," Louise called after her. "Have a nice day." Louise's satisfied laughter filled the air.

Chapter Sixteen

"Well, there it is. Bisbee, queen of the copper camps."

From her vantage point atop the pass, Sabra viewed the town with delight. Bisbee was even more enchanting than she'd imagined from Logan's descriptions.

The small community nestled at the bottom of Mule Gulch, a narrow gorge in the compact aggregate of ridges and peaks that comprised the Mule Mountains. Lining the two main streets was a picturesque hodgepodge of buildings, new brick structures rubbing shoulders with ramshackle frame edifices. Beyond the main section of town, clusters of wooden or adobe miners' cabins were packed along the tiered switchback trails. Other cabins were scattered haphazardly about the ocher-colored hillsides, perched precariously on stone-reinforced terraces or held aloft by long wooden pilings.

Taking it slow and easy down the sloping trail, the trio began their descent into the valley. The thick stands of cottonwood, walnut, and oak found on the mountain began to disappear, giving way to larger and larger patches of bare stump-dotted ground as they got closer to the town.

"Look, Logan," Sabra said, pointing first to one side of the pass and then to the other. "See the distinct changes in color? How strange. And this side is tilted at such a crazy angle. It looks like some giant squashed two different-colored lumps of clay together."

Logan smiled and shook his head in amusement. Leave it to his sister to distill nature's cataclysmic forces into such terms.

4 BESTSELLING HISTORICAL ROMANCES BY YOUR FAVORITE AUTHORS CAN BE YOURS, FREE!

Kensington Choice, our newest book club now brings you historical romances by your favorite bestselling authors including Janelle Taylor, Shannon Drake, Rosanne Bittner, Jo Beverley, and Georgina Gentry, just to name a few! Each book is filled with passion, adventure and the excitement of bygone times!

To introduce you to this great new club which is part of Zebra Home Subscription Service, we'd like to send you your first 4 bestselling historical romances, absolutely free!   And once you get these 4 free books to savor at home, we'll rush you the next 4 brand-new books at the lowest prices available, as soon as they are published.

The way the club works is that after your initial FREE shipment, you will get our 4 newest bestselling historical romances delivered to your doorstep each month at the

preferred subscriber's rate of only $4.20 per book, a savings of up to $7.16 per month (since these titles sell in bookstores for $4.99-$5.99)! All books are sent on a 10-day free examination basis and there is no minimum number of books to buy. (A postage and handling charge of $1.50 is added to each shipment.) Plus as a regular subscriber, you'll receive our FREE monthly newsletter, *Zebra/Pinnacle Romance News*, which features author profiles, contests, subscriber benefits, book previews and more!

So start today by returning the FREE BOOK CERTIFICATE provided. We'll send you 4 FREE BOOKS with no further obligation: A FREE gift offering you hours of reading pleasure with no obligation...how can you lose?

We have 4 FREE BOOKS for you
as your introduction to
KENSINGTON CHOICE!
To get your FREE BOOKS, worth
up to $23.96, mail the card below.

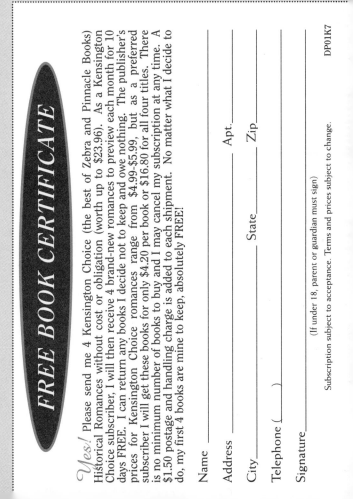

FREE BOOK CERTIFICATE

Yes! Please send me 4 Kensington Choice (the best of Zebra and Pinnacle Books) Historical Romances without cost or obligation (worth up to $23.96). As a Kensington Choice subscriber, I will then receive 4 brand-new romances to preview each month for 10 days FREE. I can return any books I decide not to keep and owe nothing. The publisher's prices for Kensington Choice romances range from $4.99-$5.99, but as a preferred subscriber I will get these books for only $4.20 per book or $16.80 for all four titles. There is no minimum number of books to buy and I may cancel my subscription at any time. A $1.50 postage and handling charge is added to each shipment. No matter what I decide to do, my first 4 books are mine to keep, absolutely FREE!

Name _____

Address _____ Apt._____

City _____ State_____ Zip._____

Telephone ( ) _____

Signature_____

(If under 18, parent or guardian must sign)

Subscription subject to acceptance. Terms and prices subject to change.

DP01K7

4 FREE
Historical
Romances
are waiting
for you to
claim them!

(worth up to
$23.96)

See details
inside....

KENSINGTON CHOICE
Zebra Home Subscription Service, Inc.
120 Brighton Road
P.O.Box 5214
Clifton, NJ 07015-5214

"I think it has more to do with mineral content, sis. The leaching of iron causes the russet-brown and yellow, and the rocks on this side are mostly limestone—that's why they're gray."

But Sabra's wandering gaze had already spotted a new point of interest. "Oh, how pretty," she said, pointing across the gulch to a huge rock, a massive limestone outcropping which overhung the mountainside and the town. "It looks like a castle, doesn't it?"

A small smile etched Hawk's mouth in response to that whimsical statement. He never ceased to wonder at her eternal enthusiasm. She could find beauty in anything, from ugly little horned lizards to great lumps of rock. He suddenly wished he could always view the world through Sabra's eyes; she made it so much easier to see the sunshine instead of the shadows.

Logan squinted at the pale gray mass on the side of the mountain. "H'm. Well, I guess it might look like a castle, at that."

"I quite agree," Hawk said, earning one of Sabra's brilliant smiles.

"Is that where silver was discovered? Up by that rock?" Sabra asked, remembering bits and pieces of tales she'd heard.

"Sure is."

"Tell us about it," Sabra encouraged as they carefully picked their way down the trail toward Bisbee. There was a lilt in her voice, and her face fairly shone with excitement as she turned to Hawk. "Bisbee has a fascinating history. It might provide you with some material for your book."

"Then I'd be pleased to hear all about it," Hawk replied with a smile. He'd listen to anything at all if it kept that enthralled look on Sabra's face.

Logan shifted his weight in the saddle, a pleasant jingle floating on the air as his horse shook its head in response to his movement.

"Let's see; I guess it all started in May of seventy-seven. Lieutenant Rucker and fifteen men from C Company were out scouting for sign of Indians. They came here in search of fresh water—there's a spring at the base of

193

Sabra's pretty rock."

"And that's where Rucker found the silver? At Castle Rock?"

"Not exactly, sis, not the silver itself. And it wasn't Rucker who found the first sign. George Dunn, a tracker and scout for the Army, saw a float of cerussite—"

"What's that?"

"A lead carbonate mineral . . . it's usually found around silver deposits. Anyway, Dunn poked around for a while and put some talus samples in his pocket to show Rucker. Dunn and Rucker and ol' T. D. Byrne looked 'em over. They decided it was a good sign. Plus, there was a faint green stain on the hillside—that's another strong indication of lead and copper and, most importantly, silver. They paced off a claim before they left, but it was August before Byrne got to Tucson to file papers on the mine."

"And did it all belong to them then? This whole valley? Did they get rich?"

"No, Sabra." Logan's laughter rumbled through the pass. "They weren't that lucky. Dunn told a fella named George Warren about their find. Dunn even grubstaked Warren with food and two burros. But instead of going on into the mountains to stake another claim for the two of them, Warren went looking for more partners. It was the end of September before he filed on the Mercy Mine. And he purely forgot to put Dunn's name on the claim."

"How unfair!" declared Sabra, her brow wrinkling in distress.

Fair, thought Hawk. A world of Sabra's making would always be fair and honest and compassionate. Dear God, if it could only be that way.

"No, I guess it wasn't," Logan agreed. "Not much of life is."

Hawk cut a swift glance at Logan. At least *he* was aware of the reality of life. For a moment Hawk wished Sabra weren't quite so innocent. He was very much afraid she was going to get hurt someday because of it. But deep down inside he knew that, given the opportunity, he wouldn't change her. Not one tiny bit. It was that sweet innocent belief in the goodness of life that made her so special.

"Go on with the story," Sabra prompted.

"A whole bunch of mines were staked that fall, the Silver Queen, the Mohawk, the Mammoth, the Neptune. Then silver was discovered over by Tombstone, and before long these mountains were swarming with prospectors. By seventy-nine over a hundred claims had been filed."

"But what about the silver here?" Sabra persisted. "Did they ever find it?"

"Sure, they found some. But not in quantities sufficient to make mining it worthwhile."

"Oh." There was a touch of disappointment in Sabra's voice. "But they did find copper. Right?"

"Right. And the biggest portion of it was at the site of the ol' Mercy Mine. That became the Copper Queen, the richest copper mine in the area."

"So Warren came out all right, after all," Hawk remarked.

"No. No, he didn't," Logan said with an amused shake of his head. "The ol' boy wasn't too smart. He eventually lost his share of the mine on a bet. What you might call poetic justice."

"A bet?"

"Yeah. Folks say Warren and another fellow were over at Charleston, doing a bit of heavy drinking. Warren swore he could beat a horse in a race from a starting point, around a stake, and back again."

"But that's not possible, is it?" Sabra questioned.

"Yes, it is," Hawk declared. "I've seen Ind—" He quickly amended his statement, realizing questions might be raised if he admitted seeing such a race in an Indian camp. "Uh, I've seen it done. Men can sometimes gain more ground in rounding the stake than a horse can make up for on the straightaway." Hawk let out a breath of relief when it appeared that neither Sabra nor Logan had noticed his near blunder.

"That's right. And I've heard folks say that Warren learned the trick from Indians—seems he was captured as a youth and held captive for almost two years by a band of Apaches," Logan explained. "Anyway, Warren was evidently too drunk to do it that time, because he lost the

195

race and his share of the Copper Queen."

"What happened to him then? And to Rucker and the others?"

"Don't know about Warren. Last I heard, he'd headed south into Sonora looking for another mine. Rucker drowned in a bad flood in seventy-eight. The others have scattered over the years."

"And the mines? Obviously they're still being worked," Hawk commented, his sharp eyes taking in the bustling town.

"Yep, and richer than ever. Things are changing though. The Phelps Dodge Company bought in a year or so ago, and independent mining operators are having a tough time. Lots of them are selling out, giving in to the pressure of the conglomerate. But, as you can see, that hasn't hurt the town's growth any. It's still growing by leaps and bounds. The second smelter went into production last spring." Logan paused to point toward the smudge of greenish-black smoke which hung over a cluster of buildings on a far hillside. "That's it over there, the newest smelter."

Hawk eyed the clouds of smoke billowing from the smelter's stacks and then glanced at the denuded hillside, thinking how pretty the little valley must have been before civilization overtook it. "That's what happened to the trees, isn't it? Fuel for the smelter."

"Sure is," Logan said with a nod of his head. "Used to be a lot of oak around here, as well as juniper and manzanita. The Mexican woodcutters have just about cleared this whole area of trees of any size. Every month they have to go farther and farther afield to find wood to keep the fires going."

Sabra's soft doe-eyed gaze swept the hillside. "It's kind of sad, isn't it? Cutting all those trees down, I mean."

Hawk's heart constricted at her soft words. Once again their minds seemed to have been linked.

"Can't stop progress," Logan said with a shrug of his shoulders. "And there's more coming. Last time I was here, there was talk of linking up with the railroad over at Benson. Folks who know say they'll have rail service through here in less than two years."

"Where's the community hall—the one where the entertainers will perform?" Sabra asked, suddenly tired of the talk of mines and smelters.

"That big two-story white building over there." Once again Logan pointed. "The library's on the ground floor. The show'll be upstairs."

"Oh, it's all so exciting. I can hardly wait until it's time to go."

Logan grinned. "Patience, Sabra. It'll be time before you know it. First, we'll get rooms at the hotel and have a bite to eat. Then you'd better rest a little this afternoon before it's time to get ready for the show."

"Rest?" Sabra protested. "But I'm not tired."

"Believe me, you'll be glad you did. The show will probably last until a late hour and you want to be at your best for it, don't you? Besides, I thought I'd take Hawk over to Brewery Gulch and show him—"

"But—"

"No buts, Sabra," Logan said with an emphatic shake of his head. "You're not going to Brewery Gulch with us, so just put that thought out of your pretty little head. It's no place for a lady."

Sabra knew better than to argue when Logan assumed that tone of voice.

And by the time they'd registered at the hotel and visited the restaurant, she had decided her brother was right. A nice bath and a few hours of rest were beginning to be most appealing. A word to the hotel clerk resulted in Sabra being chin-deep in a tin tub of hot water by the time Logan and Hawk had covered the distance from Main Street to the Golden Lily Saloon in the notorious Brewery Gulch.

Hawk could hardly believe his eyes. Row after row of saloons, restaurants, and gambling houses lined the streets of Brewery Gulch. These eventually gave way to roominghouses and a bevy of cribs—Bisbee's "tenderloin" district. Obviously Bisbee was a "man's town," the majority of its businesses catering to masculine needs. The saloons never closed, and money flowed around the clock. Gambling and drinking establishments were housed in everything from tents to ornate frame or brick structures.

Noise swirled around them like a sandstorm, rinky-tink pianos, bands, and orchestras all pouring music into the streets through the open doors of saloons in an effort to entice customers inside.

"You can find anything you want right here in Bisbee," Logan said as they paced by one saloon after another. "Everything from poker to women to liquor."

"I can well imagine," Hawk said, his restless eyes cataloguing everything. "Are we going anywhere in particular?"

"I wanted to show you the Gulch, of course, since it's known far and wide in this part of the country. And then I thought we'd stop by the Golden Lily for a while. I want to introduce you to a little lady I know. Sings like a bird, and twice as pretty. She told me an interesting tale one time . . . about Geronimo. Thought it might be a good anecdote for your book."

"Fine," Hawk agreed, sidestepping a group of rowdy miners.

They covered another block, and then Logan angled toward a wide doorway. "Well, there it is. The Golden Lily, one of Bisbee's finest sources of entertainment."

Just as Logan and Hawk reached the saloon's entrance, the swinging doors burst open, two brawling men spilling out onto the boardwalk. A ball of flailing fists and feet, they rolled into the street. A few people stopped to view the fight, but most simply ignored it and went on their way. Hawk gave the pair one last glance, then followed Logan inside.

Even at this hour of the day, a dozen men were bellied up to the long mahogany bar lining the left side of the saloon. Across the room, a scrawny little banty rooster of a fellow pounded away at an upright piano. The huge black cigar clamped between his teeth bobbed in rhythm to the lively tune he was coaxing from the instrument. The clink of poker chips contrasted with the music; over half the gaming tables in the saloon were in use.

Garbed in bright satin dresses, three ladies circulated

among the men, pouring drinks, joking, flirting. A fourth perched on the edge of an unoccupied table, cheering on a group of players, her fiery red hair like a torch in the dim smoke-filled room. She threw back her head and laughed at something one of the men said, gave him a playful slap on the shoulder, and then suddenly looked toward the front door as if she'd sensed the arrival of Logan and Hawk. Her light green eyes lit up immediately.

"Logan!"

The joyful greeting rang loud and clear, even over the rousing sound of the piano. Within seconds, the redhead had maneuvered an obstacle course of tables and had flung herself into Logan's outstretched arms.

"Della, honey," he exclaimed, holding her out from him. "H'm-Ummm. You look good enough to eat. You had any time to miss me, or have all these other fellas been keeping you too busy?"

Della planted a resounding kiss on Logan's lips. "Miss you? Why, you big galoot! Why would I do that?" But the way she threaded her arm possessively through Logan's, pressing one full breast against his bicep, belied her words. She threw a glance in Hawk's direction. "Come on in here, and get comfortable. No need to be standing around like strangers."

Logan chuckled as Della tugged gently at his arm, but with no argument he gave in to her urging. Hawk followed after them.

"Hey, Johnny. A bottle of the best for my friends, here," the redhead called as they passed the long bar on their way to an empty table.

"Right away, Della."

They'd barely gotten seated before the bartender brought a tray of glasses and a tall bottle of amber liquid. Della poured for everyone, then slid her chair closer to Logan and snuggled against his arm once more.

Hawk watched the byplay with interest. The woman was undeniably beautiful. Her eyes were the color of new spring leaves, her skin flawless and creamy white. A beauty mark hovered provocatively near the corner of her full red mouth. The low cut and tight fit of her spangled gown left little doubt as to her lush female form. But her charms moved Hawk not one iota. The memory of sun-kissed hair and deep brown eyes was too strong.

"Aren't you gonna introduce me to your friend?" Della probed, giving Logan a little prod with her elbow. Her eyes raked over Hawk, inquisitive but friendly.

"Sorry, honey. Della Maxwell, meet Sterling Hawkins—or Hawk, as his friends call him."

"Howdy, Hawk," Della said, a twinkle in her eye. "How'd you ever get hooked up with this scalawag?"

Once again, Hawk told his prepared tale. Once again, it was accepted without question.

"That's one reason we stopped by, Della," Logan explained. "Remember that story you told me . . . the one about Bill Davis' wife and Geronimo?"

"You mean when she was a kid?"

"Yeah. Tell Hawk what Bill told you."

"All right." Della took a dainty sip from her glass. "Well, must have been around seventy from what Bill said. Molly was just a kid, although she was the oldest of the four in the family. They had 'em a little place out by the San Pedro River, down toward Tombstone. They fished and cut wild grass for the calvary over at the fort for a living. Seems Molly's dad left the kids alone at home, went into Tucson after supplies. He was a long time coming back, and the kids had run out of everything. They were living off fish—whatever they could catch each day. This one particular day, they saw some Indians coming—"

"This was back when there were a lot of Apaches in the area," Logan interjected.

"Yeah." Della took time to sip her drink again. "Anyway, the kids saw these Indians coming, and one of the boys hid behind the door with a butcher knife while Molly answered it. The Indians wanted food. Molly told them she didn't have any—this was all done in sign language, you understand—but the Indians didn't believe her. They barged on in and poked through the boxes and cupboards until they saw that those kids really didn't have anything to eat but a few fish. Well, one of the Indians just looked at the kids and shook his head. He said a few words to his companions; then they all just up and left. Molly thought she'd seen the last of them."

"But she hadn't?" Hawk asked.

"Nope. About two hours later, they came back. They'd evidently been to some ranch farther down the river. They had jerky and salt and flour—quite a bit of stuff—and they gave it all to Molly."

"Great story, huh?" Logan asked. "Not exactly what folks back East would expect of Indians; they'd be more likely to think the Apaches would scalp those kids or something."

Hawk's eyes narrowed for a split second before he realized that Logan's statement was innocent—and truthful. A great many people would be reluctant to believe Indians could be so compassionate.

"Tell him the rest, honey," Logan prodded, slinging an arm around Della's creamy shoulders.

"Years later, Molly recognized the Indian who'd been responsible for bringing them the supplies. He was none other than Geronimo. Even after Geronimo broke from the reservation and ran the whole damn Army ragged while it was trying to catch him, Molly would never tolerate anyone saying a bad word about him. She was his champion from the day she recognized him."

"I think I'd like Molly. Very much."

"Say," Logan said. "Maybe I could arrange an introduction for you before we leave Bisbee. Does Bill still drop by pretty regular?"

"Sure. You know Bill, always looking for a card game to help pass the time. I imagine he'll be in over the next day or so. I'll ask him about your meeting Molly, if you want me to."

"Thanks, honey." Logan gave Della a quick hug.

Then she turned bright eyes on him. "How long are you going to be in town?"

"Two, three days. We brought Sabra with us. Got us some rooms over at the hotel."

"Oh." Della's face was crestfallen. "Then you won't be here for the show tonight?" Disappointment thickened her voice.

"Not tonight, honey. I promised Sabra we'd take her over to the community building to see that troop of

201

traveling entertainers. Say, sugar," Logan said, finally noticing Della's less than happy expression. "Don't look so sad." He tucked a long finger under her chin and tipped her face upward for a quick kiss. "That vaudeville show won't last all night. After I get Sabra back to the hotel all safe and sound, I'll be over to see you."

Della's face lit up with pleasure. "Really? Oh, Logan, I'm so glad. Tell you what, I'll trade off with Irene, get her to take the last number tonight. That'll give us a little more time . . . alone."

Logan's mouth tilted in a roguish grin. "I'm looking forward to it," he said, his voice soft and full of suggestion. Then he nuzzled Della's neck, bringing from her a squeal of delight.

Hawk silently watched this affectionate byplay, and wondered if Logan was even slightly aware that Della was in love with him. Somehow he didn't think so. She put on a good act, and was careful to hide her true feelings. Maybe she knew Logan well enough to realize he'd run like the wind at the first hint that there was more to her side of their relationship than friendship and great affection.

"Well, I do declare, if it ain't some of the folks from the fort. Small world, ain't it?"

As Julian Hobart's booming voice shattered Hawk's reverie, his head snapped around and his gaze speared the rotund little salesman who was wending his way toward their table.

"Good to see you again." Hobart snared Hawk's hand and pumped it up and down; then he reached across the table to grasp Logan's. "Always nice to see a familiar face when I'm making calls in a new territory."

Hawk knew there was nothing they could do but ask him to join them. Still, he winced inwardly as Logan voiced the invitation. The words were barely out of Powers' mouth before the little drummer plopped into a chair and its legs thumped against the wooden floor as he edged it closer to the table.

"Speaking of familiar faces," Hobart said, squinting at Hawk through his thick lenses, "I'm still working on where I've seen you before."

Not again. "I'm sure we've never met, Mr. Hobart," Hawk said quickly; yet he became more nervous as the little man continued to study him.

"I never forget a face. Nope. Sometimes it takes a while. But I'll remember one of these days. Say, you ever been in Atlanta? Spent some time there a couple of years ago."

"No," Hawk said with an emphatic shake of his head. "No, I've never been in Atlanta."

"Ummm," Julian Hobart mused. "How about St. Louis or Kansas City?"

"No. I really think you have me mixed up with someone else. I'm sure we've never met."

Suddenly it was all too much. The piano's tinny tune pounded painfully against Hawk's ears; the smoke-filled air burned his lungs, making him long for the clean, quiet purity of the open land. Across the table, Julian Hobart continued his myopic scrutiny. Hawk was aware that a fine sheen of perspiration was now covering his brow. With a quick gesture, he downed the fiery contents of his previously untouched glass.

"How about Memphis?" Ever been there?"

"No." Hawk cast a beseeching look toward Logan.

With a small shrug of his shoulders, Powers lifted one brow in amused acknowledgment of the drummer's tenacity. "Say now, Mr. Hobart. Why don't you tell Della here about all those pretty baubles you've got in your suitcases? If she's real sweet, I just might be persuaded to buy the lady a gift."

Responding as if on cue, the little salesman went right into his spiel.

Hawk breathed a sigh of relief, grateful that Logan had gained him a moment of respite. Ruefully, he noted Powers' relaxed position in the chair, one arm still casually draped over Della's shoulders. It was obvious Logan wasn't yet ready to leave.

But Hawk was. He could go back to the hotel or he could roam the town for a while. It didn't matter. But he had to get out of the Golden Lily before Julian Hobart's errant memory was sparked by a look or a word.

Hawk's chair rasped harshly against the floor as he

surged to his feet. "Logan, if you'll excuse me, I believe I'll have a look around the town. Miss Maxwell—"

"Della, please," the redhead insisted. "Any friend of Logan's is a friend of mine."

Hawk's smile was fleeting but sincere. "Della it is then. It's been a pleasure to meet you." He forced himself to turn toward the little drummer. "And, Mr. Hobart, good to see you again. I hope your continued journey is pleasant. If you'll all excuse me now . . ."

"Good to see you, too, young fella." Hobart reared back in his chair, tucking his thumbs into his vest pockets in a familiar gesture. "I'll keep on thinking. . . ."

Hawk nodded sharply. "You do that, Mr. Hobart." It was an effort to keep the desperation out of his voice. "See you back at the hotel later, Logan." With that remark, Hawk spun on his heel and strode from the saloon.

Chapter Seventeen

Sabra reveled in the intriguing pleasure of Hawk's nearness as they sat shoulder to shoulder, thigh to thigh, on the small chairs in the crowded community center. Even through his black broadcloth jacket, the heat from his body warmed her arm and sent little tingles up and down her spine. The spicy scent of his cologne teased her senses, making it difficult for her to follow the simple one-act melodrama unfolding on the makeshift stage, and within seconds of being seated she'd quite forgotten that Logan was on her other side.

The skit finally ended, capped by the enthusiastic applause of the audience. As Hawk and Sabra raised their hands to join in, the movement brought her arm into even closer contact with the hard muscular length of his. Her heart gave a peculiar little hitch as she felt him hesitate for a fraction of a second and then make an almost imperceptible shift in his chair. The movement caused his arm to rest even more firmly against hers. Joy, like sweet warm honey, flowed through her at the small reassuring gesture. Sabra's eyes never left the platform as new performers took center stage, but the gravity-defying feats of the brightly costumed jugglers barely registered on her mind. Her attention was riveted on the man beside her.

The pressure of Sabra's soft warm flesh sent Hawk's mind whirling. A thousand thoughts tumbled through his brain, all of Sabra.

That first smile at the park and the way it had warmed his heart. No reservations, no restraints. Just

205

simple acceptance.

The ball at the San Xavier . . . how beautiful she'd looked and how glad he'd been when she accepted his rather improper invitation to dance. The feel of her in his arms as they'd waltzed across the floor.

The silver music of her laughter as they'd escaped into the desert night. Sabra, eager and brave and full of delight, ready to thumb her nose at propriety just to be with him. And the utter magic of their first kiss.

The gentle touch of her finger on the scaly head of the little horned lizard as she'd instructed Hezekiah to set the creature free. Compassion and warmth and caring.

And that afternoon, after the picnic, when they were all alone. The wonderful, mind-stunning texture of her breast against his palm. How could he even begin to sort out how she'd made him feel? She hadn't acted coy or feigned sudden capitulation to unexpected ardor as some women might. She had simply given—no, *shared*—herself with him. Openly, honestly, totally. Asking nothing in return.

And what was he going to give her in return? Sorrow. He was going to take her world and turn it upside down. The death of her father would leave her alone and floundering in a world that could be cruel. Oh, she'd have Logan. But for how long? Until he found someone who could win his love or until the dangers of Army life caught up with him and a bullet, an arrow, or a knife ended his life. Then she'd have no one.

Somewhere between the jugglers and the magician, Hawk realized he couldn't do it. Somehow, in some way, Sabra Powers had inched her way into his heart and had melted the cold hatred that had filled it for so long.

There was no way in hell he could take her father's life.

A strange sense of relief seeped through Hawk, and he felt almost at peace for the first time in many years. His sadness at the thought of breaking the vow he'd made so long ago was alleviated by the certainty that his parents would understand and approve.

He could now see the foolishness of years of hatred, could realize that the lust for revenge had crippled his mind and his heart. It had taken Sabra's sweet caring to heal his awful scars. At last he could put the past behind him.

But the cost of his redemption was great . . . almost too great to bear. Still, bear it he must. Sabra had healed him, and in a few days he must leave her, return to Hawkinsville. He felt obliged to let her get on with her life since he could offer her nothing. The truth would surely destroy her feelings for him, and perhaps make her as bitter as he once had been. *That* he couldn't bear.

He knew what he was going to do—what he *had* to do.

As soon as they returned to Fort Huachuca, he'd leave on the very next stage. In the meantime, he'd wring every possible ounce of joy out of the next few days.

It would soon be all he had.

The walk back to the hotel was pleasant, the air was crisp but not cold enough to make their stroll uncomfortable. Sabra talked excitedly about the evening's entertainment, recalling this act and that as they walked, and Hawk soaked up each silver note of laughter, each breathless comment, storing these golden nuggets away in his mind.

A dark sadness flowed through him when they reached their destination, for within minutes he'd be separated from Sabra.

It had been obvious during the course of their walk that Logan was eager to get Sabra back to the hotel and tucked into her room. He'd already told Hawk he'd be back early in the morning, before his sister awoke, and when he said not a word to Sabra about his late-night rendezvous with Della Maxwell, Hawk realized Logan had no intention of telling her he was going out again. Possibly a small sop for his brotherly conscience, or reluctance to offend Sabra's sensibilities with the knowledge that he was headed for a tryst.

In far too short a time, they were in the upstairs hall of the hotel. Sabra, reluctant for the night to end, lingered outside her door, offering a few final remarks about the play and the variety of entertainment offered afterwards. She again said how enjoyable the evening had been, and gently badgered Logan about his plans for the next day.

Hawk was just as opposed to parting as Sabra, but he could think of no logical way to prolong the evening. Sabra appeared oblivious to her brother's agitation, although Logan had spent the last five minutes shifting from one foot to the other and his answers to his sister's questions had become shorter and shorter.

Hawk finally took pity on his friend. Disinclined though he was to abandon Sabra's company, he stepped toward the door to his room. Logan took advantage of the gesture and quickly inserted Sabra's key in the lock, gave it a turn, and then pushed the door open.

"Well, sweet dreams, sis," he said with a grin, propelling her gently toward the open doorway. "Get a good night's sleep. There'll be lots of things to do tomorrow. And, if you're good, we might even go see the show again tomorrow night."

"Really?" Sabra stopped, hesitating just outside her room, her face aglow. "That would be wonderful."

Logan lightly nudged her again. "Lock your door," he admonished sternly.

"I will."

Sabra rose on tiptoe to place a kiss on her brother's cheek and then slipped through the door, turning at the very last second to call good night to Hawk and gift him with one final smile.

Meanwhile, Logan had hurried to the door to his room and was fumbling with the lock. The tumblers gave way with a loud click. Having no intention of going inside, he simply paused in the doorway, hand upon the knob, until Sabra obediently closed her door. As soon as he heard her turn the key on her side of the door, he pulled his own shut again.

"See you in the morning," he whispered to Hawk,

repocketing his key.

"Sure. See you then." A grin wreathed Hawk's face at the ridiculous sight of Logan easing his way down the hall on tiptoe so Sabra wouldn't suspect his departure.

As Powers rounded the corner of the stairwell, Hawk let out a sigh and stepped inside his room. The door snapped shut, and for a long moment Hawk stood, his back against the smooth wooden panel, and stared bleakly at the gloomy interior. Finally, he pushed away from the door and strode purposefully to the table, bending down to light the lantern.

The springs of the big double bed creaked under his weight as he sat down to jerk his boots off. They fell to the floor with dull thuds. Rising once again, Hawk paced the room, discarding articles of clothing as he went. His coat was placed on the back of a chair, his shirt on the cross-stitched seat cushion. Still clad in trousers, he threw himself across the bed, and clasped his hands behind his head.

On the other side of the wall, Sabra slipped out of her russet-colored gown and petticoats, and hung them in the cavernous wardrobe. One by one she undid the ribbon knots on her chemise. The ties of her pantaloons were freed next, and the garment slid downward to puddle around her feet alongside the chemise until she scooped both up and stuffed them in her traveling bag.

Naked, she padded across the room, retrieved her white dimity nightdress from the dresser and slipped it over her head. The gossamer cotton gown extended almost to the floor, barely allowing Sabra's toes to peek from under its full ruffle.

For some time Sabra sat before the mirrored dressing table, pulling her silver-backed brush through long curls. The gentle motion reminded her of that afternoon on the blanket, the feel of Hawk's long fingers stroking through her hair. The brush hung motionless as she remembered the taste of his mouth upon hers, and a puff of heat erupted in the pit of her stomach, a tingly warmth that spread inch by inch through her body.

With a sigh Sabra abandoned the brush on the dresser and pattered to the bed. Lying across it on her stomach, chin in her hands, she gazed out the window, time passing as she watched wisps of lacy cloud float across the silver face of the moon.

As she did so, something new and sweet and wonderful blossomed inside her—a certain knowledge, a total acceptance of her love for Sterling Hawkins.

He was the man she wanted to spend the rest of her life with. No doubt about it.

Oh, she knew there were obstacles. Her father, for one. And the fact that Hawk was scheduled to leave Fort Huachuca in a week or so. But she was serenely positive those complications could be overcome.

Fate, destiny . . . call it whatever you will. Some magic had brought him to the Arizona Territory. They had to meet in this lifetime.

It was meant to be. As simple as that.

There was just one other small problem to consider. She sensed something in Hawk . . . a hesitation, a fear. Whatever it was, it held him back, kept them separated; and it put a halt to the master plan that had brought them together.

Sabra nibbled at her bottom lip as she tried to unravel that unknown element. She knew in her heart, knew without a doubt, that he cared for her. It showed every time he looked at her, every time he touched her. And whatever it was, whatever was holding him back, they could overcome it. She just had to let him know how she felt.

A gasp slipped from her lips. Could that be it? Could it really be that he was just not sure of how she felt?

Could that be? She was positive she hadn't misread his feelings. How could he not know hers?

With a puzzled frown Sabra rolled on to her back. The thought continued to pluck at her mind. Maybe it wasn't anybody's fault. Maybe men simply weren't as perceptive about such things.

Why did everything have to be so confusing? How much easier the mysteries of life must be if you have a mother to talk to. Suddenly Sabra missed her mother very much. Not that Gramma hadn't been sweet and loving. But she'd been so old-fashioned and timid when it came to such matters. Sabra had certainly gained no clues about man-woman things from her. And her girl friends back East, they'd all been as innocent and ignorant as she. Oh, they'd done a great deal of speculating, but that was all it had been, guesswork.

She desperately needed someone to talk to, someone who might tell her what to do, what to say, how to convince Hawk to stay. But who?

Who indeed? a small inner voice teased. Who had always been there for her? Who had listened to her dreams and fears during her younger years? Who had soothed away her nightmares and answered a million and one questions?

Logan. Always Logan. Why had she waited so long to confide in him? He'd listen without censure. He'd understand—and help.

In the room next door, Hawk once again changed position. He'd wallowed and rolled and turned until the linens of the bed were rumpled, for during the last hour he'd tormented himself with thoughts of Sabra.

Wondering if she were still awake.

Thinking how her hair would look spread across the pristine white of the pillow slip.

Did she sleep with the covers tucked clear to her chin? Or did she kick them to the bottom of the bed as he sometimes did?

Was the moon as bright and beautiful from her window? Was its silvery light touching her, ghosting over the soft curve of her shoulder, feathering across the lush fullness of her breast? . . .

"Dammit!"

Hawk exploded from the bed. There'd be no sleep for him that night, not with Sabra on the other side of that wall. He might as well go back to Brewery Gulch. There just might be enough whiskey in this town to ease his frustration.

He stopped long enough to shove his feet into his boots and thrust his arms into the sleeves of his wrinkled shirt. Ignoring the buttons, he grabbed up his coat, stormed across the floor, and reached for the doorknob.

Sabra slipped from her bed and padded quickly across the floor to the wardrobe. Opening it, she grabbed her wrapper. She slid her arms into the sleeves, but in her eagerness to talk with Logan neglected to tie the dangling sash.

Quick as a wink, she went in to the hallway, stopping only long enough to peer up and down it. *Thank goodness. Not a soul in sight.* Being ever so quiet Sabra pulled her door shut and scurried down the hall to Logan's room.

Tap, tap, tap. her knuckles softly grazed the wood.

"Logan," she whispered, poking her tip-tilted nose toward the crack in the doorframe. "Logan, it's me. Are you asleep?"

"He's gone."

The sudden creak of Hawk's door and the unexpected sound of his voice startled Sabra. She gave a little gasp of surprise, then whirled to face him, delight swiftly replacing the alarm in her eyes.

"I'm sorry," Hawk said. "I didn't mean to frighten you." *Sweet heaven, but she's beautiful.*

Her gown and wrapper hugged each womanly curve, the delicate cotton fabric barely concealing the delights that lay beneath. And her hair hung long and loose, one curl lying intimately against her breast, which rose and fell with each breath.

"I . . . I'm not frightened," Sabra said with a small self-conscious smile. "I just didn't expect anyone else to be up at this late hour." *He's so handsome, it makes my heart ache just to look at him.* Hawk's shirt hung open, bracketing a strip of bare bronze chest so enticing that Sabra's mouth went dry. Invisible bonds tightened, making it hard for her to breathe. Unknowingly, she took a small step toward him, then another.

"Do you need something? Maybe I can help." Concern filled Hawk's eyes, and he abandoned his position in the open doorway, stepping into the hall. *Tell me. What do you want, Sabra? Do you want the moon? The stars? Just tell me. I'll get them for you.*

"I . . . I was just going to talk to Logan about . . . something." *Yes, you can help. Take me in your arms. Make this crazy ache disappear.* Her feet moved on their own, taking her closer to him.

"Logan went back to . . . uh . . . he went to visit a friend for a while. Did you need him for something important? I could get him for you." *I need you. I need you more than life itself. Leaving you will be the hardest thing I'll ever do.*

"It wasn't important." *But you're important . . . the most important thing in my life.* Her gaze clung to his; and she felt she was drowning in the deep blue depths of his eyes.

"Are you sure?" He watched the tiny pulsebeat at the base of her throat, caught by a spell as old as time. *Go back, Sabra. Go back. Lock yourself away behind that door while I can still stop myself.*

"Sure?" she repeated, her voice dulcet, almost breathless. *I'm sure I belong with you. I'm sure there's nothing else I want but to feel your arms around me.* "Yes, I'm sure."

The last two steps brought her within touching distance. Her lashes shuttered downward, causing fan-shaped shadows on the soft velvet of her cheeks. Then she raised her eyes to his, eyes so dark with emotion that pupil and iris seemed one and the same.

"Would . . ."—a blush climbed up her throat, stained her cheeks palest rose—" . . . would you mind very much if I asked you to kiss me good night?"

Hawk's groan was a deep, echoing rumble in his chest. His arms instantly went about her, molding her soft curves to the hard lines of his body, and he captured her lips, glorying in the taste and texture of her mouth.

Sabra's hands slid upward, her hands caressing the back of his neck, stroking the thick shock of hair that nestled against it. Then her fingers tangled in those dark locks, urging him closer and closer still, binding him to her.

His hands skimmed over her back, across her ribs, and she whimpered, ever so softly, when his fingers grazed the sweet swell of a breast.

A shift of weight. A step here. A half-turn there. Neither knew who made the first move or how they maneuvered the few steps that took them from the hallway to the inside of Hawk's room.

Suddenly, magically, they were all alone, the darkness cradling them, the door shut against the rest of the world.

"Sabra, Sabra," he murmured against mouth. "So sweet, so soft."

"Hold me, Hawk, hold me. Tighter." Her voice was a satin whisper in the dark.

With an answering moan, Hawk tilted Sabra against him, cupping the gentle curve of her buttocks, pulling her up hard against the throbbing ache of his man-hood. Then, unaware of anything but the desperate need to touch her, feel her next to him, he bent and slid his arm under her legs. Scooping her up, he cra-dled her against his chest as he strode across the room. Then he set her on the bed.

It was the dip of the mattress, the slight squeaking protest of the springs that brought a moment of sanity back to Hawk's desire-muddled brain. He snatched his hands away and sank down on the edge of the bed, his back toward Sabra.

His long fingers ravaged his hair, then he pressed the heels of his palms against his burning eyes. When he finally spoke, his voice was ragged, harsh. "Oh, God, Sabra. This is madness."

She came to her knees to kneel behind him, her cheek pressed to his back, her arms slipping around to lock gently against his chest. The utter sweetness of the gesture nearly broke Hawk's heart.

He shifted, bending his leg and turning so he could face Sabra, and his hands grasped the tender flesh of her arms, giving her a little shake. Her head tilted back, the cascade of long blond curls shimmering like molten gold in the moonlight.

"This has got to stop," Hawk beseeched. "I don't deserve . . . I mean . . . Oh, lord, you don't understand. You don't know."

Her gaze never wavered. Her words were rose-petal soft but full of conviction. "I know everything that's important. I know I've never felt like this before in my life, that you're the only man who'll ever make me feel this way."

Hawk froze at her words. A muscle ticked at the corner of his jaw as he hung between heaven and hell. Haunted, hopeful, his eyes searched hers, wanting to believe she knew what she was doing, wanting to believe they had a chance, wanting to believe in miracles.

Chapter Eighteen

Time ticked by as Hawk wrestled with himself. It could have been seconds, minutes, hours. He never knew how long. Later, much later, he wasn't sure whether he would ever have come to a decision, would ever have made the first move. But, once again, Sabra gave of herself.

She said not a word, simply raised one small hand and placed her palm against his cheek. Hawk's breath caught in his chest, his heart trying to hammer its way to freedom. He tilted his head a fraction, moving it back and forth, a mere millimeter each way, stroking his cheek against the warmth of her hand, relishing the feel of her fingertips against his temple, against the curve of his jaw. Then, turning his head, he pressed a kiss into Sabra's palm, his lips lingering against her sweet flesh.

Cloaked in silence, they sat facing each other on the bed, suffused in the moon's luminescence, their bodies and faces painted with velvety sable shadows and splashes of shimmery silver, each savoring the sheer breathtaking anticipation of what was to come.

Finally, with fingers that trembled, Hawk reached out and caught the edges of Sabra's wrapper, easing the soft cotton fabric from her shoulders. Her arms slipped free, and the robe slid forgotten to the floor, leaving her in a gossamer gown that barely veiled the temptations of her body—pristine white, virginal, but at the same time utterly provocative. The lace-bedecked neckline swept low across the lush swell of her bosom, and

216

narrow straps left creamy shoulders and softly rounded upper arms bare. She looked like some sort of angel, all shining and silver and alabaster in the captured moonglow.

With one swift movement, Hawk shed his shirt, tossing it aside to reveal muscles bunching under smooth coppery skin.

Tremulously he reached out and brushed his knuckles across the beguiling swell of Sabra's breast, gently, reverently. His gaze lifted, meeting eyes as dark as midnight. She smiled, a soft, small, utterly beatific smile, and his heart soared with a joy he'd never known. Then she raised her hand, trailing fingertips over the hard bulge of shoulder muscle, tracing the firm ridges of sinew that undulated down Hawk's arm.

Once again his hands clasped her shoulders, but this time they drew her toward him.

Bracing her hands gently on his hard thighs, his flesh quivering under her touch, Sabra leaned into him, tilting her face, parting her lips, waiting breathlessly for the alluring touch of his mouth.

It came none too soon, his lips capturing hers, warm and moist and possessive. His tongue teased at the edges of her mouth, feathered across small pearly teeth, stroked the soft silken inner lining until she whimpered with delight.

Hawk's tongue danced with hers, touching, tasting, caressing, coaxing until Sabra's responded in kind. Her shy duplication of his moves evoked a low moan from him.

With gentle pressure he shifted Sabra, pulling her toward him, turning her so she lay cuddled in his lap, her hip pressed hard against the firm evidence of his desire. His mouth stayed locked to hers while one trembling hand fumbled at the tiny pearl buttons at the front of her gown.

One by one they came free.

Brushing the fabric aside, he cupped the lush mound of her breast, glorying in the velvet texture of her skin, the heat of her pearled nipple against his palm. Beneath his fingertips he could feel the staccato beat of her heart. White-hot desire washed through him as Sabra moaned and arched against his hand.

He relinquished her lips to dust tiny kisses across the line of her jaw, and her head fell back against the strong bend of his shoulder, in a silent plea for more. A dozen kisses were sprinkled down the delicate curve of her throat before his tongue explored the soft purple-shadowed hollow at its base.

Gently he cradled her, curling her body against the solid haven of his chest. Then his hand dipped to the hem of the gown bunched about her knees, stealing beneath, ghosting up the curve of her calf, gliding over the sensitive flesh at the back of her thigh, gently squeezing the soft mound of her derrière.

"Sweet heaven," Hawk whispered against Sabra's lips, emotion congesting his throat. "I can't believe this is happening. You feel like satin, so soft, so warm. I can't get enough of you. I want to brand every inch of your body with my touch, savor every line and curve—mark you as mine. Only mine."

"Yes, oh yes," Sabra murmured.

Her every nerve-ending tingled at Hawk's touch, rejoiced at his honeyed words. And when his fingers tiptoed over the gentle curve of her hip to skim toward the heart of her womanhood, a surge of glorious heat exploded deep within her, the intoxicating flames leaping higher and higher, coursing through her veins like a prairie fire.

Suddenly, Hawk's fingers stilled, lingering against the silken flesh of Sabra's stomach. With a groan of despair, he buried his face in the pale golden curls at the side of her neck.

"Ah, Sabra, Sabra. Sweet love. I wish you knew how very much I care, how special you are to me. I wish I could be sure you'd understand . . . I couldn't bear it if you were sorry—"

"Hush," she said, gently pressing her fingers against his mouth, stilling his agonized voice. "I'll never be sorry. I couldn't be."

Her soft, loving words dissolved the last barrier of restraint.

"I love you," Hawk whispered. "Never, never forget that. Promise me, no matter what happens, you'll never forget that I love you."

"I promise," she answered, quite positive that she'd never have reason to doubt his love.

Ever so tenderly, Hawk brought her upright, drew her gown over her head before easing her down among the tumbled pillows. Then with one powerful lunge, he rose from the bed, his hands already at the fastenings of his trousers. A flick of the wrist, a small bend, a tug at the fabric, and his pants fell to the floor to nestle atop Sabra's discarded garments.

At last Hawk stood straight and proud before her, his darkly gold skin cloaked only in silver incandescence.

Sabra's heart leaped into her throat at his magnificence, and her hungry eyes roamed his tall, beautifully proportioned form, savoring every masculine inch of him.

Massive shoulders.

Strong arms that could hold her with unbelievable tenderness.

A broad chest, underlaid with muscles that rippled with each lissome movement.

Narrow waist and flat stomach.

Slim hips that cradled the unashamed evidence of his desire.

Long, hard legs, roped with sinews.

His beauty took her breath away.

Moonlight flowed and rippled, chasing shadows over copper planes and bulging muscles, as Hawk bent one leg and placed his knee on the edge of the bed. Then, in one fluid movement, he lay side by side with Sabra, her head cradled on his shoulder.

For a long ponderous moment, they remained still, staring at each other, marveling at the joy of simply being together. But soon desire overcame the final small shreds of shyness.

Fingertips traced gentle curves and quivering muscles.

Mouths touched and tasted.

Tongues dueled, eliciting soft moans of pleasure.

Hawk's firm muscular leg slid between satin thighs,

hooked over Sabra's calf and snugged her closer.

A long sigh of contentment escaped Sabra's parted lips as the mighty wall of Hawk's chest pressed against the ultra sensitive skin of her breasts. Her nipples hardened, became tight knots of excitement that responded to every subtle move, the tiniest amounts of pressure, the slightest rasp of flesh upon flesh.

And just when she thought that nothing could feel any better, Hawk dipped his head, brushing moist airy kisses across the slope of her breasts. Her fingers tangled in his hair, and his name rode the sigh that slipped from her lips.

Hawk feasted on the glorious sight of Sabra naked beneath him, her breasts high, rounded, taut, tipped with palest coral. She felt like velvet and tasted like honeyed wine.

Lovingly, his tongue laved the moon-kissed areola of each breast, then flicked the pouty nipples. Once again her fingers tightened in his hair, chaining him to her.

At last, when she thought she would die from the want of him, his lips closed over one proffered bud and he took the sweet flesh into the hot moistness of his mouth. Desire cavorted in the pit of her stomach, skipped from nerve to nerve as he gently suckled.

The feelings he elicited were exquisite. Shivers of delight danced and capered in the blood that raced through Sabra's veins. Shards of white-hot rapture exploded in the pit of her stomach. But these sensations seemed pale shadows of feelings when a gentle hand slipped between their bodies to fondle the flaxen curls at the apex of her thighs.

As Hawk stroked the silken petals of her womanhood, Sabra opened to him like a flower seeking the sun. Ever so gently, one long finger probed within the dewy blossom, finding the secret bud, stroking, teasing, caressing until she quivered with passion.

Then, amidst whispered words of love and desire, and the dusting of a thousand kisses on lips, shoulders, throat, and breasts, Hawk bracketed his hands on either side of Sabra's shoulders and lowered his long, hard body atop hers, easing her legs apart with his powerful thighs.

She eagerly accepted his weight, reveling in the feel of his hard strong body, and lifted her hips to meet him as the rigid shaft of his desire probed at the roseate entrance to her inner core of wanting.

Hawk's mouth captured Sabra's in a searing kiss as his body sank into hers, catching the soft cry of pain that rang forth as he made her his.

"It's all right, my love," he whispered against her lips, each word a tiny caress of warm breath against her heated flesh. "It's over. It won't hurt anymore. I promise."

Convulsively, her arms tightened around his neck, her legs lifted to wrap around his, and she met him in a rhythm as bright and new as their love, as old as time itself.

Ever so gently, Hawk readjusted his weight. Slipping his hands under Sabra's buttocks, he clutched her soft warm flesh, drawing her upward, tighter, closer, as he stroked her silken recesses with long, rapturous strokes. Their breaths came in short, harsh rasps as they rode a timeless wave of passion.

And when the storm was over, when they surrendered the stars and sank back to earth, their bodies sheened with the urgency of their merging and replete with satisfaction, Hawk drew a rumpled sheet over them and enfolded Sabra in his arms.

She breathed a small sigh of contentment, and snuggled closer to his warmth. "I love you," she whispered, pressing one last kiss against his chest before her eyes closed and she drifted into sweet dream-filled sleep.

Hawk lay awake for a long time, savoring the gentle caress of Sabra's slow, even breathing against his chest, relishing the exquisite feel of silken tresses against his cheek, and glorying in the sweet female scent, the warmth that emanated from the marvelous, giving woman in his arms.

And as he held her, the words to a song his mother used to sing rang in his memory.

He had thought of it as his childhood lullaby, but now he remembered the husky tone of his mother's voice, the gentle delivery of the words, the way her bright blue eyes had always found her husband as she'd sat beside their son and sung him to sleep, and he knew the truth. It had been an Indian love song, learned and sung for the man who'd won her heart.

As Hawk drifted into sweet slumber, the melody and the words echoed in his mind and in his heart.

How, then, can I tell you of my love? Strong as the eagle, soft as the dove. Patient as the pine tree that stands in the sun, and whispers to the wind . . . you are the one.

An insistent knock at his door jerked Hawk from deep slumber. For a moment he panicked, his first instinct to protect Sabra from discovery, but in the next second, a great gasp of relief escaped his lips and he fell back against the pillows. He'd remembered waking before dawn and carrying Sabra back to her room.

It had been hard to leave her, especially when she'd sleepily protested. But he'd known it was necessary. And the sound of Logan's voice, calling from the other side of his door, was proof positive.

Hawk flung back the covers, shoved his legs into his trousers, and padded barefoot to the door.

"Hey," Logan said brightly when Hawk's door finally creaked open, his face wreathed in his usual devil-may-care smile. "You mean to tell me you're still asleep on this glorious morning? Aren't you ready for some breakfast? I know I am. Need to rebuild my strength." He waggled his eyebrows comically, and Hawk had to laugh.

"Sure. Come on in while I get my clothes on."

Hawk swung the door wide, and Logan sauntered in. "Well, I hope you slept well," he said.

"Uh . . . sure." Hawk stumbled over the words. What would Logan think if he knew just how little sleeping Hawk had done?

Even after he'd made sure Sabra was tucked in her own bed safe and sound, Hawk had lain awake for a long time, his mind once again raking through the bevy of complications facing them. But this time the gift of Sabra's sweet love had made it easy for Hawk to convince himself that those problems could be solved. How and when that would be done, his tired mind hadn't yet dealt with. When he'd finally fallen asleep, his nose had been buried in the pillow that still held Sabra's scent.

He didn't have all the answers. He just knew that somehow—some way—he'd find the right time, the right way to tell her the truth.

And he had to believe that their love could withstand the revelation.

While Hawk washed and brushed and dressed, Logan prattled on. Hawk barely listened, simply murmured an occasional "mmm" in response during a momentary pause. It took the mention of Sabra's name to drag his attention back to the matters at hand.

"Oh," Hawk said. "Is she awake yet?"

"Barely," Logan answered with a chuckle. "She was almost as bad as you about sleeping in."

Hawk averted his face at Logan's innocent comment, gratefully turning his attention to dragging tumbled covers from the floor in search of his discarded boots. By the time he had the boots on, he'd regained a modicum of composure.

"Well, I'm ready."

"Great." Logan unfolded his long length from the chair he'd been perched on. "Sabra said she'd meet us in the dining room in a few minutes. Myself, I'm ready for a hot cup of coffee. How about you?"

"Uh . . . sure. Sounds good. Let's go."

Hawk wasted no time in exiting the memory-filled room, Logan shadowing him down the stairs and across the dining room to a corner table. Steaming cups of coffee were delivered, and Hawk had just hoisted his, the tempting aroma teasing his nose, when Sabra entered the door and paused to scan the room.

Hawk's heart melted and pooled in the pit of his stomach. She'd never looked more beautiful. A becoming flush tinted her face, and the sparkle in her eyes when she caught sight of them rivaled heaven's own stars. The smile that curved her lips washed over Hawk like warm sunshine.

Heads turned to deliver appreciative glances as Sabra wove her way between tables to join them, her apricot-colored gown swaying with each graceful step. As if aware of Hawk's penchant for seeing her long curls cascading down her back, she'd caught her hair up at the sides with matching ribbons. Desire bloomed as Hawk remembered twining his fingers in those thick golden locks only hours ago.

He and Logan rose as Sabra approached, and Hawk quickly stepped to the side of the table and pulled out her chair so she could be seated. Her shoulders brushed against his knuckles as she settled herself against the back of the chair, and he fought the temptation to caress the tender flesh of her neck.

Midst a bevy of good-morning greetings, Hawk reclaimed his chair and raised his wary gaze to hers, suddenly afraid of what he might read in her eyes. Had the harsh morning brought a sense of shame about what had happened between them? Was she sorry?

Sabra's eyes met his across the table. They were full of love and joy and utter contentment, and Hawk breathed a silent prayer of thanks. Then, afraid that Logan might read something in their glance, he forced his attention back to his coffee. Luckily Logan was too caught up in his own good mood to pay much attention to the sizzling glance exchanged by Hawk and Sabra.

When breakfast was finished, the trio decided to take a walking tour of the small town. The weather was beautiful, the sun even brighter than usual in a cloudless periwinkle sky . . . or so the lovers thought.

They spent the morning ambling slowly, aimlessly about Bisbee, poking into this store or that, standing in awe before the gaping entrance of the Glory Hole mine, exclaiming in amazement at the precarious positions of the cabins perched on the side of the mountain.

"I hear tell," Logan recounted with a chuckle, "that the local authorities use the stairs to judge the degree of a man's intoxication. If a man can negotiate these steep steps and make it up to his house, he's allowed to do so. If he's too potted to make it, off to jail he goes."

The story served to further pique Sabra's interest in the infamous Brewery Gulch, and Logan finally relented enough to allow her a quick peek down the length of the notorious street, from a safe distance, of course.

Along the way there were a hundred opportunities for touching, and Sabra and Hawk took advantage of every one of them. She never stepped off a boardwalk without tucking her hand securely in the crook of Hawk's arm for just a moment, and as they dodged miners on the crowded walkways, Hawk's hand was ever at the small of her back, exerting a gentle guiding pressure.

In a dry-goods store Sabra fell in love with a saucy little straw bonnet, and Hawk insisted that she have it. Betwixt half-hearted refusals, he placed it on her bright golden curls, his fingers lingering overlong to savor the silken texture of her skin as he tied the pert blue satin ribbon beneath her chin.

A brief stop for a late midday meal offered even more possibilities. Hawk's leather boot just happened to creep forward until it nudged the toe of Sabra's slipper. Knees bumped deliciously. Fingers brushed during the passing of dishes. And the air fairly crackled as a million and one wonderful, heart-slowing, heat-building glances were exchanged.

And all the while they ached for the opportunity to be alone again.

"Well, what do you want to do now?" Logan asked as they exited the restaurant. "We've got a couple of hours left before we should go back to the hotel to get ready for tonight."

Sabra was just about to answer when a woman's voice broke in.

"Logan! I'm so glad I found you. And Hawk. Wait till you hear the news I have for you."

Sabra bristled at the familiarity of the woman's tone, and her gaze raked the stranger hurrying toward them. *Who is that? And that hair! I never saw hair quite that color before.*

"Della," Logan said, a grin tilting his mouth. "What are you doing up so early?"

"Taking care of Hawk, that's what," she answered with a saucy toss of her red curls.

Sabra's mouth thinned to a hard line. The woman was dressed well enough, the material of her frock obviously expensive, the lines well cut and fashionable. But the color was just a shade on the loud side for a morning dress. And her face . . . *Why, that's makeup!* Sabra realized with a start. She didn't know anyone who painted her cheeks and lips or highlighted her eyes in such a manner.

Who *was* this woman and what was she to Hawk? Unconsciously, Sabra moved a few paces closer to him.

Della, experienced in the nuances and subtleties of human nature, recognized Sabra's reaction for what it was. Jealousy. Quickly, she sought a way to defuse the situation.

Stepping to Logan's side, she slipped her hand through the crook of his arm and gifted him with a glittering smile before turning back to Sabra. "You must be Logan's sister. He's told me so much about you."

"Wha—? Uh . . . yes. Yes, I am," Sabra stammered, relief sweeping through her as she instantly realized that her suspicions had been unfounded. Whoever this woman was, she was interested in Logan, not Hawk.

"Sabra, this is Della Maxwell, a . . . a friend of mine."

"How do you do, Miss Maxwell," Sabra said, noting the suddenly sheepish look on her brother's face. For some odd reason it called to mind the time he'd been caught with a sticky tablespoon and an almost-empty quart jar of Gramma's prized orange marmalade.

"I'm sorry to accost you like this, but Bill Davis dropped by a while ago. He was sure Molly would be happy to talk with Hawk. He said to just drop by anytime this afternoon. I thought you'd want to know."

Hawk expressed his thanks, though he was chagrined that it had taken him a minute to connect the names with the story Della had told at the Golden Lily. He intended to keep this unexpected appointment; it was all part of maintaining his cover.

Meanwhile, Logan's eyes had brightened at Della's statement. If Hawk and Sabra spent the afternoon visiting with Molly Davis, he would be free to spend a little additional time with Della. The opportunity was simply too tempting to pass up.

Gathering his courage, Logan made his suggestion. The words had barely left his mouth when Della slipped him a wicked little wink, acknowledging that she knew full well what he had in mind and was looking forward to it. Hawk and Sabra quickly agreed to the plan. In fact, their capitulation had proven almost too easy. . . .

Nah, Logan thought with a little shake of his head, quickly shrugging the idea away. He was too intent on covering up his own objective to question whether Sabra and Hawk might have motives of their own.

After Della gave Hawk directions to the Davis house, Logan, acting the part of a properly mannered gentleman, graciously offered to escort her home. It was all so simple. Within a few minutes Hawk and Sabra were headed up the hill to Molly's house, and Logan and Della were on their way back to the Golden Lily for an afternoon romp.

Chapter Nineteen

Molly Davis was a delight. Hawk had knocked at her door with the thought of completing the "interview" as fast as possible and then escaping, but under the on-slaught of Molly's charm his intention melted as fast as snow on the desert.

Small, lovely, and imbued with a sparkling vitality, Molly insisted they stay to share tea and cake with her. One cup became two, then three, as Molly regaled them with tales of her childhood, a fascinating potpourri of events.

She'd spent her younger years in the wilderness on the river banks of the San Pedro, had witnessed the birth of the infamous town of Tombstone, had rubbed shoulders with such folks as Wyatt Earp and Doc Holi-day and Bat Masterson. Her plentiful tales were vivid, alive with color and texture, and before he quite knew what was happening, Hawk was as caught up as Sabra in Molly's narration. She told of roaming the high mountain passes as a child, of swimming in hidden spring pools and exploring secret caves, of caring for her younger brothers and sister while her father searched for the elusive promise of silver.

From the very first moment, something about Molly put Hawk totally at ease. Outwardly, in direct contra-diction to her frontier upbringing, she was very much the eloquent lady. Clad in a fashionable gown of forest green velvet, her long hair coiled demurely at the back of her neck, she could have been a gently raised South-erner pouring afternoon tea on a plantation veranda.

The first clue to the "real" Molly was the telltale sparkle of mischief in her eyes. As the afternoon passed, Hawk began to suspect that beneath that polished veneer lay a person of far greater substance than most people he'd met. His conviction grew stronger with each passing hour.

As Hawk glimpsed more and more evidence of her quick wit and rich sense of humor, he became convinced that Molly Davis was one of the special ones—a woman of determination and ambition, who had a great passion for life and all it had to offer, and who was utterly loyal to the people lucky enough to gain her friendship or her love.

Her steadfastness was never more evident than when she recounted the Geronimo story for Sabra. Nothing the Apache warrior had done in his later life, none of the rumors or reported episodes of cruelty on his part, could shake her belief in his better nature.

"But how do you account for all the terrible stories that surfaced about Geronimo during that fiasco with the Army?" Hawk asked Molly, curious as to how she could maintain her loyalty in the face of such condemning evidence.

"A great many people seemed to believe him guilty of those crimes," Sabra said. "Wouldn't that prove there's a bit of truth to those stories?"

Molly gave an emphatic shake of her head, and her chin rose an inch. "Is it truly necessary to remind you that most of those people had never met the man, had never spent even one minute with him? In my opinion, their judgments were all too frequently based on circumstantial evidence and hearsay."

Sabra's brow furrowed at that disturbing thought.

Molly continued. "I would also say that they had not the slightest inkling of what might have precipitated some of those actions."

"You're right about that, of course," Hawk was quick to agree. "A good number of the people who wrote those stories and newspaper articles had never even been west of the Mississippi."

"Precisely. And if given the opportunity, I would love

to ask them how they could possibly lay blame on a man who struck out at those who came to steal the land of his birth, the land his forefathers had roamed for countless generations." Molly's eyes took on a hard, proud glint.

I just bet you'd do it, too, Hawk thought, the corner of his mouth tilting upward as he listened to the feisty little woman.

"Would we not defend our homes against any such aggressors? Wouldn't you do anything you could to protect your way of life, your home, your children?" Molly aimed the words at Sabra, her gentle gaze defiant.

Sabra's cup clattered against the saucer, and she turned wide startled eyes on Molly, her mind grappling with a question she'd never before considered.

"Yes, of course . . . I'm sure I would," she finally responded, her words coming slowly, as if she were still contemplating the portent of what Molly had said. "I . . . I never quite thought of what happened—I mean, all the terrible things that took place between Indians and whites—in quite that way."

Molly's bright eyes probed Sabra's. "If *we* would attempt to protect the things and people precious to us, why should the Indian be blamed and condemned for doing the exact same thing?"

Sabra simply shook her head.

Molly's voice softened. "We should strive to remember that there are always two sides to a story. People forget that, more often than not, there's a right and there's a wrong, on *both* sides."

Hawk smiled a gentle smile. "You're very brave to voice such compassion for a people much maligned. I'm afraid there are many who would not approve."

Molly's determined little chin lifted higher still. "I never put much stock in what other people approved or disapproved. I live my life according to the dictates of my heart. And I don't believe it's bravery, or sympathy, or anything like that. It's simply that, because of my mother, I understand a little bit of how they might feel. You see, I'm half-Navajo myself."

At first Hawk was stunned by Molly's revelation, but within minutes he realized he should have guessed in spite of the few visible clues. Her skin was a soft golden tone and her hair a rich warm brown, but Molly Davis evidently favored her white father. It was her personality that should have alerted Hawk. Her inner strength, proud carriage, inquisitive nature, and devotion to her family—the childhood one and the one she'd cared for with her beloved husband Bill. These traits were reminiscent of the people he'd known many years ago in his father's village.

The clock over the mantel struck the hour, dragging Hawk back to the present. He frowned as he noted how late it was, experiencing a flash of regret that there would be no opportunity to delve any deeper into the gentle magic that was Molly Davis.

He longed to ask her how she'd managed to weather the circumstances of her birth and maintain such a marvelous attitude. What had enabled her to become so self-assured, so content with herself and her lot in life? Was it possible that the enduring love she shared with Bill Davis was the answer?

Hawk's gaze went to Sabra. She'd had an impact on him from the first moment he'd seen her. Was she the rhyme and reason behind this whole crazy situation? Was Sabra the key to the end of the crooked, confusing path he'd been following? Had the spirits seen fit to place him here so that her love could be the talisman that would at last provide his salvation?

Troubling questions still whirling through his mind, Hawk felt Molly's intent gaze on him. He turned his head and their eyes met and held for a long time. Was he being foolish, was he grasping at will-o'-the-wisp hopes, or was there really a message of some sort in Molly's eyes?

Almost sadly Hawk realized he'd never know for sure.

The hour was late and, even if it hadn't been, it would have been impossible with Sabra in attendance to discuss the issues weighing so heavily on his mind. Logan was probably already at the hotel, waiting for them and wondering where they were. And tomorrow they were returning to Fort Huachuca. There'd be no opportunity to talk with Molly again.

With great reluctance, Hawk reminded Sabra that they'd best be on their way.

"I'm so glad you dropped by," Molly said as she escorted them to the door. "The afternoon has passed much too fast. I wish we'd had more time to talk."

"So do I," Hawk said, his words utterly sincere.

"I feel that I've made two new friends this day." As if to emphasize the truth of her statement, Molly gave Sabra a warm hug. "I hope we have the opportunity to meet again someday."

"That would be lovely," Sabra agreed. "Thank you so much. For everything."

"And you," Molly said, tilting her head to gaze up at Hawk with shrewd brown eyes. One small hand reached out and lay warm against his arm for just a moment. "I hope circumstances go well for you."

"Thank you." Somehow he didn't think she was talking about his supposed writing aspirations.

Once again, Hawk and Sabra thanked Molly for her kindness and hospitality; then they bid her goodbye. At the end of the path leading to the dirt road, they turned and waved to her one last time.

Molly returned their wave and, from her place in the open doorway, called to them. "Come back if you can. Remember that my door is always open to friends."

It would be hard to say who was the quieter during the short walk back to the hotel, for Sabra and Hawk were both ruminating over thoughts provoked by their visit with Molly.

"There you are," Logan said with relief, hurriedly rising from the depths of a wing chair as Hawk and his sister entered the lobby of the hotel. "I was beginning to get worried about you."

"No need to worry, Logan. We've been at Molly's."

"All this time?" he asked in surprise.

"Oh, yes." Sabra's voice bubbled with enthusiasm. "And you know what, it wasn't near long enough. She's so nice, Logan. And the stories she told . . . you should have been there. You missed such a lovely afternoon."

"Well, I'm glad you had such an enjoyable time. I'm truly sorry I missed it."

Logan's gaze met Hawk's over the top of Sabra's head as they began to climb the stairs to their rooms. The quasi-innocent look caused Hawk's brow to quirk in amusement, and he gave Logan a questioning glance that clearly said, *Am I supposed to believe you really meant that?*

Logan just grinned.

Hawk spent the long hours at the community center in glorious anticipation. The players, the singers and dancers, the jugglers and magician were barely noticed, for his mind dwelt on far more pleasurable thoughts.

With Logan once again planning to spend the night with Della, Hawk knew that no force on earth could keep him from Sabra. It would be their last night for a while and he meant to make the most of it. Their return to Fort Huachuca would put an end to such opportunities for more reasons than one.

To begin with, Major Powers would be returning at any time. But foremost in Hawk's mind was the desire to protect Sabra. He would take no chance of jeopardizing her reputation on the post.

No, this would probably be the last time he'd be able to hold her in his arms through the long velvet hours of the night.

Until they were married.

Hawk now had it all worked out in his mind. As soon as Andrew Powers returned, he was going to have a long talk with him, perhaps the most important conversation he'd ever had in his life. Hawk had spent years blaming Andrew Powers for what had happened to his family, but he'd now put that part of his life to rest, and he wanted to make peace with the man himself—for Sabra's sake.

He wasn't sure how much he would tell Powers. Although he certainly would not broach the real reason behind his journey to Arizona, he did intend to tell the major of his love for Sabra, and to say what he must to convince the man that he would cherish and care for her forever.

Hawk intended to do this right, to secure the major's blessing and then ask Sabra to marry him.

With all his heart, he believed his plan would work. The spirits wouldn't have brought him this far, given him a glimpse of heaven, a promise of inner peace, only to snatch it from his grasp at the last possible moment.

Andrew Powers would listen to his pleas and understand.

He had to.

Hawk lay upon his bed, fully awake, fully alert, waiting for the sound of Logan's departure. His head told him it had only been minutes since they'd all gone to their individual rooms; but his heart insisted that it had been forever.

Click. At last. Hawk's keen hearing caught the sound of Logan's door being pulled to, and then the stealthy sound of steps heading for the staircase. He lay perfectly still, counting each footfall, mapping Logan's progress down the hall, the slightly different sound of his boot heel taking the first step downward. Then another and another and another, until the sounds faded into nothingness.

Cat-quiet, Hawk rose from the bed, crossed the dark room, and checked the hall. Empty. A dozen softly trod, barefooted steps and he was in front of Sabra's door, his heartbeat sounding louder in his ears than his knuckles against the wood.

His heart lurched when he heard the turn of her key in the lock. The door swung open, and in the next instant he was inside the shadowed room, his back hard against the closed door and Sabra in his arms.

"Sweet heaven, I can't believe we're alone at last," Hawk breathed against her lips. "I thought the time would never pass."

"I know," Sabra whispered, melting into his warm embrace. "Hold me, Hawk. Hold me. I've missed you so."

His strong arms tightened around her, pulling her close as he rubbed his cheek against the silken wisps of hair feathering her temple.

"Ummm, you smell wonderful," he said, burying his nose in curls.

His hands skimmed across her back, eliciting little shivers of ecstasy up and down her spine.

"And your skin feels like satin."

She gave a small squeak of surprise, then purred her contentment as Hawk nuzzled the side of her neck and nipped playfully at her earlobe.

"And you taste even better."

Soft laughter bubbled forth from Sabra, but it soon faded into little moans of pleasure as his lips found hers.

"Do you . . . remember . . . the first time . . . I held you . . . in my arms?" he asked in a husky whisper, his words punctuated by kisses.

"I'll never forget."

The gentle puffs of breath that accompanied her words were sweet and warm against his lips.

"The band was playing and you stepped into my arms and we went gliding across the floor."

"Yes," she answered, the sound more sigh than word.

"And before I knew it, you'd danced your way right into my heart."

With that, he danced her away from the door, their figures pale shades of gray in the ebony-cloaked room. His slow, sensuous steps took them nearer and nearer the corner that held the dim bulk of the bed.

"Oh, yes. I remember," Sabra said. "And I remember how lost I felt when you walked away. Like you'd taken a part of me with you."

They turned and twirled in the darkness, each movement languorous, almost dreamlike, as they progressed inch by tiny inch across the floor, savoring every step, every brush of flesh upon flesh.

Thigh whisked against thigh.

Fingers traced soft hollows and muscular ridges.

Gently swelling breasts pressed warmly, enticingly, against the rigid expanse of male chest.

Soft kisses were exchanged, lips touching, parting, returning to drink again and again.

"I didn't want to go," Hawk murmured. "I had to make myself walk away."

"Why?"

"Because of something foolish, something that doesn't even exist anymore. I know better now."

"Do you?"

"Yes. And I'll never leave you again."

"I'm glad."

As the backs of Sabra's legs bumped the soft edge of the mattress, Hawk's hands edged around from her back to stroke her arms and caress her shoulders, then drift up the slender column of her neck to tenderly cup her cheeks. Her features were barely discernible in the velvet shadows of his room.

"May I ask a favor of you, sweet love?"

"Anything."

"A candle. One small candle, here on the table by the bed—so I can see you. So I can burn the memory of this night into my heart to keep me warm during the lonely nights to come back at the fort."

"Oh, Hawk." Sabra sighed and dropped her head forward in a forlorn gesture, letting her forehead rest against the hard strength of his chest. "I don't want to think of being without you."

"It won't be for long, Sabra. I promise. And when we're together again, things will be right. Very, very right."

Hawk's fingers threaded through her hair, his thumbs lovingly tracing the delicate ridge of her jaw, exerting just enough pressure to bring her head up until their lips clung once again.

When the kiss ended, Sabra stepped away from him without a word, turning and bending to light the candle while Hawk moved toward the window and reached to pull the curtains tightly shut.

The small flame flickered and caught, glowing bright,

chasing the obsidian shadows away.

Sabra straightened and raised her eyes to Hawk's, and for a long, long moment they simply stood and gazed at one another while the dancing light bathed them with a golden aura.

Then slowly, ever so slowly, of one accord and with no words spoken, they began to discard their garments.

Hawk's fingers fumbled with the buttons on his shirt, pushing them through their openings, baring inch after tantalizing inch of bronze flesh. Each brush of his knuckles against that hard-muscled expanse evoked memories in Sabra of how his warm skin had felt under her own fingertips, and little frissons of pleasure raced through her when the shirt finally fell to the floor.

Sabra reached up, her long, slim fingers easing the wrapper from her shoulders. The soft material slithered down her arms and fell in a pale pool at her feet. Candlelight haloed the soft blur of her figure visible through the gossamer gown, taking Hawk's breath away.

He unfastened his pants, pushing the fabric down the firm, muscular length of his thighs. A step. A tug. A kick. And then he was gloriously, beautifully naked before her, his smooth, satin-textured skin painted in shades of copper and gold and bronze, the proud thrust of his manhood declaring the strength of his desire.

Sabra's lashes feathered downward, lacy shadows fanning across her cheeks. Then her fingers gripped the narrow shoulder straps of her nightdress.

Gracefully, she raised her arms and the gown floated upward, slowly revealing the hidden delights of her body. Dainty feet, trim ankles, soft curve of calf and knee. Satin thighs bracketing tangled taffy curls. Delicately rounded hip, tiny waist, proud high breasts.

A lift, a turn, the drop of an arm, and Sabra's waist-length hair, momentarily pulled upward by the skyward path of her garment, at last spilled free. Then, capturing a million sparks of light, it cascaded downward, floating into place, brushing against Sabra's back and shoulders in a ripple of softest gold, falling forward to shield her slightly bowed head, to hide her color-stained cheeks.

"You're more beautiful than anything I ever imagined," Hawk murmured reverently.

Sabra's head lifted, her dark lashes fluttering upward as she finally met Hawk's eyes. And the love she saw shining in those midnight blue orbs gave her courage. Tilting her chin a tiny bit higher, she squared her shoulders and surrendered herself to his gaze, all shyness suddenly melted away.

"I love you." The words reached across space to caress her as surely as his touch would have done.

"And I love you."

Hawk closed the distance between them, enfolding Sabra in his arms, cradling her cheek against the naked warmth of his broad chest. Her arms went tight about his body; her hands splayed against the smooth expanse of his back.

His heart beat like a trip-hammer beneath Sabra's ear, and she gloried in his response to her nearness. When she allowed one hand to drift downward, fingertips exploring the intriguing area where narrow waist flared and became hard-muscled buttocks, Hawk's breath caught and held. And when she turned her head, tentatively flicking the tip of her warm pink tongue against the small copper nodule nuzzling her cheek, that breath became a harsh rasp deep in his throat.

Tangling one hand in her golden curls, he tugged until her face tilted to his, and lowering his head, he claimed her mouth with a fiery kiss. Then he led her to the bed.

Chapter Twenty

Sabra and Hawk had three wonderful, carefree days after their return to Fort Huachuca. Three days to roam the foothills, usually in the company of Logan or Hezekiah and Jasmine, but sometimes for an hour or two all by themselves. Days of haphazard fun-filled mealtimes at Logan's, where time and rules didn't matter, and all felt welcome and at home. A golden time when friends and lovers, relaxed, teased, laughed, and learned about each other. Three days to bask in the warm magic of new love.

And then the major returned.

Hawk lay awake far into the early morning hours on the night the stage had brought Sabra's father back to Fort Huachuca, trying to formulate what he was going to say when he confronted Powers.

Not too much. Not too little. Just enough to convince the major to give his approval for their marriage. Hawk's mind would go no further than that. The rest he put out of his head, placating himself with assurances that he'd find a solution to all that "later."

Through the long dark hours of the night he rehearsed the speech in his mind, discarding this sentence, revising that one. It was bad enough that Powers had apparently disliked him on sight, but Hawk also had to convince him that true love could be found in the short time he and Sabra had known each other. Almost any father would question the validity of such a claim; Hawk expected Andrew Powers to do so more strongly than most.

And so, his weary brain probed and planned, concocted and modified, until he was exhausted. Finally, still dissatisfied with the arguments he'd composed but too weary to wrestle with the matter any longer, he fell into a restless sleep.

The boom of the reveille cannon sent Hawk tumbling from his rumpled bed, groggy, disoriented, but determined. Despite his fatigue, he shaved and dressed and arrived at the major's office not too long after the young clerk unlocked the door.

Hawk had hoped to see Powers early, before the major became enmeshed in the work of the fort . . . and before he himself lost his nerve. But all his careful planning went for naught. Although Hawk suspected Sabra's father was closeted behind the closed door leading to his office, the snippy little clerk in the anteroom was most uncooperative and would give him no information whatsoever.

Hawk wondered if the major was trying to avoid him, or if it was simply that the young soldier was naturally contrary.

Swallowing back the words of protest that were forming on his tongue, Hawk tried again, politely requesting an appointment for later in the day. This effort, too, failed to produce results.

"Impossible," the ferret-faced clerk declared in his nasal voice. "Simply impossible for today. However, you might call back tomorrow. I'll see what I can do for you then."

"But this is important," Hawk insisted, more than slightly tempted to take the self-important little fellow by his scrawny shoulders and give him a good shake. "Couldn't you just take a message in to Major Powers, tell him I'm here? Perhaps he can spare me a few minutes later on this afternoon—"

"Really, Mr. Hawkins, I've already told you that today is out of the question. I don't see how I can say it any plainer."

Hawk's nervous fingers dug furrows in his dark hair

240

as he turned away and began to pace the floor in agitation.

From his safe position behind the desk, the clerk eyed Hawk's stormy countenance. Resentment swept through him as he remembered Sterling Hawkins's rumored wealth.

They're all alike, the wealthy ones, the clerk thought with a disdainful sniff. *Pushy. Think their money can buy them anything. Well, his riches don't mean diddlysquat here. No, siree. In this office, Homer Kornsberg calls the shots.*

"I'm afraid you have no choice, sir," Kornsberg said, thoroughly enjoying the power his words conveyed. "I have strict orders not to bother Major Powers today. And I *always* follow orders. Perhaps you could come back tomorrow."

"Tomorrow . . . like hell!" Hawk muttered vehemently under his breath as he strode from the room, his boot heels thunking against the plank floor.

A small, self-satisfied smile tilted Kornsberg's thin lips. *Ha! Put the bastard in his place, all right. Showed him how important his money is to me. He can wait, just like everybody else.*

Smugly content with his petty victory, the clerk went back to shuffling his papers.

Hawk's frustration built throughout the day. He roamed the fort, but saw no sign of Powers. Where the hell was the man? He wasn't at the house he shared with Sabra; she hadn't seen her father except for a few minutes right after he'd arrived on the stage. And there was no sign of him at the office of the fort's commanding officer, or out by the stables, or over at the mess hall.

Hawk paced the length of the parade ground for the third time that day, growing more and more positive that the major was still closeted in his office, working on God only knew what.

What could possibly be that important?

A sudden thought brought Hawk up dead in his

tracks, so unexpectedly that the soldier walking behind him crashed into his back.

"Sorry," Hawk mumbled to the man, his mind still grappling with a disturbing possibility. Troubled, he walked over to the trading-post porch and propped himself against a support pole, his gaze roaming unseeingly over the autumn-yellowed grass while he examined the issue.

Had Powers somehow found out who he was? Was that why he was locked away in his office? Was he formulating some devious plot for telling Sabra about Hawk's past, aspiring to destroy any hope for happiness they might have?

Son-of-a-bitch, Hawk thought, giving himself a mental shake, what's wrong with me? I'm acting like a pure jackass!

What had gotten into him? If there was one sliver of truth to the crazy thoughts racing through his head, the major would already have done something about it. He damn well wouldn't be locked away in his office. He'd have told Sabra long before now. Hell, he'd probably have called out the guards the first thing that morning and demanded that they arrest Hawk!

Totally irritated by his irrational behavior, so uncharacteristic of his nature and upbringing, Hawk pushed away from the rough-hewn post and stomped into the store, desperate to find some way to pass the time.

At first glance the place seemed deserted. Hawk didn't care. He could use a few minutes by himself. He wandered aimlessly up and down the aisles, fingering a plaid wool shirt, testing the edge of a Bowie knife, poking at this and that, willing his tension to seep away.

On a bottom shelf in a far corner of the store, Hawk found a stack of shopworn books. Squatting down, he flipped through them. Several penny dreadfuls, a literary history of ancient Greece, a small book of sonnets.

Hawk stacked all but the last volume back on the shelf. He was thumbing through the pages, trying to decide whether Sabra might enjoy it, when he heard the creak of a door and then voices.

". . . stopped by early this morning. Said he had all the ammunition he needed."

"What kind of ammunition?"

A derisive snort. "I didn't ask."

"So now what?"

"Follow the plan. But the schedule moves up."

"Right away?"

"As soon as possible."

"No problem. Just leave it to me."

Hawk rose to his feet as two men rounded the end of the long wooden counter at the back of the room.

Henderson's head jerked around as he caught the movement from the corner of his eye.

"Sorry," Hawk said, recognizing the store's proprietor. The sergeant on Henderson's other side was a stranger to Hawk. "I didn't mean to startle you."

"No, no," Henderson blustered. "That's fine. Just didn't think anyone was in here, that's all. Uh . . . I was just taking care of a special order for Sergeant Jennings. We're all finished. Now, is there something I can help you with?"

Hawk held up the small volume of poetry as if in explanation of his presence, then gave a wry smile and a shake of his head. "No, I don't think so. I was just browsing, but it's not what I had in mind." What he had in mind was a little solitude, a little peace and quiet, not a discussion of weapons and ammunition. Well, he'd picked the wrong place for that. He bent and returned the book to its dusty shelf. "Thanks anyway."

And with that, he left the store.

The sun hung like a huge orange ball on the horizon, ready to plunge out of sight. The sky above was already turning indigo, the darkness bleeding downward, chasing away the last bright streaks of color. A chill breeze teased the tufts of yellowed grass on the parade ground and rattled the ocotillo branches, a lonely hollow sound in the gathering dusk.

Hawk watched the snooty little clerk leave the office, noting with relief that a light still burned within. This was as good a time as any to approach Powers. Perhaps better, since they'd have a bit of privacy now that the major's arrogant guardian had left his post for the night.

Squaring his shoulders, Hawk girded himself for the task ahead, even more determined to speak with Andrew Powers before the night was out.

In the twilight, he crossed the parade ground, stepped up on the small porch and knocked at the door. There was no answer, but then he hadn't really expected one. If Powers was still in his inner office, he might not even be able to hear Hawk's light knock.

Hawk tried the door. It was unlocked. He slipped inside.

His footsteps sounded unnaturally loud to his ears as he crossed the room with slow determined steps. In front of the door to Major Powers's inner sanctum, Hawk paused and drew a deep fortifying breath. Then he raised his hand and rapped his knuckles against the wood.

"Who is it?"

The irritable words made Hawk jump.

"Sterling Hawkins, Major Powers."

The muffled sound of a chair being pushed back followed, then the tock-tock-tock of heels across the floor, the scrape of a key in the lock. Finally the door was flung open.

"What do you want?" Powers's expression matched his barely civil tone. "Your timing is most inopportune. I'm quite busy at the moment."

"I'm sure you are, sir," Hawk replied. "But I've been trying to see you all day. If you could just spare me a few minutes?"

Powers's dark eyes raked over Hawk, and his lips compressed into a single thin line. As an exasperated sigh sounded, Hawk waited for the door to be slammed in his face. But it didn't happen. Instead, the major finally stepped backward, grudgingly making room for Hawk to enter the dimly lighted room.

"Oh, very well. But make it short. I have a great many things to take care of."

"Yes, sir."

Hawk stepped inside before Powers could change his mind. Standing in front of the cluttered desk, he waited nervously for the major to resume his place behind it.

The major sat down, chair legs rasping against the floor as he pulled his seat forward. The lone lantern's flickering light cast eerie shadows on the whitewashed walls of the small room.

"Sit down." Powers's words were curt.

"Thank you."

"Now, get to the point, please."

Powers didn't even bother to look at Hawk. Taking up his pen, he bent his head toward his desk and began to edit the top page of a stack of papers.

All right, Hawk thought irritably. If that's the way you want it. Short, and to the point. No beating around the bush.

He had hoped for a little softer opening, some sort of opportunity to lay the groundwork for his plea, but it was obvious that Powers wasn't going to allow such niceties. Fine. He'd dispense with all the extras.

"I came to ask your approval to marry Sabra."

Hawk delivered the line, expecting fireworks in response. Instead, the major just lifted his head and looked at him with those cold flat eyes of his.

"You can't be serious," Powers finally said.

"I am, sir. Very serious."

"Ridiculous. The answer is no."

"No?" Hawk repeated incredulously. "No, just like that? No questions, no discussions, no thought as to what Sabra wants?"

Powers leaned back in his chair, pinning Hawk with a piercing look. The pen bobbed between his fingers.

"Sabra is too young to know what's best for her."

"Best for her? You can't mean that. She loves me, and I love her. I wanted your approval, your blessing. But we don't have to have it. I can marry her without it, you know." Hawk's growing anger was evidenced by the syncopated tick of muscle at the corner of his jaw.

The major's mouth tilted upward in an amused sneer. "I'm quite confident that my daughter will not go against my wishes."

Hawk glared at him. "Are you so sure? Do you really believe you can manipulate her like that? Do you honestly believe she'll just stand by and let you make all her decisions for her?"

"I can assure you, she's been quite happy with her life since she came here. And once you're gone, things will go on just as before."

"And what if I refuse to leave without her?" Hawk's chin lifted to a belligerent angle.

The major threw his pen down on the desk, black splotches of ink spattering across the sheaf of papers. "How dare you threaten me? You bastard! I knew you were trouble the moment I laid eyes on you."

Anger welled up inside Hawk, and he leaned forward in his chair. "You *knew?* Just a look and you knew all about me?"

"Yes."

Hawk threw back his head and gave a derisive snort. "Well, pardon me! I didn't realize that I was dealing with the Almighty. Read minds, do you? See right through people? Think you know all there is to know and that you never make a mistake?"

"I know what you are. And I know my daughter," the major replied with deadly calm. "That's all I need to know."

"Really?" Hawk shook his head in disbelief. "Hell, man! You don't even know that she's afraid of you."

"Afraid of me?" Now it was the major's turn to be incredulous. He gave a quick dismissive flip of his hand. "Don't be ridiculous."

"She is. I've seen her reactions," Hawk insisted, remembering the afternoon they'd toured the fort and the day of the picnic. He knew for Sabra's sake he couldn't discuss the circumstances of the latter episode, but he was too angry not to pursue the crux of the matter.

"I find that highly unlikely."

"I saw it with my own eyes!" Hawk persisted. "A casual mention was made of the time, as I recall, and she absolutely panicked. Her face went pale and she began to stammer excuses . . . that you'd wonder where she was, be upset with her for being late to dinner. Logan had to calm her down."

"And just when—and where—did this all supposedly take place?" The major's condescending tone of voice emphasized his refusal to give any credence to such an absurd accusation.

"The day after I arrived. The day Logan and Sabra took me on a tour of the fort. We were out by the northwest corral, the one closest to the Indian village."

"Ah," said the major, leaning back in his chair, a smug look on his face. "That explains it."

"Explains what? What the hell are you talking about? Didn't you understand what I said? She was afraid to take the time to go to the Indian village, afraid you'd be angry with her."

"No." The major shook his head. "That's not the case at all, Mr. Hawkins. I'm afraid *you're* the one who doesn't understand what's going on. *You're* the one who draws unwarranted conclusions, not I."

"Dammit—"

"Mr. Hawkins, you profess a desire to marry my daughter—a somewhat absurd aspiration since you know next to nothing about her."

"What are you talking about?"

"Sabra's not afraid of me. She wasn't worried about being late. That was an excuse, that's all."

"An excuse? We'd been having a grand time up till that moment!"

"Precisely. Everything was fine until you suggested

247

going into the Indian village. The fear you saw pertained to the Indians, not to me. Sabra is deathly afraid of Indians."

Hawk's mouth dropped open, his mind refusing to accept what was being said.

"That's . . . that's ridiculous," he sputtered, unaware that he was using the major's expression.

"Not when you understand the circumstances behind that fear," declared the major. "Sabra's mother—my wife—and her baby sister were killed by a band of renegade Indians when she was but a child. She witnessed the whole thing . . . she and Logan, that is. They were playing up in the hayloft and somehow miraculously missed being discovered by the Indians. But she saw it all. Every last bloody detail. She's been terrified of Indians ever since."

"But . . . but she's not!" Hawk insisted, the revelation too bitter to accept. "I know she's not. We spent the afternoon with a lady who is half-Navajo. She wasn't afraid of her."

"Oh, women and children don't have such a strong effect on her," the major said with a small shrug. "It's the men, the braves, that remind her of that awful day. She'll do anything to avoid getting anywhere close to one of them."

Hawk remembered the afternoon of the picnic, the way Sabra had cowered behind him when the Indian scouts had ridden near. He'd been so sure she was simply afraid the men would tell her father she was out unescorted. So sure it was her father who'd caused her fear.

Never in his wildest imaginings had he considered the real reason behind her apprehension.

My God! What would she do when she found out he was half-Indian? Would she be afraid of him? Would she see him as nothing more than one of those savages?

The painful thought was too much to bear, and the pompous look on the major's face made it doubly hard for Hawk.

248

"So, you see," Powers said, "you don't know my daughter nearly as well as you thought you did. She didn't even confide in you, trust you with the truth about her past. I think that speaks for itself. Why, if my own daughter weren't involved, I'd find the whole situation rather amusing."

"B-but—"

"You've been a diversion, Mr. Hawkins. Nothing more. And you're foolish to have thought otherwise. Sabra has no need for the likes of you."

No need for the likes of you. The words pounded in Hawk's head.

Suddenly he could stand no more. He had to get out of there—fast. Escape. He needed the solitude of the desert, the quiet peace of the heavens above him. He needed the free singing wind to clear his spinning mind. He needed . . .

Oh, God! Oh, dear God! He needed Sabra.

Hawk rose with such speed that his chair crashed to the floor. He spun and lurched toward the door. Heedless of the major's startled look, he grappled with the knob, unable to get the door open fast enough. His trembling fingers gave a final vicious twist to the knob, and the wooden panel flew backward, slamming against the wall.

Hawk rushed across the outer office, burst through the door, and fled into the night, heedless of the major's final words, heedless of the shadowy figure at the corner of the building, heedless of anything save the pain that burned in his heart.

Chapter Twenty-one

Logan was awakened by a loud pounding on the front door. "Damn it, what is it now?" he mumbled, rolling from his bed.

He fumbled his way across the night-shadowed room in search of the chair that held his clothing. "Hell!" The word scorched the air as his little toe cracked against the corner of the bureau.

Finally locating his pants, Logan poked one long leg after the other through the opening and then tugged the britches upward. He barely managed to get them fastened by the time he groped his way down the stygian hall to the front door.

"I'm coming!" he shouted above the insistent din. "Give it a rest, will ya?"

The pounding stopped just as Logan turned the lock and wrenched the door open. Hezekiah stumbled in from the dark, his breath coming in great gulps as if he'd been running.

"Logan," he rasped, reaching out to steady himself against the doorjamb. "There's trouble . . . your daddy . . ." It was all he could manage to get out until he caught his breath.

"Oh, hell. What's the ol' man pissed about now, Hezekiah? Come on in here and sit down."

"What's wrong?" Hawk's voice echoed from the hallway. He, like Logan, was barefoot and shirtless, his hastily donned pants half-buttoned and hanging on his hipbones.

"I don't know," Logan said. "Hezekiah just got here. Something about my father . . ."

Hawk's mouth thinned. Here it was. It had to be something about his meeting with Powers earlier that night. It had to be. Maybe Powers was calling Logan in for reinforcement. Maybe he was afraid Hawk meant what he'd said about not leaving without Sabra.

A bitter smile rimmed Hawk's mouth. Oh, he'd meant it all right, meant it one hundred percent when he'd said it. But that was before the major had dropped his bombshell.

Well, Powers could quit worrying about that now. No matter how Hawk had agonized over the situation, turning it inside out in search of an answer, he'd come to a conclusion.

It was hopeless.

There were too many lies between him and Powers, him and Sabra, too many memories, too much to overcome. The major's gloating explanation had been the final blow. Although Hawk knew he'd be leaving his heart behind, in the wee dark hours of the morning he'd finally decided that there was nothing he could do but get on the next stage—alone—and go home. Get out of Sabra's life; give her an opportunity to find someone worthy of her love, someone who could make her happy.

Hawk cast a troubled glance in Logan's direction. He'd hoped to slip away quietly. He didn't want any more problems, any more lies. He just wanted to escape . . . go home, back to the nothingness his life had been before Sabra.

Why couldn't the major have waited? Why had he sent for Logan now? In just a few hours Hawk would have been gone. *Damn!* If Hezekiah had only arrived after the stage had left. Now there'd be questions that required explanations he didn't have. There'd be more lies, because he couldn't bear to tell them the truth.

Hawk drew in a steadying breath. Get it over with,

he thought. Just get it the hell over with. He stood quietly by, sadly, waiting like a condemned man for Hezekiah to relay the major's message.

"Logan." Hezekiah's big hand found Power's shoulder. "Logan, you gotta listen to me."

Logan's brows drew together in a puzzled frown at the strange tone of Hezekiah's voice. "I'm listening. What's the problem?"

"It's your daddy. He's . . . he's been shot."

"Shot?" Hawk gasped.

"Shot?" Logan echoed uncomprehendingly. He stared blankly at the big black soldier for a minute, then, as if he'd finally gotten the punch line to a joke, a wry grin tipped one corner of his mouth. "What'd he do, shoot himself in the foot? Drop his gun? Accidentally discharge it while he was cleaning it? What?"

"No." Hezekiah's woolly head swung back and forth. "He's dead, Logan . . . murdered. I'm sorry. Lord, I'm sorry."

Hawk saw the blood drain from Logan's face, felt his own knees go wobbly.

"Murdered?" Hawk repeated, his voice hardly more than a whisper. "But how? When?"

"Yes," Logan said, finally finding his voice. "Yes, what the hell happened?"

He stumbled toward the living room, the others following behind. Dead. His father was dead. He could hardly believe it. They hadn't been close in years; Logan had even convinced himself that he no longer cared. But now, strangely, he was sorry, sorry he'd never have the chance to try to rebuild a relationship that had died years ago, as certainly as his mother and his baby sister had died.

"Nobody knows what happened. One of the sentries noticed that a light was still burning in his office. When he got a little closer, he saw that the outer door was ajar. He went inside to investigate and . . . and that's when he found him."

Logan sank into a chair. "Murdered," he repeated, his voice toneless. "How can that be?"

Hezekiah perched on the edge of the couch, his cap dangling from his big hands as he continued his story.

"Looks like there'd been a fight of some sort. The chair was turned over, and his papers were scattered all about. The desk drawers had been pulled open, the contents rifled."

Hawk felt something lurch deep in his belly as he remembered the discordant crash of his chair when he'd run from the office.

Wait! his befuddled mind protested. *That's not right! That's not how it was.*

Logan raised his head, his dark eyes full of confusion. "But why? To what purpose? This doesn't make sense. No sense at all."

Hawk pressed his lips together, as if to stop the flow of incriminating words that threatened to spill forth. It didn't make sense to him either.

When he'd left, the major had been alive—haughty, disdainful, and utterly remorseless . . . but alive. What had happened after that?

Who else had gone to the major's office after he had left? Perhaps Powers had been murdered while Hawk was pounding bareback over the night-shrouded desert in a desperate attempt to rid his soul of the man's hateful words. Or during the long hours Hawk had sat on a tumble of rocks, his mind endlessly groping for answers to his dilemma. Or perhaps during the early morning hours, after Hawk had returned his horse to the corral and had wearily made his way back to Logan's house, convinced that he had no choice but to leave on the morning stage.

"No, it doesn't make sense. It surely doesn't," Hezekiah said, watching his friend closely, his dark eyes filled with concern. God, how he hated to be the one to deliver such news.

"Sabra," Hawk said suddenly, his head jerking up-

253

ward, his eyes searching Hezekiah's. "Does she know? Has anyone told her?"

"No. I thought I should come to Logan first."

Logan tilted his head back and squeezed his eyes shut, a dreadful thought surfacing in his numb brain. It would be up to him to tell her. Naturally. But how? How? His breath huffed out in an explosive sigh; his bewildered eyes swept the room . . . and settled on Hawk. A tiny blossom of hope uncurled within.

"Hawk," Logan croaked, "you'll go with me, won't you? To tell Sabra, I mean."

"Me?" Hawk asked, surprised to be included in such a private family matter. "Sure," he said finally, "sure I will, if you think it will help."

"It will," Logan assured him. "She'll need you. I'm not blind. I know how you two feel about each other. She'll want you with her."

Hawk's stomach tensed for a moment; then he forced the muscles to relax. There was no condemnation in Logan's tone, only gentle acceptance.

But Hawk's initial flash of pleasure at Logan's attitude slipped quickly away. What did it matter? The major no longer stood in his way, but the rest of the lies still did. Nothing else had changed. Nothing except the date of his departure. He wouldn't be boarding the morning stage after all. Not today. He couldn't run out on Sabra at a time like this.

"Having you there will make it easier on her," Logan was saying when Hawk forced his mind back to the present. "I know it will."

"I can get Jasmine," Hezekiah volunteered. "She'll be happy to stay with Sabra today."

Logan nodded his head, then raked his hands through his tumbled taffy curls. "Good idea. She probably shouldn't be alone. And we can't stick around all day. We've got to get busy and find the bastard who did this."

"Do they"—Hawk's voice caught in his throat, as if

balking at the words he was about to ask—"do they have any clues? Any witnesses?" His heart tripped, halted, then lurched into rhythm again as he waited for the answer.

Why did he feel such guilt? Because he'd been at the office just hours before the major died or because Powers's death fulfilled his own secret wish?

"Nothing yet," Hezekiah said. "But Sergeant Jennings went to Lieutenant Colonel Forsyth and volunteered to head up a committee to look into the matter. Way I understood it, they're going to start questioning people right away. Try to find out if anyone saw somebody hanging around, anything suspicious . . . that kind of thing."

Merciful heaven, thought Hawk. Would they question him, too? Should he tell them he'd been to the major's office? Or should he keep quiet? He didn't know. He simply didn't.

"Well, that's a start," Logan said, his long length unfolding from the chair. "Give us a few minutes to get dressed, Hezekiah. Then, soon as we're ready, I'd appreciate it if you'd fetch Jasmine and meet Hawk and me at Sabra's."

"All right." Hezekiah stood up and began to move toward the door. "I'll go on to Jasmine's so she'll have a chance to get ready, then we'll head over to your da—to the house. But we'll wait outside until you get there."

"Thank you," Logan said, another ragged sigh coming after the words as he left the living room to return to his bedroom and finish dressing.

Hezekiah watched his friend's exit; then his keen eyes went to Hawk. "Are you all right?"

"I'm fine," Hawk answered, almost too quickly. "Just a little shocked by all this." He spread his hands in punctuation.

"Yeah, I know. We all are."

"How could it happen? I mean, right in the middle

255

of the fort."

Hezekiah gave a morose shake of his head. "Don't know. All I can figure is, it had to be someone the major knew."

"Someone he knew?" Hawk repeated blankly. "But . . . but why do you think that?"

"The door wasn't forced, so the major evidently let his killer in. And he made no attempt to get to his gun. Hell, I don't know. It doesn't look like he was in a fight. But the room . . . it's torn up like somebody was hunting for something."

"But what?"

"Who knows?" Hezekiah cast a wary eye toward Logan's bedroom door. "The major wasn't the most popular officer on the post. He could be mighty hard to get along with at times. But I can't imagine anyone just settin' out to murder him."

Hawk didn't answer. He was still groping for an answer to the question of whether or not to disclose his presence at the major's office. He was torn with uncertainty. He had noting to hide; there was no reason he shouldn't admit to having talked with the major. But wouldn't it be misconstrued? Could he take that chance?

Hezekiah, jamming his hat back on his head, turned toward the door again. "Well, there's a lot to do. I'd best be on my way."

Hawk's head jerked upward. "Yeah. Sure. We'll meet you there."

Twenty minutes later, Logan roused Sabra from slumber and led her to the living room of the house she'd shared with her father, where Hawk and Hezekiah and Jasmine waited in silence.

As she stepped through the door, her eyes swept the room, growing larger and more apprehensive by the second. "Something's happened." It was a statement, not a question. The fingers of one hand crept upward to clutch the lapels of her wrapper, holding it close to her throat in an unconscious gesture of defense. "Hawk," she whispered, holding her other hand out to him.

He hurried to her side, one arm going around her shoulders, protectively pulling her against the hard security of his chest. His grip never wavered while Logan delivered the shocking news, and when she turned to him, burying her face against his shoulder, he held her close, rocking her, stroking her long tumble of golden curls, whispering soft words. As she wept bitter tears, tears that stained the front of his shirt and dampened the skin beneath, he uttered a silent prayer of gratitude that he'd seen the light and abandoned his plan before it came to this. He knew he couldn't have borne it if he'd been the one to cause her such pain.

An hour later, the three men left Sabra to Jasmine's gentle care, promising to return as soon as possible.

Logan was anxious to talk with Jennings, to find out if anything new had turned up. His heels clattered sharply against the wooden steps as he hastily descended the stairs and struck out across the parade ground.

The nebulous thoughts swirling in Hawk's head suddenly took form, and he knew that he had to tell Logan about last night. Not for his own sake, but because the telling might provide a further clue to the mystery of the major's death.

So much was being misconstrued already. The overturned chair . . . the assumption that it indicated some sort of fight with the killer. The unlocked door . . . not necessarily proof that Powers had known his killer, as Hezekiah had presumed. Perhaps the major had merely neglected to lock it after Hawk's hasty departure. If the culprit was going to be found, they needed every possible shred of information.

"Logan, wait." The words sounded sharp, almost

anxious on the cool morning air.

Slowing his purposeful stride, Logan half turned and looked over his shoulder in Hawk's direction. "What is it?"

"Wait up a minute," Hawk said. "I want to talk with you—alone—before we get around all those other people."

Puzzled, Logan halted and waited for Hawk. Hezekiah hesitated, unsure whether he should go on without them or simply move out of hearing range. Hawk read the dilemma on his face.

"Stay, Hezekiah," he said. "You need to hear this, too."

"What is it, Hawk?" Logan asked again, the perplexity in his voice underlined by the deep furrowing of his brow.

"I saw your father last night. I thought you might want to know before the questioning starts."

Logan's frown deepened while Hezekiah's face remained stoic, unreadable.

"Last night?" Logan repeated. "When?"

"Late." Hawk raised one hand to smooth back the shock of dark hair the teasing morning breeze ruffled against his forehead. "I'd tried to talk to him all day. Hadn't been able to. So I waited until that guard dog that calls himself a corporal left the office, and I went in to see him."

"You did?"

"Some of the 'evidence' Hezekiah mentioned really has nothing to do with you father's death. You see, I was the one he unlocked the door for. I didn't want you going off on the wrong tangent."

"I appreciate that."

"There's more."

"What?"

"I have to be honest with you. We argued. Rather bitterly. About Sabra," Hawk explained as he saw Logan's brow rise questioningly. "I asked for his approval

258

to marry her. He didn't like the idea."

An acerbic grin tilted one corner of Logan's mouth. "I can just imagine."

"And I was the one who knocked over the chair—it didn't happen in a fight, as everyone seems to think. I was angry at something he said, and I . . . I just bolted from the room. I heard the chair hit the floor, but I didn't stop to pick it up."

Hawk's words died away. His hands dropped to his sides, and he silently, patiently, waited for the questions he knew would come, should come.

But the questions Logan asked weren't the ones Hawk was expecting.

"All right. That clears up a couple of points. Now, think hard. Did you see anyone when you left? Hear anything that might give us a clue about my father's final visitor?"

Hawk could hardly believe what he was hearing. Not once, not even for a fraction of a second, had Logan considered that Hawk himself might be the culprit. His trust was unwavering, and totally unexpected.

Hawk's eyes met Hezekiah's dark-eyed gaze, and he read understanding in the black-brown depths. Hawk realized that Hezekiah was a man who would understand groundless suspicion, and fear of condemnation without justification. Perhaps years of enduring such treatment, or of simply watching his fellows be subjected to it, had made him keenly receptive to the wary feelings within Hawk.

The big black soldier gave a shallow dip of his head, his eyes never leaving Hawk's face, as if in total agreement with Logan's assessment that Hawk could not possibly have had anything to do with the major's death.

Hawk felt as if a giant weight had been lifted from his chest. He pulled a draught of cool night air deep into his lungs and applied his mind to Logan's questions.

259

After some moments of thought, he shook his head. "No. No, I'm sorry. But I don't recall anything. I wish I did. I guess I was just too upset at the time."

Logan nodded. "I figured something was wrong when you came in so late."

"I went riding. Had to do something to clear the cobwebs."

"I understand." Logan tugged at the bottom of his coat, unconsciously making sure that the line of his uniform was as faultless as would have been required by his father. "Maybe you'll think of something later," he said. "Come on, let's get this over with." He turned on his heel and proceeded toward his father's office.

A dozen men were clustered on the porch fronting the major's office. A low murmur ran through the crowd when Logan was spied, and it parted like the Red Sea as the three men drew near.

"Sorry, Lieutenant," one small sandy-haired man called out. Logan nodded an acknowledgment of the private's condolence but kept on going.

Once inside the small anteroom, Hawk noticed immediately that the fussy little clerk had lost his hallowed place behind the outer office desk to Sergeant Jennings. Kornsberg hovered over the spot like a mother whose precious only child is being dandled on the knee of a stranger.

"Anything to report?" Logan demanded of the sergeant as he came to a halt in front of the desk, his thighs almost pressed against the wooden edge.

"Nothing yet," Jennings answered, stacking a sheaf of papers to one side.

Hawk's mind had just begun to register recognition of the man behind the desk when Kornsberg gave a muffled squawk and pointed one bony finger in his direction.

"That's the man," the clerk declared, his thin nostrils quivering with distaste. "That Hawkins fellow. He's the one who insisted on seeing the major yesterday morning. Wouldn't hardly take no for an answer, either. Acted exceedingly peculiar, if you ask me."

Jennings halted his paper shuffling, raised his head to turn speculative eyes on Hawk.

Logan threw Kornsberg an annoyed glance, remembering the clerk's thirst for power and his occasional penchant for theatrics when vexed. He never had understood how his father had put up with the man. Personally, Kornsberg's nasal whine and habitual toadying had always rubbed Logan the wrong way.

"Calm down, Corporal," Logan instructed. "Mr. Hawkins is a friend of the family. There was nothing peculiar in his seeking an appointment with my father."

Kornsberg sniffed. "Well, the man was rude. Quite rude," he insisted, delivering the last words with a disdainful tilt of his head.

Hawk breathed a prayer of gratitude for having had the good sense to tell Logan of his visit with the major

Logan bristled at the tone of the clerk's voice. "I've heard quite enough, Kornsberg. The subject is closed. Do you understand?"

Kornsberg puffed up like an irate banty rooster, but he knew better than to argue with a senior officer. "Yes, sir." The words were spoken grudgingly.

Jennings watched the exchange with bright interested eyes, a nebulous plan forming in the back of his head.

Animosity hung heavy in the room, but finally Logan turned away to stalk to the open doorway leading to the inner office. He viewed the disarray for a moment, thankful that his father's body had already been taken to the post hospital.

"Is there anything missing?" he called back over his shoulder.

Kornsberg stepped forward, full of self-importance

261

once again. "Nothing as far as I can tell." Then, suddenly, he pursed his mouth. "No. Wait. There was a small leather case . . . I don't remember seeing it when Sergeant Jennings had me check the room."

Logan pounced on the statement. "What case?"

"Well, just this little case . . ." Kornsberg's hands fluttered in the air. "I believe the major must have brought it with him from Tucson. I don't recall ever seeing it before."

"What did it look like?" Logan snapped. "What was in it?"

Kornsberg frowned. "Uh . . . it looked rather expensive . . . was sort of a maroon color. Flat and not too big. Similar to a dispatch case. I suppose it held papers; at least it was the right size. However, I have no idea what was in it. I *never* touched the major's private possessions unless instructed to do so." The words were punctuated by another of the little clerk's reproachful sniffs.

"Naturally," Logan said with a barely concealed grimace. "But back to the case . . . where did you last see it?"

"The major had it on his desk when I arrived at the office yesterday morning. I remember it clearly. However, I don't recall seeing it later in the day. Perhaps he took it home."

"Did you see him leave with it?"

"No." Kornsberg shook his head. "But I wasn't here the entire day. I did leave at noon, and again for supper—as instructed by the major, of course."

"Of course," Logan parroted, rolling his eyes heavenward.

"I ate my meals, and then I brought something back for Major Powers. He ate at his desk. I don't recall the case being in the same place on his desk when I set the supper tray down." The clerk tapped a finger against his chin. "I suppose he could have taken it somewhere while I was out, or perhaps put it in a drawer."

"Check the drawers," Logan instructed Hezekiah.

They all gathered just inside the doorway of the major's private office, waiting expectantly as Hezekiah did Logan's bidding. But a thorough search of the desk provided nothing.

"Does anyone else know about the case?" Logan asked Kornsberg, after the fruitless search.

"No, I don't think so. Your father said he went right home when he got off the stage. And that morning, as far as I know, he came straight to the office—very early, evidently, because he was already here when I arrived."

"And you haven't mentioned it to anyone else?"

"No. Actually, I hadn't thought of it before now. Do you think I should tell Lieutenant Colonel Forsyth?"

"No." Logan's voice was emphatic. "As far as we know, no one knows about the case except us"—his sweeping gaze took in Hezekiah, Hawk, Jennings, and Kornsberg—"and in all likelihood, my father's killer."

"You think it'll provide a clue eventually?" Hawk asked.

Logan shrugged his shoulders. "I'm probably clutching at straws, but it seems to be the only out-of-the-ordinary thing right now. Let's wait and see if it turns up. Meanwhile, I don't want the case mentioned to a single soul who isn't in this room. Not anyone. Do you all understand?"

Words of agreement were punctuated by the nodding of heads, but Jennings's head halted in mid bob when a movement just outside the window caught his eye.

It couldn't be, he thought with alarm. He narrowed his eyes and watched the sliver of light between the wall and the window drape. The figure moved again, and this time the face was clear. *Goddammit!*

Jennings began easing toward the door. "Uh . . . Lieutenant Powers, there're some things I need to take care of. If it's all right with you, I'll see to them and be back in an hour or so to begin the questioning again."

"Fine," Logan said.

"Thank you, sir."

Jennings turned on his heel, forcing his steps to remain slow and even all the way across the outer office. Once on the porch he brusquely told the waiting men to return in two hours, then shouldered his way through the throng. Quickening his pace on the path at the bottom of the steps, he made a hurried left turn at the corner of the building.

"What the hell are you doing here?" Jennings demanded, his hand closing around soft flesh and swinging the woman around to face him.

"Ouch!" Melissa protested, prying at the fingers digging into her arm. "You're hurting me!"

"Shhh!" Jennings warned, his hand dropping away as if he'd been burned. He quickly glanced around to assure himself that no one had seen them. "Keep walking, Melissa. And smile. Make it look like we just accidentally ran into each other."

She did as she was told, but her forced smile did little to conceal her irritation.

Jennings fell into step beside her, far enough away to look respectful but close enough to carry on a whispered conversation.

"What are you doing here?" he repeated. "I saw you eavesdropping outside the window. My God, anyone could have seen you. How would you have explained that?"

"So what?" she retaliated. "Don't I have a right to take a walk if I want to?"

"You know as well as I do that's not what you were doing. For crissake, Melissa, there's been a murder! Things are going to be all out of sorts for a while. Don't you understand that?"

"No," she said with a pout. "I only understand that I miss seeing you."

"Well, you'd better get used to it. I'm going to be

264

busy with this for a while."

"Daddy said you actually volunteered for this job. I don't understand why you'd do something so foolish. Colonel Forsyth would have assigned somebody else, and you could have spent the morning with me as we'd planned—"

"There was a good reason for what I did, but I have no intention of trying to explain it. And you, if you know what's good for you, quit trying to pry information out of your daddy before he gets suspicious. You're tampering with things you don't even begin to understand."

Melissa cut a sideways glance at Jennings, suddenly wary at hearing so much anger in his voice. Deciding to change her tack, she assumed a provocative little-girl pout and sugar-coated her next words.

"Don't be so fussy, darlin'. It's just that I was worried—and disappointed—when you didn't show up this morning. That's all. Edward was over again last night; he keeps pressing me to give him an answer to his marriage proposal—"

"So marry him," Jennings said curtly.

Melissa threw him a scathing look. "Well, I certainly have considered it. He does have money—"

"Then that ought to settle it. We both know I don't have the funds to claim you permanently. Not that your daddy'd allow it anyway. Besides, I'm not so sure I'd even want to, if he did. I'd be afraid to turn my back on you for fear of getting the same treatment you've been dishing out to Woodley."

"Now you're being crude," Melissa snapped, as they neared a small storage shed. "For your information, I may very well marry Edward. It's just that he's so . . . so boring. Why, he spends more time talking to Daddy than he does paying attention to me."

Suddenly, Jennings whipped the door of the shed open and jerked Melissa inside. She stumbled and fell against him, and his arms clamped around her.

265

"Boring, is he? What's the matter? Don't his kisses satisfy you?" He stamped his mouth hard across hers. "Doesn't his touch set you on fire?" One hand raked over her back while the other palmed her breast, squeezing, rubbing, tweaking her nipple until she gasped with pleasure.

"Leroy," she moaned against his lips.

"Listen to me, you little hellcat. I enjoy this as much as you do. But you knew from the first that your daddy wasn't going to approve of you seeing me."

"But I don't understand why."

"You don't have to understand; just accept the fact. You also knew that I wasn't going to jeopardize my business dealings with him on your account. I have ambitions, and I'm not giving up what I've been working for just because of you."

"But if you had money, we could—"

"I'm not going to argue the point any longer, Melissa. You made the decision to settle for what little time we could manage to steal. Besides that, have you forgotten how eager you were to keep dear ol' Edward believing he was the only one? The situation worked out for both of us. Let's just leave it that way."

"But, Leroy—"

"But nothing." Jennings silenced her with another scorching kiss before he continued his litany. "What's the matter, Melissa? Has the game with Woodley lost its charm? He's finally proposed, and now you don't want the poor fool."

"You don't understand," she protested weakly, tilting her head back to allow him greater access to the sensitive flesh of her throat.

"I understand you completely. We're two of a kind," Jennings rasped. His teeth nipped at the curve of Melissa's shoulder, and a shiver ran through her, a little mew sounded low in her throat. "You're selfish and spoiled—"

"But you want me, just like I want you," she taunted

266

softly.

"Hell, yes. I want you. But it's going to be on my terms, or none at all. Do you understand?"

"Yes," she whimpered. "Yes."

Chapter Twenty-two

The sun hid its face on the afternoon Andrew Powers
was buried in the small cemetery northwest of the post.
Towering cotton-boll clouds hung over the darkly shadowed mountains, their underbellies sooty with the threat
of rain. Occasionally a fat raindrop fell from the gun-
metal gray sky, plopping down to be hungrily sucked
into the sandy soil. And a chill wind blew sporadically,
rattling the leaves overhead, plucking at the hem of
Sabra's somber black cloak, then dying away and leaving a sudden eerie stillness, only to rise again within a
few minutes.

Hawk felt the renewed trembling of Sabra's fingers
against his arm when the chaplain intoned one last
prayer as the raw wood coffin was lowered into the
ground. When he reached his free hand across and
cupped it over hers, she leaned even closer to his side,
as if gathering strength as well as warmth from his
nearness.

Tilting his head slightly, Hawk cut his eyes to the
side, searching Sabra's pale, drawn countenance with
concern. The sheen of unshed tears in her eyes brought
an ache to his throat that no amount of swallowing
would abolish. She'd been so brave, not even crying
after that first heartbreaking release of emotion.

Hawk's gaze finally left Sabra and traveled to Logan,
who stood stiff and still on the other side of his sister.
Although Powers' face was motionless and unreadable,
his dark eyes moved restlessly over the crowd, and
Hawk knew that he, too, was wondering if one or

another of the mourners was the person responsible for the major's death.

The last words the chaplain uttered were snatched away by a fresh gust of wind. And a miniature dust devil whirled across the ground, bobbing and weaving as it hurled tiny grains of sand against anything in its path.

Eying the darkening sky, Hawk gritted his teeth and mentally harangued the people filing by, urging them to hurry up and finish their customary handshakes, hugs, and softly murmured condolences. All he wanted to do was get Sabra away from the sorrow-filled place, out of the cold and back inside the safe confines of the house—away from the probing, sympathetic eyes of the fort's inhabitants.

Finally, endless minutes later, Lieutenant Colonel Forsyth, the last of the mourners, murmured "I'm so sorry" and Hawk was able to lead Sabra home.

They were barely inside the house when the skies opened up and loosed a torrent of silver-gray water.

"Just in time," Hawk said, shutting the front door against the driving rain and ushering Sabra into the living room.

"I'll help Jasmine and Hezekiah," Logan called over his shoulder as the three of them disappeared down the hall.

Hawk grunted an acknowledgment, and hurriedly poked the embers in the fireplace to blazing life before slipping Sabra's cape from her shoulders. Gratefully, she bent toward the dancing flames, a sheaf of golden hair spilling over her shoulder as she held her hands out to the warmth.

"Here, let me help," Hawk said, stepping toward her and taking her hands between his, chafing them gently. "Do you want something to drink? Something warm perhaps? Or a little glass of wine?"

"No," she said, her voice soft. She tugged her hands free and stepped into his embrace. "I've got all I need right here."

Hawk's arms wrapped around her, and he laid his cheek against the honey-colored curls at her temple. Once again, he felt a rush of pure relief at not having been the one to cause her such sorrow.

"I wish I could make all this hurt go away," he murmured against her ear, the words he spoke utterly sincere.

She turned her face into his neck, the arms about his waist tightening. "Just having you here helps more than you'll ever know," she replied, the warm puffs of her breath caressing his throat. "As long as I have you, I'll be all right."

Once again Hawk tottered between heaven and hell. Should he marry Sabra and pray with everything he had that she'd understand when he told her the truth? Or should he stay long enough to help get her over the initial shock of her father's death and then sneak out of her life like a craven coward?

He didn't know.

He simply didn't know.

The muted thud of heels against the polished wooden floor rescued Hawk from his tormenting thoughts.

"Jasmine's heated up some of that food the ladies brought by. Logan says you're to come in and eat, Sabra, and no arguments." Hezekiah delivered his message with the stern mien of an old family retainer.

Hawk was grateful to see a small smile tip Sabra's mouth. It held but a faint hint of its usual glory, but it was a smile nevertheless. Hawk trailed at her heels as she stepped from his arms and obediently followed Hezekiah to the kitchen.

The five friends gathered around the table, where, despite a succession of protests — from all but Hezekiah, whose stomach was rumored to be bottomless — Jasmine served them plates that all but groaned under the weight of their contents.

Sabra, her mind far away, merely toyed with her food. She felt as though her life had been turned upside down, and she couldn't help worrying about what the future held for her.

Would she still be here next week, next month? She supposed she could stay with Logan, if she so desired. Or with Gramma and Gramps. She knew she could go back East to live with them, but she honestly didn't want to.

What she wanted,—with all her heart, was for Hawk to propose. She'd been positive that he was thinking about it before her father's death. What else could all those sweet words in Bisbee have meant? But somehow her father's death seemed to have had a great impact on Hawk.

Maybe he felt it would be improper to bring up the subject at this time, thinking she'd want time to herself, time to mourn.

But, if that was what he believed, he was wrong. Mourning wouldn't bring her father back. And putting this new sorrow out of her mind would be so much easier if she and Hawk were building a life together. She didn't care if they stayed at the fort, if they traveled while he continued the research for his book, or if they returned to his hometown, just as long as they were together.

That random thought about Hawk's home brought a small frown as Sabra realized she knew hardly anything about his background, not even where his hometown was, or whether he had any family at all since his parents were dead. Well, it didn't matter. Wherever Hawk was, that would be home to Sabra. She just wanted to be with him.

A tiny flash of guilt stabbed through her as she turned to Logan. Would he feel abandoned if she left with Hawk? Surely not. He was used to being on his own. He'd spent years at West Point, and he'd made no bones about there being no sense of "family" between him and their father before Sabra had arrived. Actually, despite the closeness between Sabra and Logan, there had been no change at all in the relationship of the two men even after she came to the fort.

She'd miss Logan, miss him terribly, but she knew her brother would want her to be happy. And for her, happiness was centered squarely on Sterling Hawkins.

She cast another lash-sheltered look at Hawk, wishing she could express how grateful she was that he'd been beside her to shore up her emotions when this terrible thing had happened. How very lost and alone she would have been if she hadn't had his arms to shelter her.

That thought filled her with a sudden determination. She knew what she was going to do.

She'd thrown caution and propriety to the winds that first night in Bisbee. Why should she stand on foolish ceremony now?

As soon as she got the chance, Sabra was determined to find a way to let Hawk know that she had no desire to postpone the rest of her life because of her father's death.

Across the rain-swept parade ground, two men huddled near a single lantern sitting on the trading-post counter.

"I'm telling you, it would be like insurance."

"I don't know, Jennings. I'm not crazy about the idea of sneaking into Logan Powers's house. Not now. Not with everybody so on edge. Maybe he'll get tired of playing detective and give it up. They're never going to find out who killed the old man. There's no evidence, no link, no reason to suspect anyone."

Jennings gave a derisive snort. "You don't know Powers like I do. You haven't spent the best part of the last few days with him. He's like an old hound dog with a coon's scent in his nose. I tell you, he's not going to give up. Not now, not ever. Something is driving the man."

"But he can't prove anything."

"I'm not willing to take that chance," Jennings insisted. He pinned his companion with a hard, probing stare. "What the hell do you care that Hawkins is innocent? Jeez, Henderson, you developing a conscience at this late date?"

"No, it's not that—"

"Then I say we give Powers a decoy. Make sure he never sniffs out the truth."

"All right, all right. Do it first chance you get, but be damn careful when you do."

Logan lifted the edge of the red brocade drape and peered out the living-room window. "Look's like it's slacking off a little. Think we ought to head out while we have a chance?"

"Might be a good idea," Hezekiah agreed. "I can get Jasmine back to Suds Row before it's pitch black out there."

Jasmine turned to Sabra, the skirt of her dress whispering against the horsehair sofa she shared with her friend. Concern etched her lovely café au lait face. "Are you sure you don't want me to stay tonight? I don't mind. Really."

Sabra reached out and gave Jasmine's hand a reassuring squeeze. "I'm positive. I'll be just fine. And I won't be alone. Hawk's going to stay for a while. And tired as I am, I'm sure I'll go right to sleep. No sense in you getting any further behind in your work than you already have."

Jasmine gave an elegant shake of her head. "That doesn't matter."

"I know. But I'm fine. Go on home. And you, too, Logan."

Logan cast a long look at Hawk. Then, evidently satisfied with the silent message he read in the other man's dark blue eyes, he shrugged and abandoned his hold on the drape. Crossing the room, he gathered up his coat and hat and bent to drop a kiss on his sister's forehead.

Sabra stayed by the fire while Hawk followed the

other three to the door. Hezekiah and Jasmine bid them a quick goodbye and slipped into the deepening shadows, but Logan hesitated at the doorway, his hand on the knob.

"Uh . . . don't let her run you off too early. She thinks she's ready to be alone in the house, but I'm not so sure."

"I won't leave until I'm positive she's asleep," Hawk promised.

"She doesn't want me hovering over her, says I treat her like a baby," Logan confessed with a wry smile. "But she'll take it from you."

"Don't worry, Logan. I'll take care of her. You know I will."

"Yeah, I know I can trust you." Logan took a step, then turned back one last time. "Listen, if she gets edgy, I'd just as soon you not leave her. The sofa won't make a very comfortable bed, but I'd feel better knowing someone was here."

"Sure."

"Thanks. You're a good friend." With that, Logan finally stepped over the threshold and pulled the door closed behind him.

Sabra appeared so lost in thought when Hawk returned to her that he wondered if she'd even heard him come back. But when he sat down beside her and slipped an arm around her shoulders, she immediately curled against him with a contented sigh.

To make her more comfortable, Hawk shifted position, turning his back against the corner of the sofa, stretching his long legs out. At his hands' gentle urgings, Sabra moved with him until her legs paralleled his and the dark skirt of her gown billowed and flowed over him from thigh to ankle. A few more wriggles, a tiny adjustment here and there, and Sabra lay cuddled against his hard reassuring length, her head cradled against the curve of his shoulder.

The gentle rise and fall of Hawk's chest imparted a sense of security Sabra knew only in his arms, and she snuggled closer against him.

"Are you warm enough?" he asked.

"Ummm," she murmured, nodding her head just enough to feather a wing of golden curls against the underside of his chin.

For a long moment, they lay locked together, very still, simply staring into the crackling flames within the fireplace. Then Sabra sighed deeply, her breath fanning out against the front of Hawk's shirt.

"Penny for your thoughts," he whispered against the top of her head.

She stilled against him, save for the gentle rhythm of her breathing and the sudden nervous fiddling of one hand with the middle button of his shirt.

Hawk's heart beat softly beneath her ear; the warm male scent of him filled her nostrils. She knew there was no place else on earth she wanted to be, no other man in whose arms she'd want to lie. This was no time for coy answers or simpering little-girl silliness. If she wanted her heart's desire, she must ask for it.

Sabra tilted her head back so she could look into his eyes. "I'm thinking about the future . . . about us," she answered, her manner utterly honest.

Midnight blue eyes bored into orbs of deepest brown. Her softly spoken words needed no further clarification. He felt totally attuned to Sabra, as if their souls were one. He could read her love—her need, her hopes—in the bottomless magic of her eyes. And he knew at last that he had to take the chance.

Leaving Sabra was something that was now totally beyond him. In an instant his weary mind had solved as many of his problems as it could manage at one time.

He was going to stay.

He'd brought sufficient funds with him to remain in the area for an indefinite period. He'd carried a large portion of his cash to Fort Huachuca; the remainder was safely deposited in a bank in Tucson. He had enough to support them for several years, if necessary.

He'd write a letter to his uncles tomorrow, explain to them that his trip was going to take much longer than he'd first thought, tell them the lumber business was in their hands and that they should keep managing it as they saw fit until he returned. *If* he returned.

Why had he thought himself so indispensable? They'd run the business for years during his childhood and adolescence. They could certainly do it again. Hell, as far as that went, in any city large enough to have a lawyer, he could have papers giving them full ownership drawn up and simply put them in the mail.

It might be nice to travel for a while . . . go to California or maybe Oregon or Washington. He'd heard that was great lumber country. There was nothing to keep him from starting another business.

The future might be vague, nebulous, but the present was firmly settled in his mind. He was going to ask Sabra to marry him, then wait patiently until the mourning period she set was over. That was as far as he could logically plan. Up to their marriage. After that, he would take one day at a time, waiting, hoping for an appropriate moment to tell her the truth, a time when he'd know beyond a shadow of a doubt that what they'd built between them would stand the shock of his revelation.

And if that time never came, then so be it; for Hawk had come to realize that living with his lie would be easier than living without Sabra.

Sabra watched the play of emotions on his face, her heart fluttering in her throat as she waited. When he suddenly smiled and pressed a kiss against her forehead, her heart stilled with expectation.

"I'm afraid this is a rather unconventional position for what I'm about to say . . . I think I'm supposed to be on my knees."

The catch in Hawk's voice made his lightly teasing words unbelievably endearing to Sabra. And when he tensed his muscles, as if to rise, she tightened her arm across his chest.

"No," she whispered. "Please don't move. I'd rather be in your arms."

His hold on her tightened. "In that case, my love, would you do me the very great honor of becoming my bride?"

Crystal tears of joy gathered at the corners of Sabra's eyes, clung tenuously to the thick fringe of her lashes.

"Yes, oh yes," she sighed. "Nothing would please me more."

Her mouth lifted eagerly to his when Hawk bent his head to seal their pledge with a devastatingly tender kiss. And when they at last drew apart, with a contented sigh he nestled her head back against his shoulder.

"Could . . . could we talk about when?" Sabra asked timidly, her voice muffled against his shirt front, her finger rimming the middle button of his rumpled cotton shirt.

Hawk chuckled softly. "Of course we can, sweetheart. What do you think about June? Would that be too soon?"

"June?" Sabra jerked upright, her hand braced against his chest, her eyes wide and round with consternation. "That won't do at all."

Crestfallen, Hawk hastened to retract the suggestion. "I'm sorry, love, I should have realized you'd want to wait longer. Just name the date. Whatever you want."

"Longer?" Sabra repeated, aghast at the very idea. "Oh, no, you don't understand. I don't want to wait at all. I want to get married right away."

"B-but" Hawk sputtered, "I thought . . . I mean . . . do you think people will . . . "

"Talk?" Sabra supplied. "Probably. But I don't care what anyone might say. Those who are important to me will understand. Besides, my father would have wanted me to be happy, I'm absolutely positive of that."

Hawk nodded his head in agreement, pushing ugly memories of his last confrontation with the major far to the back of his mind. "Of course he would. He loved you very much."

"Don't you see? Why should we let convention stand in our way? Being happy means being with you. I want to talk with Logan first, of course, but if he's in agreement then I want to make arrangements with the chaplain as soon as possible."

Hawk blinked in surprise, but said not a word.

An almost comic look of concern flashed in Sabra's eyes. "Oh, dear. I mean, if it's all right with you." Her voice was now tiny and tentative, but filled with hope. "It is, isn't it?"

Pure unadulterated joy blossomed on Hawk's face as he wrapped his arms around Sabra and dragged her back down against his chest.

"Of course it is. As long as Logan gives his approval, tomorrow wouldn't be too soon for me, my love."

Chapter Twenty-three

Hawk almost got his wish, but in the end it took three days to make all the arrangements for the wedding, simple though it was to be.

"You don't think I'm being foolish, thumbing my nose at propriety like this?" Sabra asked Logan the day after Hawk proposed, her heart in her eyes as she waited for her brother's reaction to the news.

"Is this what *you* want?" Logan asked.

"Yes. Oh, yes, it is."

"Then that's good enough for me."

"I've thought about it, Logan, really I have. I just have this feeling . . . I can't explain it. I belong with Hawk. I . . . I don't know how else to say it." Sabra ducked her head, her fingers plucking at one end of her sash. Then she looked him square in the eye. "I'm not going into this blind. I'm aware that some people won't approve—the ones that set so much store in etiquette and social formalities."

Logan cocked an eyebrow. "And who gives a damn what any of those people might say? I sure don't. Do you?"

"Yours is the only opinion I care about. If you disapprove—"

"Well, I don't," Logan declared, giving her a big bearhug and then swinging her round and round until she was almost dizzy. "I think it's a grand idea, and what's more I demand to give the bride away."

"Oh, Logan! Would you?" A wide smile wreathed Sabra's face. "That would be lovely."

"You bet I will. And if anyone says one word about your plans, you just tell them to go straight to the devil."

Hawk's heart soared at the sound of Sabra's soft laughter. They were doing the right thing. He was positive they were. The radiant look on her face was evidence enough for him.

"Do you think you can wear two hats for this ceremony?" he asked Logan. "I mean, give the bride away and stand up as my best man?"

Logan's big hand closed around Hawk's and pumped it up and down with enthusiasm. "I'd be proud to." Then, casting an eye in Sabra's direction, he asked, "Who's going to be the maid of honor?"

This time the saucy little dimple appeared along with Sabra's smile. "Well, if I'm going to give this post something to talk about, I might as well do it up good and proper. Since this is obviously destined to be a rather unorthodox wedding—to say the least—what would you think if I asked Jasmine to stand up with me?" Her eyes swept from Hawk to Logan and back again.

"I think it's an absolutely marvelous idea," Hawk said.

"And so do I."

"Good, then it's all settled."

News of the coming event spread across the post like a prairie-grass fire in August. Sabra had let it be known that any who felt so inclined would be welcome to attend. There would be no individual invitations.

While some declared their support of Sabra's decision, others professed shock at the very thought of holding a wedding a mere three days after a funeral.

Had Logan known of Melissa Henderson's reactions, he'd have placed her name at the top of his list for ol' Beelzebub's attention. The black-haired beauty jumped at every opportunity to proclaim—at length and loudly—her personal repugnance of the situation.

When Louise Penrod and Mary Ruth Randall

dropped into the trading post to purchase a spool of thread, Melissa took advantage of her captive audience to once again voice her horror at Sabra's lack of good taste.

That was all it took for Louise to make up her own mind. If Melissa was against the wedding, then she was for it.

"I don't see anything wrong with what Sabra's doing," Louise declared, her voice full of conviction.

Melissa's hand flew upward to flutter over her heart as if she were about to have an attack of the vapors. "I can't believe you could say such a thing," she said in a stricken, self-righteous voice. "Why, Louise Penrod, where's your good sense gone to? The girl's daddy just died."

"So?" Louise lifted her chin another stubborn inch. "I suppose you'd prefer she throw herself on the grave and spend the next year wailing at the top of her lungs."

"Well, a little decorum would hardly hurt. Makes us all look like we don't have the manners God gave a goose."

Louise and Mary Ruth exchanged quick exasperated glances as if to say, Look who's talking about proper social behavior . . . good grief!

Too caught up in her tirade to notice the other girls' sudden silence, Melissa continued. "And surely you've heard who's going to be her maid of honor. I can hardly believe it myself. After all, she had all of us to choose from. It's an insult, that's what it is. A pure and proper insult to each and every one of us that she had the gall to actually ask a ni—"

"That's it," Louise declared, slamming the wooden spool onto the counter so hard that Mary Ruth and Melissa both jumped. "I swear, Melissa, if you say one more thing about Sabra Powers, I'm going to snatch you baldheaded."

Melissa's mouth snapped shut. When the shock of Louise's words began to wear off, she narrowed her eyes, spoiling for a fight. "I can't believe you would condone such trashy behavior."

Louise bristled with indignation. "What's so trashy about falling in love and getting married? Humph! At least someone wants Sabra. The way I see it, all this blow and bluster is just because you're jealous because she's getting married and you're not!"

Melissa gave a small screech of fury. "For your information, Edward Woodley has already asked for my hand in marriage. I'm simply trying to make up my mind."

Louise gave a disdainful toss of her curls. "Well, you'd better make it up quick. If the man's got any brains at all, he'll figure out that you're no prize catch and withdraw the offer!" She snatched up the spool of thread and spun on her heel. "You can put this on our account."

Head high, shoulders back, Louise Penrod marched from the store, Mary Ruth Randall scurrying behind.

Hawk was positive there'd never been a more beautiful bride. His heart danced and capered in his chest as he took Sabra's right hand in his and stood facing her in front of the simple altar.

The sun speared through the windows at the back of the small chapel, crisscrossing the interior with beams of pale light that seemed to meet and meld in a golden sun-kissed halo surrounding the starry-eyed couple.

Sabra wore a simple sateen gown of palest blue, a mantilla of cream-colored lace gently framing her face. Hawk was attired in the same dark suit he'd worn the first time he'd held her in his arms.

Although Sabra's fingers trembled slightly against his palm as the chaplain's voice droned on, her voice was as firm and strong as Hawk's when she repeated the vows that would make them man and wife.

The hours before the ceremony had seemed endless, minute after minute spinning out into perpetual time. But now, as their eyes held and worshiped, and their voices rose and fell, promising to love and cherish, to belong to, each other until death alone would part them, the universe seemed to double back upon itself, and time ticked by with a speed that matched the staccato beat of their love-filled hearts.

Eventually, the chaplain's gentle voice penetrated the misty haze of happiness that enveloped them, asking if there was a ring. Sabra was just about to shake her head no when Hawk answered the question with a nod.

But how? she wondered. There's been no time, no sources, for wedding gowns or flowers or rings. She's cared little about the first two and, as far as a ring was concerned, had simply assumed they'd buy a ring at some later date. Confused, Sabra watched him dip into his pocket and withdraw a delicate gold band.

"It was my mother's," Hawk murmured softly in response to her bewildered look. "I want you to have it."

A ray of sunlight caught and splintered on the ring's golden surface as he slid the band onto her finger, and Sabra fleetingly thought her heart might burst with the happiness that filled it.

"I now pronounce you man and wife. You may kiss your bride, Mr. Hawkins."

Hawk's strong arms enfolded Sabra, sheltering her as if she were the most precious thing on earth. His lips were soft, warm, utterly tender as he placed them upon hers to seal their marriage vows.

At one instant, they were lost in the wonder of their first kiss as husband and wife; in the next, they were surrounded by Lieutenant Colonel Forsyth and a handful of noisy wedding guests, eager to impart congratulations. Logan and Jasmine escaped through the crush, happy to leave the newly wedded couple to the well-wishers. Grinning with satisfaction, they joined Hezekiah at the back of the room.

Meanwhile, the babble was getting louder and louder as each guest tried to outdo the others' sentimental wishes for long life and happiness. Sabra was hugged by the ladies and kissed by the gentlemen, while Hawk received enough hearty claps on his shoulder to make it sting.

When he finally managed to extricate himself from the crush, he stepped back a little and let his dark eyes sweep the boisterous scene, spotting Logan, Jasmine and Hezekiah near the back of the room. Logan gestured toward him, his signals questioning whether Hawk wanted to join them, away from the crowd. But Hawk quickly shook his head, preferring to stay near Sabra should she need him.

Propping one shoulder against a wall, he drew a deep, satisfied breath as he watched his bride. His heart swelled with pride when he saw her eagerly hold her hand out for two young ladies to view her wedding band.

Sabra must have felt Hawk watching her, for she lifted her head, and those dark brown eyes connected with his immediately. From her tender gaze, he could feel the love flowing to him. Never had he felt so good inside, so complete. She'd given him so much more than she could imagine; and he vowed to protect her from harm or unhappiness with every ounce of his being, to forever keep their love as bright and wonderful as it was at this moment.

Slowly Hawk and Sabra made their way out of the chapel and through the foyer, their progress impeded time and again by one well-wisher or another, or by the necessity for the larger than expected crowd to funnel down to ones and two in order to squeeze through the doorways.

Then, at last, they were outside, and the bright afternoon sun was shining down on a happy couple and the crowd lingering about them to give them more hugs, more rounds of congratulations. In fact, the assemblage began to grow larger, as folks who had not attended the ceremony drifted by and, drawn by the festive air, lingered to stop and talk and offer their own felicitations. From a distance, a few—Melissa Henderson, for one; Leroy Jennings, for another—simply watched with hard, disapproving eyes.

Hawk didn't try to rush Sabra. Under the circumstances, it had been impossible to provide her with the elaborate ceremony he would have wanted for her, but she certainly deserved the opportunity to enjoy every possible minute of pleasure she could squeeze from the afternoon. He was standing at her side, Logan to his right, when an all-too-familiar voice caught his ear.

"Say there, young fellow. Hold up a minute. Am I ever glad I ran across you again." Julian Hobart's voice, extra loud to overcome the buzz of the crowd, sliced through the air like a knife.

Hawk's heart gave a sick little lurch, then sank to the pit of his stomach. His mouth went cotton-dry, and for a long moment his legs failed to respond to the signals from his brain. Then, finally, his muscles obeyed as best they could, answering Hawk's mental demands with movements so leaded he might as well have been mired in quicksand. Slowly, he turned to face the man he was somehow sure would be his undoing.

Hobart's face was split in a broad, self-satisfied smile. His step was so brisk as he strode the final stretch of the path leading to Hawk, his little round potbelly bobbed with each footfall and his glasses slid ever farther down his nose. He looked like a man who'd just drawn the card to fill a straight flush.

Hawk knew, with gut-wrenching certainty, what the persistent little drummer was going to say before the man opened his mouth; still, his mind silently begged for reprieve. *Please, please, please.* The words drummed in his brain. *Don't let this happen. Dear heaven, don't let this happen.*

His thoughts were not for himself; it never even entered his head that he might be in jeopardy because of Hobart's comments. His fears centered on Sabra and what the coming words would do to her.

As panic set in, Hawk's mind, desperate as that of a wild animal caught in a trap, sought some way to stop Hobart from speaking his piece. He considered grabbing Sabra's hand, pleading sudden illness, and escaping to the house before the drummer could utter the fatal words.

With frantic eyes, Hawk measured the distance the man still had to travel to reach them. Next he surveyed the position and density of the crowd that surrounded them, and was grateful for the people who were inadvertently separating them from Hobart—at least for the moment.

285

Escape wasn't possible. There wasn't enough time, there wasn't enough room. Still, Hawk refused to give up, to surrender to the bitter eventuality. Hurriedly he bent and whispered in Logan's ear.

"I need your help, Logan. Run interference for us. Just keep Hobart occupied until we can get out of here. Please."

What he'd do if this one chance in a million worked, Hawk had no idea. The stage didn't leave until morning, so that wasn't a viable solution. Could he convince his bride of only a few minutes to climb on a horse and ride away on some crazy impromptu honeymoon? Now. Immediately. As soon as he could get them to the corral.

Logan responded to the raw urgency in Hawk's voice, his gaze quickly honing in on the subject under discussion. Sure enough, the tenacious salesman was churning toward them, determination written all over his face.

Logan could well understand why Hawk wouldn't want to spend the afternoon listening to the same old spiel about familiar faces and remembrances. Well, he'd do what he could to help.

The next few seconds were a blur to Hawk. As Logan stepped forward to intercept Hobart, he took Sabra's hand in a desperate grip. He could hear snatches of Logan's conversation. "They just got married . . . need a little privacy . . . tired . . . why don't you wait till tomorrow?"

Hawk gave Sabra's hand a persistent tug, hoping, praying she'd follow without question. She looked up at him, slightly startled by his desire to leave so hastily. Then, miraculously, she began to move with him.

But that was the last thing that went right.

Hobart sidestepped Logan, still jovially intent on reaching his quarry. And now, while he walked, he talked—loud and clear—as he tried to get Hawk's attention.

"Say there, young fellow, I finally remembered where I'd seen you before. I knew I would, if I thought about it long enough."

"Hawk, I think that man is speaking to you," Sabra

286

said, casting a perplexed look first at her husband and then back at the salesman's vaguely familiar figure.

"I know. I don't want to talk with him. Not now. Come on, honey. Please." Hawk ignored Hobart and kept on moving, tugging a bewildered Sabra behind him.

Then, just when Hawk thought they had a clear path to freedom, an elderly lady stepped from the fringes of the crowd and laid her wrinkled hand on Sabra's arm. Acting on natural instinct, Sabra hesitated and politely bent her head toward the little woman so she could hear what she was saying.

By then it was too late.

Still trying to persuade Hobart to wait until a more opportune time, Logan was hot on his heels as the salesman finally reached his goal, practically bowling the newlyweds over in the haste of his arrival.

As if sensing something out of the ordinary was about to take place, the people closest to Hawk and Sabra hushed their talking and turned to stare with mildly curious eyes.

"Well, now. Isn't this nice? Running into you again like this. Oh, and congratulations, young fella. Hear you just got married."

"Yes." Hawk's voice was flat, weary.

"That's just wonderful. Me and my missus were married almost ten years before I lost her. That's why I travel so much now. Keeps me from being so lonely." He gave a quick wave of one hand. "But that's neither here nor there. I'm sure you don't want to hear about me. Just let me wish you both the best."

"Thank you." Sabra's smile was genuine.

A tiny bud of hope flickered in Hawk's chest. Was that it? Could it possibly be that the man was satisfied, now that he'd delivered his message . . . that he'd go away? *Please, please, let him go away.*

But that was not to be.

"Did you hear what I said before, young fella?" Hobart inquired.

"Yes, I heard you," Hawk answered, the small flame of hope growing dimmer with each successive word

Hobart spoke.

"Yep, I remembered, just like I said I would," Hobart said again, shoving his thumbs into his vest pockets and rocking back on his heels. His round face glowed with satisfaction. "Knew I would if I kept at it. Hawkinsville. That was the name of the town. Hawkinsville." The drummer punctuated his words with a continual nod of his head.

Silence rippled from the center of the crowd, fanning out in concentric circles until the whole gathering was straining to listen to the peculiar exchange.

Hawk made one more effort. "That's right, Mr. Hobart. You certainly have a good memory. Maybe we'll have time to talk about it later, but right now we really have to be on our way—"

Hobart's double chin quivered as his smile spread wider still. "Yes, siree. Got a great memory, I do. I even remembered the story I heard about you while I was there."

Oh, no. Please. No.

"Quite a surprise it was, too. I certainly never would have figured you to be half-Indian just from your looks. Guess you must take more after your mama."

Someone nearby gasped.

Logan frowned, his brows almost meeting over the bridge of his nose as he tried to digest what he'd just heard.

Sabra just looked at Hawk blankly, as if the whole conversation were being carried on in some foreign language.

Hawk cringed. But the worse was yet to come.

"Once I got the name of the town right, the rest just started seeping back in—even the part about the Stone River Battle . . . sad thing, that was. Even sadder for you, I guess."

By now the crowd was beginning to close in. In excited whispers, people repeated the words uttered by the little salesman. Then murmurs began to ripple through the crowd. Leroy Jennings pushed his way into the throng, shouldering through the tightly packed bodies until he stood almost next to Hawk.

Little by little, the crowd began to shift, stand on tiptoe, shove closer, all to get a better look at what was happening, to see firsthand the reactions of the main characters in the scene being played out before their very eyes.

"What the hell is he talking about?" Logan growled at Hawk. Then, without even waiting for an answer, he turned on Hobart, anger blazing in his eyes. "What are you talking about, old man? You don't even know what you're saying. You've got Hawk mixed up with someone else."

Hawk just stood there while his world fell apart around him.

As offended by the slur cast upon his precious memory as by the tone of Logan's voice, Hobart drew himself up and fixed them all with a myopic look of utter self-righteousness.

"I beg your pardon, sir," the drummer said, his voice more than a little huffy. "I know exactly what I'm talking about. I recall every word of the story . . . how the young man's mother and father were killed in the Stone River Battle. A sad and tragic occurrence, especially considering his mother was from one of the finer families in Hawkinsville."

Logan took a menacing step toward Hobart, and his big hands clutched the drummer's lapels. An excited babble raced through the crowd.

Sabra gasped at her brother's move, her fingers flying upward to tremble against her mouth. The whole scene was beyond her comprehension; nothing Hobart was saying made sense. Her eyes widened in a perplexing mixture of confusion and shock and the waning vestiges of denial.

"See here, sir!" Hobart protested, making a few weak attempts to dislodge Logan's tangled fingers. "I must insist you unhand me immediately."

Logan's face was a thundercloud. "I don't know what you're trying to pull, but I'm not buying it." He gave Hobart a none too gentle shake. "Whatever your scheme, you've got your story all mixed up. My father was the one involved in the Stone River Battle . . . he

289

was the commanding officer of the batallion."

Hobart danced on his toes as Logan yanked him higher. "Really, I must insist—" he began, but Logan cut him off with another shake.

"This is my sister's wedding day, you bastard. I suggest you apologize for your malicious lies. Whatever the purpose of this whole charade, it's not going to work here. I can promise you that."

Hobart's bottom lip stuck out stubbornly. His voice had a squeak of fear in it, but he had no intention of retracting his story—not when he knew he was right. "I'm not wrong!" His eyes searched for Hawk through the bobbling lenses on the end of his nose. "See here, young fella, why don't you tell him I know what I'm talking about? Tell him your Indian name is Silver Hawk—"

Logan let out a roar. "You'd better shut up! Right now. Or so help me, God, I'm going to break your neck."

Logan drew back a fist. Sabra screamed. Hawk surrendered to his fate.

"Let him go."

Logan's head jerked around and he stared at Hawk. "Let him go?" he repeated in disbelief. "The little son-of-a-bitch comes in here telling lies and I should just let him go? Like hell I will!"

"Let him go, Logan," Hawk said, his voice deadly calm. "He's telling the truth."

Chapter Twenty-four

"He's *what?*"

"He's telling the truth, Logan. Let him go." From far, far away Hawk heard a small stunned gasp. He didn't even have to turn around to know it emanated from Sabra.

Reaction swept through the crowd in waves, followed by moments of silence while everyone tried to hear what was being said, then incessant buzzing as information was zealously passed from person to person.

Hezekiah held tight to Jasmine's arm, the glowering looks he cast about the shrinking circle keeping the eager spectators from closing in completely.

Melissa Henderson finally burrowed her way through the inner ring of onlookers, weaving through the crush of bodies until she gained her objective—a position beside Leroy Jennings. Taking full advantage of the packed bodies, she sidled even closer to him, standing so near that the side of her breast pressed against his arm.

"Can you believe all this?" she whispered in properly horrified tones, her eyes full of gleeful satisfaction at the probability of Sabra's imminent downfall. "I suspected all along."

Jennings, totally oblivious of her until she spoke, whipped his head sideways and pinned Melissa with an exasperated glare. "Will you shut up, for God's, sake?" he hissed under his breath. "I want to hear this."

"Well!" Melissa responded, indignation sizzling through the word. The congestion surrounding them kept her from flouncing as far away as she would have preferred, but she managed to shift enough to turn a cold shoulder to Jennings. Her black mood showed plainly in the angry tilt of her chin and the malevolent stare she fixed on the principal players in the continuing drama.

Melissa would have been doubly provoked had she realized that Jennings was too fascinated with the possibilities presented by the unfolding spectacle to even notice her show of pique.

In the center of the circle, Logan stared openmouthed at Hawk for a long, long moment before reluctantly releasing his hold on Julian Hobart's crumpled lapels.

Once freed, the little drummer stumbled backward, pinwheeling his arms to catch his balance. His eyes were huge, watery blue blurs behind his thick lenses, and his fingers trembled more than a little when he tried to brush his jacket into shape.

As soon as Logan took his hands off Hobart, Hawk's gaze immediately turned to Sabra. His heart sank at what he saw. All color had drained from her face, and from the peculiar brittle fashion with which she held herself, Hawk feared that her knees might buckle at any moment. Her eyes, overly large in her ashen face, were filled with a look of utter confusion.

Hawk would have sold his soul to buy back the last few minutes, to spare Sabra this pain.

For several seconds, they all simply stood there: Logan, head bent, a deep furrow marring his brow as he tried to make some sense of what had been said, Sabra with glazed eyes veering from Hawk to Hobart to Logan and back again, Hawk wishing the ground would open up and swallow him.

Logan finally broke the uncomfortable silence. "Would you mind telling me what in hell is going on here? Would that be too much to ask?"

"No, of course it wouldn't." Even as he voiced the

weary, sighing reply, Hawk's eyes never left Sabra's pale face. "I'll tell you anything you want to know, but, please, let's take Sabra to the house."

Logan's gaze snapped to his sister. He immediately perceived the reason for the concern in Hawk's voice. "Let's go," he said. "We'll discuss the rest in private."

Murmurs of disappointment rippled through the crowd when they realized they were going to miss the drama's conclusion, and Hawk eyed the loudest protestors with distaste as he reached for Sabra's arm. A shaft of pain lanced through him when she flinched slightly as he cupped her elbow.

Hezekiah led the way, barreling down on the greedy-eyed spectators with such a wrathful look that they stumbled over one another to get out of his way. Hawk and Sabra followed, with Logan pacing protectively by her side every step of the way as if he didn't quite trust Hawk to see to her safety.

A bewildered Julian Hobart was left standing alone in the middle of the small circle of open ground . . . but not for long. As soon as the others cleared the outer edge of the crowd, people closed in, showering the little drummer with endless questions, greedily demanding a rehash of all the details. Before it was over, Hobart would tell his story dozens of times.

And the person who asked the most probing questions, who had the most attentive ear, was Leroy Jennings.

Once inside his house, Logan insisted that Hezekiah and Jasmine stay, stating that there was a need for them since they might be able to look at the situation objectively. They perched, close together, on one end of the sofa, not at all sure they wanted to witness what was about to take place.

Huddled in the corner of one of the big easy chairs, Sabra looked everywhere but at her new husband.

Almost unnaturally motionless, Hawk stood by the unlit fireplace, the only clue to his emotional status the undeniably desperate look in his eyes as he searched his wife's face.

Too agitated to sit still, Logan stopped only long enough to splash a huge portion of whiskey into a glass before he began to pace again. The amber liquid sloshed alarmingly as he stomped about the room. Finally, he paused near the doorway, took a large swallow, and pinned Hawk with a hard stare.

"Well?"

At the sound of Logan's voice, Hawk shifted slightly, his shoulders in resignation. "It's all true. What more do you want to hear?"

"Wait just a damn minute," Logan rasped, long fingers raking through his hair. "Let me see if I can make any sense of this mess. You're from a town called Hawkinsville, not back East as I assumed?"

"Yes."

"Are you a writer? Did you come to Fort Huachuca for research?"

"No. I run a lumber business. I . . . I lied about the research."

"Your parents—what Hobart said about them—is it true?"

"Which concerns you the most?" Hawk asked softly, a flash of the old pain in his eyes. "The part about my father being an Indian, meaning, of course, that I must be half-Indian, that I also answer to the name of Silver Hawk, my Indian name? Or the part about my parents dying in the Stone River Battle?"

Logan's only response to Hawk's questions was to raise his glass and gulp another large portion of whiskey.

"It's all true," Hawk said, a bitter smile touching the corners of his mouth.

"Jesus," Logan breathed.

Sabra's gaze flew to Hawk. *Indian!* Her beloved

294

Hawk half-Indian. How could that be? The thought was almost totally incomprehensible.

She waited for the fear, the revulsion to come. For a mental replay of that bloody afternoon when those filthy renegades had butchered her mother and her baby sister. But it didn't happen. The memories, the fear, didn't come. And that added to the confusion she was already awash in. A maelstrom of emotions swirled in Sabra's head . . . but, for some unfathomable reason, fear of Hawk wasn't one of them.

Her bewilderment grew stronger, and finally she pulled her eyes away, curling even tighter into the corner of her chair, her arms held close across her middle as if she might fly apart at any minute.

Logan looked beseechingly at Hezekiah, but his friend's dark eyes held no answer. Instead, he seemed to be quietly waiting for Logan's response to Hawk's revelation.

But, if truth be told, Logan didn't know what he was feeling. Shock. Of course. A sense of betrayal. Certainly. Hawk had lied to them! Anger. Yes. But not because Indian blood ran in the veins of the man who'd married his beloved sister.

Logan had never been one to judge a man's value by such unfair standards. White skin didn't guarantee honor or sincerity or worth. And "different" didn't mean unworthy—just look at Hezekiah. But Logan knew there were complications to such a union as his sister had made, no matter how worthy the man. A good portion of the population would condemn the couple out of hand because "it just wasn't done." Educated, mannerly, handsome though he was, to some people Hawk would always be "one of those savages." Which would mean problems and pain for Sabra. And that was what was hard for Logan to forgive.

Hawk felt strangely remote as he watched the reactions of the room's inhabitants, as if he were viewing the proceedings from a far, far distance. He thought he recognized a small flicker of empathy—almost kinship—in Hezekiah's calm gaze, but worry etched Jasmine's face as she closely observed Sabra. She was simply concerned for her friend rather than reacting to the answers Hawk had given. Logan's agitation was obvious in his continued pacing, in the jerky movements of hand to mouth as he downed the contents of his glass, swallow by swallow.

And Sabra, what was Sabra thinking? Hawk wondered. What was she feeling? Guilt surged through him as he quietly watched her. Bewilderment filled her eyes, etched her face . . . and pain. Such pain. Was she sorry? Did she wish she'd never met him? Never loved him? Never married him? Dear God, he didn't think he could bear it if she regretted the vows they'd taken.

He loved her so much. Needed her so desperately. Now she was probably lost to him forever. And it was nobody's fault but his own. Why hadn't he told her the truth before the wedding? Why hadn't he given her a chance to listen, to understand, to perhaps accept?

Why, indeed. Hawk knew exactly why. Because if Sabra didn't accept, then she would reject. Reject him. Reject his love. And that was what had kept him from telling her, had made him believe he was justified in his actions.

He had lied to all of them, but most foolish of all he'd lied to himself.

Well, he was paying for his dishonesty. And the price was higher than he'd ever imagined. He'd wanted to keep Sabra safe and happy, to protect her at all costs. And look at her now. The anguish, the sorrow, the confusion.

His fault.

All his fault.

"Why . . . why did you come here?" Logan forced himself to ask.

Hawk wouldn't lie again. Not ever. "I came here to—"

His answer was interrupted by an insistent knocking on the door. "Son-of-a-bitch!" Logan muttered under his breath. "What now?" He slammed his glass down on a table, then stormed over and threw the door open.

"I'm truly sorry to interrupt, Lieutenant Powers," Sergeant Jennings said. "I know this is a difficult time for your family. But I feel I must speak with you. Immediately."

"Couldn't it wait?"

"No, sir. I'm afraid it can't. If you'll just give me a minute, I think you'll see why I'm so concerned."

"Oh, all right. All right," Logan said with a weary sigh. "Come in. Get it over with. Fast. We've got other things to tend to."

Jennings whipped his hat from his head and sidled through the door. Drawing a deep breath, he steeled himself for what was to come. His insides were aquiver, but his step was strong and sure as he followed Logan down the hall.

The occupants of the living room looked up in surprise when Logan ushered Jennings through the door.

"My apologies again, for this disruption. But I felt it my duty, as an investigating officer, to . . . uh . . . broach an unpleasant subject."

"Sergeant." Logan's tone of voice brooked no further delay.

Nervously turning his hat round and round in his hands, Jennings began. "I happened to be passing the chapel this afternoon when . . . when Mr. Hobart . . . uh . . ."

"When you heard Mr. Hobart's tale. Right, Sergeant?" Logan prompted, irritation edging his voice. *You, and half the population of the fort.* God, it was starting already. Was Jennings here as the delegate of an enraged citizenry? What did they want him to do? Throw Hawk off the post? Ask him to move to the Indian village? Have the marriage annulled?

That sudden thought caused Logan to cast a quick

297

glance at his sister. He hadn't considered such a possibility before. Would Sabra want to end her marriage? Now? Before it had even begun? Logan was suddenly filled with a surge of hope that they'd be able to find a satisfactory solution to this problem.

"Yes, sir. That's right," Jennings continued, oblivious to the fact that he'd lost Logan's attention for a moment. "And I felt it my duty to stay and talk with Mr. Hobart after you left—to get all the facts, you understand."

"Fine. Fine. Now, what is it you found so urgent to discuss?"

Jennings eyes widened with surprise. "Well, sir . . . I'm a bit taken back that you hadn't thought of the implications yourself. I assumed—"

"You assumed what, Sergeant?" Logan queried, his patience wearing thin.

"That you'd put two and two together, just like I did. About Mr. Hawkins's arrival and your father's death."

"What the hell are you talking about?" Logan thundered.

"Well, it's obvious, isn't it?" Jennings declared, backing up a step or two. "Mr. Hawkins' family was killed at the Stone River Battle. Your father was the commanding officer; he gave the order to attack. Hawkins shows up here and two weeks later your father is found murdered."

"No!" Sabra's denial ripped the air. She was hurt by Hawk's lies, bewildered by the reason behind them, and even angry that he'd trusted her so little. But she didn't believe he was a murderer.

Jennings surveyed her with sympathetic eyes. "Miss Powers . . . uh, Mrs. Hawkins . . . I'm truly sorry to be the bearer of such bad news, but it's my duty to find the person responsible for your father's death. Mr. Hawkins appears to be the only suspect. And you have to admit that he had one hell of a motive—"

"I don't believe it. Hawk, tell him," Sabra demanded.

"Tell him you didn't do it."

All eyes were on Hawk as his gaze met Sabra's. "I didn't do it, Sabra," he said with a small sad shake of his head. "I'm guilty of a lot of things ... coming here under false pretenses, misleading all of you, and most of all of being grossly unfair to you, but I'm not guilty of killing your father."

The breath Sabra had been holding slipped past her parted lips.

Jennings drew himself up, his face a study of shocked indignation as he turned to Logan. "You don't mean to tell me that you're simply going to accept the fellow's word on this? Lieutenant Powers, I really must protest. This is hardly what I'd call proper handling of such a serious matter."

"And just what would you suggest, Sergeant?"

Jennings stared at his superior officer as if he couldn't believe Logan didn't understand the gravity of the situation. "My heavens, you've at least got to ask him some questions. You can't just turn a blind eye to the evidence."

"What evidence are you talking about?" Hezekiah's inquiry was a rumble.

Jennings stifled a look of irritation. He had to remember not to appear too eager. He was, after all, supposed to be searching for answers with the open mind required in an investigation such as he was "conducting."

"Well," Jennings answered, "first of all, I don't think we can dismiss what Kornsberg told us. Hawkins stopped by the major's office the day he died. He practically demanded to see him, and, according to Kornsberg, he was highly agitated when informed he couldn't." When silence met his testament, Jennings spread his hands. "Don't you wonder what was going on? What was so important that he would insist on seeing the major?"

Hawk interrupted Jennings's eloquence. "If you must

know, I went to the major's office that afternoon to ask his permission to marry Sabra."

Startled, Sabra looked up at Hawk. She'd had no idea he planned to speak with her father. Her anger softened just a little. Had he planned to tell the major the truth before asking to marry her? Surely, oh surely that was the answer. He was going to tell her father, and then tell her.

Of course. It made perfect sense. But then things got all muddled. Her father had died before Hawk could make amends. And she was at fault, too. Rushing things the way she had. Sabra felt a burst of relief when Logan finally responded to Jennings' denunciations.

"I think that would account for Mr. Hawkins's anxiety. Don't you, Jennings?"

Jennings shrugged. "Possibly." He turned and scrutinized Hawk. "Mr. Hawkins, where were you the night of the murder? We know Kornsberg left the office about six, and the body was discovered just before dawn. Can you tell us where you were during those hours? Particularly around midnight."

Hawk's gaze held steady. "I was riding. Out on the desert. I had some thinking to do."

"H'm. How convenient," Jennings said pointedly. "Perhaps . . . just perhaps, someone saw you leave? Was anyone at the stable when you got your horse?"

"No."

"When you returned?"

"No."

"I see." After those two words, Jennings let the ominous silence hang.

"You're reading too much into this, Jennings," Logan said. "Hawk has been staying with me. I heard him come in that night. It was after midnight, but it was certainly long before dawn."

Jennings shook his head sadly. "Your father could have been killed anytime between six and sunrise, Lieutenant. I can understand why you're trying so hard to absolve Mr. Hawkins of any guilt. And I can't say I blame you. If it was my sister's husband, I'd do the same—"

"Goddammit! I'm not absolving anybody of anything!" Logan protested. "I just don't want you going off half-cocked because of what that silly twit Kornsberg said."

"You're quite right," Jennings said, emphatically, nodding his head. "It's important that we look at this fairly, from all points of view. That we cover all possible questions. And, speaking of questions, Mr. Hawkins, how do we know that you didn't drop by Major Powers's office later that night?"

Sabra spoke up. "He didn't—"

"I did," Hawk interrupted. He had promised himself there'd be no more lies, and he meant to keep that promise. "I'm sorry," he added, when he saw the look of dismay on Sabra's face. "I did go back. After dark. And I talked with Major Powers."

"About your marriage to Miss Powers?"

"Yes."

"I see." Jennings laid one finger beside his chin. "Tell me, did he give his approval?"

"No."

"Oh, my," Sabra said softly, sadly.

"And what transpired after that?"

"We had words. I left the office—"

Jennings pounced. "You had *words?*"

"Enough, Sergeant!" Logan demanded after one look at Sabra's stricken face. "Mr. Hawkins had already told me about the visit to my father, and about the argument that ensued. I doubt if he would have done that had he been guilty."

"Not unless he is very, very clever," Jennings pointed out.

"Hawk, Logan, please," Sabra implored, her wide, bewildered eyes sweeping from brother to husband. She

301

felt she might scream if either one said another word. If they'd all just be quiet, go away, and let her think, she might yet make some sense out of this horrible muddle.

"I think we've heard enough, Sergeant," Logan declared. "My sister is understandably upset. She needs some peace and quiet and some time alone with her husband. We can finish discussing this another day."

"I'd like to make one last request, Lieutenant Powers, and then I'll drop the subject altogether, if you so wish."

"What is it, Jennings?" Logan's tone revealed utter weariness.

"I suggest we search Mr. Hawkins' belongings. It might set all our minds at ease."

"Oh, for pity's sake, Jennings," Logan growled. "Is this really necessary?"

"Go ahead." Hawk's soft response brought Logan up short.

"What?"

"Let him search. It doesn't matter to me. I have nothing to hide."

Logan's scowl grew darker, but he turned to Jennings and gave his permission. "Go ahead. Right now. Do it yourself. That way you'll be sure we didn't hide any evidence from you, or trick someone into covering up what was found."

Jennings looked remorseful. "I'm truly sorry to have to put your family through this, Lieutenant Powers. But surely you understand, sir . . . it *is* my duty. And I think Mr. Hawkins is handling this admirably. I'm sure we'll all feel better after the search is over and we can lay these suspicions to rest."

As if indulging in a game of follow-the-leader, the room's occupants trailed Logan down the hallway to the back bedroom. Hezekiah, Jasmine, and Logan stood outside, Hawk and Sabra just inside the entrance to the room.

302

Sabra's thoughts were still amuddle, but she moved a little closer to Hawk as Jennings began his exploration. She didn't even protest when Hawk stepped nearer, not quite touching her but close enough so that she could feel his warmth against her back. She closed her eyes for a moment, wishing that the damned investigation were over, craving a few minutes alone with Hawk. Perhaps, given those, she'd begin to understand what she felt and what she wanted. All she knew for sure at this particular moment was that she still loved him. Despite everything.

Jennings was slow and thorough. He began with the bureau, opening each drawer, ruffling through every garment within, running his fingers along the edges and into the corners and even against the bottom of the drawers.

Next he searched the wardrobe, dragging Hawk's clothing out piece by piece, shaking, feeling, digging in pockets. The bottom of the wardrobe and the shelf within received the same careful scrutiny as the bureau. Jennings even requested that Hezekiah fetch a chair from the kitchen so he might climb up and peer at the top of the cabinet.

Then the bed came under scrutiny. The linens were stripped, the pillows pounded and squeezed, the mattress checked, top and bottom, for openings which might be used to conceal something.

The sergeant poked, prodded, lifted, fingered. Nothing was left unturned, untouched. The lamp was hefted, the crocheted doily flipped up, the drapes drawn back, the rug peeked under. But nothing was found.

"There," Logan said. "Are you satisfied now?"

Jennings stood, hands on his hips. "Well, it certainly appears that everything is in order. His head swiveled as he gave the room one last perusal. The only item left was the suitcase upended in the far corner of the room. "Wait," he said, one eyebrow quirked in surprise at having missed something. "There's still the bag. I might as well check that, too." He started across the room.

"It's empty," said Hawk.

Jennings glanced over his shoulder. "Then I'm certain you won't mind if I look inside."

"Not at all."

The sergeant squatted in front of the case, tipped it onto its side, and began to unbuckle the straps which held it closed. His fingers caught the edge, drawing the top slowly upward as he leaned forward to peer within.

"Well, well," Jennings murmured, "What have we here?"

Chapter Twenty-five

Jennings dipped his hand into the gloomy recesses of Hawk's suitcase and slowly withdrew a small maroon leather case.

Sabra emitted one frail gasp and backed away in shock, seeking solace in her brother's nearness.

"Son-of-a-bitch," Logan muttered.

Jasmine whispered a soft "Oh, no!" and moved closer to Hezekiah, who automatically put his arm around Jasmine's shoulders but said nothing as he carefully watched Hawk's reaction to the discovery.

Hawk stood stock-still as Jennings gradually rose to his feet, then turned and held the case out toward them. The room had become deadly quiet — so quiet that Hawk fancied he could hear the rush of suddenly ice-cold blood through his own veins.

A dozen retorts flashed through his mind. *I didn't put it there. This doesn't make any sense. Don't believe it, Sabra. Please don't believe it.* But for a moment he was so stunned that his tongue refused to work.

"What do you say now, Lieutenant Powers?" Jennings queried, his tone smug, his eyes glittering with self-importance and satisfaction.

Logan's mouth opened, snapped shut, opened again as he stared in confusion, first at the case in Jennings hand, then at his sister's husband. "Hawk, say something, goddammit! Don't just stand there! How do you explain this?"

"I can't," Hawk answered. "I have no idea how that

305

case got into my luggage."

Jennings snorted. "A likely story."

Logan's gaze jerked toward Jennings. "Shut up, Sergeant! Listen, Hawk, this doesn't look good. You know it doesn't. There's got to be some sort of explanation. Ah, dammit, man! Say something!"

Logan fought a war within himself. He didn't want to believe Hawk guilty, but the evidence—the damned evidence—just kept piling up. The furrows in Logan's brow deepened as he peered expectantly at Hawk. Why the hell didn't the man defend himself?

Sweet Jesus, Logan wondered, *could I have been so wrong about him?* He'd liked Hawk from the very first day. That might be coloring his judgment. And Sabra. What about her? Logan had suspected all along how she'd felt about Hawk. Why, he'd even encouraged it. He'd been so sure Sterling Hawkins was a man worthy of his sister. Could he have misjudged the man that badly?

Sabra was crying quietly. She held her trembling fingers to her lips, as if trying to hold the sobs inside. A ray of light glinted on the thin gold band on her finger, and Hawk felt something twist in his gut.

Since Logan had failed to respond in the way he'd hoped, Jennings switched tactics. "Well, Mr. Hawkins? What do you have to say for yourself? Surely you're now prepared to abandon that story about not being guilty."

Hawk ignored Jennings's taunts, and riveted his attention on his wife. "Sabra, please," he said softly, pleadingly.

Sabra's gaze slowly lifted to her husband's anguished face. Tears clung stubbornly to her lashes in diamond-bright droplets before sliding slowly down her pale cheeks.

"I didn't do it," Hawk said, his eyes boring into hers, dark and stormy as thunderclouds. "You've got to believe that."

"I d-don't know what to b-believe anymore," she

306

managed to say between sobs and little strangled hitches of breath.

The knifing words plunged into Hawk's soul.

The five of them stood in an uncomfortable little huddle in the doorway, eyes glancing here and there, feet shuffling, fingers curling and uncurling, Logan cursing softly under his breath. And no one seemed to know what to do, what to say.

Except Jennings.

The tap of the sergeant's boot heels against the plank floor as he shifted his weight finally drew the others' attention.

"Lieutenant Powers, I'm sure you'll agree that the evidence is too damning to ignore. The man obviously came here with one purpose in mind, to kill your father. I'm just sorry that he was callous enough to use your family to accomplish his goal." Jennings's gaze flickered to Hawk. "That's rather a rotten trick, Hawkins . . . even for an Indian. Courting the lady— even going so far as to marry her—to achieve your plans."

Hawk's head snapped up. "That's not true!" he roared, muscles coiling as he prepared to launch himself at Jennings.

Sabra screamed as Jennings quickly drew his gun, all the while backing away from Hawk as fast as his legs would take him. Logan and Hezekiah sprang forward, each of them taking hold of one of Hawk's arms, digging their heels in, and holding him in place.

The awful words hung in the air, tiny seeds of doubt that found fertile ground in the raw flesh of Sabra's already aching heart. She stared at Hawk with wide, wounded eyes and wondered if what Jennings had said was true.

"Damn you to hell!" Hawk growled, his voice full of bitter frustration. "Damn you for saying such a vile thing."

Jennings's eyes narrowed dangerously. "You'd better calm down, right now, you half-breed bastard." He leveled his gun menacingly at Hawk. "It would please me greatly to shoot you where you stand instead of taking you off to the guardhouse." There was the tiniest hint of a smile on Jennings' lips as he cocked the gun.

"No! Don't!" Sabra cried.

For a second Hawk strained against the hold of Logan and Hezekiah, but not hard enough to break free. He longed to get his hands on Jennings, to smash his fist into the sergeant's lying mouth, but he didn't want to endanger Sabra or the others. With an iron will, Hawk tamped down the white-hot rage that boiled inside him, all too aware what might happen if Jennings began firing wildly.

Somewhere behind him, Sabra sobbed harder. Hawk could hear the gentle murmur of Jasmine's voice as she tried to comfort her.

He drew in a deep breath and forced his tense body to relax. "You can let go now. I'll cooperate."

Logan and Hezekiah exchanged questioning glances. Logan gave a quick little lift of one shoulder, as if to debate the wisdom of such a move. In answer, Hezekiah slowly nodded. Carefully, they loosened their fingers and stepped away . . . but only a few inches. Both held themselves ready, just in case Hawk tried anything else.

"Shall we go, *Mr.* Hawkins?" Jennings inquired softly, his emphasis on the word making it a slur. The gun barrel made a small arc toward the door. "Too bad your quarters in the guardhouse won't be as comfortable as those you've enjoyed here in the lieutenant's house." A wicked grin spread over the sergeant's face. "But don't worry. You probably won't have to suffer such indignities for long. I have a strong feeling you'll be swinging at the end of a rope soon. Quite soon."

A wail sounded from Sabra and her tears fell even faster at Jennings crude pronouncement.

"Will you shut up, Jennings?" Logan snapped. "My

308

God, man, there're ladies present."

Jennings looked at him, amazement on his face. "I would think you'd be overjoyed to see your father's murderer hang, Lieutenant."

"Jennings," Logan rasped, the word full of warning.

"Of course, Lieutenant, whatever you say," the sergeant agreed, his voice suddenly solicitous. "Now, if you'll allow me to carry out my duties, sir, I'll escort the prisoner to a cell."

Logan hardened himself against the mournful weeping of his sister. Guilty or not—and right now Hawk certainly looked guilty—he had to be locked away. Logan dared not risk his escaping. In the end, a trial would determine the facts.

"I'm afraid there's no choice," Logan said, his voice gravelly. "You'll have to go with him, Hawk."

Hawk pulled his attention away from Jennings's mocking gaze, his dark blue eyes locking with Logan's. "I'll go," he said. "But tell me one thing first . . . do you believe I did it?"

Logan pulled a ragged breath into his chest, and his fingers raked nervously at his already disheveled hair. "I don't know," he finally answered. "I can't even think straight right now. All I can say for sure is, if there's any truth to this and if you did kill my father, I will see that you pay—dearly."

"I see," said Hawk with a very small nod of his head, his voice almost emotionless. And then his sad gaze moved to his new wife, "Sabra?" The word carried endless questions.

A tear slipped down her cheek as she raised her eyes to his. The endless seconds ticked away.

"D-did you?" she finally asked, her voice so full of emotion she could barely speak. For a minute he thought she was asking if he'd killed the major. But her final words delivered the cruelest blow of all. "Did you use me? Is that all it was?"

Pain blossomed deep in Hawk's gut, clawed upward, raked his insides to tattered ribbons. He tried to swal-

309

low but couldn't; the huge hurtful lump in his throat made it impossible. He held himself tightly in control, forbidding the smallest movement of his body. Only the peculiar ashen tone of his bronze skin and the agony in his eyes betrayed his inner turmoil. His eyes were filled with a desperate pleading.

Sabra's heart was breaking as she watched her husband, waiting, still hoping even when she was afraid there was no hope. Yet he didn't answer. He didn't deny it.

Why did she still love him, even in the face of the most damning evidence?

She wanted him to tell her that everything was all right, that he'd done nothing wrong. That it was all a misunderstanding. That everything they'd shared was real and true and totally honest. She wanted to tell him she believed in him, that she could never doubt him.

She wanted to.

But she couldn't.

And suddenly Sabra could stand no more. She jerked her eyes from Hawk's and buried her face in her hands.

Hawk kept his hands clenched tightly at his sides; it was the only way he could keep from touching Sabra. He desperately wanted to pat the shoulders that shook with her weeping, to smooth the bright golden hair that tumbled over her tear-stricken face. He longed to take her in his arms, deny the ugly accusations, convince her that everything he'd said and done where she was concerned was utterly true. Most of all, he wanted to tell her that he loved her beyond measure, that he would give his life to have saved her from this agony.

But he did none of those things. He knew she was too torn at this time to hear anything he had to say. He wondered if there'd ever be a time when she would listen and understand . . . if there'd even be that opportunity to explain.

"I'm ready to go," Hawk said, numb and defeated.

* * *

With a metallic clank the door clanged shut behind him.

"Enjoy your stay, half-breed," Jennings said.

A satisfied chuckle accompanied the sergeant's retreating footsteps down the hallway and across the little office where the soldier on duty sat. The outside door slammed shut with a muffled thud, and Jennings was gone.

Expelling a deep breath, Hawk surveyed the small square area of his cell . . . a bunk with a lumpy mattress and one thin blanket, a single chair, a scarred table, and a chipped porcelain chamber pot.

The back and one side wall were solid adobe, the other side and the front were rods of blue steel, spaced too close for even the thinnest prisoner to slip through. The cell next to his was empty. The whole place smelled of stale sweat and urine and despair.

The soft shuffling of feet on the other side of the bars caught Hawk's attention, reminding him that he was not alone. He turned, wrapping his fingers around the cold metal, and did his best to give Hezekiah a jaunty smile. The effort was a failure.

"I haven't quite figured out why Logan sent you with us," Hawk said, attempting a cheerful tone. "Not that I wasn't pleased to have a friendly face along. Do you suppose he thought I'd try to escape?"

Hezekiah's big head shook slowly from side to side. "No, I think he thought Jennings was a bit too trigger happy."

"Ah."

Hezekiah looked miserable. He cleared his throat twice before trying to speak again. "For what it's worth, I don't think Logan believes you're guilty."

"Oh?" Hawk raised his head, a tiny flame of curiosity in his dark eyes, "Why's that?"

"I know him and his daddy didn't get along, but Logan feels a real loyalty to his family. If he'd honestly believed you killed the major . . . well, I don't think you'd be standing in this cell right now."

"A little vigilante justice?" Hawk asked, one corner of his mouth lifting just a tad.

"Could be."

Hawk sighed, nodding his head in agreement. "Can't say as I'd blame him. That's exactly what I wanted to do to the man guilty of killing my parents."

"Yeah, I figured that."

Hawk's startled gaze jerked upward. "You knew?"

"Nah," Hezekiah shook his head again. "Not before. It just makes too much sense now that I know all the background."

"And?" Hawk's knuckles went white as his fingers tightened on the bars.

"And I don't believe you did it. You might have thought about it. You might even have come out here for that purpose. But you're a better man than that. I think you found out you couldn't do it."

Hawk sagged against the bars. "Thank you, Hezekiah. Thank you. I didn't realize how much I wanted to hear those words."

"What are you going to do now?"

Hawk's gaze swept the small enclosure. "What can I do?" He shrugged. "Hope that Logan decides to follow his instincts. Pray that Sabra realizes how important she is to me. Wish that they find the real culprit.

"Well . . ."

"Think about it, Hezekiah," Hawk said. "How hard do you think anyone is going to look for the killer, now that I'm locked up?"

Hezekiah frowned, his bushy black brows gathering in one straight line. "Well, there's always the trial. All they've got is circumstantial evidence. Maybe they'll find you not guilty."

Hawk's laugh was mirthless, bitter. "Since when can an Indian expect a fair trial in a white man's court?"

Hezekiah had no answer.

Sabra bent over the white china basin, her hands cupped to scoop up another palmful of cool water to soothe her swollen and gritty eyes. Despite the cups of hot tea Jasmine had forced her to drink, her throat was still raw and achy. It was late and she was utterly exhausted, weary in body and soul, yet she prayed that she would be able to sleep.

With a deep sigh, she pushed herself upright, reaching for the towel to pat the moisture from her face. From habit, her eyes strayed to the small oval mirror. Suddenly she stilled, struck by the reflection of her wedding ring on the silvery surface. The burning behind her eyes began anew, the invisible cords that had sealed her throat drew tight once again, and she knew there'd be no rest for her that night.

Hawk lay upon the lumpy, musty mattress, his hands behind his head. From the small outer office he heard a soft snore, a loud snuffle, and then a flurry of movement, a sequence which had happened several times in the past hour. Hawk had long ago decided that the young guard was having trouble staying awake. He'd doze off, wake with a start, and then pace the floor or busy himself with things at the desk. But eventually things would grow quiet once more, and the process would start all over again. The fellow was either already tired from the day's activities when he'd come on duty, or was a new recruit, green and inexperienced at having to stay alert in the wee hours of the night.

Hawk stared at the ceiling, recollections of the afternoon cartwheeling in his head. How had things gone so wrong? And how had that damn leather case gotten into his bag? But it was hard for him to concentrate on such things. Memories of Sabra kept flooding his mind. He couldn't forget the look on her face as she'd whispered those last dreadful words. *Did you use me?*

Was that all it was?

Ah, God! He could beat almost anything—anything but Sabra not believing he loved her. But there was no way he could convince her of the truth. He probably wouldn't even see her again until the trial. He certainly didn't expect her to come to the guardhouse. But what if he sent a note, pleaded with her to visit him just once? Hawk unconsciously tensed at the thought, then slumped back against his thin pallet as he realized how little it would help. Even if she did come, how long would they have? Five minutes? Ten? What could he say in that short length of time that would make the least difference? Nothing. It was impossible.

He needed an opportunity to hold her, to show her he'd meant every word he'd ever said to her, every caress, every kiss. He needed to spill forth his whole story. If he could just explain it all in the right words, the right way, then surely she'd understand why he'd felt the way he had. Why he'd come. And then she'd have to understand that the love they shared was what had made him whole again.

If only he had enough time to explain, she'd have to believe. She'd have to.

Time. A bitter smile edged Hawk's mouth. Time was what he didn't have, locked up in this godforsaken cell where he could never get close to Sabra.

But what if? . . .

Hawk sat up with a jerk. The dirty gray blanket slithered to the floor. If he escaped, how long would it take for them to realize he was gone? He reckoned it to be about two in the morning. All right. Suppose he found a way to get out. Then what? If he went to the major's house, would he have enough time to talk to Sabra before they caught him again? Probably not. That would be one of the first places they'd look. And how did he know Sabra was alone? No. He couldn't count on that. Jasmine was probably staying with her again. He couldn't subdue Sabra *and* Jasmine long

314

enough to say what he had to say. Hell, even if she were alone, the most he could hope for was a couple of hours. But that wouldn't do. He needed days.

All right. All right. Think, dammit, think! Providing he could get out — and he'd worry about that later — how was it possible to get those days? Where could he go, and who could he turn to? Before Hezekiah had left the guardhouse, he'd promised to keep looking for evidence that would exonerate Hawk. The big soldier believed in Hawk's innocence, but he wouldn't hide him. That would smack too much of betrayal of Logan.

All right. Hezekiah was out. Logan was out. Jasmine was out. Who the hell did that leave? He hardly knew anyone else. Especially someone who'd stand by him *if* convinced of his innocence.

Wait! A thought exploded in his brain. Molly. Molly Davis. God, if anyone was ever steadfast and loyal to her convictions, it was Molly. Look how she'd championed Geronimo all these years. And being half-Indian herself, she just might understand what had driven Hawk to such folly. If he could just get to her, talk to her, then maybe she would help him.

He didn't even consider staying at her house. No. He wouldn't expect that of her. Even if she thought Bill would agree, there were the children to consider. He wouldn't put them in any danger. It had to be someplace else. But where?

The cave. Molly's secret cave. The one she'd played in as a child. Up in the Mule Mountains, not far from Bisbee, but so far back in a high steep gulch that few people even knew it existed. He remembered her talking about how pretty it was up there, about the flowers in the spring and summer, the stand of shady trees, the small waterfalls and catch basins of a cold mountain spring. Well, pretty wasn't important, but water and security sure as hell were.

So what did he have so far? *If* he could get out . . . *if* Molly would help him . . . *if* he could stay in the

315

cave undetected for a while. Then what?

Wait. That was what. Wait until he could figure out a way to talk with Sabra.

And Hawk knew he was going to do it. His chances were slim, his plan almost nonexistent, but he was going to follow through on it. It was his only chance to make things right with Sabra.

Hawk turned his head, listening hard. The cell and hallway were dim, shadowed, the only source of light the rectangle of pale yellow reflected from the office where the guard was. It was quiet again. Soon Hawk knew he'd hear the soft raspy snore of the guard as the young man nodded off one more time. The soldier was tired and, hopefully, fuzzy-headed from lack of sleep. There'd probably be a change of guard after reveille. He couldn't hope to escape in the daytime, and the next night's guard might be more alert, more experienced.

It was tonight or never. And suddenly Hawk had a plan.

Curling himself into a tight ball, Hawk clutched his stomach and groaned. The snores in the outer office hesitated, then continued. Hawk groaned again, louder, longer. There was a snort, a snuffle, and then silence. A wary listening kind of silence. This time Hawk groaned as if the hounds of hell had hold of him.

His heart quickened at the whispery shuffle of foot-steps, and through squinted eyes, he could see the silhouette of the guard poised warily against the rectangle of light. Another moan, and the guard scurried closer, his concerned face barely discernible in the gloom.

"Say there, fella. Something wrong?" he croaked.

Hawk groaned and thrashed about.

"Hey. Hey there, you want me to go get the doc?"

Another long agonized moan, an unintelligible mumble. Hawk prayed it sounded like delirium. He twisted, clutched his stomach harder, and rolled to the

316

edge of the bunk.

"Hey, fella, talk to me. You gotta tell me what's wrong. If you'll just talk to me, I'll get help. I'll get the doc. I'll . . ." The guard's voice, full of panic and confusion, wheezed to silence.

Hawk carefully peeked through the narrow slit of his eyes. The guard's hand nervously hovered near the ring of keys hanging from his belt.

Releasing a brief groan, a gasp, and then a blood-curdling gurgle, Hawk fell from the bed, landing in a limp heap on the floor.

Chapter Twenty-six

"Aw crap!"

Horrified, the young soldier peered through the bars at the lifeless lump of humanity on the cell floor. Then instinct took command over discipline. Hauling the large ring from his belt, he jammed a key into the lock, metal clanging discordantly against metal as he forced it to turn. As soon as the mechanism clicked free, he jerked the door open. The barrier swung back, screeching in protest, and with a loud crash slammed against the wall. He rushed toward his stricken prisoner.

Ashen-faced, the soldier knelt at Hawk's side, one hand reaching out. Hawk didn't even breathe until the guard's fingers touched his shoulder. Then, in one mighty lunge, he sprang up. Before the guard could even think about reacting, Hawk had him disarmed and flat on his back, and was sitting astride his chest, his steel-muscled thighs pinning the soldier's arms to his sides.

"Oh, jeez, oh jeez," the young guard whimpered, his eyes so wide with fright that white showed all the way around. Hawk pressed the gun barrel against the end of the soldier's nose, and the poor fellow's eyes almost crossed as he followed the movement.

"Please, please," he blubbered, near hysteria now. "Don't shoot me. For crissake, don't shoot me. I ain't done nothing to you. Jeez, I was only gonna try and help you."

"Just shut up," Hawk instructed, striving hard to

make his voice sound as merciless as possible. He didn't want the soldier to get any last-minute urges to resist. "You play your cards right, and maybe I won't hurt you . . . as long as you follow my instructions exactly."

"Yeah. S-sure. Anything you say." The area around the guard's nostrils was pinched and white, and his scared eyes continuously flashed from Hawk's face to the gun and back again.

When Hawk increased the pressure against the tip of the soldier's nose, the guard whimpered like a small boy.

"Listen to me, very carefully," Hawk said, "and do exactly what I say."

"S-s-sure."

Hawk had the distinct feeling that if the guard had dared to move his head even once, it would have started to bob like a cork on water.

"I'm going to ease up, just a little, so I can unbuckle your belt and pull it loose. Then, after I've moved clear, I want you to turn over on your stomach and put your hands behind you. And don't make one unnecessary move. Not one. Do you understand?"

"Y-yes."

Except for the tremor that ran through his whole body and the wild shifting of his eyes, the guard didn't move a muscle as he was relieved of his belt. Then Hawk eased to one side, taking his weight off the supine body, and slowly withdrew the gun from its constraining position against the guard's quivering nostrils. Frightened eyes fastened on the merciless black opening of the receding gun barrel, the soldier didn't move one inch.

"Over. Now." Hawk sketched a half-circle with the end of the gun that had so recently been snug against the soldier's red-tipped proboscis.

The guard flopped like a fish out of water. His peach-fuzzed cheek hard against the cold floor, he crossed his hands behind his back like an obedient child and then lay perfectly still.

"Good," Hawk growled.

Once again he straddled the soldier, this time placing his weight on the back of the man's legs. In that position he felt secure enough to slide the gun into the waistband of his pants. Within a few seconds Hawk had the guard's hands secured with the looped and buckled belt. Next, he unknotted the colorful handkerchief hanging around the soldier's neck and balled one corner of it.

"Open," Hawk instructed. The guard obeyed and Hawk stuffed the wad of cloth into his mouth.

Hawk stood up, grabbed the seat of the fellow's pants and the back of his jacket, and hoisted him onto the cot. After tearing a long narrow strip off the tattered blanket, Hawk bound the guard's feet with the remnant and threw the remainder of the blanket over his prone body.

Leaning over him, Hawk checked the gag to be sure it was still secure. "Can you breathe all right?"

The guard answered with an unintelligible "Mmff," and nodded his head.

"Comfortable enough . . . well, considering the circumstances, that is?"

Another "mff," another nod.

"Good. They'll find you in a few hours. Just lie still, take a nap, and you'll be free before you know it."

"Glumfphllk."

Hawk had a sudden inspiration. "If things go well, I'll be half way to Tucson before they even miss me." *Good!* Maybe that would send any pursuers off in the wrong direction.

"Sweet dreams," Hawk said, closing the cell door and turning the key in the lock.

He threw the key ring into the far corner of the hallway. Even if the guard managed to escape his bonds, he wouldn't be able to reach the keys.

Within minutes Hawk was out of the guardhouse and slinking through the night-shrouded fort. All the old skills his father had taught him came back. He catalogued every sound—the soft rustle of leaves, the snuffle of a horse, the distant howl of a coyote—as he moved silently from building to building, keeping in the shadows. The moon hid behind a cloud, and only a handful of silver stars peeped through; but Hawk's keen eyes easily separated onyx rectangles of barracks from obsidian clumps of foliage.

On his way to the corral Hawk stopped only long enough to slip into several storage sheds. The post slumbered unsuspectingly as the fugitive rolled blankets and filled stolen haversacks with a variety of supplies and extra ammunition. If there were any patrols about, he didn't encounter them.

Hawk made it to the corral without a hitch, and in just a few minutes, he had his horse saddled and the packs loaded. Upon leaving the fort, he laid an obvious trail in the direction of Tucson.

Half a mile or so from the post, Hawk stopped and cut several long, willowy limbs with bushy tops. He looped one end of his rope around the trunks, leaving the foliage ends free. Back atop his horse, he cradled his makeshift "broom" until he found a large patch of flat rock. The tracks of Hawk's horse led to the slabs of stone, but there were none moving away—only the random brush marks of wispy foliage upon the sandy soil.

As a further precaution, Hawk headed north at first and then angled to the west. Finally content that he had done all he could to cover his tracks, he circled around until his horse's nose was pointed east. Within minutes he was riding like the wind across the Chihuahuan Desert in the direction of Bisbee.

Sunlight rimmed the Mule Mountains with pink and deep gold by the time Hawk reached his destination. Except for the ever-busy area of Brewery Gulch, the town was fairly quiet, just now beginning to stir itself in preparation for the new day.

Hawk led his weary mount up the steep hill to Molly's, securing the stallion in a clump of trees across the dirt path that served as a road. Finding a secure lookout point from which he could easily view the comings and goings at the Davis house, he settled down to wait.

Hawk calculated that the children should already have left for their lessons at the schoolhouse, and it wasn't too long until a man Hawk assumed to be Bill Davis came from the house. Nattily attired in a dark suit, a bowler hat atop his head, the gentleman struck off down the path and soon disappeared from view.

Hawk waited another fifteen minutes before approaching the dwelling. Then he himself eased across the porch, making not a sound, and knocked softly on the door. There was a muffled "Just a minute" from within and in a few seconds the door was pulled open.

"Mr. Hawkins," Molly said in surprise, her dark eyes widening at the unexpected sight of her recent guest. "Well, my goodness, what a pleasant surprise. Come on in."

Hawk gave the road one last wary glance, then slipped into the Davis residence.

"You may not think this is such a pleasant surprise," Hawk warned once they were seated in the parlor.

"Oh?" Molly asked, one eyebrow rising. "And why is that?"

Hawk told her. Everything.

". . . and that's the whole story." His cup clattered against the saucer, the coffee finished along with the tale.

"Would you like some more?" Molly asked politely,

322

lifting the coffee pot from the tray she'd fetched while he'd talked.

"No, thank you. Look, Mrs. Davis—"

"Molly. Remember?" she prompted with a smile.

"Molly. If you don't feel you can help me, or if you simply don't want to, I'll understand. I'm asking a lot, I know. I covered my tracks real well, but there's no guarantee the Army won't eventually come this way looking for me. I don't want to put you in any jeopardy. So, if the answer's no . . ."

Head cocked slightly to one side, Molly watched Hawk with bright shoe-button eyes. "I pride myself on being a very good judge of character, Mr. Hawkins."

Hawk held his breath.

She gave a final tiny nod of her head. "I'll take you to the cave."

Molly had been right about the path to the cave being almost nonexistent. Beginning at the back edge of a dense clump of bushes, it worked itself up the mountain in a series of steep switch-back turns. The loose, rock-filled soil made walking difficult, even for someone as sure-footed as Hawk. More than once his boots threatened to slip out from under him as a pebble unexpectedly rolled beneath his foot, but scattered brush and random outcroppings of tumbled rock made each successive zigzag almost invisible to anyone standing below.

From the looks of it; Hawk guessed the trail hadn't been traveled since Molly used it to visit the cave. He marveled that no one had stumbled across it in the last few years, but after making the trip he decided that the tough going on the path would deter all but the most ardent adventurer from exploring this high hidden gulch.

Eventually they traversed the last section of the trail and topped the final ridge. A section of fairly flat

323

land stretched away into a small vee-shaped canyon.

At first Hawk couldn't spot the entrance to the cave, but his keen eyes eventually picked out a sliver of darker shadow in the far corner of the gulch. A shoulder-high clump of gray rocks shielded the entry. Nature had created an ideal arrangement. Once inside the cave, a man could peer through sections of the rock pile's uneven top and see anything approaching the hideaway.

Past the entrance to the cave and up another incline, there was a very small box canyon, almost a rock-lined corral. The floor was covered with a rich abundance of grass, and seepage from a nearby spring provided a pool of water. His horse would be safe, well fed, and sheltered.

Off to one side of the gulch, not far from the cave and in a stair-step arrangement, were three rock-lined catch basins, the natural formations growing successively larger from top to bottom. Clear mountain spring water cascaded from the top one into the next and from that into the third and largest basin. From there the water must have seeped back into the ground because none spilled from the bottom pool.

The cave itself was large and high ceilinged, its entrance opening into a wide oval-shaped room. Toward the back, several narrow passages led off into the dark. Two opened onto smaller anterooms and still more passages, the others pinched off after several feet. The cave may have gone undiscovered by white men, but there were obvious signs of Indian usage in the past. Bits of broken pottery, a scattering of arrow heads, some scratchings on the cave walls—in all likelihood the residue of many generations of Indian visitors.

A sooty trail along the top of the main room led back to one of rear passages, making Hawk believe there was a natural chimney somewhere down that long, dark corridor. At least the smoke from a campfire wouldn't plume out through the front entrance, another positive factor as far as safety and concealment were concerned.

Hawk had seen ample sign of rabbit, deer, and other small animals. It would be easy for him to supplement the supplies he'd brought with fresh meat. A well-placed trap or two — he'd learned hunting skills from his father — and he could forgo the necessity of firing a gun. There were plenty of mesquites and a variety of cactus to provide seeds or possibly some late-blooming fruit. And prickly pear pads, when relieved of their spines, peeled, diced, and cooked, would also produce an acceptable change of menu.

It was perfect.

Molly left soon after they arrived, anxious to return home before her children got back from school. Then Hawk unloaded his horse at the entrance to the cave before leading the animal to the small box canyon, where he hobbled his mount and left him to graze. He spent the rest of the afternoon carrying the supplies into the cave and arranging rocks of like size into "shelves" to hold his provisions. The extra weapons and ammunition were placed in a safe place near the entrance.

Night descended, enveloping the little canyon in a cloak of darkness, and the mountain air turned chilly at the sun's departure. After a quick supper and one last check on his horse, there was nothing for Hawk to do but lie upon his blankets in front of the small campfire and think about Sabra.

Once again his mind skittered like that of a trapped animal. One minute, he'd wish he'd never succumbed to the urge to track and kill the major. The next, he would realize it was that very goal, perverse though it had been, that had brought him to Arizona and to Sabra. He finally gave up trying to puzzle that out and simply accepted that some force greater than he had purposely led him here. And Sabra, and the effect she'd had on his attitudes and on his life, had to be the reason.

They were meant to be together. The spirits had ordained it. Now it was up to him to take the next step. But what was it? He saw no hope of returning to Fort Huachuca and spending any time with Sabra, especially enough time to convince her of his innocence and his love. To attempt that would result in his arrest. So, unless they caught the real murderer, he was forced to stay where he was.

Hawk fell asleep pondering his seemingly hopeless situation. And as he slept, he dreamed.

Well into the night when he awoke, his hands reaching for the woman who'd been beside him in the dream world, he knew what he was going to do.

Chapter Twenty-seven

As the hours turned into weeks, Sabra spent her days in bitter self-denouncement for so easily falling prey to Hawk's lies. But each night she awoke with tears on her face, tears born of the Hawk-filled dreams that haunted her sleep. Nonetheless, she refused to admit they might mean she still loved him, would love him until the day she died. It was easier to believe that he'd used her from the beginning than to acknowledge that she might have let him down when he most needed her love and trust.

By choice, and with the kind urgings of the fort's commanding officer, Sabra continued to stay in the house she'd shared with her father, unable at this point to make any firm decision regarding her future. On most evenings Logan stopped by and shared supper with her, and when their duties permitted, Hezekiah and Jasmine also joined them. Such gatherings were bittersweet, for they reminded Sabra far too much of the times when five friends had been together, and of how promising and wonderful the future had seemed such a short time ago.

Meanwhile, life for the rest of Fort Huachuca's inhabitants gradually returned to normal. Once the initial manhunt for Hawk was pronounced futile, the consensus being that he'd long since reached Tucson and had managed to slip on a train headed out of there, the formal investigation was abandoned. Telegrams were sent to other forts and to sheriffs in nearby towns, but there was little hope that these would produce any results.

Gossip, as always, persisted for a while, but eventually the post's inhabitants found other things to occupy their attention.

Logan resumed his normal duties, the long hours passing in an almost mechanical manner. Although he'd spent a good many of his adult years in the military, he was beginning to realize that he had done it to please his father. With that impetus gone, he seemed to question more and more whether he wanted to stay in the service after his present term of enlistment expired.

Only Hezekiah, in his own quiet way, was still searching for answers to the major's death. Although Jasmine was the only person with whom he'd actually discussed his preoccupation, Hezekiah suspected that Logan was aware of what he was doing. Despite that, the black soldier chose to leave his friend to his own devices, taking as a positive sign the fact that Logan didn't interfere or discourage him.

The big soldier was sure that somewhere in the back of his mind Logan also believed in Hawk's innocence, and was happy to see the quest for the real killer continue. For the moment Hezekiah was satisfied to wait until such time as Logan could work through the situation. He'd long ago decided that prodding did no good; Logan seemed to fare better when allowed to handle things in his own good time.

Jasmine, on the other hand, approached the matter from an entirely different point of view. She was positive that a man who loved a woman as much as Hawk loved Sabra would not kill his love's father. She was also sure Sabra still loved Hawk, and always would; and she felt it her duty as Sabra's friend to offer whatever positive thoughts she could.

Late one afternoon, as the two women worked in the kitchen preparing the evening meal which would be shared with Logan and Hezekiah after the men had finished their duties, Jasmine told Sabra of Hezekiah's quest for clues to clear Hawk.

"But whatever for? What can he hope to accomplish

by dragging this out?" Sabra inquired in response to the startling news. "And how can Hezekiah possibly believe that Hawk is innocent? Just look at the evidence."

Jasmine's lips thinned. "He can and he does, and that's all there is to it. Sometimes you just have to follow your instincts."

Sabra threaded her fingers through the hair at her temples, lightly massaging her suddenly flushed skin with tight little circular movements of her fingertips. "Really, Jasmine," she said in a soft, mournful tone. "I have such a headache. Do you mind if we don't discuss this right now?"

Jasmine bit her lower lip, wondering what to do. If she acceded to Sabra's wishes, her friend would continue to avoid facing the issue. If she pushed Sabra into a painful confrontation, memories were bound to cause even more distress before the healing process could begin.

Finally, with a heartfelt sigh, Jasmine dropped the subject.

Meanwhile, on the far side of the post, Leroy Jennings knocked lightly on the back door of Mortimer Henderson's house.

"Where's your daddy?" he asked immediately when Melissa opened the door.

"Gone to Lieutenant Colonel Forsyth's." Automatically her hand reached up to fluff the ebony curls hanging on her shoulder, and her little pink tongue flicked out to moisten her lips.

"Damn!" Leroy swore under his breath.

"Why don't you come in and wait for him?" Melissa knew her father would probably be perturbed when he found Jennings there, but she'd worry about placating him later. Jennings was within her reach, and that was all that mattered. Besides, it might be days before she had another opportunity to speak to Leroy alone, and patience wasn't one of Melissa's virtues.

When Jennings hesitated, Melissa quickly stepped

aside, swinging the door open wider.

"Come on in," she urged with an inviting smile. "I promise it'll be all right."

Bored to tears with Edward Woodley's insipid attentions and hungry for the hot thrills that Leroy had always been able to evoke, Melissa was more than eager to reestablish their relationship. Never one to pass up an opportunity that might be turned to her own benefit, she was determined to lure Jennings inside so they might have a fair amount of time to talk privately before her daddy returned.

With an acerbic lift of his brows, the sergeant finally slipped through the opening, and Melissa smothered a quick flash of elation.

She'd hardly seen Jennings since the afternoon in front of the chapel when he'd been so rude and hateful. At first he'd been busy leading search parties in pursuit of Sterling Hawkins, and when those efforts had been abandoned, Melissa had chosen to avoid him for a few more days as punishment for his treatment of her. But somehow the tables had turned, and Jennings, much to her chagrin, had thereafter gone out of his way to dodge her.

Suddenly Melissa's little game of retaliation had lost its luster. She'd been trying to find a way to patch things up ever since.

"What's wrong, Leroy?" she asked, placing a small solicitous hand on his arm. "You seem disturbed. Can I do anything to help?"

Leroy's frown deepened. "Dammit, Melissa, your father wants me to keep a low profile, not hang around the store during regular hours, all that crap. But when I try to see him at any other time, he's never here. I'd like to know what the hell is going on!"

Melissa knew Jennings and her father had some sort of business deal going, something they didn't want the rest of the fort to know about, but that was of concern to her only because those dealings had led Leroy to insist on seeing her in secret. As for the rest of it, Melissa had always been too self-centered to pay much attention to anything that didn't directly affect her.

She hadn't concerned herself with her father's multifaceted business. Therefore she had no answer for the exasperated Jennings.

"Well, darling', I'm sure I don't know. I don't understand any of this in the first place." She didn't, and she didn't care in the least about that. She just wanted to soothe Leroy so she could get on to more important matters. "Why would he ask you to stay away, sugar? For what reason?"

Jennings had no intention of answering Melissa's question. He had too many of his own. "Is it normal for your father to drop by Forsyth's like this?"

Two tiny lines furrowed the space between Melissa's brows. "Well, he has a time or two before. I never thought much about it. However, now that you mention it, he's been over there three times this week. I guess you could say that's fairly unusual."

"Do you have any idea why your father's gone to talk to the colonel?"

"No," Melissa answered, giving her curls a dismissive shake. "He's been awfully quiet lately, but he takes spells like that every once in a while. It'll pass. It always does."

Jennings' frown deepened. Something was going on. He could feel it in his bones. What did Henderson know—or suspect—that he wasn't sharing with his partner? Perhaps the trader was thinking of leaving him holding the bag.

"Leroy. Leroy, darlin'!"

Melissa's plaintive calls and the provocative press of her bosom against his chest finally pricked the sergeant's awareness. Instinctively his arms looped around her small warm body. Not only was Melissa's soft flesh a means of solace for the frustration Leroy was experiencing, but after all the weeks of sneaking around and being careful, it gave him a perverse sense of satisfaction to embrace her right in Henderson's own house. The act was sort of a symbolic nose-thumbing.

In the throes of a growing anger fueled by his fear of an impending betrayal by Henderson, not to mention his extended abstinence due to recent events, Jennings let his emotions rule and not his head. With a growl, he hauled Melissa hard against him, stamping his mouth down on hers.

Surprised and thrilled by Jennings's ardent response, Melissa made a mewing sound low in her throat and pressed even closer against his hard male body. The expert hands raking her back and gripping the plump flesh of her rump sent shivers up and down her spine.

"What the hell is going on?"

Henderson's thunderous roar startled the lovers and they quickly broke their feverish clench.

Melissa's wide apprehensive eyes flew to her father's face. One look at the wrathful expression that twisted his countenance and she knew it was going to be far more difficult to get out of this scrape than she'd imagined. Not that she wouldn't give it her best try.

The very real alarm she felt made it easy to bring the first sheen of tears to her eyes. She let her bottom lip quiver, and folded her hands demurely at her waist —becoming the picture of innocence, she hoped.

"How dare you?" Henderson raged, his gaze raking Jennings up and down. As his eyes encountered the telltale bulge at the front of the sergeant's pants, he let out a screech of fury and lunged forward. "I'll kill you with my own two hands!"

Jennings' gun was in his hand and pointed dead at Henderson's chest before Melissa's scream died away.

"Back off, ol' man, unless you want a gut full of lead."

"You sorry, sniveling little son-of-a-bitch," Henderson wheezed. "I oughta—"

"Save it. You're not going to do anything. Melissa, get out of here." With the gun barrel, Jennings gestured toward the door. "Now. Your daddy and I have some strong talkin' to do."

By this time, Melissa's tears were very real. "B-b-but, Daddy . . . L-Leroy . . ."

"Get the hell out of here, Melissa, before you hear more than your dear ol' daddy wants you to."

An ugly mottled purple suffused Henderson's face.

"Go on, Melissa. Do as you're told. We've got things to settle."

Melissa gave each of them a swift, frightened glance, then scurried from the room, grateful that her father had seemed inclined to place the blame for what they'd been doing square on Leroy's shoulders. The door to the hallway slammed shut behind her.

Keeping his gun carefully trained on Henderson, Jennings tiptoed to the door and pushed it open a crack, making sure that Melissa wasn't listening on the other side. Finding the hall was deserted, he let the door swing shut again.

"You dirty, low-down—"

"I'd watch what I was sayin', if I was you," Leroy retorted with a smirk. "I'm the one with the gun."

Henderson's face grew redder. "Goddammit, Jennings! How dare you touch my daughter? Who the hell do you think you are, taking advantage of a sweet innocent little girl like that? Christ, man!"

Jennings stared at the trader in disbelief, then he shook his head. "I'm certainly not going to stand here and discuss Melissa's innocence with you, Mortimer. I have other things on my mind that are more important—"

"Important!" roared Henderson. "More important than my daughter's virtue? Like hell!"

"You'd better believe it, ol' man. Now, I suggest you set your butt down in one of those chairs before I lose my patience and shoot you anyway." Leroy jerked his head in the direction of the kitchen table. "Remember, I've got nothing to lose at this point."

Henderson's cheeks quivered with the force of his rage, but he obeyed Jennings, slinking to the table with rapid, nervous steps. Folding his bulk into a cane-back chair, he gritted his teeth and waited.

Jennings sauntered to the other side of the table and pulled out another chair. Then he sat down, keeping the gun leveled at his partner's heart. For a moment or two, he simply stared at the trader, a bitter smile tilting one corner of his mouth.

"First thing I want to know, Henderson, is what you

were doing at Forsyth's."

The flash of guilt in Henderson's eyes confirmed Jennings' earlier fears. He jiggled the gun just a tad. The storekeeper's eyes followed the movement.

"You'd better tell the truth, ol' man—the *whole* truth, if you know what's good for you. I've been suspecting that somethin' was mighty wrong for several days now."

"Jesus Christ!" Henderson muttered. "I don't know why I ever teamed up with you in the first place."

Jennings sneered. "Because you had access to government supplies and I could find a way to smuggle them over to the Mexican settlements along the border and sell them. Quick profit. Little hassle. I think it's called greed."

"Smart-ass bastard," Henderson muttered under his breath.

Leroy just grinned. "Then there was the fact that I kept you informed about any problems concerning the sale of whiskey to the men in the barracks. Not to mention bringing shipments of cheaper rotgut from Bisbee to mix with your stock, and sometimes even hiding it out in the barracks until we could get it moved to your store without anybody seeing it."

Henderson only glared.

"Now, answer my question. What were you doing at Forsyth's?"

"Trying to bail our asses out of hot water, that's what, you dumb little peckerwood! And what do I get for my efforts? Huh? I ask you that! What do I get? I come home and find you forcing yourself on my daughter."

When Leroy threw back his head and roared with laughter, Henderson turned so purple with rage, the sergeant wondered if he was going to have a stroke.

"Forget your stupid fairy tales, Henderson." Jennings waved the gun again. "I want to know just how you were supposed to be saving our asses."

"Evidently Powers telegraphed some messages when he was in Tucson. The answers are coming in now. There's not enough in them to do much more than prove that Powers and I had a grudge fight going about the whiskey sales — and most everybody already knew that — but I've been hanging around, trying to find out if Powers had caught on about the missing supplies. It would only take one mention of that in these responses for Forsyth to decide to do an inventory check. We can't afford to have that happen."

"How the hell did you expect to talk him out of it?" Jennings asked.

"I didn't say I intended to talk him out of it," Henderson growled. "But if I found out the issue had been broached, then I'd pack up and get the hell out of here. Quick."

Leroy's eyes narrowed. "And me. What about me, Mortimer?"

"I'd have told you, Jennings. Christ! Do you think I'd have left without telling you?" Henderson looked shocked at the thought.

"Maybe."

Henderson started to rise, then remembered the gun and thought better of it. He sank back onto his chair. "Goddammit, man, I don't take kindly to slurs on my loyalty, especially not from a man who's just been doing what you were about."

"Mortimer, Mortimer," Jennings said wearily. "I wasn't doing anything Melissa didn't want done. Open your eyes, man."

Henderson's chin jerked upward. "I'm not going to listen to your trashy — "

"Suit yourself, Henderson." Jennings rose to his feet. "Just keep this in mind . . . you're as guilty of Powers's death as I am. Right now, we can't afford to be at each other's throats. We're forced to call a truce until this issue is resolved. Best I can see, you'd better keep watching out for what's happening with Forsyth, just like you been doing. I'll keep up my normal routine. And, in the meantime, we'll prepare for the worst."

Henderson knew Jennings spoke the truth. "All right," he said grudgingly.

Jennings holstered his gun as he walked toward the

door, a gesture of bravado that proved he had no fear of Henderson, armed or not. Hand on the knob, he paused. "Oh, by the way, I'll be needing an extra sum of cash."

"I already gave you your last payment!" Henderson protested.

"Things have changed. If we gotta run for it, I intend to have enough money to get me set up way down in Mexico. I don't intend to be hauled back for desertion, much less a murder rap. Just get the money ready. I'll stop by the store one day soon and you can slip it to me with the purchase I make. Nice and easy. No one will be the wiser. Right, partner?"

Henderson didn't bother to answer.

Once Hawk had made up his mind regarding what he was going to do about Sabra, he relaxed. He spent almost two weeks readying the cave, making it as comfortable as possible. That entailed stacking great heaps of extra wood in one of the small back chambers of the cave, trapping a number of rabbits, and cleaning and smoking them so he'd have a good supply of meat.

He even made a couple of furtive trips into Bisbee, first to leave lists and money with Molly, then to pick up his supplies a day or two later. He almost believed he could have gone to the stores himself without being noticed, for no one seemed to pay the slightest attention to strangers.

The busy little mining community was accustomed to the comings and goings of mining officials, prospectors, and peddlers. Still Hawk refused to take any chances. He was especially careful to avoid the area around Brewery Gulch. Della Maxwell was the last person on earth he wanted to run into.

Molly assured him that there was no suspicion of his actual whereabouts. News of his escape had reached Bisbee, but public opinion held that Hawk had headed for Tucson and had taken a train out of the territory. Rumor had it that things at Fort Huachuca were back to normal. Evidently Hawk was still the only suspect in the death of Major Powers, for little else was being done about his killing — unless Hezekiah was doing some probing on his own, as he'd promised.

But Hawk didn't have time to worry about that; he had other plans to make.

…the…
…the…

Chapter Twenty-eight

Well, this is it. Hawk knew there was now no turning back.

One more time he ticked off, in his head, items of concern. There'd been no alarm when he'd sneaked back into Fort Huachuca. And getting the ether from the hospital supply shed had been easy. The small bottle and a soft cloth were clutched securely in his hand. His horse was waiting patiently by the screened back porch.

Hawk had managed to slip into the dark kitchen of the major's house undetected. He'd even thought to leave the back door ajar an inch so he wouldn't have to grapple with the knob on his way out. The straps of the pack which would hold Sabra's clothing were slung over his shoulder, and the note he'd composed for Logan was on the table.

All he now had to do was get his wife.

Hawk released a sigh, grateful that the layout of this house and the one Logan occupied were identical. Sabra's bedroom was just a few feet away.

His fingers trembled ever so slightly as he unscrewed the cap and tilted the bottle until he heard a soft gurgle. He felt the cloth grow damp in his hand, and his nostrils quivered at the slightly sweet aroma that pervaded the night air.

Slipping the recapped bottle into his pocket, Hawk turned his head aside and took a deep fortifying breath, then silently crossed the kitchen.

A sliver of moonlight spilled through the open

drapes into Sabra's bedroom. It fell across the bed, an illuminating stripe that displayed a portion of patchwork quilt, an edge of white linen, and a tangle of golden curls. Half in shadow, Sabra's face was turned to the side, one small hand lying on the pillow beside it.

As a board creaked slightly beneath Hawk's feet, Sabra moaned softly. He froze. The hand on the pillow twitched and slid into the pale slice of light. Something glinted in the dark, and Hawk's heart leaped into his throat.

The ring! Sabra was still wearing her wedding ring! If he'd had any doubt that what he was doing was right, it was gone now.

She had to care. Why else would his ring still be on her finger?

"This won't hurt, darling," he whispered, more to himself than to her. "I promise."

On cat-quiet feet he slipped to the side of the bed and eased the cloth over Sabra's nose. She mumbled something incoherent, and, still deeply asleep, tried to turn her head away. Hawk matched her movements. The covers made a slithery sound as she shifted her legs. Her hand came up and pushed feebly at the cloth for just a second, then fluttered down again to lie, open and palm up, on the pillow.

Sabra was unconscious.

Hawk quickly snatched the cloth away. He wanted her out only long enough to get several miles from the fort. He allowed himself the luxury of pressing a fervent kiss on her forehead before proceeding with the next step.

A quick forage through the bureau and the wardrobe provided shoes, a hodgepodge of underthings, several dresses, and a shawl. Hawk stuffed these into the pack as fast as he could.

When he'd finished, he slipped his arms through the straps and settled the full pack securely against his back, much like a peddler assuming the burden of his wares. Then he hurried to the side of the bed and bundled the quilt around Sabra before lifting her in his arms. Quickly, silently, he made his way to the back door, and eased it open with the toe of his boot.

It was a little tricky getting Sabra's limp form atop the bare back of his mount, but Hawk managed. He carefully positioned her so that she slumped forward over the horse's neck, her arms dangling down either side, and then he looped the reins around her. Tightly clutching the thin strips of leather in his fist, he braced her with that hand and used the other to swing himself astride behind her.

Once up, Hawk gently pulled Sabra back against his chest, supporting her within the circle of his arms. Then he painstakingly arranged the quilt around her so she wouldn't get chilled.

Sweet heaven! I did it! I can't believe I did it!

Elation filled Hawk's heart as the natural heat of Sabra's body began to seep through the layers separating them, warming his chest and the insides of his thighs. Limply, she slumped against him, her head lolling against the hollow of his shoulder. Hawk found temptation too strong to resist.

For just a moment, he nuzzled the delicate curve of her neck, inhaling the unique woman-scent of her, savoring the silky texture of pale moon-kissed curls. Then, with a reluctant sigh, he abandoned the sweet self-torture.

His inclination was to kick his heels into the horse's flanks and ride like hell before someone found them and took her from him again. But he squelched that impulse, knowing it would be far safer—and smarter— to slip quietly through the night until he was back on the open desert. He snuggled Sabra more securely against him, then clucked softly to his patient mount.

Staying in the shadows, keeping the horse at its slowest gait, he guided them past the dark, slumber-still buildings to the edge of the fort. There was nothing to betray their passage but the dulcet plop of hooves against the ground and an occasional jingle of the harness.

As an extra measure of precaution, Hawk back-tracked through the lazy flow of Huachuca Creek for a good distance before striking out in the direction of Bisbee. He maintained the same slow, even pace until Fort Huachuca was far behind them.

He couldn't use the "broom" trick again this time — not and balance Sabra, too — so he used other means to throw any pursuers off track. He circled about, crisscrossing the horse's hoofprints until they were nothing but a muddle of comings and goings; he searched out soft sand that would seep back into the hoofprints, and large areas of thick desert grass that he hoped wouldn't hold an impression for more than an hour or so. It was the best he could do.

As they rode on, Sabra occasionally sighed and shifted against him, but for the most part she was quiet and supple in his arms, the ether having done its job well. They were halfway to the Mule Mountains before she began to stir.

"Shh," Hawk crooned against her ear. "Sleep, darling, sleep. Everything is all right."

She grumbled like a sleepy child, but eventually slumped back against his shoulder and settled once again into blissful slumber.

Each time Sabra stirred, coming closer and closer to awakening, Hawk braced himself for the moment when she would realize that something was terribly amiss. About half an hour before they reached the cave, he felt subtle changes in her as she began to come out of her stupor.

Finally Sabra blinked a half-dozen times. Her eyelids felt heavy, so very, very heavy. She could barely force them open. What a strange dream she'd been having . . . she'd seemed to be floating . . . gliding across the desert under a black velvet sky. . . . On a horse? Yes. That was right, a horse . . . just riding along . . . drifting over the silent land . . . oh, so slowly.

How funny, she mused, her eyes repeatedly sliding shut. The sensation of riding had been so real she could still feel the sway of the horse. She forced her rebellious eyes open again.

There! What's that? She wondered woozily. Ears. *A horse's ears*. How very peculiar. Maybe I'm dreaming that I'm awake.

She squinted to bring the pointy objects into clear view as they bobbed along in front of her.

Such a strange dream.

Floating. No, no, that wasn't it . . . riding. Yes, riding along. Not floating. Completely relaxed . . . curled into a soft, safe corner of strength. No, that wasn't exactly right either . . . leaning against something. Something warm . . . granite hardness overlaid with satin. Something . . . someone? . . . whose nearness made her feel utterly safe. She smiled a crooked little smile.

"Ummm," she murmured, snuggling even tighter against Hawk's chest, relishing the feel of strong arms about her. "Nice. So nice." The words were so soft he barely could hear them.

"I love you," Hawk whispered against the wisps of hair on Sabra's temple.

He felt her indulge in a deep, satisfied sigh. "I love you, too." She turned just enough so that she could tilt her head back against his arm and lift her mouth to his.

Hawk could no more refuse the enticing invitation than he could stop breathing.

The beating of his heart clamored in his ears as his lips claimed hers. So sweet, so pliant—everything he'd been dreaming of as he'd lain on his lonely bed.

Something in the back of Sabra's mind kept tweaking at her consciousness, pleading for attention. She tiptoed around the edges of the thought, considered giving it attention, tossed that idea aside. The dream was too wonderful to abandon.

She shifted again, trying to get closer to him, little whimpers of regret sounding in her throat when she couldn't quite reach her goal.

The horse plodded to a stop as Hawk's grip tightened on the reins. As quickly as possible he looped the ends together in front of his wife and dropped the knotted lines on the stallion's neck.

With one fluid movement he lifted Sabra and turned her so that she was cradled against the vee of his thighs, her back supported by one strong arm, both legs now on one side of the horse.

He was unbelievably hungry for the feel of her beneath his hands, the soft silkiness of her skin, the fragrance of her hair, the honeyed warmth of her. His arms tightened around Sabra, crushing her against his chest. His mouth covered hers, his tongue delving deep, touching, dancing, dueling with hers.

His arms. His sweet mouth. Nothing had ever felt so good, tasted so fine. Sabra pushed aside the swaddling cloth and freed her arms. One slid under his arm and around his waist, the other lifted upward to curve about his neck. Her fingers tangled in the soft thatch of hair at his nape, burying themselves in its silky texture, gliding against the back of his head, pulling him closer and closer and . . .

But the persistent little voice at the back of her mind was chanting ever louder. *This is too real . . . too warm . . . too heartstoppingly sweet. It can't be a dream. It can't. Don't be a fool . . . fool.*

She suddenly went stiff in his arms.

"Where am I? What's happening?" Fear and confusion filled Sabra's voice.

"It's all right. It's all right," Hawk crooned between ragged breaths. "You're safe. I wouldn't let anything happen to you. You know that. Hush, my darling, you're safe. You're safe."

Her eyes grew wide as the velvet words were whispered into her ear. *Oh, my God! Hawk!*

Like bands of steel, his arms kept her from falling from her perch as she jerked upright to stare into the midnight blue eyes of her husband.

"What do you think you're doing?" Her words were charged with shock and anger. "H-how did I get here? Oh, my God! Where am I?"

"You're safe. Just stay calm. Everything is all right. Please believe me."

Hawk's arms remained firmly about Sabra as she struggled weakly to free herself, and his knees squeezed tighter against his mount's barrel as he fought to keep his balance.

The horse's ears flicked back and forth, and then the large creature turned its head to eye the strange apparition on its back, all flapping arms and legs. A shiver ran from its flank to its muzzle, and then the horse shifted its weight nervously, pawing at the sandy soil.

"Sabra, calm down," Hawk pleaded. The stallion sidestepped in alarm. "Sabra! Sit still before this damn horse bolts and we both wind up on the ground!"

She stilled for just a second, long enough for Hawk to grab the reins again. But he felt her muscles coil in preparation for the next round.

"No! Sit still, I said. I don't think you'd relish being out here in the wilderness without a mount. It's a hell of a long walk—"

"Walk? To where?" she demanded.

Her head swiveled as she surveyed the moon-washed terrain, the indigo sky spattered with diamond-bright stars. Her eyes grew larger still as she picked out silhouettes of cactus and paloverde, agave and yucca.

Her position slowly began to dawn on her.

No buildings.

No sign of the fort in any direction.

Just the dark thrust of mountains on all four sides, but they were no clue. There were mountain ranges all over this part of the territory, ringing and overlapping and paralleling one another, so close that it was often hard to tell where one left off and another began. She only knew one thing for sure: they were out in the desert, far from the fort.

A little sob escaped her. "Why? How? I . . . I don't understand. Why did you do this?"

Hawk nudged the horse into motion again. He was anxious to get to the cave before the first sign of dawn. Keeping Sabra disoriented was a major part of his plan. He didn't want her to know that Bisbee was within walking distance, albeit a very long walk, from where they'd be staying. He was counting on her being unsure of their location so she wouldn't try to run away before he had a chance to convince her of his innocence and his love.

"I did it because I love you."

"Love me?" she repeated, staring at him. "You can't be serious. You come here, lie to me, k-k—" But she couldn't say it. She couldn't say he'd killed her father . . . maybe because she didn't believe it deep down.

But Hawk knew what words had been on the tip of her tongue. "I didn't do it, Sabra. You've got to believe that."

Her mouth thinned to a stubborn line. "I don't have to believe anything. Take me home. I demand you take me home. Right now!"

"No." The word was velvet steel.

She glared at him "They . . . they'll come looking for you. Logan won't stand by and let you get away with this. *He'll* search until he finds me!"

"They haven't found me yet."

Sabra's mouth snapped shut at this succinct statement. It was true. They'd thought he'd gone to Tucson, that he'd long ago left the territory. But here he was. Big as life. Strong . . . warm . . . tempting. *No!* Absolutely not! She'd believed him once before. But she wouldn't again. Not ever. It hurt too much.

They rode in silence for a long while. Then Sabra finally voiced one of the hundreds of questions buzzing in her head.

"Where are we going?"

"To a safe place. Where we can spend some time together."

"Even if I don't want to?"

"That's right. You're my wife."

"In name only," she protested.

His eyes probed hers. "Have you forgotten so soon?" There was a long pause. "I haven't."

Sabra felt a flush begin to climb her throat and she turned her head, refusing to look at him.

"There are a lot of things I need to tell you. Explanations that should have been given a long time ago. And I've been thinking about all this . . . about some peculiar coincidences that seem too good to be true."

"Nothing you say is going to change my mind," she declared stubbornly.

"Maybe not. But I have to take the chance. You see, I know I didn't do it, and I might be correct about who's guilty. Besides, I love you far too much to just give up and ride away."

A little lump formed at the back of Sabra's throat. "They don't think anyone else is guilty."

"I may have to convince them differently."

Her head whipped around and she stared at him in disbelief. "You go anywhere near there and they'll catch you. Then they'll hang you!" The lump in her throat grew larger, aggravated by the very real fear that what she said was true. Why hadn't he kept going? He could have been far away by now . . . out of harm's reach.

No. She couldn't think like that. She hardened her heart, refusing to allow any tenderness in. If he got caught, it was his own stupid fault. She wouldn't care. Why should she?

But she did. And that made her more determined than ever.

"I'll run away the first chance I get."

"I suspected as much. It's a chance I'll have to take."

"You're crazy if you think I'm going to be kept hidden in some hotel or boardinghouse. I'll scream for help at the first sign of people."

"I figured on that, too. That's why we're not going anywhere close to civilization."

"But . . . where will we stay? We can't just camp out. The days are still warm most of the time, but the weather could turn nasty any day now. You don't know how cold it gets sometimes. We'd freeze. And Logan's told me all about the storms. Sometimes it snows. And food, what about food?"

He chuckled over her efforts to discourage him. "Don't worry. I've taken all that into consideration. We'll be safe and sound. And well fed."

"You can't watch me every minute of every day. The first time you turn your back, I'll be gone!"

"I don't intend to turn my back on you. I'm going to talk to you, and discuss my theories; and nothing on this earth is going to stop me. I hope with every fiber of my being that I can convince you of my sincerity, but if, after all is said and done, I can't . . . well, it won't be because I didn't try."

"It won't work," she muttered, folding her arms stubbornly across her chest.

Moonlight glinted on the thin golden band. "We'll see," said Hawk. "We'll see."

They didn't speak again until Hawk halted the stallion halfway up the side of the mountain, at the beginning of the imperceptible path to the cave.

"We'll have to walk from here," he said.

"Walk?" Sabra protested.

"Yes, it's too steep, and the horse is tired from carrying both of us such a long distance." He slid from his mount and then reached up to lift Sabra down.

"Oh, it's cold!" she said, as her bare toes touched the ground.

"Be still and I'll find your shoes." He slipped the straps of the pack from his arms, and began to rummage around inside.

Sabra's mouth dropped open. "My shoes? You even brought my shoes?"

Hawk stopped digging and pinned her with an amused look. "You would have preferred to have nothing but a nightgown and a quilt to wear for the duration of your stay?" He pursed his lips as if pleased at the novel idea, and then shrugged in acceptance. "Well, it's all right by me. In fact, it might be much more fun that way. I can get rid of this stuff easily enough." He lifted the pack as if to toss it down the side of the mountain.

"No!"

The forward movement of Hawk's arm halted at her cry. "No?" he asked.

"I . . . I want the shoes." Sabra drew the blanket tighter about her shoulders. "And the rest of my things."

"I thought you might." Hawk nodded, then resumed his digging in the pack. "Ah. Here they are." He held out a pair of black kid slippers. "Brace your hand against my shoulder while you slip them on."

"I'll manage," Sabra said in a gritty voice as she leaned against the side of the horse and bent to slip the shoes on her feet.

Hawk let her have her way. He slung the pack onto his back again. "Let's go," he said, offering her his hand.

She pointedly ignored the gesture.

"Very well. Stay on the inside, and don't stray. It can get rather rough in places."

"I'll manage," Sabra once again insisted.

And she tried. Valiantly. But several times she had to accept to his help to keep her balance. Perhaps it was only wishful thinking, but it seemed to Hawk that by the end of their trek she had become just a little less reluctant to accept his touch.

Sabra's breath was rapid by the time they'd climbed to the canyon floor, and little feathery plumes of mist puffed into the night air every time she opened her mouth. She tugged the quilt tighter about herself as she trudged alongside Hawk, and as soon as the horse was secured in the makeshift corral, Hawk hurried her to the mouth of the cave.

It was pitch black inside, and Sabra balked at entering.

"I'm not going in *there*," she protested. "Good heavens, how do I know what's *in* there?"

"There's nothing in there. It's just a cave . . . a rather nice one."

"No."

"All right." Hawk sighed. "Just stand still. There's a lantern just a step or two inside. Maybe a little light will convince you it's all right."

Sabra gave a faint squeak of alarm as Hawk disappeared into the inky blackness. It was just a natural response to being left alone, she assured herself. It had nothing to do with the eerie manner in which Hawk had faded from her sight—or her sudden flash of concern for his safety. Absolutely nothing.

She heard a scuffle of sounds, the rasp of a match, and then a tiny circle of golden light blossomed in the darkness, bringing sweet relief to Sabra's flip-flopping stomach.

"Come on in," Hawk urged.

Sabra slowly shuffled through the entrance and into the gloomy gray interior, her eyes large and curious as she turned her head this way and that, taking everything in. There were makeshift shelves, full of provisions—enough to last several weeks. And an abundance of crocks and buckets, which she presumed held water. Cooking utensils were stacked neatly on a separate slab of rock, along with folded clothing and extra blankets, a coil of rope, an axe, and some other tools. There was even a soft pile of blankets arranged in front of the rock-ringed fire.

Well, she thought, he certainly meant it when he said he'd taken everything into consideration.

While Sabra gaped at Hawk's handiwork, he worked on the campfire, and soon had a blaze going. It filled the cave with pale yellow light and the beginnings of warmth.

Dejected to realize that her prospects for escape were limited, Sabra finally ceased exploring the cave and plopped down on a rock by the fire to stare morosely into the dancing flames.

Within a few minutes the residual effects of the ether combined with the wearisome ride began to take a toll. Hawk watched with tender amusement as Sabra fought to keep her eyes open. Each time her lids fluttered down, it took her longer to force them up again. When her head began to nod, she propped an elbow on one knee and rested her chin on it; but that didn't work either. Her head nodded again. With the third bob, her chin dropped off her hand and bumped against her chest.

"Oh!" She said, sitting up with a start and looking around in surprise.

"Let's go to bed, Sabra," Hawk said softly. "You're worn out. Tomorrow will be soon enough to talk." He crossed to her side, took her hands, and pulled her to her feet. The quilt slid to the ground.

"No," she mumbled sleepily, eying the one bed with trepidation. "I . . . I don't want to go to bed. I'm not tired"—a huge yawn interrupted her protest—"at all."

"Come on," he said, tugging her along with him. Sabra followed even though she continued to grumble.

Within seconds, Hawk had gently set her on the pile of blankets. Then he squatted beside her, fussing with the covers until she was tucked in tight on the side nearest the fire. Sabra managed a word of protest every now and then, but for the most part she let him do what he wanted.

Her eyes had just begun to drift shut when he stood and yanked his boots off. Then his shirt fell to the floor of the cave.

Sabra's eyelids flew up, and she sat bolt upright. "Wh-what are you doing?" Her eyes grew even wider as she watched him unfasten the buttons of his britches and push them down his legs.

"I'm going to bed, too."

"Here?" she asked in a shaky voice, pulling the blanket more tightly under her chin.

She tried desperately to keep her eyes from his body, to keep her mind from thinking how magnificent he looked. The firelight licked across his skin, making it all coppery bronze and deep gold, and the soft ripple of muscles brought a catch to her throat. Despite all her efforts, her eyes slid over the wide expanse of chest, the massive shoulders and bulging biceps, the waist that tapered to narrow hips. She jerked her gaze from the abundant evidence of his maleness nestled at the juncture of rock-hard thighs. Then he turned to toss his pants aside and the powerful muscles of his buttocks clenched with the movement.

Sabra swallowed hard. "But . . . but I don't . . . I won't . . . I mean—"

"I'm not going to force you to do anything, Sabra. I told you, I brought you here to talk. I won't lie and say that I don't want you—desperately. I do, but I won't force you. Ever. All I'm going to do is lie down beside you and go to sleep."

"You could make another bed . . . sleep over there." She pointed a trembling finger toward the other side of the fire.

"What? And allow you to escape while I'm asleep?" Hawk shook his head. "Not on your life. I went to a lot of trouble to arrange all this, and I have no intention of letting you get away so easily."

"But—"

"We'll sleep together." The subject was closed.

Eyes wide and round, Sabra watched him throw a few more logs on the fire and then walk to the pallet. Without another word, he slid under the blankets, then turned to face her, lying on his side, one arm looped over her waist.

"Just remember," he said softly, "I'll be able to feel it if you try to get out of bed." His arm tightened slightly around her body.

Sabra knew it was useless to protest. She held herself as rigid as possible, afraid to relax for fear her arm would brush his chest or her leg would encounter his. Despite her firm intentions, at the moment when sleep claimed her, she turned toward her husband, curving into his warmth and burrowing against his body, instinctively seeking the safety and contentment of his nearness.

Chapter Twenty-nine

"I don't care what the note says!" Logan roared, slamming his fist against the kitchen table. The piece of paper Hawk had left bounced in response.

Hezekiah and Jasmine exchanged worried glances. Logan had been like this ever since Jasmine had discovered Sabra was missing.

"Look," Hezekiah pleaded. "Just think about it for a minute, would you? He promised that she'd be all right. You don't really think Hawk would harm Sabra, now do you?"

"How the hell do I know?" Logan grumbled, slumping against the back of his chair. "Oh, lord, you're right, I suppose." He rumpled his already ragged hair. "I don't honestly believe he'd hurt her. But . . . but, why'd he have to come slinking in here in the middle of the night and take her off like that? It's not right, dammit. It's not right! I can't just sit here and let him get away with that."

Jasmine sighed, her dark, slanted eyes full of compassion. "Logan, I know you're upset, but I'm positive Sabra is safe with Hawk. Think about what the note says. All he wants is some time alone with her, time to try and put things straight. That's not a lot to ask. She is his wife."

Brows drawn together in a frown, Logan peered up at the dusky beauty. "But, Jasmine—"

"Think about it, Logan," Hezekiah put in. "Just consider what he said. He promised she'd be safe, and he also promised to return her in three weeks, if that was her choice."

"And I'm just supposed to sit here and wait?" Logan asked belligerently. "For three goddamn weeks?"

Hezekiah threw his hands up. "All right, all right. For argument's sake, let's say you put troops out to search for them. Which way are you going to send them? And how often are you going to have them check the same locations?"

"It would be hopeless," Jasmine interjected.

"Two people, traveling light—they can move at the first sign of soldiers. Be gone in minutes. Don't you remember how Geronimo kept us run ragged?" Hezekiah reminded his friend. "Do you think you could find Hawk any easier? He's half-Indian, Logan. He knows every trick in the book. Just look at how he covered his trail—both times."

"Yeah, but—"

Jasmine's soft voice interrupted him. "Have you ever considered that Sabra went with him of her own free will?"

Logan shook his head. "I find that hard to believe, not when he snuck in like this . . . in the middle of the damn night."

Jasmine shrugged her elegant shoulders. "He could hardly come in the daylight, could he?"

Logan didn't answer.

"I think you have to consider the possibility she might have, Logan. There's no sign of struggle. And enough of her clothes were packed to make it appear—to me, at least—that she meant to go. He couldn't have packed and held on to a struggling woman at the same time," Jasmine reasoned.

"And why didn't anyone hear any screams?" Hezekiah questioned. "You'd think she'd have hollered at the top of her lungs if he was forcing her to go against her will."

Logan dropped his head into his hands. "I don't know what to believe. I just don't know."

"You know more than you realize, Logan," Jasmine said softly. He raised his head and looked at her with puzzled eyes. "You know they love each other."

Logan sighed. "Yeah, I can't deny that."

"And I think you know that he's not guilty of your daddy's murder. Don't you?"

Hezekiah's question brought Logan up short. "You think he's innocent, don't you?" Logan asked.

"You bet I do. And someday we'll prove it."

Logan rubbed a hand across his face. "Aw, hell. Maybe I should go with my instinct on this. I don't think he did it, either. The problem is, who did?"

The fire was nothing more than a pile of embers, leaving the cave cloaked in an early morning chill. Sabra pulled the covers higher and snuggled closer to the warm body at her side. Strong arms hugged her tighter, and she sighed in contentment, nestling her head against the firm shoulder she'd been using as a pillow. She hadn't slept so well since . . .

Oh, no! Sabra's eyes flew open. She couldn't have! Oh, but she had.

She was as close to Hawk as she could possibly get. She held her breath, not daring to move a muscle, afraid that he would wake at any moment. How could this have happened? She remembered the events of the past night, holding herself rigid and as far away from him as possible. And now they were all tangled together . . . too tangled for Hawk to have done it alone.

Granted, his arms were around her, but hers were around his waist. Her nightgown had worked up around her hips and her leg was snugged between the two of his, and somehow she knew she'd placed it there herself — willingly. Suddenly she realized that the top of her thigh was pressed firmly against . . . against parts she'd rather not think about.

354

How could she have done this? How could she have given in so easily? She'd planned to stay far from him, aloof, unfeeling. And just look! One night, that was all it had taken. One night in his arms and her resolutions had disappeared like rain upon the desert.

Well, it wasn't going to happen again! She'd been putty in Hawk's hands from the first minute she'd seen him. He'd lied, he'd pretended, he'd fooled them all. And she'd fallen for every word he'd said, believed him, loved him. But she had promised herself that it would never, ever happen again.

Hawk murmured her name in his sleep, stirring ever so slightly. His hand slid down the curve of her back and cupped one plump cheek, pulling her up against the hard evidence of his desire. Heat blossomed deep in the pit of Sabra's stomach, a thousand butterflies took wing inside her chest. Her back arched and her lower body rocked toward him in instinctive response. And then she froze, overcome by the undeniable knowledge that she was headed straight for disaster.

"Get your hands off me!" she cried, placing her palms against his chest and shoving as hard as she could.

Hawk rolled onto his back, coming awake instantly as Sabra scrambled to a sitting position.

"What the hell?" Wild-eyed, he sat up and scanned the dim room for danger. His bewildered gaze finally settled on Sabra. "Good lord, don't ever do that again. I thought something was wrong—"

"Something *was* wrong," she announced, her voice icy. "I want a separate bed tonight. I refuse to be subjected to your . . . your attentions."

"I wasn't doing anything, Sabra. I was sound asleep. What's the matter? Did you find out you still like the feel of my arms around you?"

"No. I certainly did not." She jumped to her feet, giving Hawk a tantalizing glimpse of firm, round thigh before the cotton gown slid down. The ground was chilly, and without the extra warmth of Hawk's body next to hers, her teeth began to chatter.

Concern flooded his face. "I'll build up the fire," he said, throwing the covers back and starting to rise.

Sabra quickly averted her eyes. "Would you have the decency to put some clothes on first?"

"Whatever you want." Reaching for the trousers he'd discarded the previous night, he slipped them on.

Not that it helped much, Sabra was morosely thinking. His chest was still bare, muscles rippling under his bronze skin with each movement he made. And the pants rode low—too low—on his lean hips. When he bent over to add wood to the fire, the fabric pulled down in back, revealing two beguiling little dimples at the base of his spine. It was all Sabra could do to yank her gaze away.

It was happening. Again. Whatever magic Hawk possessed, it was slowly but surely weaving its spell once more.

She had to get away from him. And soon. Already her heart was trying to convince her that she should at least listen to his explanations. And her head knew she didn't dare. If she stayed much longer, her heart was going to win, in more ways than one.

"I'll start the coffee while you get dressed," Hawk was saying. "Here, let me get a lantern for you."

As soon as he moved away, Sabra slipped on her shoes and snatched up a blanket, draping it over her shoulders. Hawk hurried to one of the rock shelves. He struck a match, adjusted the wick, and returned with a glowing lantern, which he handed to Sabra.

"See that opening on the left," he said, nodding his head toward a gloomy passage in the wall. "I fixed some . . . uh . . . private facilities for you. And I put a bucket of water and some soap in there, too. The towels are stacked on the ledge. A good amount of light filters through from here, but you'd better take the lantern with you. You'll feel safer. Meanwhile, I'll

356

start breakfast."

"I need some clothes."

"Oh. Sure." Once again he hurried to the side of the cave, retrieving the bag he'd packed for Sabra.

Sabra accepted the offering, being very, very careful that her fingers did not touch Hawk's in the transfer. Then, head held high, back ramrod stiff, she marched off toward the entranceway Hawk had indicated.

The adjoining chamber was much smaller than the main room. She was grateful for the lantern. The golden light helped dispel the deeper shadows. She availed herself of the "facilities," then hurriedly washed and pulled her clothes on to ward off the chill morning air.

Hawk was busy over the fire when she returned. His eyes lit with pleasure at the sight of her, and a hopeful smile etched his face. When Sabra felt her own mouth begin to respond, she clamped her teeth together and averted her eyes. She wasn't going to give in. She wasn't! No matter how her heart lurched when he looked at her like that, she wasn't going to succumb.

Pulling her shawl more tightly about her shoulders, she took a seat on the same rock she'd used last night. She tried hard to concentrate on a plan of escape, but her traitorous gaze kept going to Hawk.

When the food was ready, he fixed her a plate and took it to her. She accepted it, but refused to participate in the casual chitchat he tried to carry on during the meal. Afterward he cleaned up, and Sabra sat and tried not to watch him. By then the sun was up and Hawk took her out into the sunshine to view the beauty of the small canyon. She trudged along beside him, responding to his litany with muffled monosyllables.

And so the pattern was set—Hawk doing his best to make her comfortable; Sabra doing her utmost to ignore the way she felt inside every time he came near her. He was tender and loving and attentive; she refused to meet his gaze, turning a cold shoulder to his every effort, and fighting to keep from falling into his arms.

And each night, as they lay side by side, Hawk having steadfastly refused to listen to her pleas for a separate bed, it became harder and harder for her to deny how very much she still loved him. Each night he banked the fire and then slipped under the blankets, draping his arm across her waist. And each night she forced herself to remain rigid and remote . . . until she fell asleep.

Always she awoke to find herself once again in his embrace.

Deep down Sabra knew she couldn't put the blame on Hawk. He hadn't forced her. She knew perfectly well that when sleep overtook her stubborn mind, the true desires of her heart took command.

It had been five days. And Hawk wasn't sure if he'd made any progress at all with Sabra. If anything, she was colder, more distant now than she had been in the beginning. He'd been unable to bring himself to really talk with her, fearing she wouldn't yet be open to what he had to say. The nights, when she turned to him in her sleep, clinging, cuddling, pressing herself as close as possible against him and murmuring his name, were all that kept Hawk believing that his plan could still work.

It was midmorning. Breakfast was over, and he was on his way to the corral area to check the horse, as he did every day. Sabra accompanied him, as usual— alternately silent or surly, as usual.

Hawk was giving himself a mental lecture on being patient and trying harder when he felt a tiny vibration beneath his feet. His brow wrinkled and he slowed his pace, then stopped altogether, looking around in bafflement.

"Did you feel that?" he asked Sabra.

"Feel what?" she asked warily, uncharitably wondering what trick he was trying to pull.

Hawk listened, concentrating hard for a few more seconds. Then, giving himself a mental shake, he continued on his way.

"I guess it was nothing. Never mind."

Two hours later it happened again. Hawk watched the bucketful of water he had recently set down. The previously placid surface shimmied in response to an almost imperceptible force. It wasn't his imagination. The trembling water was proof of that. His gaze flew to Sabra, but once again she seemed not to notice.

Each nerve ending on high alert, Hawk continued with his morning chores, finishing the preparation of the noon meal. They'd just sat down to eat when he felt it again.

This time there was less than an hour between the shocks, and this one was considerably stronger.

Eyes full of puzzlement, Sabra watched her fork vibrate against the rim of the tin plate she was holding.

"Hawk?" she said, a touch of fear in her voice as she sought to assure herself of his nearness. "What was that?"

"I'm not sure," he answered, setting his own plate down by the fire. "Maybe . . . maybe they're doing some really heavy blasting over at the mines." Damn! he thought. I shouldn't have said that. But it was too late, so he hurried on with his explanation, hoping Sabra hadn't noticed. "There could be a fault line. That might account for the concussions being felt this far away."

"Mines?" she repeated, her mind momentarily snatched from its current worries. "That means we're near Bisbee, doesn't it?"

Hawk refused to lie, but he wasn't going to answer her either. Thoroughly irritated with himself, he gathered up his half-finished meal and stalked to the cave's outer entrance.

Hawk's hasty departure confirmed Sabra's guess. Bisbee. That put a whole new light on her situation. Not having the least idea where they were, she'd been too afraid to make a sincere effort at escape. But, if Bisbee were nearby, then surely she could reach help. She was trying to decide whether she should attempt to sneak away at night while Hawk slept or risk trying it during the daylight hours when the tremors began anew.

"Hawk!" she cried in fright. She jumped to her feet, fervently wishing he hadn't left her alone.

Outside, he froze in his tracks. The ground was dancing under his feet. Never in his life had he experienced anything like this. *Earthquake.* That had be to the only explanation.

"Oh, my God!" he muttered, the plate dropping unheeded from his fingers. "Sabra! The cave might collapse. I've got to get her out of there!"

He whirled and began running.

"Hawk!" Sabra's frightened voice vibrated through the cavern. The ground lurched drunkenly and she lost her balance, falling heavily.

"Sabra!"

She could barely hear Hawk's voice above the terrifying rumble that surrounded her. She struggled to stand up, but lost her balance again almost immediately. Dust sifted from the ceiling, turning the air hazy, filling her nose and throat. Clumps of dirt and rock began to fall, clicking and clacking as they tumbled down the walls and skittered across the floor.

"Sabra! Get out of there!"

Hawk's voice was nearer. Sabra's frightened eyes jerked to the cave entrance. She could barely discern his wildly weaving silhouette through the gloom of dust and raining debris.

"Hawk! Help me!" she cried, scrambling to her

knees, desperate to get to him.

And suddenly the whole world went crazy right before her eyes. A large chunk of rock tore loose from the ceiling just as Hawk lurched through the opening. He heard—or sensed—the danger and threw his arms up to protect his head. But it was too late. Sabra's terrified scream echoed and reechoed as she watched him crumple to the ground.

She never knew how she got to his side. Whether she crawled or whether the ground's violent shaking abated enough to allow her to regain her feet and run. The only thing she was conscious of when the world finally stopped tilting and grew silent again was that she was on her knees beside him, her body bent protectively over his motionless form.

She kept perfectly still for a minute or two after the tremor was over, afraid the ground would begin to heave again. When it didn't, she raised up and looked at Hawk. There was a lump on the side of his head, and a trickle of scarlet blood seeped slowly from his forehead. A surge of fear made her stomach flop sickeningly.

She leaned over him, her hands frantically gripping his shoulders, stroking his cheeks. "Hawk! Oh, no! Hawk. Please, talk to me. Say something!" Tears made dusty streaks down her cheeks, dripped from her chin, plopped unheeded on his face, his chest.

For an unbelievably frightening moment, she thought he was dead, and suddenly felt hollow, as if something had scooped out her insides and left nothing but a shell.

And she knew, without Hawk, that was the way she'd feel for the rest of her life.

Sobs interspersed her prayerful words. "Please, God, please. Don't let him be dead. Don't let this happen. I can't bear to lose him. I can't. . . ."

When he groaned and rolled his head from side to side, Sabra's tears fell even harder.

Hawk woke to the lingering smell of dust in the air, the hazy flicker of firelight, and the feel of a cool, damp cloth against his forehead. A pale oval blur hung suspended above him. As his eyes began to focus, Sabra's face swam into view.

"You're still here," he marveled.

"Yes," she answered softly.

"You could have left." He tried to sit up, wincing at the effort. His head throbbed with a dull ache.

"Lie still," she instructed. "I don't want you moving around for a while. You've got a big lump on your head." She pressed her hand against his shoulder, and reluctantly he sank back against the blankets.

Hawk gingerly fingered the swollen place. "Have I been out long?"

"Most of the afternoon. It's almost dark now."

"I don't understand. You knew Bisbee was nearby, and the horse was right outside. There was nothing to stop you."

Sabra shrugged, a small smile tipping her mouth up. "Nothing but the way I feel about you." She ran freshly dipped cloth over his face. "I . . . I couldn't go."

"I'm glad," he whispered.

"So am I."

His eyes searched her face. "You look tired."

"I'm fine. Really."

"It must have been scary. I don't remember getting this far into the cave."

"You didn't. I dragged you here when it was over. I even started the fire again. And fetched fresh water." She looked like an eager little child, pleased at her accomplishment.

You did a wonderful job."

She blushed. "Do you want something to eat?"

Hawk shook his head. "No. I want you to lie down

362

beside me. Just let me hold you for a while. Please."

Happily she granted his request. And nestled in each other arms, they talked long into the night. He insisted on telling her all of it — every last detail and inner thought that had driven him to come to Arizona, and how he changed when he'd fallen in love with her.

He said he wanted no more lies between them, ever.

She listened and began to understand, to believe.

And eventually she turned in her husband's arms, whispering "I love you," letting him know that there was nothing in the world she wanted more than him.

Their loving was gentle, sweet, all the more precious because they knew how close they'd come to losing one another. And when the loving was over, they fell asleep wrapped tightly in each other's arms.

The next morning the talking began again, interspersed with frequent pauses for long kisses, gentle reassuring touches. They shared their innermost thoughts while sweeping the scattered debris from the cave. Explanations and questions were exchanged as Hawk checked for structural damage, the heady flow of conversation barely stopped even when Hawk pointed out what looked like a smattering of silver ore on the wall of the rear chamber where a large chunk of rock had fallen away.

All through the day they talked, taking out the good memories and polishing them, or discussing their fears and hurts until they dissolved.

It was night again when Hawk brought up the afternoon of his arrest. They'd finished supper, washed and put away the dishes. The fire was blazing high, yellow and orange and amber flames leaping and dancing, casting cavorting shadows on the walls of the cave. Hawk had pulled the blankets closer to the rock Sabra used as a chair, and now they were stretched out on the makeshift pallet. His back was against the rock, and Sabra was tucked securely in his arms, her head on his chest, her arms around his waist.

"I couldn't believe I was in jail. I couldn't think about how it happened or why at first," he said, his fingertips unconsciously tracing the soft flesh of her arm as he spoke. "I was too shocked by everything that had happened. And, to be honest, my main concern was what you were feeling, thinking. . . ."

Sabra's arm tightened around him, and she snuggled closer still. She savored the gentle rise and fall of his chest beneath her cheek, and marveled at how secure she felt with his arms around her.

"That first night, all I wanted to do was get out of that damn guardhouse and get to you. That's all I could think about. Even after I arrived here, the only thing on my mind was making things right with you. After I came up with that crazy plan to get you here—"

"It was crazy, you know," Sabra gently chided. "I don't understand why you'd take such a terrible risk. You could have been caught."

Eyes full of love searched hers. "I did it because I had to," he said softly. "You had saved me from myself, stopped me from doing something I'd have hated myself for doing. I knew if I couldn't have your love, then nothing else mattered. Not being falsely accused, not prison, not even dying, if it came to that."

Sabra pressed her fingers against his mouth to silence the awful words. "Shh. It's over. We'll never be parted again. Never."

Hawk gently kissed her fingertips, then continued his story. "My mind wasn't quite so muddled once I believed I was going to see you again. I started to think about everything else that had happened. And I realized how crazy—how implausible—that last afternoon was. Jennings showing up like he did, drumming it into everyone's head that I was the only suspect. And the search—why did he insist on that search? Not

364

that I cared. I didn't have anything to hide. But he was so thorough, almost as if his every move was calculated."

Sabra frowned in remembrance. "Do you think Jennings is guilty? It's hard to understand why he'd be involved. As far as I know, he and my father got along fine. He had no motive."

"I don't know, Sabra. Maybe he isn't guilty. Maybe he's covering for someone else. Or he's being forced to cover for the killer. But I can't get it out of my mind—the way he left the bag till last. Something makes me believe he knew the case was in it. It was just too staged, too planned . . . like he was saving the discovery, working toward a big finale."

Sabra nibbled at her bottom lip, one slim finger pressed against her chin. "Well, maybe. I guess if you think about it that way, it makes sense. But why did he do it?"

"That's where I come up against a brick wall." Hawk sighed. "And I don't have the slightest idea how we can convince him to tell."

Sabra tilted her head so she could look into her husband's troubled eyes. "So what do we do now?"

"I don't know. I just don't know." Unconsciously, Hawk tightened his hold on Sabra, as if she might be snatched from his arms.

"We could just go away, far away, where we wouldn't have to think about this anymore."

"Do you have any idea what that would mean, Sabra? Running for the rest of our lives. You wouldn't be able to see Logan again, or even write him, for fear that someone would track us down. I couldn't ask that of you."

She swallowed hard. "I . . . I wouldn't mind."

But Hawk knew better, he could hear the tremor of sadness in her voice. She'd do it for him, but he wouldn't ask it of her.

"No. We've got to go back—"

"Back!" Sabra exclaimed, pushing away from him. "Don't even think that!" Her brown eyes were wide with apprehension.

Hawk gripped her arms, holding her still, his eyes probing hers. "We have to, Sabra. I've had this crazy thought floating around in the back of my mind for the last hour. It's all I can come up with."

"Wh-what are you talking about?"

"We've got to go back and find a way to get Jennings to talk. A lot depends on whether we can convince Logan and Hezekiah to help us. If they will, then maybe we can trick Jennings into revealing what he knows."

Chapter Thirty

"Logan." Sabra spoke softly, reaching out to poke his shoulder. "Wake up."

Logan sat bolt upright in bed, his eyes widening in disbelief. At first he thought he was dreaming. He shook his head to clear the cobwebs of sleep, and stared at her again. No. By God, she was real! Sabra was actually standing beside his bed, her hand cupped protectively around a flickering candle.

"Good lord," he rasped in wonder. "It's you. It's really you."

With one wild swoop, he threw the covers back and bounded out of bed. Sabra suppressed a smile at seeing in the baggy union suit he was sleeping in.

"Damn it, girl," he murmured in awe. She managed to place the candle on the night stand before he pulled her into his arms and began pounding her on the back. "You scared me out of ten years' growth. God, I'm glad to see you!" Logan squeezed her so hard he threatened to cut off her breathing. Then suddenly he gripped her arms and held her away from him, a dark scowl on his face. "How the *hell* did you get in here?"

Sabra smiled. "Hawk's really quite good at that sort of thing."

"Hawk!" Logan's sleep-swollen eyes swept the room. "Where is that ba—"

"Shh!" Sabra scolded. "You'll wake up the whole fort."

Although he continued to glower, Logan obeyed and lowered his voice. "Where is he?" he asked again in a gravelly whisper. "I think it's time I had a little talk with Mr. Hawkins."

"All in good time," Sabra said calmly. "First I want you to promise that you'll listen to what we have to say, and that you'll help us. We have a plan, but it requires a lot of work."

Logan's mouth dropped open. "Listen? Plan? What the hell are you talking about?"

"Logan! Lower your voice!" Sabra hissed. "If you don't give me your solemn promise that you'll help, I'm going to turn around and walk right out of this house."

Brother and sister glared at one another, and Logan was the first to falter. He'd never been able to deny Sabra anything. He wasn't going to start now. He was too damned glad to see her.

He took a deep breath. Then another. "All right, all right. I promise. Now, where is he?"

"Right here." Hawk materialized out of the dark, stepping through the bedroom doorway. He crossed the room to stand beside his wife, his arm possessively around her waist.

"I oughta punch you out," Logan growled, his fingers flexing at his side. "I've been worried out of my mind."

Hawk nodded. "I'm sure you have. And I'm sorry. Really."

Sabra's eyes swung from husband to brother. "You two can squabble later. Right now, there are more important things to take care of. Namely, clearing my husband of false charges." Her chin tilted stubbornly when Logan's eyes snapped to her. "He didn't do it, Logan. And I won't hear otherwise. Do you understand?"

Logan's mouth thinned, but he nodded his head. "You can get off your soapbox, Sabra. I'd already decided he was innocent." His gaze swung toward Hawk. "But I'm still genuinely angry at you for taking my sister off like that—and don't you forget it!"

Hawk barely managed to get out "I won't" before Logan threw his arms around the both of them. "God, I'm glad to see the two of you! Now," he demanded, "would you please tell me what the hell is going on?"

Over cups of hot coffee in Logan's semidark kitchen, Sabra and Hawk did just that.

When they'd finished their story, Logan sat quietly, turning his empty cup round and round on the table. The single candle flickered in the middle. "All right. I'll go along with you. The deal with Jennings does seem fishy, but it's all supposition. There's nothing solid to go on. Even if he suspects who the killer is, I don't know what we can do to get him to tell us. If he was going to talk, he'd have done it already."

"Sabra and I keep trying to come up with some sort of trap, something that could be said or done that would make him believe we're on to the whole story."

"That's going to be hard, considering what little you have to go on," Logan reminded Hawk. "Besides, you don't dare show your face. Jennings would be hollering for help to get you back in the guardhouse before you ever got the words out of your mouth. And he knows damn well that I wouldn't be playing games with anyone who might know who murdered my father."

"There's still Hezekiah. If we can think of a plausible scheme, he might be our best bet to carry it out," Hawk said. "I don't have it all worked out yet . . . there's something else in the back of my mind, something I can't quite put my finger on. I thought it might come back to me if we all had a chance to talk, really hash this over."

Logan lifted one brow. "I guess it can't hurt. We won't be any worse off afterward than we are now."

"Reveille will sound any minute now," Hawk reminded him. "First off, we've got to keep everything looking normal. We don't want Jennings to pick up any kind of a warning. I think it would be best if you went on about your daily business—Sabra and I will lay low here—and then this evening we can all get together and see what we can come up with. You can get Hezekiah to drop by, can't you?"

Logan nodded. "Sure. He's here on a fairly regular basis anyway. Nobody'll think anything of it. At least no more than usual," he added with a grin, recalling how many of the officers frowned upon their close association.

Sabra spoke up. "Tell him to bring Jasmine. She might be able to help."

"All right."

"And meanwhile, keep your eyes peeled for anything that might be useful. Pass the word to Hezekiah and Jasmine. Just be careful, real careful, that Jennings doesn't suspect anything."

It was almost dark by the time the five friends gathered around Logan's kitchen table. Once again Hawk and Sabra told their story.

"You might be right," Hezekiah said when they had finished putting forth their suspicions about Jennings. "Scuttlebutt among the enlisted men is that Jennings has been acting mighty peculiar lately. Something is definitely on his mind."

"I hate to be the bearer of bad news," Jasmine interrupted, "but what's bothering Jennings might have nothing to do with the murder."

"What do you mean?"

"Jennings has been messing around with Melissa Henderson—that is, till lately. Seems they've had a fallin' out or something. He hasn't seen her the last couple of days. I suppose that's why he's been acting so down in the mouth."

"How do you know that?" Sabra asked.

"All the laundresses know. Gossip's a way of life on

Suds Row. Seems Sukey Taylor was passing one of the equipment sheds late one evening and she heard this moaning coming from inside. She thought someone was hurt, so she peeked in. Well, let's just say she got a real eyeful. Sukey does the Hendersons' laundry, and Melissa's always been real snooty to her—that's one spoiled gal, for sure. Anyway, it kinda got to be a game with Sukey, seeing if she could catch Melissa sneaking around. And she did, several times. Mr. Henderson would have himself a genuine fit if he knew what his little girl's been up to lately."

"Henderson," Logan said with a snort. "Now, there's someone who might have had a motive. My father was out to get him, for sure. Too bad we can't tie him and Jennings together, besides the connection with Melissa, I mean."

"Wait a minute. Maybe we can." Hezekiah's bushy black brows drew together. "A while back, a cache of liquor was found in one of the barracks . . . Jennings's barracks. No one owned up to hiding it there. Seems a couple of privates had found it and got drunk. The major was almighty mad about it—marched everybody away from post in the middle of the night and made the culprits bury that trunk full of whiskey six feet down. There was talk that it was some of the same stuff Henderson sells on credit."

"That's still damn little to go on—Melissa and Jennings playing house, and Henderson's whiskey in Jennings's barracks. Not much to string a case on, if that's all we've got." Logan rumpled his hair in vexation.

"What about the fact that Jennings up and volunteered so fast for the investigation? Might have expected that if he and your daddy had been close," Hezekiah said. "But they weren't. And since when does a soldier run out and volunteer for extra duty?"

Logan nodded. "That's another good point. Maybe he did it so he could keep abreast of anything that turned up."

371

"Like the case!" Sabra exclaimed.

"That's right! Hawk, do you remember that morning in my father's office, when Kornsberg told us about the case?"

"Yes," Hawk said, his eyes brightening. "I sure do. There were five of us there: you, me, Hezekiah, Kornsberg, and Jennings."

"All right," Logan said. "What have we got so far?" He raised his hand, spread his fingers, and ticked off the points one by one. "The connection with Melissa. Henderson's liquor in Jennings's barracks. And Jennings's knowledge about the case." He gave a deep sigh. "That's still not enough."

"Wait a minute." Hawk's face lit up. "We've got something else. I just remembered."

"What?" the others asked in unison.

"The day I tried to see the major, I went into Henderson's store to kill some time. Jennings and Henderson were in the back talking. They didn't see me. And when they came out, Henderson was telling Jennings that someone had stopped by early that morning—"

"The morning after Father arrived from Tucson!" Sabra said excitedly.

"—and had told him he had all the ammunition he needed. I didn't think too much about it, Henderson being a storekeeper and all. But what if the 'ammunition' he was talking about was evidence?"

Hezekiah grinned. "Evidence to force Henderson off the post. Major Powers had been trying to do that for months."

"He might have brought it back in that case," Hawk ventured.

Logan shook his head. "We'll never know. The case was empty. If it ever held anything, the contents were destroyed before it was planted in Hawk's baggage."

Sabra's shoulders slumped. "So we still don't have anything."

"Maybe we do," Hezekiah said. "Maybe we do. I have an idea."

"Evenin', Sergeant," Hezekiah said. "Sorry to interrupt you like this, but I need to speak with you in private."

Jennings looked up from his paperwork, surprised to see Hezekiah before him. "Can't it wait, Kane? I have this supply list to finish tonight. Forsyth insisted —"

"I don't think so. And I don't think you want to discuss it here." Hezekiah turned his head and looked pointedly at the common room of the barracks, where soldiers were sprawled on beds or lounging in chairs.

Jennings eyed Hezekiah somewhat suspiciously, then shrugged his shoulders. He stacked his papers to one side of the desk, shoved his arms in the coat that had been draped over the back of his chair, and followed Hezekiah out of the barracks.

The air was crisp with the chill of approaching winter, and a huge silver moon floated over the mountains, surrounded by stars that looked close enough to pluck from the skies.

But Jennings was oblivious to the beauty of the night. "What is it you want, Private?" he demanded, his legs working hard to keep up with Hezekiah's long strides.

"Not here." Hezekiah kept walking. He passed the moon-drenched steps of the recreation building, then turned to walk along the side of it, seeking the deeper shadows at the rear.

Jennings's patience was fast growing short. "Isn't this a bit melodramatic, Kane?" he grumbled when Hezekiah finally halted. "You'd best tell me what you're up to, before I put you on report."

Hezekiah shoved his hands into his pockets and leaned his shoulders against the adobe wall. His teeth gleamed against the darkness of his face as he spoke. "I think I've got something you'll be interested in buying, Jennings."

Jennings gave him a scornful look. "What are you talking about? What could you possibly have that I'd pay you for?"

"My continued silence." Hezekiah watched the sergeant closely. So much hinged on Jennings reading the right things into that small sentence. If the man had something to hide, as they hoped, it might work. If he didn't, they were out of luck, and Hezekiah would probably be spending the next couple of days in the guardhouse.

Jennings stood silent for a long moment, his face an emotionless mask except for the tiny muscle that bunched and jumped at the corner of his jaw. He swallowed, hard enough so that Hezekiah could see his Adam's apple work against his throat, and pinned Hezekiah with a direct gaze. "What if I decide not to make this . . . uh . . . purchase?"

"Then I see no choice but to talk." Hezekiah's voice was calm, almost icy, but his insides were turning cartwheels.

A ragged sigh escaped Jennings. "And what figure did you have in mind?"

The muscle at the corner of the sergeant's cheek danced in double time when Hezekiah quoted his price. Then Jennings drew a long, deep breath. "How long do I have to think about this?"

Hezekiah decided to push. Hard. "No time. It's take it or leave it. But I will give you the opportunity to get your funds together. Shall we say midnight?"

There was another sharp hiss from Jennings. "You're asking for a lot—"

"You're getting a lot in return, Sergeant. You might consider the consequences. If I don't get the money, I go to the man in charge. Tomorrow." Hezekiah gloated inwardly over his last statement. Let Jennings figure out what it might mean, since the reference could be to Lieutenant Colonel Forsyth, Henderson, or even Logan.

"One last question, Kane, if you don't mind? Where'd you get your information?"

Hezekiah's grin was wide and white. "From a friend of yours. *A real close friend.*" Hezekiah didn't care if Jennings thought Henderson or some other accomplice had spilled the beans, as long as the ploy worked.

And it did. Perfectly. Jennings muttered a foul curse under his breath and turned to stalk off.

"See you at midnight, Sergeant," Hezekiah called after him, elation in his voice. "Right here."

Jennings didn't bother to answer. Hunching his shoulders against the chilly wind, he strode angrily back toward the barracks.

Hezekiah hurried off. Now all they could do was wait.

Jennings threw a cursory look over his shoulder as he stepped onto Henderson's back porch. His knuckles rapped sharply against the door.

It soon creaked open and Henderson poked his head around the edge of the panel, anger lining his face when he saw who his visitor was. "I told you not to come back here. Ever." He jerked his head away from the opening and started to shove the door shut.

Jennings stabbed his foot through the narrowing crack just before it closed. "I'm coming in."

"You're not," Henderson insisted, pushing even harder against the door.

Jennings applied his shoulder to the wooden panel and shoved. The door flew open, crashing back against the wall. The trader stumbled backward, arms flailing.

Then the door slammed shut.

Two silent figures slipped from their shadowy hiding

place and crept forward to peek through the high kitchen window.

Henderson's jowls quivered with indignation. "Get out of my house, you bastard. We have nothing more to say."

"I have plenty to say, ol' man. We have a problem, and since it appears to be your flappin' mouth that caused it—"

"Say what you have to say, Jennings, and then get the hell out of my house before I call for help."

Leroy's laugh was mirthless. "We both know you won't do that." His snide gaze raked Henderson up and down. "You bringing in a new partner? Is that what this is all about? You too greedy to wait until the flap over Powers dies down? Well, you're playin' with my life now, ol' man, and I'm not going to let you get away with it."

"I don't know what you're talking about."

"You expect me to believe that, Henderson? Well, I don't. Not by a long shot. You're going to give me the money to pay Kane off, plus a whole lot more, and then I'm getting the hell out of here. At least they don't hang deserters."

Henderson grew still, his brows pinched together in perplexity. "Kane? That big darky?"

"One and the same."

"What's he got to do with any of this?"

"He knows all about it. He wants money to keep quiet. Hell, Henderson, it's your neck, too. I won't stand trial alone. So quit bellyachin' and give me the money so I can pay him off."

Henderson's mind was racing. He wasn't sure he even believed Jennings's wild story about Kane. It could be just a ploy to get more money. But either way there was a big problem. Henderson knew one thing for sure. He had to get rid of Jennings. The man had become a threat. A plan began to form in the trader's mind, a desperate one but better than nothing.

"Did you hear me?" Jennings growled. "I want the money. Now!"

Henderson bobbed his head. "Sure. Sure. I'm going to get it for you. I was just trying to remember where I put it. It's in my desk. That's where." Henderson began edging toward the hallway. "Wait right here. I'll go get it."

"What kind of a fool do you take me for? I'm not about to let you out of my sight. We'll go together."

Jennings shadowed Henderson as they left the room.

Crouched beneath the kitchen window, Logan and Hawk watched the two men disappear from view.

"Crap!" whispered Logan. "Now what do we do? They've danced all around the subject. You know and I know that they're guilty. But neither one of them has said enough to give us any evidence."

Hawk shrugged. "I guess we go inside. I don't know what else to do. We can't hear from out here."

"If they see us, it'll blow the whole thing," Logan warned. "If Hezekiah's in place at the front of the house, maybe he can hear the rest of the conversation."

"I can't take that chance," Hawk whispered, shaking his head. "I'm going in."

"Then I'm going with you."

Hawk didn't argue.

They slipped up the stairs and across the porch to the door. Hawk's knuckles were white as he gripped the knob, turning it ever so slowly. His stomach flopped when the latch clicked, sounding far too loud to his apprehensive ears. When there was no response from the house's occupants, Hawk eased the door open, praying it wouldn't squeak. It seemed like an eternity, but it only took them a few seconds to slip through the opening and tiptoe across the room. Loud voices were coming from the room across the hall.

Jennings was flipping through the bundle of bills Henderson had handed him. "It isn't enough, Mortimer. This paltry amount will barely pay Kane. Dig out some more, ol' man. I want enough to get way down in Mexico."

"Sure, Jennings, whatever you say. Why don't you have a drink?" Henderson jerked his head in the direction of the whiskey decanter on a side table. "Relax a minute while I look for some more. I think I've got some cash stashed in the back of this top drawer." He held his breath as he began to slide the drawer open. Would Jennings cooperate?

Relief surged through Henderson as Jennings stomped to the table and lifted the bottle to pour himself a drink. This was what he had been hoping for. His hand darted into the drawer.

Jennings raised the glass to his lips. The amber liquid slid toward the crystal rim. Henderson smiled gloatingly as he leveled the gun directly at Jennings's heart.

"Enjoy it, Leroy. It's going to be your last."

The sergeant lowered the glass, his eyes wide with a mixture of surprise and fear. "I should have known better than to trust you."

"Guess we're even then. I shouldn't have trusted you either. I thought you were smart, that you'd enjoy making a little extra money. But you weren't smart enough to keep your hands off my daughter—"

"Speaking of Melissa," Jennings said, trying to take Henderson's mind off the gun in his hand. "Where is our little darlin'?" The glass was in his gun hand, but if he could drop it and draw, he might have a chance. He lowered his hand ever so slightly, hoping Henderson wouldn't notice.

"She's gone to a friend's house, not that it's any of your concern. We should have plenty of time to transact our business before she returns. And I advise you not to go for that gun, Jennings."

Jennings's hand halted in midair. "You won't get away with it, Henderson. How are you going to explain shooting a man in cold blood? You forget Kane knows. He'll guess that I came here. You may not swing for Powers's murder, but you'll swing anyway."

"No," Henderson answered smugly. "I have it all worked out. If this story about Kane is real, he'll be just as happy to get his money from me as you. I can worry about him later. But my instincts tell me you're lying."

"I'm not, you dumb bastard. But even if I were, you still couldn't explain why you'd want to kill me."

"Sure I can. You came here drunk, intent on robbing me. You blubbered about how you'd done this terrible thing, confessed to killing Major Powers. Said you couldn't take the pressure anymore. You knew I had money and you were going to steal it and hightail it out of the country. We struggled. And you were so drunk I managed to get the gun away from you. Too bad it went off in the middle of the fight. You'll be dead, but that'll save the army the time and trouble of a trial."

"You bastard! I wouldn't have killed Powers if you hadn't put me up to it. You're just as guilty as I am!"

"Ah, but no one else knows that." Henderson raised the gun. "Say your pray—"

At the sound of the front door opening, the trader froze. He knew who it was. Panicked at the thought that Melissa was going to walk in just in time to see him shoot Leroy Jennings, Henderson hesitated one moment too long.

Jennings was coiled tight as a steel spring. And when Henderson cut his eyes toward the door, he dropped the glass and lunged—not at Henderson, who would surely have pulled the trigger, but toward the door.

"Daddy—"

Melissa barely had the word out of her mouth before Jennings grabbed her. Her scream was cut off by an arm clamped across her throat, and with one swift movement Jennings hauled the struggling woman in front of him, drew his gun, and pressed it to her head.

"What are you going to do now, Henderson?" His chuckle was wicked. Melissa sobbed, her eyes wild with terror and confusion.

Henderson's face turned sickly white, his hand began to tremble, and the gun fell from his limp fingers.

"Kick it over here," Jennings instructed.

The trader obeyed and then slumped against the desk, all the fight gone out of him.

At that very instant, Hawk and Logan stepped through the doorway from the kitchen.

"Let her go, Jennings," Hawk said, his voice low and menacing.

Jennings laughed. "Well, half-breed. Fancy seeing you again. And you, too, Lieutenant." The sergeant made a clucking sound. "Shoulda known that big black bastard was too dumb to come up with this scheme on his own."

Hawk's hands clenched into fists, but he overcame the urge to try to slam Jennings' teeth down his throat.

"You two might as well save your breath," the sergeant continued. "I have no intention of turning Melissa loose. I'm taking the little lady with me. All I need is a horse and I'll be long gone." Leroy began backing toward the door, dragging Melissa along. He carefully watched Hawk and Logan.

Something moved just outside the still-gaping front door. Hawk kept his gaze aimed straight at Jennings's retreating figure. "You'll never get away with it, Sergeant. We heard everything. We know you shot the major. Give it up." Hawk kept talking and slowly walking forward, one slow step at a time, desperate to keep Jennings' attention on himself.

"No good, half-breed." Jennings grinned and shook his head. "I'm walkin' out of here. Just remember, I'll have the gun on her all the way. If anyone comes near, I'll shoot her—"

"I don't think so."

Jennings's gun was suddenly snatched from his grasp before he realized what was happening. Shocked beyond measure, he dropped his hold on Melissa and whirled to look behind him. He stared in openmouthed disbelief at the towering figure of Hezekiah Kane, as Melissa collapsed in a sobbing heap upon the floor.

"Now who's the dumb one?" Hezekiah asked, a huge grin wreathing his face.

Epilogue

San Xavier Hotel — Tucson, Arizona Territory

"Penny for your thoughts."

Hawk joined Sabra at the window, slipping his arms around her from behind, savoring the feel of her soft warm body through her silken night dress. She sighed with pleasure as he drew her against his chest and then nestled his cheek against her hair. Moonlight streamed through the window, illuminating the hotel room with a pale silver light that made lanterns superfluous.

Sabra tilted her head, looking back over her shoulder to smile up at her husband. Her glorious smile set Hawk's heart to galloping.

"I seem to remember another time when you made that offer. I never did collect."

"I thought you might let me work my debts off in trade," Hawk whispered in her ear. His hands brushed softly against her midriff and then slipped upward for just a moment to cup the lush fullness of her breasts in a teasing tempting promise of what was to come.

"In that case, it may take you a long, long time."

"An eminently fair proposition."

"Then I'd best give you an answer so I can begin collecting on the debt."

"Absolutely," Hawk agreed, nuzzling her neck and again wrapping his arms tightly about her waist.

"I was thinking how much has changed since we were last here, the night of the ball."

"Ummm. I thought you were the most beautiful woman I'd ever seen." He pressed a kiss against her temple. "But

382

I was lost long before the band struck up the waltz and I took you in my arms. I'm afraid my destiny was set at the moment of that very first smile in the park."

"Destiny." The word sounded soft and silky on Sabra's lips. Her arms were crossed on top of her husband's and she tightened her hold, snuggling even closer to him, reveling in the feel of his long muscular body pressed against her back, of his heat warming her through the gossamer silk of her nightgown. "I felt it, too. From the very beginning. We were meant to be."

"You were my gift from the spirits." This time Hawk rained gentle kisses from the soft wisp of curls at her temple to the delicate slope of her shoulder.

"I'm so glad we stayed at Fort Huachuca for a while," Sabra murmured, relishing the beginning frissons of excitement skipping through her veins. "Not that I'm not looking forward to going to Hawkinsville," she quickly assured him. "But I would have hated to miss Jasmine's and Hezekiah's wedding."

"I'm glad we stayed, too. I think they're going to be very happy."

"*Almost* as happy as we are. I'm going to miss them. And Molly. I'm sorry we only had time for one short visit with her before we left. But at least I got to thank her for doing what she did for you . . . for us."

"Yes, I'll miss all of them. And Logan."

"Especially Logan. But he's promised to come for a visit when his enlistment is up. I was surprised when he told me he intends to come back here and live in Bisbee for a while."

Hawk chuckled softly.

"What?" Sabra asked, casting a questioning glance over her shoulder.

"I think Logan must be planning to do a little silver mining."

"Silver mining? Why do you think that?"

"I told him about that vein we saw in the cave after the earthquake. He casually asked where it was, so I drew him a map."

Sabra's soft laughter joined her husband's, then she turned to more serious thoughts. "Do you think your family will like me?"

"My family will adore you. Like I do. There's no doubt in my mind."

"I hope so." Sabra pressed closer to Hawk. "I guess they're getting anxious for you to come home."

"They'll understand. We had more important things to take care of first."

"That awful trial, for one." Sabra shuddered. "Thank heaven, Henderson and Jennings are on their way to the territorial prison. When I think of the harm those two greedy men did—"

Hawk turned Sabra within his arms until she was facing him, and his hands cupped her face with unbelievable tenderness. The tiniest pressure of his thumbs tilted her head so that midnight blue eyes meshed with brown.

"That's all over now. Put it from your mind. They'll be in prison for many years. By the time they get out, they'll be too old to cause any trouble."

"Poor Melissa," Sabra said with a sigh.

"I'd be more apt to say poor Woodley. I'm afraid that man got more than he bargained for when he married her."

"Well, maybe they'll be happy since he's received his transfer. I rather hope so. Right now, I'm so gloriously happy I want everyone else to feel this way, too."

Hawk's heart did a little hitch-step. His Sabra, innocent and forgiving and loving, was still trying to fix the world. He bent toward her, his lips claiming hers in a kiss that rocked their universe.

When he finally broke from her, Sabra sighed with contentment and then sank into her husband's embrace, pillowing her head against the reassuring expanse of his chest, wrapping her arms about his waist; grateful that she had his strength and his love to depend upon.

"Well, I don't know about everyone, but I know how you can make your husband happy tonight." Hawk's voice was husky with desire.

"Oh? And what would that take?"

"Come back to bed, Mrs. Hawkins."